American Harlot

Rebecca Flynt

ASHES TO ROSES PRESS

ASHES TO ROSES
PRESS

*To my children, Katie and Conner,
for their unwavering support and encouragement
in all their mother's endeavors, no matter how crazy they may seem*

Prologue

July 13, 1804
Philadelphia, Pennsylvania

Mary stood on the top step of the fashionable Society Hill townhouse looking down the busy cobblestone street as she twisted her fingers anxiously in the folds of her skirt. Horses, carriages, wagons, and pedestrians all created a cacophony of sound and activity that swirled around her. This morning was still pleasant, but she knew that in a few hours the summer heat and humidity would make things unbearable. Everyone went about their business as if it were just another ordinary day. As if her world hadn't suddenly stopped when she heard the news.

She felt disconnected from this city she had made her home, like she was standing on the outside looking in through a dirty window that distorted things once so familiar. This city where everything began all those years ago.

She scanned the streets, trying to catch sight of the young boy she had sent to buy a copy of today's paper. She had already heard the news, of course, but she needed to see it in print. *If it's not in writing, perhaps it didn't really happen.*

The boy returned quickly, and Mary wiped her sweaty palms on her crisp white apron. She tucked an errant blonde curl back under her linen cap before taking the paper from his hands with shaking fingers, handed him a small coin from her pocket, and sent him on his way. She clutched the paper to her chest without looking at it, opened the front door, and stepped across the threshold into the elegantly appointed reception area.

Mary heard footsteps on the staircase and quickly ducked into the empty parlor, closing the door softly behind her. It was early Friday morning, and Dr. Mathew would begin seeing patients soon—but right now she needed a moment alone before she was forced to face the busy day ahead. Knowing she couldn't put it off any longer, she took a deep breath, pulled the paper away from her chest, and stared down at the headline.

The words swam in front of her, and Mary felt slightly queasy. She sat down on the sofa and sank back into the velvet upholstery, feeling like a wilted flower among the green and gilt finery. A soft knock at the door made her jump.

"Mrs. Clement, is everything all right?"

"Yes, Abby. Everything is fine. I'll be out in a moment." Her voice sounded distant, as if she were watching the scene from outside her body.

Mary heard a slight pause before the click of the maid's shoes retreated down the polished marble entryway. Even at the age of thirty-six, somehow people still felt the need to worry about her, as if she were some fragile little thing. If they only knew, they would realize she was far stronger than she appeared.

Alone once again, Mary looked back down at the newspaper on her lap. Two men, both so tightly woven into the fabric of her life.

Each had played the parts of both hero and villain in her story. Both had betrayed her, and both she had betrayed. But only one had she loved.

Now, that one was dead, killed by the other.

She felt like she was going to retch.

Mary took a deep breath and lifted a shaking hand to her chest, her fingers outlining the slight bulge of the silver locket she had worn over her heart, pinned to her stays, and hidden under her gown for the past twelve years. A lock of auburn hair rested safely inside. That's all she had left now.

She anticipated tears, but none came. Perhaps she was still in shock, and those would come later. Or perhaps the tears were Maria's to shed, not Mary's, and the wall she had built around her heart was truly impenetrable. Even after all these years, Mary wore Maria's pain and disgrace around her like a protective cloak, visceral and ever-present.

The shame and public humiliation had almost destroyed her, but somehow, she survived. She had returned to Philadelphia four years ago and reinvented herself once again. A new name and a new life, her scandalous past hidden beneath a thin veneer of respectability. Her daughter was grown now and had moved away, lost to her own vices—a constant ache that Mary was unable to soothe.

She closed her eyes and leaned her head against the back of the couch. A sob escaped her lips as the memories hit her all at once, a swirl of images and sensations . . . love, loss, revenge, betrayal, and scandal.

She knew rampant speculation would rear its ugly head in the coming days concerning the origin of the long-standing feud between those two powerful men. And now, she was one of two remaining who knew the whole truth behind it. And, heaven help her, she intended to take her secret with her to the grave.

One

Maria stepped out of the coach and looked up at the boarding house that, if only temporarily, was to be their new home. *Not* a very encouraging sight. Tightly pressed on either side by much taller rowhouses, the plain, two-story red brick building was small and simple. A thin coating of dust and smoke residue darkened the exterior bricks, the portico weathered and badly in need of a fresh coat of paint. Two brick chimneys jutted out from either end of the slate roof, grey smoke billowing into the sky.

She opened the drawstring on her delicate satin reticule and pulled out the note Mr. Burr had sent—along with money for their passage from New York—to confirm the address.

154 South Fourth Street.

She glanced up at the numbers painted on the side of the house in front of her, slightly disheartened to see that they matched. *This is the right place.*

Not nearly as nice as what she was used to, but at least the small size meant fewer tenants to poke around in her business, she thought to herself. She always tried to look for the positives. Mr. Burr had also assured her that she could count on the landlady for a certain level of discretion. Difficult to go back to living in a single room again, but it would have to do for the time being. Hopefully, they would be able to move to larger quarters soon.

When Susan poked her head out of the coach, Maria lifted her daughter out and set her on the street beside her. She also righted the hat that was about to fall off the fidgety six-year-old's head, tightening its ribbon before reaching up to pull her own wide-brimmed hat onto her own blonde curls more securely. Susan's grey eyes were wide with excitement. She had never been out of New York before, and this was a new adventure.

"Is this where we'll be living now, Mama?"

Maria squeezed her hand and smiled down at her. "Yes, sweetheart."

She had spent the long coach ride telling her daughter all about the city that was to be their new home. She told her stories of the Pennsylvania State House and of the Declaration of Independence that had been signed there during the War before Susan was born, and of the new constitution that had been created in the same place just four years ago.

They had been among the thousands of people who had crowded onto the streets of New York City two years ago to see General Washington inaugurated as the new president. Maria still counted it as one of the most exciting days of her life. And now they were in the new capital, a city newly swollen with hundreds of congressmen and government officials. Burr had advised her that he was lucky to have found a room for them at all.

Susan smiled back, revealing a gap where she had recently lost a tooth, a constant reminder to Maria that she wasn't a baby anymore. The pretty blonde child was good-natured, compliant, and the light of her doting mother's eyes. She was smart too. Maria had already taught her letters and numbers, and she could read and write her name. Maria's own education had been rudimentary, and she knew there was not much more that she could teach her inquisitive daughter. Hopefully, she would soon have enough money to hire a tutor here in the capital.

The driver jumped off the front of the coach and began dragging their baggage out of the back. Everything they owned was packed neatly into three trunks that were quickly deposited on the brick sidewalk in front of the boardinghouse. Their baggage unloaded, the driver jumped back up onto the seat and slapped the long reins, sending the team of four horses out into the street. Maria watched the coach disappear into the traffic, leaving them alone with their belongings.

A woman stepped out of the front door of the boardinghouse to greet her. "Mrs. Reynolds?"

Maria turned and looked at her. "Yes. Mrs. Folwell, I presume?"

She nodded. Her new landlady was stout, middle-aged, and wore a red jacket and a serviceable yellow wool skirt with a well-used apron tied around her waist. Her complexion was ruddy, her salt and pepper hair tucked up into a plain linen cap. Maria smoothed the skirt of her fashionable green silk gown (carefully chosen to match the color of her eyes) down over her stomach and hips and adjusted the sheer fichu covering the top of her decolletage that spilled out above her stays. She hoped she didn't look too rumpled from the long coach ride.

She pulled her daughter closer to her side. "This is my daughter, Susan."

"Pleased to meet you both," Mrs. Folwell said, giving a little curtsy. "Senator Burr told me to be expecting you today. Please, come inside. I'll show you to your room."

"Thank you." Maria looked back at their luggage. "I don't suppose there is anyone who can help with our trunks?"

Mrs. Folwell nodded. "My son will get them for you." She turned and yelled over her shoulder, "John! Come get Mrs. Reynolds's baggage."

A few seconds later, a gangly young man of about twenty came bounding down the stairs and began dragging the trunks out of the street and onto the wide sidewalk.

Leaving him to wrangle their luggage, Maria took Susan's hand to follow Mrs. Folwell up the narrow stairway inside. Maria ran her free hand along the worn smoothness of the wooden banister as they went along, taking it all in. The boardinghouse was small and dimly lit, but so far, it looked clean. The fragrant aroma of roasting meat drifted up from the back. Maria's stomach growled. She couldn't remember the last time she had eaten a full meal.

They got to the top of the stairs and turned down the upstairs hallway. Mrs. Folwell stopped in front of one of the doors. "You have room number five," she said, inserting a key into the lock. She opened the door, and Maria and Susan stepped inside.

"Will your husband be arriving soon?" Mrs. Folwell asked.

"Mr. Reynolds is currently out of the state on business and will be joining us later," Maria said, the lie coming easily to her lips. She left out the fact that her estranged husband had been out of state on "business" for the past year. She wasn't sure what story Burr had used when he procured the room for her, so it was best to keep things vague. She had also learned the value of telling a little white lie up front to avoid further questions down the road.

Maria looked around, taking stock of their new lodgings. The room was small but well-furnished and clean. A colorful quilt covered the bed, a simple dresser and washstand opposite it. Two wooden chairs and a small round table completed the furnishings. She had certainly lived in worse.

The sounds of John Folwell dragging her first trunk up the stairs caught her attention, and Maria stuck her head out into the hallway. He had stopped at the top of the stairs to catch his breath.

"Where do you want it?" he asked.

"You can put all three trunks against the wall," Maria said, stepping out into the hall. She would unpack later. The only dresser in the room was not going to be nearly large enough for all their clothing. It looked like they would be living out of their trunks for a while—not long, she hoped.

She stepped out of the way as John dragged the trunk into the room. Mrs. Folwell pulled a watch from her pocket.

"It's three-thirty now. Supper is served in the dining room at five o'clock," Mrs. Folwell said, "and breakfast is set out at six."

"Thank you, Mrs. Folwell, it smells delicious." After three days of travel, Maria was ready for a hot meal and a good night's sleep.

"I'll leave you to settle in, then. Please let me know if you need anything."

"Thank you."

Mrs. Folwell turned and walked back down the stairs while Maria stepped inside the room, leaving the door open for the young man to finish bringing in the other two trunks.

She walked to the window and pulled the curtains aside. Their room was in the front of the building, so her window looked out onto the street below. Although the city had a much larger population, the streets here somehow seemed less chaotic than in New

York City. Well-dressed men and women walked along the sidewalks, and the soft clang of carriages and horses' hooves on the cobblestone street floated up to her on the breeze that came in through the open window.

Maria took a deep breath to soothe her nerves and looked down at her daughter. She put her hand on the child's delicate shoulders. Everything she had ever done was to provide a better life and future for Susan; she had to remember that. The idea of starting over in a new city was frightening, but there were more opportunities for her here—now that Maria was alone once again.

At the age of twenty-three, she was far removed from the impulsive, naive teenager named Mary Lewis who had run away from her respectable Dutch family to marry at the age of fifteen. In her relatively short years, it seemed like she had already lived three separate lives. And now she was embarking on a new adventure.

Maria had been a mother by the age of seventeen, and at nineteen, her husband had left her for the first of many times. Alone and with a young child to care for, Maria had done what she needed to do to provide for them. Not a life she would have first chosen for herself, but it really wasn't such a difficult way to make a living, either.

Of course, there was a price to pay for her choice. By making the decision to exchange sexual favors for pecuniary compensation with men other than her husband she was now a harlot, an adulteress, and a whore in society's eyes. But it hadn't been about morals or scruples—it was about survival—and once she had made the decision, there was no turning back. Besides, she was not working on the street or in a brothel, so thus far she had at least been able to pretend she was still respectable. In New York, she had less than a dozen regular customers, and new ones were added only upon recommendation. The money she earned gave her the security she craved. Her income also provided a more comfortable life for herself and her daughter than she had ever had with her husband.

The first time she took a man who was not her husband into her bed, Mary had ceased to exist, and she became Maria. Maria was worldly, slightly jaded, and understood far more about the way things worked than young Mary could have ever imagined. Despite her attempts over the years to quell them, she had never completely dispelled Mary's fanciful notions of love and romance—however unrealistic they were for a woman in her position.

When her husband returned and discovered how his wife had been making her way, he didn't seem as put off as she expected. Instead, he seemed quite content to allow her to continue her lucrative new profession while he attended meetings at the local tavern and occasionally worked at the docks. Only after she refused to grant him the same privileges she sold to others did he leave for good, taking Susan with him as retaliation.

But she had not been about to sit by passively and allow him to take the one thing she loved more than anything else in life away from her. Within twenty-four hours of her husband's disappearance, she had enlisted the help of a powerful new benefactor, and Susan was found and returned. Her new patron was a wealthy merchant named Elijah Wagstaff, a man older than her own father and her husband's off-and-on employer. He offered monetary support and protection in exchange for exclusive access to her charms, which she gladly granted.

After that, James Reynolds seemingly dropped off the face of the earth, and she had been assured by her powerful new lover that he would not bother them again as long as she stayed in New York. She supposed he had made his way to the Carolinas, for James had often talked about going south to make his fortune, although she wasn't certain—and didn't really want to know. She had Susan, and that's all that really mattered.

The change in circumstance from a being a "bride" of many to a kept woman of one was welcome, though, even if it was somewhat isolated and lonely at times. But her new life had its perks. As soon as their agreement was struck, Mr. Wagstaff moved Maria and Susan from the boarding house where they had been staying to a modest house close to his office. Wagstaff employed an elderly lady who could be trusted to be discreet to come in every day to cook and clean for them. It wasn't extravagant, but far nicer than anything else Maria had lived in. She had accounts at the dressmakers, apothecary, dry goods shop, and several local merchants—all paid monthly by his personal attorney and rising political star, Aaron Burr.

Their arrangement had lasted for over a year. Although not prone to affectionate words or gestures, Elijah had been kind and had never treated her harshly. She was thankful for her lover's generosity. In return, she was always willing and available to him.

Elijah visited twice a week and usually stayed for a couple hours, but never overnight. She slept alone, often tightly clutching a pillow in her arms for comfort. On some nights after her lover left her bed to return home, she cried herself to sleep, her body aching for genuine touch and affection, or just the physical presence of having someone beside her. Some nights Maria was lonely enough to crawl into bed beside her sleeping daughter and hold her close until sleep finally claimed her. And then, this past winter, Elijah became ill with a sore throat and was dead within a week.

Her future suddenly in question, Maria had grieved alone. Before he died, Elijah had arranged with Mr. Burr for her rent and accounts in New York to be paid through the spring but made no further concessions for them. Although she had been well taken care of, her lover had never given her any cash money. So after his death, they were left with nothing except their clothing, books, and a few personal effects.

Maria's parents had both died two years ago, only a few months apart. Although she had not spoken to them since running away years earlier, their deaths left her feeling rudderless. Her remaining siblings were now scattered across the Hudson River Valley. Her half-brother wrote to her occasionally, but she had too much pride to ask his family or her other siblings for help after all these years. She was truly alone for the first time in her life and felt as if she had nowhere to go.

Then, Mr. Burr offered to pay their passage to Philadelphia. He also offered to pay her room and board here in the new city, but she didn't know how long that would last—or what sort of conditions were attached to his sudden generosity. She was certain there were some.

As her lover's personal attorney, Burr had paid all her bills for the past year, even after he was appointed Attorney General of New York by Governor Clinton and elected to the Senate only a few months ago. Their relationship had always been strictly business, though. Burr had thus far treated her fairly, and she trusted him. Not having a lot of other options, she accepted his offer, packed up everything they owned, and left New York.

Leaving her home state meant she lost the protection it provided. When she left, she told no one where she was going. She provided no forwarding address to her former housekeeper, and simply told her that she was going to stay with a sister in Albany. Only Burr knew where Maria was, and she trusted him to keep her secret.

After Elijah's death, a new dream took root, one of setting up her own boardinghouse. A respectable one in a respectable city where she could make her own way without having to sell a part of herself in exchange. A boardinghouse providing shelter to women without husbands— whether by choice, death, or desertion. A boarding-house filled with young women like herself sharing chores, struggles, and gossip. The very thing she had missed over the past several years: female company.

But Maria's dream was far from obtainable at the moment, for she was entirely dependent on whatever proposal Burr had to offer.

The sound of John dragging the next trunk into the room broke Maria out of her thoughts, and she turned and gave the winded young man an encouraging smile as he deposited the second trunk next to the first before heading back out for the final one. Suddenly chilled, she turned back to the window, crossed her arms over her chest, and shivered.

As she was unpacking their clothes, a note arrived. Maria opened the letter while the smartly dressed messenger waited in the hallway outside her door. The note was unsigned, but she knew the handwriting well. Burr was not in the habit of fixing his name to his private correspondence.

> *I trust you have found your new accommodations acceptable—Please return this letter and send word by my man if it would be convenient to meet on the morrow at nine a.m. at the Coffeehouse on the corner of Fourth and Chestnut Street—I have an interesting Proposition to present to you.*

Maria folded the letter and handed it back to the man waiting patiently by the door. "Please let Senator Burr know that I will be able to attend the meeting."

"Yes, ma'am." He nodded, bowed slightly, and left.

Only later that night—after she and Susan had eaten their fill in the dining room downstairs, washed the dust and dried sweat from their skin at the basin, and curled up together in the clean, soft bed—did Maria allow doubt to invade her thoughts. Perhaps coming here had been a mistake. Everything was so different here. It felt pretentious and flashy, like the city was covered with a shiny veneer hiding what was below. So unlike the raw, gritty energy that characterized New York.

She had met the other boarders at dinner, and they were all men—clerks and businessmen who had come to the capital to do business within the new government. They were respectful and had fallen over themselves in their efforts to get her attention. She supposed then that, if Burr's proposition wasn't to her liking, it probably wouldn't be too difficult to procure another stable of benefactors here in Philadelphia.

But despite the warm welcome, she couldn't seem to shake the feeling that she might be in over her head.

Two

M aria woke early the next morning, uncharacteristically nervous about her upcoming meeting. After a big breakfast downstairs, she unpacked Susan's lesson books and left her at the table with a graphite pencil and paper and instructions to copy out the next page in her books until Maria returned from her meeting.

The coffeehouse was a short walk, and she arrived early. The shop was busy, but Maria found a small table in the corner that allowed a certain amount of privacy. She took a seat. Today, Maria wore a cream cotton gown printed with small blue flowers and edged in lace and a sheer scarf tucked into the low, square neckline. Her curls were artfully pinned on top of her head with one long blonde curl hanging over her shoulder, the current style. She blended in perfectly with the other well-heeled customers and looked every bit the respectable wife and mother she pretended to be.

Maria didn't have to wait long. She saw Burr come in the front door and signaled to him with a raised finger. He stopped at the counter to place an order before walking over to her—his steps measured, his expression portraying his customary coolness. In the year she'd known him, she had never seen that mask of calculated indifference slip. Not once.

"Good morning, Mrs. Reynolds," Burr said. He bowed and kissed the top of her offered hand. "You're looking quite stunning this morning. I trust you're finding Philadelphia to your liking and have settled into your new lodgings? I've taken the liberty of ordering coffee. It's quite good here."

She smiled at their familiar banter, and he took a seat opposite her. "Thank you. Yes, we are settled and unpacked. The room is small, but the meals are quite good. I'm afraid I'm in danger of growing plump if I continue to indulge, though." She laughed, patting her tiny waist.

"You look well, too, Mr. Burr," she continued. "Or should I say Senator Burr? Congratulations on your recent victory. I hope you are enjoying your position in the new Congress."

"Thank you. It's a damnable business, though, Mrs. Reynolds." He gave a wry smile. "But I suppose there are some interesting and potentially profitable alliances to be made. That's where I may need to enlist your considerable talents." He looked at her pointedly, arching his dark eyebrows.

Maria laughed softly, not even trying to pretend to be shocked. He knew her far too well for her to feign offense at his comment. She had always appreciated the fact that Burr didn't waste time on small talk.

Just then, a young man delivered their coffee and set the delicate, blue transferware teacups and saucers down on the table in front of them.

Maria smiled at him. "Thank you."

The young man blushed. "Y-you're welcome, ma'am," he stammered and walked back behind the counter. Burr smiled.

Once the waiter was out of earshot she asked, "What is it that I can help you with?"

Burr leaned closer and lowered his voice. "Some high-placed

friends and I would be very much interested in seeing the Secretary of the Treasury taken down a few pegs."

Maria's eyes widened. "Colonel Hamilton? For what purpose? Has he done something to offend you?"

Burr waived his hand dismissively. "We've always gotten along well personally, but he has grown too powerful, and his financial plan has alarmed some of my new friends and colleagues. Friends who would be extremely grateful to anyone who could hinder his progress."

She remembered a brief encounter with Alexander Hamilton in New York several years ago. His office was only half a block from Burr's, she recalled. She had been pacing the sidewalk in front—and hatless, at that. He was gesticulating wildly and mumbling to himself, and she thought he'd surely gone mad—until he stopped and looked at her with the deepest blue eyes she had ever seen. Although the meeting was brief, she had never forgotten the almost magnetic energy that seemed to emanate from him.

Maria hadn't seen Colonel Hamilton since, but she had followed his career in the papers as he quickly rose to prominence over the past several years. She read accounts of his efforts to secure the ratification of the new constitution in New York, and his appointment as Secretary of the Treasury in President Washington's cabinet. She knew his new financial plan was controversial, but Maria didn't really know enough to form an opinion about it one way or another.

"How could I possibly help?"

"I want you to seduce him," Burr said matter-of-factly.

Maria's eyes widened in surprise. "For what purpose? And what makes you think he would be interested? He's a married man." Married, in fact, to the daughter of the man Burr had just defeated for his Senate seat, she realized with sudden insight. Perhaps there was more of a personal aspect to Burr's proposal than he was willing to admit.

"Oh, I think you underestimate your unique talents, Mrs. Reynolds. And you of all people should know that marriage certainly doesn't preclude a gentleman from enjoying certain indulgences. I've heard from reliable sources that our esteemed Treasury Secretary can be quite susceptible to the charms of a beautiful woman in distress."

"But I'm not in distress."

"I'm sure you could come up with something," he said with a smile.

He met her flabbergasted gaze with the same coldly sardonic smile she had seen many times over the past year.

Maria leaned forward and picked up her cup and saucer. She sat up straight as she held the saucer in her left hand, fingers curled around the handle. She took a sip of the dark, rich coffee as she tried to wrap her mind around Burr's proposal. This wasn't at all what she had expected. She was looking for a rich benefactor, not getting caught up in some political intrigue. But if she was honest with herself, the proposition wasn't without a certain appeal. She could still picture Colonel Hamilton's handsome features and the intensity in those blue eyes even now, all these years later.

"What exactly do you hope to gain if I am able to successfully bed him?"

"In a word, information. You're a smart woman, Mrs. Reynolds, and intimacy is a very powerful weapon in a lady's arsenal. Any interesting information you gather will be passed along to me, of course."

"Of course."

Although Elijah had not been prone to displays of physical affection, he occasionally discussed business matters while they lay side-by-side together after making love. She had no real interest in such things, but she had enjoyed those rare, relaxed, and intimate times with him more than the physical intimacy itself. This time, however, she would be paid not just for any physical consolation she provided, but for passing along the information she collected. Somehow that seemed much more distasteful. She took another sip of coffee.

"What sort of information are you interested in?" she asked.

"Anything regarding official business. Or pecuniary transactions of any kind. He has access to a tremendous amount of power and money, and my new friends are quite convinced there is something nefarious afoot in the Treasury."

"Do you believe that?"

Burr paused, and for a brief second, she saw something she didn't recognize flash across his face.

Second thoughts? Regrets? Hard to tell.

"It doesn't matter what I believe," he said flatly. His tone made it clear that the subject was not open for debate. "What matters is that the patronage afforded to me for providing such evidence would be considerable."

Maria was silent for several seconds as she considered Burr's proposal. "Not to sound crass, but what would I receive for my services?" she asked.

"You would be rewarded quite handsomely if you are successful."

"Successful in my attempt at seduction, or successful in finding evidence of corruption?"

"If you agree to participate in my plan, I will pay your room and board and daily expenses while you are in the city, regardless of the outcome. If you can provide proof of official misconduct, my friends and I are prepared to reward you with a cash sum of five hundred dollars, enough to allow both you and your daughter to live comfortably for some time."

Maria stifled a gasp. That amount would go a long way toward making her boardinghouse dream a reality. She sipped her coffee as she considered Burr's proposal, masking her shock and trying not to appear too eager. The idea of having enough money to live independently was incredibly appealing. But the plan wasn't without its challenges.

She considered the logistics of what he was suggesting. The fact was, she was currently sharing a small room with her six-year-old daughter. Although the room did have a trundle bed that could be pulled out for Susan to sleep on, the close quarters hardly provided privacy for the type of activities Burr was insinuating.

"And where would you propose this take place?" she asked. "My current living arrangements are hardly conducive to taking a lover, especially not one with the social standing of Colonel Hamilton. Even considering that I can accomplish what you propose, he can hardly bring me into his own home."

Burr considered the problem a moment. "Children must sleep sometime, Mrs. Reynolds, and it is my observation that when properly motivated, gentlemen are rarely concerned about the size or location of a woman's lodgings. A warm pair of thighs and a soft bed are usually sufficient." He smiled.

"Besides," he continued, "in another month, summer will be upon us, and I know that Mrs. Hamilton and their children usually leave the city to visit her father in Albany." His special edge added to the words "her father" left Maria wondering once again if there was more to this than he was letting on.

"And how do you propose I make contact?" she asked, still not convinced. "Colonel Hamilton and I don't exactly travel in the same social circles."

Burr pulled a piece of paper from his waistcoat pocket and discreetly slipped it, writing face down, across the table to her. "This is his address. He lives right around the corner from your boarding house, in fact."

"Well, isn't that convenient?" Maria asked, her words laced with a little more sarcasm than she intended. She picked up the paper and glanced at it quickly before tucking it into the front of her bodice.

79 South Third Street.

"And what, pray tell, should I say when I show up at his house?"

Burr smiled. "That you are a respectable wife and mother, alone in a new city, deserted by a scoundrel of a husband, without the means to go on. Or something of the sort. I'm sure you can come up with a convincing tale of woe. You wouldn't even have to lie. Just stretch the truth a little bit."

His dark eyes shone with amusement, and he leaned forward. "Years ago, during the War for Independence, Mrs. General Arnold stayed with Mrs. Burr and me, and regaled us with stories of how she had duped General Washington and Colonel Hamilton into believing she had no knowledge of her husband's treason. Tears, hysterics, and an artful display of just the right amount of flesh will work wonders on gentlemen who are susceptible to such things. She said that Colonel Hamilton was so taken in by her story and was so convinced of her innocence, he was ready to challenge anyone who dared besmirch her honor."

Burr laughed, and Maria felt a deep, sinking feeling in her stomach. As tempting as the money was, she had no interest in subterfuge and political intrigue. She was a courtesan, not a spy. And she certainly wasn't interested in tricking someone into bedding her. She was silent as she drained her cup and set it back down on the table in front of her.

Maria considered her options. She had no money to pay for her passage back to New York. Burr had prepaid her room and board for a month, but after that, she had no idea what she was going to do. If she stayed in the city, she had no doubt she could make her way as she had before, but she didn't really want to go back to that life. She had no real connections here, though, and when the month was out, they would no longer have a place to live.

Burr had treated her fairly in the past, and he was gaining quite a bit of political power. He could prove useful to her in the future, and she had no doubt he would prove to be a very dangerous enemy if crossed. Perhaps it wouldn't hurt to contact Secretary Hamilton. After all, he was even more politically powerful than Burr.

He could also prove to be a very formidable ally and protector. Perhaps I could even turn a simple seduction into a more profitable and lengthy connection.

Maria felt slightly queasy. She knew she shouldn't have come to Philadelphia. She missed the comfortable life she'd had only a few short months ago. She missed Elijah, and she missed New York. But she had to think of Susan. She wanted her daughter to have an education beyond what she'd been given and to have a chance at a better life. And she also knew she couldn't provide that on her own. At least not right now.

Maria wrinkled her brow and pursed her full, pink lips. "I will consider your proposal, Senator," she said as non-committedly as possible for someone who knew she really didn't have a choice.

Burr lifted his coffee cup to her in a salute. "That is all I can ask for, Mrs. Reynolds," he said with a smile as he brought the cup to his lips. "I'm sure you'll decide what is best for you and your daughter's future. I would hate for your relocation to Philadelphia to be for naught."

He set down the empty coffee cup on the table, stood, and bowed slightly. "Good day. I look forward to hearing from you soon."

Maria watched Burr stop at the counter to pay for their coffee and swore she could hear the snap of a steel trap springing closed as he walked out of the coffee shop into the street beyond.

Three

"Sometime in the summer of the year 1791,
a woman called at my house in the city of
Philadelphia and asked to speak to me
in private. I attended her into a room
apart from the family."

Alexander Hamilton, the *Reynolds Pamphlet,* 1797

A week after her meeting with Burr, Maria found herself alone in the private study of the Secretary of the Treasury. She arrived at his home shortly before sunset and was shown into his cluttered office to wait.

Much too nervous to sit, she paced back and forth on the colorful wool rug, her hands crossed over her stomach to stop the nervous fluttering. She forced herself to stop, breathe, and glance around the room. The office was much smaller and less grand than she had expected, given its owner's position. A large desk dominated the room. Papers were stacked high and scattered across its leather desktop. Bookshelves, full to overflowing, lined the wall behind his desk. Mostly law books, from what she could read on the spines.

Only one window in the room, its dark green damask curtains already drawn for the evening. A single lamp sat on a small table in front of the window. The flame cast a soft, golden hue across the office.

She moved toward the window and gasped in pain as she stepped on something hard and sharp. Maria bent down and pulled a small, metal soldier out from under the toe of her satin shoe. Then, she noticed another toy soldier standing beside it on the rug—and another, and yet another—all in a line leading toward the window.

Intrigued, she looked under the table, where she found a whole battle scenario laid out. Two rows of toy soldiers had been carefully lined up facing each other, guns pointed. One side had blue uniforms, and the other, red. She noticed that several of the red-clad soldiers had been knocked over and were lying on their sides.

Maria dropped to her knees and peered farther to find even more blue soldiers posed around the table legs and hidden behind the folds of the curtains. *This is quite an undertaking.*

She smiled, instantly charmed by the scene, no doubt the work of a young child. It seemed out of place in a room so obviously dedicated to serious work and study. She could imagine the vignette in her head, a little boy lying on his stomach on the floor, intent on setting up the soldiers while his father worked beside him.

Maria sat back on her heels and looked at the toy soldier in her hand. For the first time since agreeing to Burr's plan, she felt an unaccustomed flush of shame wash over her. Her fingers curled into a fist around the soldier as she processed the emotions the child's toy suddenly elicited.

This is a father with young children, and I am here to set him up and deliver him to his enemies.

Maria glanced up as the door opened, and Alexander Hamilton

stepped into the room. From her position on the floor, she scrambled to her feet as quickly and gracefully as her gown would allow, eyes wide, lips parted in surprise. A section of long curls had come loose from the ribbon holding her hair in place and spilled down the back of her bare neck. A flush crept over her cheeks.

"C-colonel Hamilton, sir," she stammered, embarrassed to be caught in such a position. "I was . . . uh . . . looking at the battle under your table."

Hamilton tilted his head and squinted at her in confusion. She held out her hand, palm up, the tin soldier in the center.

"I stepped on it," she offered by way of explanation.

He stood silent for a moment as he tried to sort out the scene, looking at her with those same intense blue eyes she remembered from years ago. Unable to hold his gaze, Maria lowered her head and set the soldier on the table.

"I'm sorry, sir. I know you're busy. I shouldn't have come here," she said, her voice almost a whisper. She took a step toward the door. He reached out and put a light hand on her elbow, stopping her.

"No need to be embarrassed, miss. I'm sorry, I didn't get your name."

"Mrs. Maria Reynolds, sir," she pronounced her first name with a long *i*. He let go of her arm as she tried to curtsy. Her cheeks were warm—no, *red* with embarrassment, as she self-consciously brushed the front of the fashionable white chemise gown she had chosen specifically to show off her petite frame and full bust. With its soft, unstructured bodice and sheer fabric, it had seemed to be the most appropriate thing she owned to wear to a seduction. She fixed the low ruffled neckline that had dropped off one shoulder and reached up to fix the ribbon in her hair, every nerve in her body acutely aware of his gaze.

Rather than being horrified by her unladylike behavior, though, he seemed decidedly amused by the compromising position he had caught her in. The corners of his lips turned up into a slight smile as he watched her try to compose herself.

He was dressed informally in tan breeches and a floral brocade waistcoat. Having already removed his jacket and loosened his cravat, the full sleeves of his white linen shirt were rolled up to his elbows, the neck open a couple of inches. His auburn hair was pulled into a braid at the back of his neck and tied with a black ribbon, a casual appearance that made her feel even more guilty for showing up at his house while he was obviously relaxing with his family. Thankfully, he didn't seem to be irritated by the interruption.

"Please don't go, Mrs. Reynolds," he said with a smile, gesturing toward an empty chair. "Have a seat and tell me what I can help you with."

Reluctantly, Maria sat down in the chair he indicated, still flustered from his entrance. All the words she had rehearsed in her head for the past week seemed to have left her mind entirely.

"Is your foot hurt?" he asked, breaking the uncomfortable silence. He picked up the toy soldier she had set down on the table.

"Excuse me?" she asked, momentarily confused by the abrupt change of subject.

"Your foot. You said you stepped on one of my son's toy soldiers. I've stepped on them myself, so I can attest to the pain they can inflict." He smiled, no doubt trying to put her at ease, and she couldn't help but smile back.

"My foot is uninjured, sir, thank you," she said. She tilted her chin toward the table." There is quite a serious battle going on under that table, but I do believe the Americans have it well in hand." To her relief and surprise, he laughed.

"Well, I should hope so. Although to hear my enemies tell it, I am no doubt teaching my sons to follow in my monarchist footsteps."

Although his words were light, she could detect a slight edge to his voice.

"How many do you have?" she asked as he walked around his desk to sit in the chair behind it. "Sons, I mean," she added quickly.

"Three. And a daughter." He smiled. "And you, Mrs. Reynolds, do you have children?"

"I have a daughter. She is six."

"Then you know what a godsend they are, despite their tendency to leave their toys in the most inconvenient places. I hope you and your husband are blessed with many more in the future."

Maria stiffened. Although it was only polite small talk, his words caught her off guard. She had not come here expecting to discuss children, or her ability to have them.

"What can I do for you?" he asked, quickly changing the subject.

She forced herself to focus on the task at hand. "I'm afraid I have found myself in a difficult situation, sir, and I am unsure of where to turn," she said, squeezing a tear out of her left eye. She allowed it to roll unencumbered down her cheek.

He looked stricken at the sight and reached into his waistcoat to pull out a handkerchief to hand to her.

"Thank you," she sniffed as she brought the finely made cotton cloth to her eyes to dab them.

"Where is your husband?" he asked.

"I don't know. He treated me very cruelly and has left me. My daughter and I are alone now." *At least it isn't a total lie.*

"I'm sorry," he said, his voice earnest, leaning over his desk toward her as if he wanted to comfort her. "What can I do to help you?"

Seeing his reaction, she began to sob into the handkerchief even harder. "I shouldn't have come here." She stood to leave.

Suddenly, he was there beside her, his hand on her bare arm. "Please don't leave, Mrs. Reynolds. Tell me what it is that I can do to make things right for you." His expression was sincere.

Could it really be this easy? For all his power and position, she supposed he was still just a man after all. He tightened his grip on her arm, and his fingers felt like fire on her skin.

"I want to go home."

"Where do you live?"

"I am lodging a block away," she said, "but my home is in New York. I was born in Duchess County. My late father, Mr. Lewis, owned a tavern in Poughkeepsie. My sister, Susannah, is married to Gilbert Livingston of the Hudson Valley Livingstons. My brother, Colonel DuBois, fought in the War for Independence."

She listed the family relationships like credentials that would allow her entry into another world, proof she was from a respectable family, not just some street urchin who had stumbled into his home.

Colonel Hamilton dropped his hand from her arm but remained dangerously close. "My home is also in New York," he said. "I would wish to be there too, if work didn't require me to live here. What is keeping you from returning, Mrs. Reynolds?"

"I have no money, sir." She dabbed her eyes and sniffed once again.

"Perhaps I can help, then? As one New Yorker to another." He put his hand back on her arm and smiled encouragingly. "This moment is not convenient to me, but if you tell me the street and number of the house where you are lodging, I will bring or send some money to you later tonight that should be sufficient to return you to your friends and family."

"Oh no, sir! That is too much to ask."

His fingers tightened on her arm, and he leaned toward her, holding her gaze with his. "Please, Mrs. Reynolds, let me do this for you."

He bent his head toward hers, their eyes met, and everything seemed to stop for a second—before he abruptly removed his hand and turned to walk back to his desk. He tore off the corner of one of the many pieces of paper scattered across the desktop, dipped a quill into the ink well, and held it out to her.

"Please write down your address, so I'll know where to send the money." His voice had lost its softness and had returned to a polite, businesslike tone.

Flustered by the sudden change, Maria took the quill from his fingers and leaned forward to write the number and street of the boardinghouse. A residual teardrop fell with a plop onto the paper, smearing the ink.

"Oh no, I have ruined it!" she gasped, sobbing into his handkerchief once again.

He picked up the paper and used the ruffled cuff of his shirt to dab away the offending tear. "No, you haven't," he hastened to assure her. "See. It is still legible." He held up the paper.

"I don't deserve your kindness, Colonel Hamilton," she said, looking up through her tear-clumped lashes and making a great show of gathering her emotions. "How can I ever thank you, sir?"

To her immediate gratification, he blushed and stammered slightly.

"N-no need to thank me, Mrs. Reynolds," he said, although the gleam in his eyes told her that he was already thinking of ways to accept her gratitude.

He cleared his throat. "I am presently expected at supper with my family, so I must take my leave. But you have my word that I will send the promised funds to you later tonight. My housekeeper will see you out." He picked up the scrap of paper with her address, folded it in half, and tucked it inside his waistcoat pocket.

Then he was gone, and Maria stood in the middle of his office, the corners of her lips curled into a victorious smile.

Four

Maria paced back and forth across her small bedroom. Darkness had fallen several hours ago, and the room was bathed with the soft glow of candlelight. She had returned from Colonel Hamilton's in time for supper and enjoyed a hearty meal of roast beef and carrots, too distracted to respond in kind to the other boarders' questions and banter. Colonel Hamilton had not given her a time frame for expecting him, so every time the front door opened, she turned in her chair, trying to catch sight of who was arriving.

After supper, she and Susan retired to their room early. She got her daughter ready for bed, and they sat together while Maria read aloud to her from a beautifully illustrated book of fairy tales Elijah gifted her last Christmas. Maria could barely concentrate, though, holding her breath each time she heard footsteps coming down the hall—and releasing it when the footsteps went past her door without stopping.

She had been sharing the bed with Susan since arriving in Philadelphia. Anticipating the evenings events, Maria had pulled out the small trundle bed earlier and placed it between her bed and the wall. She also set up the dressing screen between her daughter's bed and her own, a barrier allowing for a respectable amount of privacy.

Thankfully, Susan didn't question the new sleeping arrangements. Their unconventional lifestyle had often required an early bedtime or a change in beds, so this was not unusual. The only thing different tonight was that Susan had pleaded with her to read not one, but two of her favorite stories, and feeling guilty about kicking her daughter out of her bed for the night, Maria complied. When Maria was done, she tucked Susan in, and the child quickly fell asleep.

The hour grew late with still no sign of Colonel Hamilton. Perhaps something had come up, and he had been delayed in getting away. She would wait. She changed out of her gown and slipped a satin wrapper on over her shift—still respectable for receiving company—but much more comfortable without stays and petticoats. She took the ribbon from her hair and let her soft, golden curls fall loose down her back and shoulders.

Maria sat down at the table and pulled out one of her sentimental novels, hoping for a distraction while she waited. She had run out of new books several weeks ago, and with no ability to purchase more, she was rereading her favorites. Tonight, though, the words seemed to swim in front of her face.

After reading the same paragraph three times without comprehension, Maria finally gave up and closed the book in exasperation. The boardinghouse was quieter as the hour grew late, and the steady procession of footsteps up the stairs and down the hallway had slowed considerably.

She was just about to give up and go to bed when she heard muffled voices downstairs. Pulling her wrapper tightly around her, she quietly opened the door to peak out. She saw the top of his head as he came up the staircase and stepped into the hallway. Afraid that a knock on the door would wake Susan, she decided to meet him at the top of the stairs.

"Colonel Hamilton, thank you for coming. I didn't think you were going to make it."

"I apologize for the lateness of the hour, Mrs. Reynolds, but I was unable to get away any earlier." He seemed harried and distracted. He was wearing a jacket over his waistcoat now, so he reached into an interior pocket. "I've brought some funds to return you to your family as promised."

She put a hand on his arm, stopping him. "Please, not out here. Come into my room."

He hesitated. "What about your daughter?"

"She's asleep."

She let go of his arm and headed toward her room. He followed closely behind. She opened the door as quietly as she could and motioned him inside.

"As I was saying, Mrs. Reynolds," he said as soon as the door closed softly behind them, "I've brought a bank bill for you." He pulled the bill out of his pocket and handed it to her. He was standing very close, the candlelight casting flickering shadows across his sharp features.

She took the folded bill from his fingers and set it down on the top of the dresser without looking at it. "I can't thank you enough for your kindness, Colonel Hamilton," she whispered.

She looked into his eyes and reached out to put both hands on his chest, her palms flat against the cloth of his jacket. He leaned into her touch, his arms remaining respectfully at his sides.

She smiled at him. "Is there anything I can do to demonstrate my gratitude?" she asked, her meaning clear.

His eyes seemed to burn into hers as he bent his head so that their lips were only a couple of inches apart.

"I suppose that I can offer some additional consolation, if it is acceptable," he teased.

"Good, because I find myself in desperate need of such consolation, sir," she whispered back, her voice low and husky. She was rewarded by the sound of his sharp intake of breath.

"Then how can I say no? It would require a harder heart than mine to refuse a beauty in distress."

With a groan, the last of his restraint fell away and he leaned forward and claimed her lips with his. He opened the front of her wrapper and slid his hands under the delicate fabric. His fingers tightened around her waist, and he bent her back without lifting his mouth from hers.

It had been months since she had felt a man's touch, and for Maria, this was leaping off a precipice and falling into the darkness below. She curled her fingers around the lapels of his jacket and held on for dear life. She yielded to his passion, her lips parting eagerly beneath the onslaught of his tongue.

"Please, make love to me," she whispered between kisses. He needed no further invitation.

Maria had no idea how long she had been asleep when she was awakened by his lips on the back of her neck, surprised to find him still in bed beside her. Most men left as soon as it was over. The candles had burned down, and the room was covered in darkness.

She was on her side with the lean firmness of his body pressed tightly against her back. His hand rested on the curve of her hip as his mouth and tongue lazily explored the sensitive spot right behind her ear. She smiled sleepily and snuggled against him.

"I can't seem to get enough of you," he whispered against her ear.

She shivered and moaned with pleasure as she surrendered to their passion once again. Alexander woke her one more time in the night before she finally succumbed to exhaustion. He left her bed sometime before sunrise, but she was sleeping so soundly, she didn't feel him leave.

Five

Maria awoke with a start. The sun had risen already, and the bedroom was flooded with sunlight. She glanced over at the now empty side of the bed. A clear imprint of his head graced the feather pillow, proof it had not just been a dream after all.

She threw back the bedsheet and swung her legs off the side of the bed. Her shift was bunched up around her waist, leaving her bare from the waist down. She colored as she recalled the reason for that—and stood up slowly, her legs shaky.

She couldn't believe she had slept so late and was certain they had already missed breakfast. In a moment of panic, she looked around for Susan—certain the child, usually an early riser, couldn't still be asleep. Maria pushed her shift down over her hips and walked around the foot of the bed, peaking behind the screen where Susan's new bed was set up.

Relief flooded through her as she saw her daughter sitting cross legged in the middle of the trundle bed, the book of fairy tales spread open on her lap. Susan looked up when she heard her mother.

"Mama, you're awake!" she squealed. The little girl closed the book and sat it down very carefully beside her before scampering across the bed toward Maria.

"Why didn't you wake me, sweetheart?"

"I tried, but you wouldn't get up," she said. "You looked like the princess in the woods."

"The what?" Maria asked, momentarily confused.

"The sleeping princess, Mama, like in my book. The one who was put under an enchantment," she said the last word slowly, making sure to pronounce it correctly.

Maria blushed. She certainly felt like she had been put under a spell. She squatted in front of her daughter so that they were at eye level and put her hands on Susan's shoulders.

"Well, I'm awake now," she stated. "Why don't we get dressed and go down and see if there is anything left in the kitchen for breakfast? Are you hungry?" Susan nodded.

"Me too." Maria was ravenous, in fact, and her stomach growled in response.

"Go pick out a dress to wear while I get ready," she told her daughter, and Susan scampered happily toward the trunk that contained her clothing.

Maria walked to the washstand and poured some clean water into the basin. She bent forward, splashed her still-flushed cheeks, and patted her face dry with the linen toweling laying at one side. *He must have also cleaned up at the basin before he left.* She could smell his distinct aroma of cloves and musk on the towel. Maria pressed the cloth to her face, closed her eyes, and drank it in.

The scent of their lovemaking was heavy on her skin too. She quickly stripped out of her shift and replaced it with a freshly laundered one before pulling on her petticoats, stays, and gown. Later tonight, she would clean up more thoroughly, but right now, she enjoyed the comfort his scent provided.

Something on the floor under the dresser caught her attention.

She walked over and picked it up—the bank note that Alexander had brought her last night. *Knocked off the dresser in the heat of passion?* She blushed. She had completely forgotten about the initial reason for his visit.

Maria unfolded the bill. Thirty dollars. Enough to get her and Susan safely to New York, with some to spare. She smiled at his generosity, opened the top dresser drawer, and tucked the money under a pile of scarves.

After dressing, she turned her attention to the tangled mess of curls that fell around her shoulders in disarray. When she looked at her reflection in the mirror, her cheeks flushed again. She looked like a woman who had been very thoroughly bedded.

It took twice as long as normal, but Maria finally finished combing out the tangles and pinned her hair up as best she could before covering it with a linen cap. It would have to do for now. She combed Susan's fine hair—a much easier task—and tied a cap securely with a ribbon, so that her active child couldn't pull it off as she was prone to do.

Finally presentable, she and Susan made their way downstairs to the dining room, not surprised to find that the breakfast dishes had already been taken up from the sideboard. Perhaps they could eat whatever was left in the kitchen if she could talk to the cook.

"Mrs. Reynolds!"

Maria turned around to find Mrs. Folwell rushing toward her with a sealed letter in her hand. "This was delivered for you just a short time ago," she said, her curiosity evident. "You didn't come down for breakfast, so I didn't know if you had already gone out or not."

"We slept in," Maria said with chagrin as she reached out to take the note from her landlady's fingers. She popped open the wax seal—but stopped when Mrs. Folwell didn't move away.

"I apologize for missing breakfast, Mrs. Folwell. Can my daughter and I prevail on you for a plate from the kitchen? If there is anything left over, that is." Maria smiled. "We would be forever in your debt."

"Certainly, Mrs. Reynolds." She hesitated slightly before walking back to the kitchen.

"Thank you so much," Maria called after her as she and Susan took a seat on the wooden bench, alone at the large dining table.

As soon as Mrs. Folwell disappeared into the back, Maria opened the letter and read the flowing script inside.

Mrs. Reynolds,

Thank you for a most enjoyable evening. Might I have the honor of calling upon you again before you leave the city? You can send a message to my office at the Treasury with a convenient time if this would be acceptable.

A. H.

She smiled before discreetly tucking the paper into the folds of her skirt just as Mrs. Folwell returned with a plate of toast and fried pork belly. She set the food down on the table in front of them, along with a pot of homemade jam.

"This is all that was left over," the landlady said apologetically.

"It looks wonderful, Mrs. Folwell," Maria assured her. "Your kindness is much appreciated. It is our fault for sleeping in. It will not happen again."

Mrs. Folwell nodded and left.

Maria spread blackberry jam onto one of the smaller pieces of toast and handed it to Susan before fixing one for herself.

"What do you think we should we do today?" she asked her daughter as she took a bite.

"Can we walk down to the river and see the ships?" Susan asked eagerly, blackberry seeds stuck to her lips.

Maria smiled. "That sounds like a splendid idea," she said. The three-block walk to the Delaware River would take them past the newly created Bank of the United States in Carpenters' Hall, and from there it was only a short walk over to the Treasury. The subject of national finance was suddenly much more appealing than it had been only a couple of days ago.

"I just need to write a quick letter," she told her daughter. "Then we can go."

Although Susan's last memory of her father had been the night he had stolen her way, thankfully, the event was more one of excitement and adventure for her than of fear. Elijah told her that James and Susan had just boarded a ship bound for Boston when they found them. Maria still had nightmares about what would have happened had that ship sailed.

After that, Susan's fascination with ships began, so Maria assumed the memory was not as traumatic for her as it was for her mother. When they still lived in New York, Susan loved going down to the docks to watch the ships coming and going, and Maria indulged her. Although they could see the tops of the ships' masts from their room, they had yet to visit the riverfront while here in Philadelphia. Today seemed to be as good a day as any, especially since it would give her a good excuse to drop a note off along the way.

With their stomachs full, they went back up to the room, and Maria pulled out her small wooden box of paper, quills, and ink. She rarely wrote letters anymore, so it took her much longer to finish the simple missive than it should have, and Maria balled up three pieces of paper on the table beside her before she had something even close to acceptable. She reread the letter before folding and sealing it.

Col Hamilton,

If you can Come this night, I shall be up any time between nine and twelve O Clock. If you can not Call tonight, please send me a Line with a time more Convenient to you.

Maria

She wrote his name on the outside of the letter and slid it into her pocket. She knew this was probably too forward, suggesting he visit again tonight. After all, he was an incredibly busy man with a family. Even though it had only been a few hours since he left her bed, she already craved the feel of his lips on hers. Maria transferred his letter into the wooden box along with her stationery supplies and placed the box in the bottom of one of her trunks.

Patting her pocket to make sure the newly written message was secure, Maria put on her favorite wide-brimmed straw hat and tied it on over her cap with a satin ribbon. She took Susan's hand in hers as they made their way downstairs and out onto the wide, paved sidewalk.

The sun was already high, with a promise of a hot afternoon to come. Right now, though, it was still pleasant, and Maria opened her parasol to shade them from the sun as they made their way toward the Treasury. She wanted to deliver the letter before heading to the river.

They had made it less than a block before Maria saw Senator Burr's familiar, dark-clad figure on the sidewalk ahead, walking straight toward her. He held the hand of a well-dressed little girl who looked to be a couple of years older than Susan. *His daughter?* Funny, how in the year she had known him, he had never mentioned having a daughter. But, then again, she had never asked.

Maria froze, not certain what the proper response should be. *Should I ignore him, or say hello?* As it turned out, she didn't have to decide.

"Mrs. Reynolds, how nice to see you," Burr called as he waved. He came toward her, and the two stopped directly in front of them. He looked her up and down appraisingly and smiled.

"You're looking quite radiant this morning," he said with a smile. "This is my daughter, Theodosia," he quickly added. The little girl smiled politely and gave a little curtsy, definitely her father's daughter. Maria noted the similarities—the dark hair, thin lips, and eyes that seemed much older than her years.

"A pleasure to meet you, Miss Theodosia," she said, smiling at her. "This is my daughter, Susan."

Suddenly overcome with an uncharacteristic bout of shyness, Susan clung to her mother's hand and pressed herself against her skirts.

"And where are you two lovely ladies off to this fine morning?" Burr asked.

Before Maria could formulate an answer, Susan cut in, "We are going to the river to see the ships. My papa took me on a ship once."

Burr raised his eyebrows. "Yes, he did."

Susan's eyes widened. "Did you know my papa?"

"Yes, I knew your papa in New York when you were small."

Maria tightened her grip on Susan's hand. She didn't like the way this conversation was going. Not at all.

"So good to see you again, Senator Burr," Maria interjected. "I don't mean to be impolite, but we should be going. I want to get back before the day gets too hot."

Burr tipped his hat. "Yes, of course, Mrs. Reynolds," he said. "I hope you will be available for a meeting soon. I believe we still have some business to discuss," he added pointedly. "I will send a message later with a time I hope will be acceptable."

"Yes, of course," Maria responded, flustered by the familiar, coldly sardonic smile that she had seen many times in the past.

"Good day, Senator. Miss Theodosia."

"Good day, Mrs. Reynolds."

Maria stood in the middle of the sidewalk as they walked away. Her previously cheerful mood had suddenly evaporated. She knew that Burr would expect an update soon.

A little over a week ago, they had met at the coffee shop for a second time, and she had agreed to his proposal. Her dream of a financially independent life had overpowered any moral objections. He left it to her when she was going to put their plans into motion. Maria had no clue what she was going to tell him when he asked what had transpired. The thought of revealing the truth of their intimate encounter to Burr made her suddenly sick to her stomach.

And besides, she told herself, there was really nothing to report. Other than words of passion, there had been no exchange of political information. They had either been making love or sleeping the entire time. No in-between.

The whole thing made her head hurt. Maria would much rather think about more pleasant things such as a walk through the city in the sunshine with her daughter or the possibility of another visit from Alexander later tonight. She smiled to herself. Just the idea was enough to put her instantly into a better mood.

Maria was able to successfully dispel any more unpleasant thoughts for the remainder of the morning. She left the note with a clerk in the Treasury, and they strolled along the river. It felt good to be outside in the sunshine, although her nocturnal activities were already beginning to catch up with her. Maybe she could take a nap before supper.

They returned to the boarding house by early afternoon. As she opened the door to their room, she almost stepped on two envelopes underneath. She bent down and picked them up. Both were addressed to Mrs. Reynolds, in two totally different hands. Both of which she recognized immediately.

She opened the note from Colonel Hamilton first.

Mrs. Reynolds,

If it is still convenient for me to do so, I will call on you at your lodgings as soon as I am able to get away this evening.

A. H.

With much less enthusiasm, she opened the unsigned note from Burr.

I look forward to hearing the details of your recent meeting—meet me in the usual location tomorrow morning at 9 a.m.

She refolded both notes and slid the one from Colonel Hamilton into her stationery box with the first. She would burn the note from Burr later, as per their usual custom. At least she had until morning to figure out what she was going to tell Burr.

The rest of the day seemed to drag as she went about her normal activities. After a short afternoon nap and a hearty supper downstairs, Maria put Susan to bed. As soon as her daughter was asleep, she stripped out of her clothes and washed at the basin, sighing with pleasure as the cool water ran down her skin. When she finished, her skin was damp and smelled of the rose scented soap she had brought with her from New York. Moist tendrils of hair fell across her back and shoulders.

A soft knock at the door startled her. She had not expected him so early. Maria glanced over at the clock, just barely past nine. She pulled her satin wrapper over her bare skin, closed it tightly in the front, and opened the door.

Alexander stood in the hallway, his tricorn hat tucked under his arm. "Is this a convenient time, Mrs. Reynolds?" he asked.

She smiled at him. "Of course, sir. Please come in."

No sooner had the door closed behind him, than he was pulling her into his arms.

"I have been thinking about this all day," he said, his voice thick with passion as his lips found hers. He wasted no time sliding his hands beneath the flimsy wrapper to caress her damp skin. He drank in her kisses like a man dying of thirst and pushed her back onto the bed before unbuttoning and tugging at his own clothes as fast as he could.

Maria welcomed the fierceness of his ardor and matched it with her own. Within minutes, his body shuddered, and he collapsed on top of her, his breath heavy.

"My God, Maria, what have you done to me?" he whispered, his lips against her ear. "You would think I was a schoolboy and not a man of thirty and four." She had no answer and could only hold him more tightly against her, unexpectedly overwhelmed by the intensity of it all.

They remained like that for several minutes as they slowly recovered their senses. Then, he rolled over onto his side, pulling her with him so they were face-to-face. When he reached out and caressed her cheek with his fingers, she could not hide her sharp intake of breath at the feel of his touch.

"You were all I could think about today. I think you have bewitched me," he whispered as he leaned forward and pressed his forehead to hers, their lips touching, their breath mingling together.

She melted into him as the room seemed to disappear. Perhaps she too was under an enchantment, like the princess in her daughter's story book. *This is not like me at all.*

"I'm afraid my behavior was most ungentlemanly," he said after several minutes, breaking the spell. "I didn't even take the time to properly undress."

Maria laughed softly. He had been in such a hurry that he still wore his waistcoat and shirt. He sat up and unfastened the row of buttons that ran down the front of his waistcoat before shrugging out of it as well as the shirt underneath. He tossed both garments off the side of the bed on top of the pile of breeches and jacket already on the floor. Satisfied, he lay back down and pulled her into his arms, bare skin pressed against bare skin.

"There, that is much better, don't you think?" he asked contentedly. Maria could only nod and snuggle closer as he pulled the covers over them both.

"How long can you stay?" she asked.

"I am in no hurry to leave. Unless you are in a hurry to be rid of me," he teased.

"I suppose your company would be acceptable for a while longer," she teased back. "I wish you could stay all night, but I know that you will need to return home," she added more seriously.

He was silent for a moment as the truth of the statement hung between them. Then, he rolled onto his back, one arm around her shoulder.

"Truth be told," he said, "I am often awake late into the night and usually retire to my office to write. Mrs. Hamilton is quite used to my absence from our bed. My presence here will not be noticed."

His voice had changed, and he stared up at the ceiling. Apparently, she had hit on a sensitive topic. Maria made a mental note not to bring it up again. Not knowing what else to say, she laid her head in the hollow of his shoulder and pressed her face against the side of his neck, breathing in his now familiar scent. She placed an open palm on his bare chest.

He lifted her hand and intertwined her fingers with his. The cold metal of his wedding band pressed into the tender flesh of her fingers as he lifted their interwoven hands and kissed the top of hers before returning them to his chest.

"I already fear that you will be my undoing, Maria," he whispered into the darkness as she began kissing the side of his neck.

When he could no longer withstand her ministrations, he rolled onto her with a groan, and soon they were both so lost to pleasure that the entire house could have come down on top of them without their knowing.

Six

Maria walked to the busy coffeehouse and found a seat shortly before nine the following morning. Alexander had left her bed in the night with a kiss and a promise to return in a few days. Unable to go back to sleep, she had clutched his pillow to her chest and tossed fitfully until daybreak. Everything had suddenly gotten so much more complicated, and she had no idea what she was going to say when Burr arrived for their meeting.

She hadn't bothered trying to fix her hair, opting instead to hide the unruly curls under a linen cap. She was dressed in her plainest gown. Her face was flushed, her eyes puffy from lack of sleep. Normally confident, she felt like a lamb headed for slaughter.

Burr entered the coffeehouse only a few minutes after she did. He acknowledged her with a nod and stopped at the counter to speak to someone. A few minutes later, a cup and saucer carefully balanced in each hand, he walked over and set them down on the table before taking a seat across from her. He took a sip and looked her up and down over the rim of the coffee cup.

"Rough night, Mrs. Reynolds?" he asked with a knowing smile. His voice had a hint of something that could almost be described as glee.

Maria didn't rise to take the bait. She raised the coffee cup to her lips, took a fortifying sip, and gave her most pleasant smile.

"My night was quite pleasant, Senator Burr. It is only the morning that has left something to be desired."

Burr raised his eyebrows questioningly. "A lover's tiff, already?" he asked.

She knew he was fishing for information, and she was not in the mood to play his little cat-and-mouse games. "Not at all. I am just feeling a little under the weather this morning. It is nothing more than that."

Burr was not about to let her off that easily, though. "I assume you were able to obtain a private meeting with Colonel Hamilton?"

The question she had been dreading for the past several hours. Maria took another sip of the rich, dark coffee before answering.

"Yes," she said. Even the simple admission felt like a betrayal, and she looked down at her half-empty cup.

Burr waited for her to elaborate, but she remained silent.

"Did you take him into your bed?" he asked finally.

Maria could sense his growing frustration, and she knew she had better tread carefully. "Yes. But there is nothing of political or pecuniary interest to report," she added quickly, and in a much more defensive tone than she had intended.

Burr smiled and leaned back in his chair. "No matter. There will be time for that. I am willing to wait. I'm assuming you have another assignation planned soon?"

Maria nodded. "Yes. But the day has not yet been settled." That wasn't a lie. Unless she was asked about it directly, though, she was not going to volunteer the information that she had already seen him twice in as many days, or that he had given her money to return to New York at the end of the month.

"I am certain you will keep me informed of any progress on that front," he said. *That* was not meant to be a question.

"Of course," she answered quickly, unable to meet his eyes. She took another sip of coffee. At least she and Alexander had not discussed business when they were together, and Burr didn't seem to be interested in any intimate details.

Only a few days ago, she would have never questioned her loyalty to Burr. He had kept her secrets and been responsible for her day-to-day sustenance for the past year. He always behaved respectfully toward her and had never given her a reason to distrust him.

But something changed now, and every part of her wanted to be away from him. As distasteful as this plan was, though, she had agreed to it.

What does that make me?

Maria struggled to keep her emotions in check, and her fingers tightened around the delicate handle as she sat the empty cup back down on the saucer. She stood up and smoothed her skirt down over her hips and stomach.

"I will be sure to inform you if anything changes, Senator," she said, giving her most convincing smile. "I'm afraid I must get back to my daughter now. Good day, sir."

Burr smiled and stood to his feet, seemingly unaffected by her abrupt exit. "Good day, Mrs. Reynolds," he said as he bowed slightly. The sides of this mouth had turned up into a cynical smile. "I look forward to hearing about any future developments."

The moment she got back to her room, Maria's first instinct was to crawl back into bed and forget about the entire morning. But Susan was ready to show off her newest page of handwritten lessons when Maria walked in the door.

She took the page of crude, but carefully copied letters from her daughter's fingers and smiled down at her. "That's beautiful, sweetheart. I'm so proud of you." Susan beamed at her mother's words of praise. Maria's eyes unexpectedly welled up with tears.

What is happening to me?

Maria angrily wiped them away. However useful tears could be at times, there was no sense in wasting them on herself. She had to stay focused on what was important, and that was to provide Susan with a better life so that she would never be faced with a similar situation.

But those emotions gnawed at her insides and wouldn't let her be. She ached to feel Alexander's arms around her once more. She had never felt the things he made her feel, not even in the early days of her marriage, when she was still in love with James.

Whatever she may have once felt for James, it wasn't the same thing she felt now. Hers seemed like another lifetime ago when James Reynolds first walked into her family's tavern in Poughkeepsie. He had been so different from the local boys who had clambered over each other to get her attention. So handsome and worldly, full of dreams and grand ideas. He was twice her age, thirty then. Although he wasn't a soldier like her older brothers, he helped with the war effort. He rented out his sloop and services as skipper to transport much needed supplies up the Hudson River to the Continental Army and worked in the commissary with his father. She'd thought he was a hero. Tall and slender, always clean shaven and smartly dressed, his grey eyes flashed with excitement when he talked.

In those early days of their courtship, he showered her with attention. He would come into the tavern and stay all evening, just waiting for her to get a break so he could talk to her. And talk he did. He told her wonderful stories about the places he'd seen during the War. He told her all of his plans for the future. And she believed him. He'd told her that he loved her and kissed her like his very life depended upon it. He'd asked her to marry him within the first month.

Her parents didn't approve. They questioned his character and said she was too young. So in the end, she and James ran away together, south to New York City. Susan was born a little over a year later. But their marriage turned difficult from the very beginning. Despite the opportunities the booming city presented, James's plans never seemed to work out the way he thought they would. They moved from boarding house to boarding house—sometimes willingly, sometimes not.

They fought often, and he'd begun spending more and more time in the local tavern with his friends, coming home late at night smelling like tobacco and rum to join her in bed. When Susan was just over a year old, Maria discovered she was expecting again, and things went from bad to worse. Although James often threatened to leave them, he finally made good on that threat in her fourth month of pregnancy, and her life quickly descended into chaos and disaster. Only two weeks after James left, she lost the baby and almost died from the accompanying infection. Maria barely had time to recover before she was forced to set herself up on a course that ended in her current situation somehow.

A knock at the door startled her out of her thoughts. She walked over to answer it, opening the door to find John Folwell on the other side. In his hand was a letter, a stationery and seal Maria recognized even before she saw the handwriting. Her heart leapt.

"This was just delivered for you, Mrs. Reynolds."

She took the letter from his fingers, but he didn't move. "Thank you, John," she said. "We'll be down later for supper." He nodded and walked away as she closed the door.

Maria opened the red wax seal and ran her finger over the elegant script inside.

Maria,

I regret that I will not be able to call on you for the next several days. There are some plans in the works, however, that may allow for more frequent visits soon, as I very much hope to continue our Friendship. If it is within your power to do so, I also humbly request that you consider remaining in the Capital for the duration of the Summer, if you are not too anxious to return to your Family, that is. I will, of course, be happy to forward any funds needed for your continued residence in the City. I eagerly await your reply.

A. H.

Maria could not help but smile as she read the words, suddenly giddy at the idea of being able to see him more often. *What is happening here?* She had never allowed herself to become emotionally attached before, not even to Elijah. Maria knew she was on dangerous footing.

She wrote a quick reply, gathered Susan, and left to deliver it. They returned from a walk through the city several hours later to find another note under the door, this one without a name on the outside. Maria opened the letter, surprised to see a twenty-dollar bank note tucked inside.

I regret that our earlier interview was cut short—I hope you are feeling much revived, as you seemed to be out of spirits earlier—I am very pleased with the recent progresses made toward our mutual goal—please accept the

*enclosed note to be used for whatever pecuniary needs you
and your daughter may have, as I wish our arrangement
to be a mutually beneficial one—I am confident you will
inform me immediately of any future developments.*

Maria felt slightly ill as she carefully refolded the letter and stood in place for several seconds, trying to sort it all out. The money in her fingers felt somehow dirty and made her stomach roil in disgust.

Why should I suddenly feel this way? Burr had been paying her bills for the past year, she reminded herself. *Why should this be any different?*

But it was different. In New York, her obligation was to Elijah. As his personal attorney, Burr was just doing what his client requested. By paying her expenses now, her debt was to Burr—and she didn't like it one bit. Maria didn't bother to reply to Burr's missive but tucked the money he had enclosed into her dresser drawer instead—next to the money Alexander had given her on that first night.

After supper, they retired to their room and quickly prepared for bed. Susan went to sleep quickly. Maria settled onto the bed with a copy of last week's issue of The *Gazette of the United States.* Another boarder had given it to her at supper, and she hoped it would distract her until she fell asleep.

She was halfway through the front-page article detailing the rousing success of the Secretary of the Treasury's new bank when she heard a knock on her door, and her heart leapt into her chest at the possibility of a particular visitor. She made a quick check in the mirror above the washstand to ensure that her hair was in place before opening the door—to an empty hallway.

Disappointed and confused, Maria opened the door a little wider and stepped outside, looking both ways for the source of the knock. No one. She glanced down at the hardwood floor and saw an envelope lying at her feet, one with handwriting she recognized. She smiled and bent down to pick it up. Glanced around again, trying to find the source of the messenger.

Satisfied she was alone, Maria popped open the seal and unfolded the paper, her fingers trembling with excitement. She tilted the letter closer to the wall-mounted sconce outside her door and read the words by the flickering candlelight.

> *Maria,*
>
> *I was delighted to receive your reply earlier today expressing your willingness to extend your stay in the Capital through the Summer. As I alluded to in my previous letter, an opportunity has presented itself that will soon allow for more frequent visits in a much more convenient and private circumstance. Mrs. Hamilton and the children are leaving in two days' time on an extended visit to her Father, and I will be alone.*
>
> *I humbly request the pleasure of your company in my bed during her absence or for however long it remains mutually agreeable. It goes without saying that your utmost discretion would be required in this endeavor. If this plan is acceptable, we will work out the details soon.*
>
> *Yrs. truly,*
> *A. H.*

Maria stared at the words on the page. The prospect of being able to share Alexander's bed every night changed everything. Suddenly, the stakes seemed so much higher.

She caught a slight movement on the staircase out of the corner of her eye and glanced up to see John Folwell standing at the bottom of the staircase, staring up at her. Maria's heart leaped into her chest. *How long has he been there, and why is he watching me?* Despite the warmth of the hallway, she felt a chill run up her spine.

Their eyes met, and John, seemingly embarrassed to be caught, immediately lowered his gaze and walked away. Flustered, Maria quickly folded the letter and slid it into the pocket in the folds of her skirt. She forced herself to take a deep breath and gather her nerve before heading back into her room as if nothing had happened.

Seven

"After this, I had frequent meetings with her,
most of them at my own house; Mrs. Hamilton
with her children being absent on a visit to her father."

Alexander Hamilton, the *Reynolds Pamphlet*, 1797

Three nights later, Maria stood on the doorstep of the Hamilton's three-story red brick home once again. The hour was late, as he had a prior dinner engagement at the president's home and had asked her to delay her arrival.

When she raised her hand to knock, the door swung open immediately. With a smile, Alexander took Maria by the elbow and quickly pulled her inside before they attracted any attention. He had her in his arms, kissing her as soon as the door closed. Still wearing his formal attire, he'd already removed his jacket and loosened his cravat. She could taste the wine on his lips.

After several seconds, he broke the kiss and held her at arm's length. "Thank you for coming, Maria. I think you will find the accommodation here to be much more comfortable than your current lodgings. If you don't mind, I still need to finish a letter to post in the morning. Please, join me in my office."

Maria nodded, looking around the elegantly appointed entryway as she followed him into his study. She was so nervous the last time, she hadn't even paid attention to her surroundings.

"Please, have a seat," he said, gesturing toward one of the chairs in front of his cluttered desk. "I will only be a few minutes."

Maria nodded and sat. She watched him walk around his desk and take a seat in front of a half-finished letter on the leather desktop. She could just make out the first line, "My Darling Betsy . . . "

She quickly averted her eyes to hide her embarrassment for prying as he dipped his quill into the ink well and continued writing. His hand moved quickly and smoothly across the paper as she shifted uncomfortably in her seat.

Maria glanced around the study. It looked much the same as it had the last time. A quick glance at the floor in front of the window assured her that the toy soldiers were gone now, no doubt taken when the children left for the summer. A leather-bound book on the corner of his desk caught her attention. She leaned forward so that she could read the title on the spine.

Poems, Dramatic and Miscellaneous.

Maria heard his quill stop, and she looked up to find him staring at her with those amazing eyes. He smiled.

"You can read it," he said. "The author is Mrs. Mercy Warren, a true patriot and champion in our fight for independence. This is her latest work. A credit to the fairer sex to be sure."

Maria's eyes widened in surprise as she picked up the book. Female authors writing under their own names were rare. Rarer still were serious works by a woman that were praiseworthy by someone of Colonel Hamilton's reputation and position. She picked up the book and opened it carefully, noting the personal inscription on the title page.

"The Ladies of Castille is my favorite," he said before turning his attention back to the letter in front of him.

She flipped through the pages to the section he recommended and started reading. Maria read frequently—mostly newspapers, overly dramatic sentimental novels, or her daughter's folk tales. She had never read political poetry or plays before, and it seemed—very unfamiliar.

They sat in companionable silence while he wrote, and she struggled through the pages of Mrs. Warren's volume. Finally, he returned his quill to the stand before dusting and folding the letter in front of him.

"Shall we retire for the night?" he asked with a smile.

Maria lifted her head from the pages and smiled back at him. "Yes, sir. I would like that." She stood, carefully closed the book, and set it back on the desk. He picked up a candle in a holder and blew out the remaining lamp, plunging the study into darkness.

It felt surreal as he offered her his hand to follow him up the staircase and down the hallway toward a large bedroom at the back of the house. The furnishings were simple, but obviously of fine quality. A large canopy bed dominated the bedroom, with panels of blue and white paisley fabric at the corners and a valance in the same fabric across the top. A highboy dresser stood in the corner, and a delicately made ladies' dressing table sat opposite the bed. Alexander set the candle down on the bedside table and began unbuttoning his waistcoat.

So strange and intimate too, to be in this space with him, behaving as if they were a proper domestic couple preparing for bed. Unsure what to do, Maria followed his example and began undressing, carefully laying her gown and petticoats over the back of the dressing table chair so that they wouldn't wrinkle. When she had unrobed down to her shift, Alexander walked over and took her into his arms.

"Thank you for agreeing to come here, Maria," he said. He lifted his hand to gently brush the side of her face with his fingers. "I look forward to becoming more familiar with you in all ways possible." She trembled slightly and leaned toward him as he claimed her lips with his, and they both surrendered to the comforting forgetfulness found in each other's embrace.

Maria woke in the middle of the night with a jolt, her eyes wide open and her heart racing. At first, she was confused by the unfamiliar surroundings, but as her eyes adjusted to the darkness, recognition dawned. She struggled to sit up, but Alexander was asleep against her, his arm thrown casually over her waist, pinning her down. They both were naked, their skin slightly damp from summer heat despite the open window.

Careful not to wake him, Maria quietly moved his arm and pushed herself into a sitting position. Her cheeks were hot and wet with tears, the vivid images from her nightmare still fresh.

She had been running through the city streets barefoot, dressed in only her thin, white shift, her hair loose around her shoulders. Crowds of well-dressed men and women stood in a line on either side of her, jeering and tearing at her clothing and hair as she ran the gauntlet between them. Her shift soon hung in tattered ribbons on her body, and she clutched the pieces together in a desperate attempt to cover her nakedness.

As she ran faster and faster, the faces of the people around her swirled and changed, turning into demon forms with red eyes and sharp teeth. In her desperation to get away, she tripped and fell to her knees on the cobblestone street. The crowd quickly surrounded her, their hands now claws. They closed in around her as she curled up into a fetal position on the ground, screaming and trying to cover her face with her hands. Then, she woke up.

Maria lifted her hands to wipe the tears from her cheeks. It still seemed so real. Alexander stirred beside her, and she slid back under the sheet. She turned on her side to face him and pressed her body against his as if he could protect her from the terrifying images in her head.

He reached for her in his sleep and pulled her to him, but the comforting warmth of his arms around her wasn't enough to dispel the images from her nightmare. She buried her face against his shoulder and whimpered softly. He woke with a start at the sound.

"What's wrong?" he asked, still somewhat sleep addled.

"I had a bad dream," she said, taking a deep breath. She pressed her face against his shoulder. He put his hand on the back of her head and tucked hers under his chin.

"Shh . . ." he said comfortingly. "I won't let anything happen to you. I promise."

Maria relaxed against him, but his assurances weren't enough to dislodge the feeling of dread inside her. She needed more. She lifted her head and began kissing the side of his neck.

He moaned and rolled onto his back. "Go back to sleep, Maria," he whispered.

But she was not to be denied. The images from her nightmare were still too real. She rolled on top of him and leaned forward to continue raining kisses across his neck, moving her body against his.

"My God, Maria," he said, his voice raw with emotion and lust as she lifted her hips to take him inside.

She felt as if she were possessed, a wild thing she didn't even recognize. She opened her eyes, looked down into his, and surrendered to the tempest inside. Her hair fell loose in front of her face as she leaned forward, creating a veil that shielded them from the rest of world.

And still, she didn't stop, couldn't stop. Not until wave upon wave of pleasure crashed across their bodies and they could do nothing more than clutch each other desperately and surrender to them.

Eight

"I myself am in good health, but I cannot
be happy without you. Yet I must not advise
you to urge your return. The confirmation of
your health is so essential to our happiness
that I am willing to make as long a sacrifice
as the season and your patience will permit."

Letter from Alexander Hamilton
to Elizabeth Hamilton, August 9, 1791

As July turned into August, the summer heat grew more and more oppressive. Those who had the means and opportunity fled to the country as Alexander's family had done. Every few days, Burr wrote to ask if Maria had been able to obtain any information, and every day, she put him off. She could also tell from the tone of his letters that he was growing impatient with her.

For the past week, Maria had spent every night in Alexander's bed and returned to her room shortly before sunset each morning. After that first night, he'd invited her to bring Susan to sleep in his daughter's room. As usual, Susan had accepted the change without question. The entire experience would have been idyllic if it hadn't been for the specter of Burr and her own betrayal hanging over them. Like a ticking clock counting down the hours until the truth would be revealed, dread consumed her—a dread when her own lies would come crashing down around her.

Maria no longer had any intention of providing Burr with information that could harm Alexander, even if she had discovered any evidence of corruption, which she had not. As her emotional connection to Alexander grew, so did her resolve to cast her lot with her lover, even if this meant temporarily giving up on her dream of a respectable ladies' boardinghouse. She could come up with another plan that didn't involve selling her soul. Maria still had not gathered the courage to inform Burr of her decision, though. Part of her hoped (albeit naively) that Burr would somehow just go away.

Lying in bed in the darkness each night, they had begun to share confidences, but nothing of the business or pecuniary kind. He had asked about her family and her estranged husband, and Maria did her best to answer honestly—avoiding the ways and means of how she had been truly supporting herself and Susan for the past several years.

When he asked her outright, she admitted to her arrangement with Elijah, just not to the scores of other men she had entertained in the years prior. Alexander had apparently done some legal work for Elijah in New York several years ago and thought highly of him, so instead of being appalled by her admission, he was surprisingly understanding. He told Maria she reminded him of his mother—who also was forced to live outside of society's rules—although he provided no further details about his family or childhood. Maria did not ask and could not tell whether this comparison was a good thing or a bad thing.

She even shared with him the details of her miscarriage and near fatality from the accompanying blood loss and fever, that the doctor attending her said she would probably never have another child as a result. Although he was sympathetic and wiped away the tears her memories still brought up, she knew that her inability to bear more children was probably a relief to him. After all, in relationships such as theirs, a child was more a complication than a blessing.

In the first few years after the loss, Maria had worried that perhaps the doctor had been wrong, and she was careful. When she became exclusive with Elijah, she no longer worried about it as there would be no doubt of paternity. In the year they were together she had not become *enceinte*, even though she knew that Elijah had fathered multiple (now grown) children with his wife. She'd given up hope of ever having another child. Considering her lifestyle, it was probably for the best.

Lying beside Alexander in the darkness, Maria gathered the courage to confide her boardinghouse idea to him, something she had not shared with anyone. He did not dismiss it as silly or unrealistic, and even suggested that perhaps he could aide her in setting it up. He did not make any promises, just like he didn't discuss many details about his domestic life. One night he did confess that Mrs. Hamilton and their youngest son had been ill in the spring and, concerned for her health, he had not slept in their martial bed for the past several months. The fact that it was the same marital bed Maria now shared with him was not lost on her. His confession gave her a brief pang of guilt, which she quickly pushed aside. He didn't elaborate on the intimate revelation, and she didn't ask.

In the year Maria was Elijah's mistress, he never brought up his wife or shared any domestic concerns. He had never talked about his family at all, in fact. Gentlemen took mistresses, and as long as they were discreet, nothing was thought of it. In certain social circles it was frequently just the way things were done.

Over the next few days, Alexander confirmed his desire to continue their arrangement even after Mrs. Hamilton and the children returned, although he warned her that he would not be able to provide for her as generously as Elijah had done. Maria knew the fact that she immediately agreed to the arrangement without even asking for the details was proof enough she was already in much too deep.

Nine

A week later, Maria left Alexander's house by the back door just after sunrise wearing the same gown she had arrived in the night before. As usual, she carried her sleeping daughter the short distance back to their boardinghouse. The fragrant aroma of freshly baked bread drifted in from the dining room as she quietly slipped inside the front door and headed up the stairs. As had become her custom, she went directly up to her room to wash and change her clothes before going back down to eat.

Balancing Susan with one hand, she unlocked the door and stepped inside. Her eyes went immediately to the letter on the top of the dresser—delivered yesterday afternoon—one she had left unopened. The letter was unaddressed, and no need to wonder who it was from, the fourth such message she had received this week. While she ignored the others, she knew she would have to deal with Burr soon.

Maria lay Susan down in the middle of the bed, quickly undressed, and bathed at the basin before slipping into a clean shift and fresh gown. Her monthly courses had started the day before, and she fixed a clean length of cotton fabric between her legs. She was surprised that Alexander still wanted her company last night. He seemed content just holding her as they slept, and she had grown used to his comforting presence beside her. Maria recognized full well the danger of such a connection, even if she didn't want to admit it.

When she started to brush her hair, the unopened letter seemed to taunt her. Knowing she couldn't avoid it any longer, she picked up the newest letter and popped open the wax seal.

> *I am disappointed you have not replied to my last messages—It is of the utmost importance that you meet with me tomorrow morning at the usual location and time to provide an update on our current project—I will expect to see you there.*

She felt instantly rebuked by Burr's tone; he had never been this short with her before. Maria glanced quickly at the clock, just after seven. She had just enough time to get Susan ready for the day and eat breakfast before heading to the coffeehouse.

Already steeling herself against Burr's expected anger, she walked into the coffeehouse shortly after nine. Burr was already there, seated at a table toward the back. He signaled to her as she walked in the door, and she made her way to him, weaving between the tables and other patrons. He stood to greet her.

"Glad to see you could make it, Mrs. Reynolds," he said. He smiled pleasantly, one that didn't quite match the intensity and irritation in his dark eyes. "I was beginning to worry."

She took a seat opposite him, her back to the door. A cup of coffee waited for her on the table.

"I apologize for being late," she said without meeting his eyes. "It's been a busy morning." She reached for the cup in front of her and took a fortifying sip of the hot liquid.

"I'm sure it has," he said, raising his eyebrows. "Let's not waste time, Mrs. Reynolds. I have it on the best authority that you have been spending your nights at Colonel Hamilton's."

Maria set the cup down and looked up at him in surprise. "Have you been spying on me?"

"Not personally," he said with a smile. "But you would be amazed at the amount of information that can be obtained from a few well-placed coins. I like to think of it as protecting my investment."

Maria's eyes narrowed.

"But, let me hasten to assure you," he added quickly, "I am quite pleased with the recent developments. I am just disappointed you have not told me about them yourself."

"I have nothing of interest to report."

"Do you expect me to believe, Mrs. Reynolds, that you are in his house and in his bed every night and have learned nothing of importance?" he asked. "Perhaps I have overestimated your talents if you have fallen victim to Colonel Hamilton's supposed charms so easily. I assumed your arrangement with Mr. Wagstaff indicated a better ability to separate business from pleasure."

"I no longer wish to be part of your plan," she blurted out, trying her best to keep her voice from shaking.

Burr grew silent, took a long sip of coffee, and leaned back in his chair. He studied her for a moment. "I must say, I am extremely disheartened by your decision," he said finally. He leaned forward and set his coffee cup down on the saucer with a loud clink, the sound the only outward indication of the extent of his irritation. "I have obviously misjudged your sense of loyalty."

Maria shifted uncomfortably and drew herself up defensively. "My loyalty was to Elijah," she said, her voice rising. "And I never once betrayed him."

"I did not suggest you had," Burr said smoothly, seemingly unaffected by her growing indignation. "I was just reminding you of the assistance that has been afforded to you in the past few months."

"I am under no obligation to you," she said flatly. "I did not agree to any conditions when you offered to sponsor my relocation to Philadelphia. And I did not ask for any additional money. You sent that on your own. I have not asked for anything more. But I will be happy to return the bank note you sent me and to repay what is owed for our first month here," she added.

Maria thought about the money Alexander had given her that first night, still safely hidden in her drawer under her scarves. More than enough to pay Burr back. All the money she had, but worth it to no longer be under any obligation to him.

Burr raised his eyebrows. "Ah," he said, "so I see Colonel Hamilton has now assumed pecuniary responsibility for you." He didn't wait for a response. "I'm impressed. Perhaps my initial assessment of your talents as a whore were correct after all."

Maria jerked her head back as if she had been slapped. Her cheeks reddened with anger and outrage.

"I may be a whore," she said, her voice shaking, "but my talents have no doubt lined your pockets as well over the past year, so what does that make you?"

Burr didn't seem affected by her outburst. "I would rather like to think of it as a philanthropic endeavor to provide aid to a mother and child in a difficult situation. Do not forget that it was your husband who left you in that position, Mrs. Reynolds, not us." He smiled. "I shouldn't have to remind you that you have always been a willing—and I daresay—enthusiastic participant."

Maria's face reddened even more as the truth of his statement hit home. She was struggling to come up with a response when saw him glance toward the front door.

"Speak of the devil. And what delightful timing!"

Confused, Maria turned and looked over her shoulder. Her heart plunged into her stomach as she saw Alexander walk through the front door. She watched in horrified awareness as he headed toward the counter to order a coffee. He glanced around the shop, obviously looking for someone.

Their eyes met over the heads of the other customers. His widened in surprise before quickly narrowing as he noted her companion. He suddenly made a beeline for their table, his chin set, his blue eyes hard.

"Secretary Hamilton, what a pleasant surprise!" Burr greeted him in a tone that could only be described as giddy.

"Senator Burr," he said tersely.

"Have you met Mrs. Reynolds?" Burr said by way of introduction.

"No, I don't believe I have," he lied easily. "How nice to meet you, Mrs. Reynolds." He turned to her and bowed slightly. His voice was polite, but his expression belayed none of the softness he usually reserved for her.

This can't be happening, she thought. Maria wished for nothing more than the floor to open up and swallow her whole in that moment.

"I don't mean to be rude," Alexander said. He glanced toward the door as two men walked in. "I am meeting some colleagues, and I see they just arrived. Good day, Senator Burr. A pleasure to meet you, Mrs. Reynolds." He bowed and quickly headed to the other side of the shop.

Maria stood up from the table as soon as he walked away, almost knocking over the remainder of her coffee in her desperation to leave. Her fingers shook as she pressed her hands to her stomach. *This—was all too much.*

"I am afraid I am not feeling well all of the sudden," she said. "Good day, Senator Burr."

Maria didn't even wait for his response before turning and heading out the front door as fast as she could without running. She hurried out onto the crowded sidewalk and turned toward the boarding house. She was halfway down the block before she felt a hand on her upper arm.

Maria spun around and gasped as she suddenly found herself looking into Alexander's face. He quickly pulled her off the sidewalk and away from a steady stream of passersby into a narrow alley.

"What are you doing here? How do you know Senator Burr?" he asked before Maria could respond. His voice was low and hard, and his eyes flashed with something she had never seen before. His fingers tightened on her arm.

Her eyes immediately welled up with tears. Verbally sparing with Burr had been difficult enough but facing the brunt of Alexander's anger threatened to undo her completely.

"I knew Senator Burr in New York. He was Elijah Wagstaff's personal attorney," she said quickly, the words spilling in a torrent out of her mouth. She desperately hoped he would recognize the truth of the statement from his own work on Elijah's behalf. "Senator Burr was the sponsor who arranged for my relocation to Philadelphia."

Trying hard to maintain control of her emotions, she looked into his eyes for signs of softening, but found none.

"Does he know about us?" Alexander's words were short and harsh, and cut her to the very core.

For a brief second, Maria considered lying. But in the end, she was unable to do it.

"Yes," she said, the admission bringing forth the tears she had been holding back. She looked down at the ground, unable to meet his eyes any longer.

"I did not tell him, but he knew I'd been spending nights at your house." Her voice broke and her body shook with sobs.

Alexander's fingers dug into her upper arms as she sobbed harder. Then, as if he could no longer trust himself to touch her, he released her and took a step back. He put his hand to his head and grabbed a handful of hair in his fist.

"I can't believe you would do this to me," he said, his voice trembling with anger. He began pacing back and forth in front of her.

She cried harder, barely able to remain on her feet.

"I'm sorry," she sobbed. "I never meant for this to happen." She reached out to grab his arm, but he shook her off.

"Are you and Burr lovers?" he asked, stopping directly in front of her. His voice shook with emotion.

She looked up at him in surprise. *That* had never occurred to her.

"No, sir! We have never shared anything other than a business relationship. I swear to you, that is the truth!"

"Don't lie to me, Maria," he said, taking a step closer, his face was only inches from hers. "I will not be played for a fool."

"I am not lying!"

He stared into her eyes, as if trying to ascertain the truth from them. This time she held his gaze, tears streaming unbidden down her cheeks. She watched his eyes soften slightly; he seemed to consider her words for several seconds before speaking.

"Burr is a dangerous man, Maria," he said finally, his voice tight and deadly serious. "He practically stole the Senate seat from my father-in-law through his scheming, and now—thanks to you—he has damning information he can use against me. I do not want you around him. Is that clear?"

Maria took a deep, shaking breath and nodded.

Seemingly satisfied with her answer, he stepped back. "I have a social engagement tonight," he said without meeting her eyes. "So

I regret that I will not be able to entertain you at my home this evening." He swallowed hard and continued. "I have much to consider."

Unable to trust her own voice, Maria could only nod. He seemed to reconsider briefly before his face hardened again. Alexander turned around and headed back into the coffeehouse, leaving her standing with trembling knees in the middle of the alley.

Ten

A persistent knock at the door woke Maria from a fitful sleep sometime after midnight. Confused, she struggled to sit up on the side of the bed before leaning over to light the candle on the table. Her face was swollen, her eyes puffy and red. Still half asleep, she stood up, adjusted her shift, and walked to the door.

She put her ear against the wood, her heart pounding in her chest. "Who is it?" she asked, her voice raw from the emotional outpourings of the past few hours.

"It's me, Maria."

Her heart leaped into her throat at the sound of Alexander's voice, and she slid the bolt to pull the door open. He quickly stepped into the room and closed the door behind him.

The candlelight cast flickering shadows across his face, and his hair stuck out from his head at various angles. She had never seen him so disheveled. Without a word, he pulled her into his arms.

"I could not stay away," he said as his lips sought hers. He sounded as if he were confessing his greatest weakness. His voice was broken and defeated.

"I'm so sorry," she whispered. She pressed her lips against the stubble on his cheek as he held her tight. She caught her breath with a sob as her knees threatened to give way beneath her. He quickly scooped her up off her feet and carried her to the bed.

Still fully dressed, he crawled in beside her, curled his body around hers, and held her tightly until the sweet forgetfulness of sleep finally claimed them both.

Alexander staggered from her bed, still wearing the wrinkled clothes he had slept in and left without a word before sunrise. Maria rolled over and buried her face in his pillow as soon as she heard the door close behind him. She felt empty and numb, but there were no more tears left to shed.

She lay awake without moving as the sun slowly rose over the horizon and filled the small bedroom with light. She didn't move even when Susan woke up and climbed into bed beside her.

The misery and guilt she felt in betraying the man she loved was overwhelming. And yes, there was no denying it anymore, even to herself. She was desperately in love with Alexander. She buried her face in his pillow and tried to forget the events of the past twenty-four hours. This time yesterday morning, she'd been blissfully happy, and her life seemed to be on solid footing. Now, everything had changed, her future once again in doubt and turmoil. In turning against Burr, she was totally reliant on Alexander. She had no idea what she was going to do if he decided to end things.

In aligning herself with her lover, Burr was now her enemy too. His words had hurt as badly as if he had struck her.

She had relied on Burr for the past year. For better or worse, he had helped to create the woman she had become—a woman the young

Mary would not even recognize. But Maria had no illusions about Burr's motivations. She knew he did those things, not because of some emotional attachment, sense of responsibility, or even friendship—but because Elijah had paid him handsomely to do it. She owed him nothing.

Now that she'd made it clear she would no longer go along with his plan, what would Burr do with the information she had provided? While embarrassing, accusations of an extramarital affair would hardly end Alexander's political career. Burr was after information, proof of financial impropriety, and corruption. She had seen no evidence of anything close to that in her time with Alexander.

Up to now, Maria had provided no information Alexander's enemies could use against him, she assured herself. Even if Burr were to tell his political allies about her, the information wouldn't be terribly useful. Merely another drop in the gossip bucket, even if some of it happened to be true.

But Burr was not a man to give up easily. She suddenly felt exposed here in this boardinghouse. She couldn't help but feel she was being watched within these walls. Obviously, someone had followed her to Alexander's home and reported it to Burr. If she were smart, she would take the money she had stashed away and leave the city immediately.

But the thought of not being able to see Alexander again was unbearable. She knew he had taken a huge risk coming here last night. Even though they had slept in each other's arms, there had been no further contact. He had not spoken a single word to her in the night, nor when he left this morning. Maria had no idea what he was thinking, and she desperately needed to talk to him.

She decided to send a message. That idea was enough to finally make her lift her head from the comforting softness of the pillow. She rolled over to see Susan, already dressed and sitting at the small table eating a piece of toast while reading from one of her lesson books. Her frilly linen cap sat upside down on the chair next to her.

Maria was quickly overcome with guilt. Susan had evidently gone downstairs alone to get something to eat; she never heard her leave.

What kind of mother am I?

Susan looked up and smiled as Maria swung her bare legs over the side of the bed. Slowly she walked over to her daughter and leaned forward to give her a kiss on the top of the head. Her entire body ached from having slept without moving, and her head pounded unmercifully.

Susan deserved so much better than this back and forth, precarious lifestyle. In New York they had been secure and comfortable, and now life seemed to bring nothing but uncertainty and turmoil. But Maria had also never known these feelings of love and desire that consumed her, either. The idea of losing Alexander was beyond comprehension. She would beg and plead and do whatever she had to do to convince him of her love and sincerity.

"I brought you some breakfast, Mama," Susan's voice broke into her thoughts. She was holding her upended cap out toward her.

Maria looked inside the white ruffles to see a thick piece of toast and a slice of boiled ham resting inside. Her stomach growled as she pulled it out with her fingers, instantly thankful for her daughter's initiative and resourcefulness—and feeling even more filled with guilt.

I am supposed to be the one taking care of my daughter, not the other way around.

"Thank you, sweetheart," she said. She sat down at the table and took a bite of the toasted bread.

"Mrs. Folwell asked me where you were."

Maria instantly stiffened. "What did you tell her?"

"That you were still asleep," Susan said, as if the answer was obvious.

She was thankful for the child's innocence and honesty, even as her cheeks reddened in embarrassment for allowing her daughter to go about the boardinghouse unaccompanied. She didn't feel safe here anymore. There were too many eyes and ears around here for her comfort.

Maria's mind raced as she laid the piece of ham on top of the toast and took a bite. She needed to come up with a plan; staying here was no longer an option. She had enough money to either leave the city or find more suitable and safer accommodations. But first, she needed to get a message to Alexander.

She popped the last bite of the improvised breakfast into her mouth as she walked over to their trunks and pulled out her stationery box. At the table she drew out a piece of paper, quill, and bottle of ink. Maria sat, took a deep breath, and dipped the quill into the ink.

Sir,

What can I say to Convince you of my love and sincerity? My heart pleads with you to Forgive me. I fear that nefarious actors are observing me with hopes of Obtaining information to injure you. I no longer feel secure here in my current longings. Please advise if you have Knowledge of where I can obtain a more Suitable arrangement where no one besides you knows where to find me. Please do not discard me in your Anger. I could not bear it.

Maria

She carefully folded the letter and sealed it, writing his name across the front before returning her stationery box to the trunk. There was no time to waste. She dressed quickly, washing her face and neck at the basin before securing a clean linen cap over her curls. Thankfully, Susan was already dressed.

She picked up the letter and slid it into the pocket of her gown. "Would you like to go for a walk?" she asked, holding her hand out. "I need to deliver a letter."

Susan grinned in response and took her mother's outstretched fingers. Maria took a quick glance around the room (*yes, no incriminating materials in plain sight*), and they left the boarding house for their short, familiar route to the Treasury.

After leaving the letter with a clerk, they walked back along the river and enjoyed the breeze coming in off the water. Not yet noon, the August heat was stifling already. But Maria was in no hurry to get back. There was nothing left to do now but wait for a reply, and patience had never been her forte. She had done all she could do, she assured herself. It was in Alexander's hands now.

By the time they made it back to the room, afternoon was upon them. Exhausted from the combination of heat, stress, and uncertainty, Maria quickly stripped down to her shift and lay on top of the covers for a quick nap with Susan. She had just drifted off to sleep when she heard someone sliding something under her door.

Instantly awake, she pushed herself up and swung her legs off the side of the bed, careful not to wake Susan. She picked the letter up off the floor, her heart beating loudly as she recognized the handwriting.

What will he say? What if he was offended by my pleas? Or worse yet, what if he no longer wants anything to do with me?

With trembling fingers, she slid her thumb under the seal. Two banknotes fell onto the floor as soon as she opened the letter. She bent down to pick them up. A closer look shocked her—*this is fifty dollars.* She put the money on top of the dresser and walked to the table to sit down. She looked at the letter.

Maria,

I have secured a small, furnished house for you at 138 Seventh Street. A Rent has been agreed upon. Pay that with the enclosed funds. You may use the remainder of the funds to purchase anything more that you may need to set up the household. I have also hired a Girl for you. She will arrive first thing in the Morning. Pack and take what you can as soon as you get this note. The Landlord, Mr. Otis, will meet you there. I have told him you are a distant Cousin from New York and that you have found yourself alone in the City with your daughter. He has not been told anything more. You are not to return to your current lodgings after you leave. I will send a wagon at first light to retrieve your trunks. I will come see you Tonight. We have much to discuss.

A. H.

Maria carefully refolded the letter as she considered its contents. Her initial reaction was profound relief and gratitude. His generosity was far more than she had expected. She was incredibly relieved he had found her a safe place to stay, even more so that he already had plans to come by later tonight to see her. If he still had doubts, she was confident in her ability to convince him of her sincerity in person.

Suddenly, there was much to do. She needed to pack their trunks and gather what they needed for tonight. Maria quickly slid back into the gown she had just removed, picked up her leather portmanteau, and began stuffing what she and Susan needed inside. Thankfully, the limited space here had not allowed them to unpack completely in the weeks since they had arrived in the city.

Maria opened the dresser drawers and emptied them out onto the bed. She pulled out the thirty-dollar bank note that Alexander had brought her that first night and added it to the money he had just sent. There was also the bank note from Burr. She briefly considered leaving it in the drawer, but that would be foolish. She had no reason to feel guilty about taking it.

Without giving herself time to reconsider, she folded the bills together carefully and tucked them into her pocket, more cash money than she had ever had in her possession her entire life. In the year she was Elijah's mistress, neither he nor Burr had ever given her cash. A decision, no doubt, intended to keep her totally dependent on them, she realized with sudden clarity.

As quickly as she could, she sorted through the stack of scarves, stockings, ribbon garters, gloves, and caps, tossing some in the trunk and others into the bag with a fresh shift. She also added a change of clothing for Susan. Awakened by the noise and activity, Susan sat up on the bed and rubbed her eyes.

"Hello, sleepyhead," Maria said with a smile.

Susan looked at her curiously. "Why are you packing?" she asked, pushing herself off the bed.

"We're moving to a new place," Maria simply said.

"Why?"

"So we can have more room and won't be so crowded," Maria said as she gathered a stack of books from the table and carefully packed them into one of the trunks. "We need to leave soon, so get your gown on as quickly as you can. You can pick out one book to take with you for tonight. The rest will come in the morning."

Susan seemed satisfied with her mother's hasty explanation and began pulling her dress on over her shift. Maria continued gathering her scented soap, hairbrush, powder, and hair pins from the washstand. She slid them all into the bag.

Maria glanced around the room once more to see if she missed anything. *The letters.* On that thought, she pulled her stationery box out of the trunk, the one with the letters from Alexander. She didn't want to leave anything that might connect him to her, so she added the most recent letter to the stack and slid them all into the portmanteau.

Satisfied she hadn't forgotten anything, Maria closed the trunks, shook the crumbs from Susan's cap, and tied it on over her daughter's long blonde curls before securing her own. She slid the book of fairy tales Susan had picked out into the portmanteau and closed it securely. She made one last glance around the room before taking Susan's hand, stepping out into the hallway, and closing the door behind them.

Maria opened her parasol for protection against the harsh afternoon sunlight as soon as they left the relative coolness of the boardinghouse and walked into the heat. Thankfully, they didn't run into Mrs. Folwell on the way out.

While feeling guilty about running out on her landlord without notice, Maria had no idea what she would say. It wasn't like she was sneaking out owing money. The rent was paid until next week. But she didn't trust Mrs. Folwell, either—so the less information she provided, the better.

Maria allowed herself to relax a bit as soon as she rounded a corner. She pulled Susan to one side and stopped, trying to orient herself. She was familiar enough with the main section of the city from her daily walks, but the address Alexander had given her was in a section where she had never been. It should be easy enough, though. Front Street ran north to south along the river, Second Street ran parallel to that, and the roads were numbered consecutively going west away from the river. The boardinghouse was on Fourth Street, so all she needed to do was to keep going away from the river until she found Seventh Street.

By the time she found the street she was looking for, her forehead and neck were wet with sweat, and she could feel beads of perspiration rolling down her back. A couple of blocks later, they arrived at the address. From what she had seen since she arrived in Philadelphia, the city's residences seemed to be almost entirely composed of red brick rowhouses, so she was not surprised to find herself in front of one fitting that exact description.

Although it was narrow, the outside was clean and well maintained. She took in the freshly painted white door and window trim. A red brick chimney jutted through the center of the gabled roof. It looked cheerful and cozy, like a proper home. A small sign with the numbers 138 painted in black hung by the front door.

A plain black carriage sat in front of the house, the driver waiting patiently atop the seat. A quick look inside assured her that the carriage was empty. Looking around for the man she was supposed to meet, she walked up the steps to the door and lifted her hand to knock. The door swung open quickly to an older and stooped, white-haired gentleman who greeted her.

"Mrs. Reynolds?" he asked.

Maria smiled. "Yes. Mr. Otis, I assume?"

He smiled back and opened the door wider. "Please, please, come inside. Colonel Hamilton told me to expect you." He said the name with respect and awe.

Taking Susan's hand in hers, Maria stepped inside as he held the door open. She could sense her new landlord's curiosity.

"Colonel Hamilton said you were a distant relation, recently come to the city?" he went on, his question rolled into a statement.

"Yes," Maria said carefully, "My brother-in-law is Mr. Livingston, of the Hudson Valley relations." Just the right amount of truth, but not too much. "My daughter and I have recently arrived, and Colonel Hamilton has been kind enough to help us secure lodgings in a respectable part of town."

"Of course, of course." Mr. Otis nodded, his curiosity apparently satisfied by her explanation. "Please make yourself at home. If there is anything else you require, please send word by Colonel Hamilton, and I will do my best to accommodate you."

"Thank you for your kindness and hospitality," she said sincerely, giving him her best smile. He blushed and looked down.

Maria glanced around the narrow entryway and gingerly pushed open the door to the front parlor on the left. The single window faced the street and filled the room with natural light. The furnishings were simple—a couch, two wooden chairs and a small tea table—but more than adequate. As Mr. Otis followed, she walked out of the parlor, down the narrow hallway, and into the kitchen located at the back of the house. A winding stairway to the upper floors was in the left corner.

Dominated by a large fireplace, the kitchen was about the same size as the parlor. An intimidating assortment of iron pots and utensils hung from a metal stand on the hearth in front of the fireplace, a worktable along the back wall. A long dining table with benches and two high-back wooden chairs arranged close to the fireplace completed the furnishings.

Maria walked to the back door and opened it. This looked out into the small, walled garden, untended and overgrown. A black, wrought iron gate opened out into the alley behind the house. She noticed a carefully stacked pile of split wood against the wall. Even though it was small, the idea of having a private outdoor space was incredibly appealing.

As Mr. Otis continued following closely behind, Maria climbed the staircase to the second story, where she found two bedrooms. The larger one in front of the house she immediately claimed as hers, excited to see that Susan would have her own room at the back of the house. As with the first floor, the rooms were clean and simply furnished. She continued up the next flight of stairs to find another, much smaller and darker bedroom tucked in the attic space, a front-facing dormer window providing its only light.

Although not as large as Elijah's house in New York, this was far better than the boarding house she had just left. She was grateful she would have a girl coming tomorrow to help. She had no idea how to set up a household on her own, even a simple one like this.

Mr. Otis tagged along after her for the entire tour, back down the stairs and into the kitchen—where Maria at last remembered that she needed to pay him. She was not used to paying her own bills, even with someone else's money. Pulling one of the bank bills out of her pocket, she held it out to him, hoping it would be enough.

"Colonel Hamilton told me you had agreed upon a rent?"

"Yes, yes," Mr. Otis said, nodding as he took the note from her. "Let me get you some change."

He pulled out some coins and handed them to her. Maria glanced at it quickly and slid the money into her pocket.

"When will your husband be arriving?" he asked.

"Mr. Reynolds is currently out of state on business and I'm not certain when he will be back," she lied easily. She'd answered *that* question the same way many times over the years.

Mr. Otis nodded. "Do you expect your belongings soon?"

"Yes, our trunks will be here first thing in the morning. Colonel

Hamilton is also sending a girl to help."

He nodded satisfactorily. "Very good. I trust everything will be to your satisfaction. Fresh linens have been laid out in all the rooms. I will leave you and your daughter to get settled in. Once again, if you need anything, please do not hesitate to send word through Colonel Hamilton."

"I will. Thank you again, Mr. Otis."

"You are most welcome, Mrs. Reynolds," he bowed slightly, turned, and left Maria standing in the center of the kitchen, unsure where to begin.

"Where are the other people who live here, Mama?"

Maria looked down at Susan, still holding her hand. "No one else lives here, sweetheart. It's just us. Just like back in New York."

Susan was silent as she digested the information. "Will I have my own bedroom?" Susan asked hopefully.

"Yes, of course. You can sleep in the one right behind mine."

Susan's eyes widened. She dropped her mother's hand and ran up the stairs to the second floor. Maria followed.

She watched her daughter climb up on the bed and dangle her feet off the side. Maria smiled at her daughter's excitement and set the heavy portmanteau down beside the bed. She opened the top and pulled out the book and change of clothing Susan had picked out.

"There," Maria said, laying them down on the bed beside her. "It's official. This bedroom is all yours."

Susan gave a delighted giggle as she reached for the book. She laid it aside and hopped off the bed to put her clothes in the small dresser on the opposite wall. Maria watched her for a moment before closing the bag and lugging it into the larger bedroom in the front of the house.

She wasn't certain whether the girl coming tomorrow would stay here in the house with them, or if she was going to stay at all. She must ask Alexander about it when he arrived tonight.

Maria put the heavy bag on the floor of her new bedroom with a sigh. Her stomach growled. The last thing she had eaten was the light breakfast Susan brought her, and it was now late afternoon. Susan was probably just as hungry.

Hopefully, they could find a tavern close by for a hot meal. First, she needed to unpack and rest a moment. Everything had happened so fast.

She carefully laid out her toiletries on the dressing table and put her clothes in the dresser. She pulled Alexander's letters out of her pocket and hid them along with the remaining bank bills in a dresser drawer underneath her stockings.

She returned Mr. Otis's change to her pocket, and after a quick check in the mirror, she called Susan, and they set off to find a respectable looking place to dine.

By the time they returned the sun had already set, and the house was quickly growing dark. The boiled mutton and potatoes she had eaten for supper settled uneasily on Maria's stomach. The tavern meal certainly wasn't as good as the food she'd grown accustomed to at the boardinghouse, but having space and privacy from prying eyes seemed a worthwhile trade-off.

As they went through the parlor and into the kitchen, Maria scouted around for a candle or a lamp. All she found was a candle stand with two half-melted beeswax tapers in the center of the dining room table. She knew they wouldn't last long, though. Maria added candles to the mental list of things she needed to find or purchase tomorrow.

She lit the candles with the tinder box on the fireplace mantel, and the room suddenly filled with flickering light. After a long day and very little sleep the night before, Maria was already exhausted. She quickly settled Susan for the night and walked to her bedroom, setting the candle stand on a table in front of the window so Alexander could see she was here. She hoped he'd arrive before it got too late.

She stripped out of her gown and sweaty shift and washed off at the basin, thankful for the clean, cool water in the pitcher and a stack of clean linen toweling beside it. The familiar and comforting aroma of rose scented soap filled the room as she dried off and slipped on a clean, dry shift.

Alexander had written that they had much to discuss, but she really had no idea what he was going to say. Since he had sent her money and secured this house for her, he likely wasn't going to set her aside. At least she hoped that's what it meant.

Now that darkness had fallen, the house was oppressively quiet. This was a much more residential area of the city than where she'd lived before, the sounds of horses and carriages on the streets slowing down considerably during the past hour. She had always lived on a busy street, so the silence was a bit unnerving. A dog barked in the distance.

Sounds of something scraping against the side of the house underneath her window startled her. Maria froze, her heart pounding in her ears as she listened intently. She heard what sounded like footsteps on the sidewalk outside. Relief flooded through her.

Maria quickly picked up the candlestick, hurried down the stairs, and opened the front door slightly, expecting to see her lover standing on the steps. But no one was there. The evening air had cooled quickly after sundown, and a light fog hovered over the ground.

She shivered involuntarily, peering into the darkness and raising the candlestick for a better look. The hour wasn't especially late, but there wasn't another soul in sight. Spooked, Maria ducked back inside, closed the door, and bolted it behind her.

The candles had already burned down to stubs, and she knew she didn't have much time before total darkness. Maybe she could find more in the kitchen, or in a drawer somewhere. She headed back down the hallway toward the kitchen, looking around for more candles.

Under the worktable, she saw a small wooden box. Inside, she was relieved to find several beeswax tapers. She pulled out two and put the box back on the shelf.

The candles in the stick were quickly burning out and starting to sputter, their warm light flickering wildly. One went out—quickly followed by the second—before she could light the new ones, and the room was suddenly cast into darkness. Maria sighed in frustration and began feeling her way across the room.

She was concentrating so hard, she didn't hear the back door open. The dark-clad figure was already inside the kitchen.

Eleven

Maria spun around and let out a started yelp as soon as she heard the door close. All she could see was a dark silhouette against the pale moonlight coming in through the window.

"Who's there?" she asked, already reaching behind her in for something—*anything*—she could use to protect herself.

"It's just me, Maria," Alexander said. She could hear him making his way slowly across the room toward her. "Why are you in the dark?"

She put her hand over her heart and sighed in relief. "Thank God it's you, sir. You gave me quite a fright. The candles burnt out, and I was trying to light new ones."

"Here, let me help." He reached out for her arm, and she trembled slightly at the feel of his fingers on her bare skin.

He began to feel his way across the room with her, the faint moonlight coming through the curtained windows just enough for him to find the tin on the mantle. He quickly lit the candles, and the orange glow of the flame illuminated his face. Maria smiled at him.

"Thank you," she said, and carried the candles back to the table where she left the candlestick. She pulled out what was left of the stubs and put the new candles in. "Why did you come in the back door?" she asked.

"I didn't see any light in the front windows, so I walked around to the back. When I saw it was dark there as well, I became concerned and let myself in. You should get in the habit of bolting the doors when you are alone. I am sorry if I frightened you."

He took a step closer, and suddenly all she could think about was the way his lips would feel on hers.

"It was my fault, sir. I did not think to look for extra candles before it got dark."

"Tis no matter," he said. "I did not come here to discuss candles." His voice was somber and serious, his eyes hard with resolve.

She trembled as he leaned forward and put his hands on either side of her face.

"Lord help me, Maria, I have tried, but I cannot seem to get you out of my head. You haunt my thoughts and my dreams, and at times I can think of nothing else. I know it is wrong, and I fear I may regret it, but I am unable to let you go."

Maria stood transfixed, staring into the bottomless depths of his eyes. He paused and took a deep breath.

"When I saw you with Burr yesterday morning, I lost my head." His fingers tightened in her hair. "I want to believe you are telling me the truth about your intentions. I need to know that you won't betray me."

She blinked back tears. "I won't. I promise."

He held her gaze for several seconds, as if he could determine everything about her if he looked hard enough. At last, he leaned forward, his lips almost touching hers.

"I pray to God that you are telling the truth," he whispered before bringing his lips to hers in a searing kiss. She moaned and melted into him, and the room around them seemed to disappear. After several minutes, he broke their kiss and pulled her closer. She sighed and buried her face in his shoulder.

"I paid a visit to Senator Burr's office this morning," he said after several seconds. He pulled away and met her eyes.

"What?" she asked, confused by the sudden change of subject.

"I asked him what he planned to do with the information concerning our *amour*."

"What did he say?"

"He gave me his word as a gentleman that he has no desire to disclose our secret passion."

"Do you believe him?"

"No. But I don't understand what benefit he might hope to gain from disclosing a private affair when he himself is well-known for his many indiscretions."

Maria's eyes widened in surprise. She had no idea Burr had such a reputation. She *did* know Burr was after more than proof of a secret affair—and that made all the difference.

"I also asked him what business he had with you," Alexander added.

Maria froze.

"What did he say?" she asked, trying hard to keep her voice from shaking.

"He told me he knew you in New York, and that you were Elijah Wagstaff's mistress," Alexander said bluntly.

Maria's face reddened. At least she'd already revealed her connection to Elijah to him.

"He also warned me about your husband."

Maria looked up at him in surprise. *Why does Alexander need to worry about my husband?*

"What did he tell you about Mr. Reynolds?"

"That he is a man without morals or character, who will do anything for money, including selling his own wife."

Maria was quiet as the words sank in. "That's not what happened," she said, more defensively than she'd intended.

"What did happen?" he asked, his fingers tightening around her upper arms. "And I want the whole truth this time, not the over-dramatic yarn you spun when you showed up on my doorstep," he warned. "I don't care what is in your past, only that you do not lie to me about it."

Maria swallowed hard but met his eyes. If she hoped to regain his trust, she was going to have to be honest about everything. Everything except Burr's conspiracy against him. Despite his assurances to the contrary, she knew he would never forgive her for her part in that.

"I told the truth when I told you Mr. Reynolds had treated me cruelly. He left me for the first time when Susan was still a babe, and I was four months gone with another." Her voice choked with emotion.

"What did you do?"

"A neighbor took pity on our situation and took us in."

"Why did you not return to your family?"

"I was embarrassed and did not know if they would receive us, as I had defied their wishes years before when I ran away to marry Mr. Reynolds."

"Is that when you suffered the miscarriage?"

Maria nodded, squeezing her eyes tight against the memory of that night. There had been so much blood. She could still remember the smell, the feel of it hot and sticky on her thighs. Maria opened her eyes to see his expression had softened, although he hadn't relaxed his grip on her arms or made any efforts to comfort her.

He is going to make me tell him everything.

"Mr. Reynolds returned a few weeks later, before I had recovered, and begged a reconciliation, which I submitted to. A couple of months later, he said the most horrible things to me and left us again."

"What reason did he give?"

Maria blushed and looked down. "That I was not behaving as a proper wife to him." She paused, humiliated by the disclosure. "I was angry, and I blamed him for causing the miscarriage and for leaving me alone," she added defensively.

Alexander's eyes softened with empathy. "I'm so sorry, Maria," he finally muttered.

Maria sniffed and cleared her throat, resolved to go on. "I determined then that I would never be in a position to depend on him again, and I would make my own way for us."

"How?" he asked, even though his eyes told her that he already knew.

He is going to make me say it.

Shame washed over Maria. One thing to admit being a mistress to one man, quite another to confess she had sold her charms to many. But no backing out now.

"By entertaining gentleman."

"Did you live in a house with others?"

"No," she said emphatically. "I worked alone. And I did not ply my trade on the streets. I only met with a small number of respectable gentlemen, customers I was certain would not do any mischief to me."

"Where was Susan?" he asked.

Maria swallowed hard. "With me. I could not bear to send her away. But I never had any visitors during the day. Only at night after she had gone to sleep." He could hardly judge her for that, she thought, since he had consented to the same arrangement himself.

"How long did this continue before your arrangement with Mr.

Wagstaff?"

"Two years." His hands were still on her arms, and she stepped forward and pressed herself against him, tilting her chin up to invite a kiss. Anything to make him stop asking questions. But he was not to be dissuaded; he held her out at arm's length once again.

"Did Mr. Reynolds return during those years?"

"Yes. He would be gone for several months, then return unexpectedly and try to effect a reconciliation, which I never agreed to. I never allowed him to share my bed again. But as he was my husband, I couldn't force him to leave."

"Did he know what you were doing?"

"Yes. Instead of being offended by it, though, he saw it as an opportunity and insisted that I seek out certain high and influential gentlemen in order to make even *more* money."

"Was Mr. Wagstaff one of those men?"

"Yes. Mr. Reynolds sought out Mr. Wagstaff, not I."

"What was Mr. Reynolds's relationship to Mr. Wagstaff?" he asked.

"Mr. Reynolds had worked off and on for Mr. Wagstaff's shipping company, but I don't know exactly what he did. I was not privy to Mr. Reynolds's financial dealings. Apparently, during one of the times while he was living apart from me, he was arrested and jailed, and Mr. Wagstaff loaned him money to pay restitution. Mr. Reynolds handled all of the negotiations for my services. I never saw any of the money from Mr. Wagstaff, so I assumed it was going to pay Mr. Reynolds's debt."

Alexander looked absolutely horrified by the very idea of her husband's actions. "How did you end up being Mr. Wagstaff's mistress, then, and how did you come to meet Senator Burr?"

Maria took a deep breath before continuing. "Mr. Reynolds and I quarreled often, and after one particularly bad argument, he left while I was sleeping and took Susan." She could still remember the panic and terror she'd felt when she woke up and discovered Susan was gone.

"What did you do?"

"I sought out Mr. Wagstaff and begged him to help me get her back."

"I'm assuming he was able to find them and affect her return to you?"

Maria nodded. "They were boarding a ship to Boston. Wagstaff notified me several hours later that Susan was safe, to meet them in Mr. Burr's office."

"Was she harmed?" Alexander's voice had an edge to it.

"No, thank the heavens. She was confused, but I think she still remembers it as a grand adventure."

"Was it then that you became Mr. Wagstaff's mistress?"

She lowered her eyes. "Yes. When I went to get Susan, Mr. Wagstaff made me a proposition. He offered to move us to a proper house instead of rented rooms and had Mr. Burr set up accounts for us at various businesses to buy whatever we needed." She remembered how cold and businesslike it had all seemed. "In exchange for exclusive access to my services." She looked down. "It was a very generous offer, and I was thankful for it," she added somewhat defensively.

"What about Mr. Reynolds? What became of him?"

"I do not know exactly. He left soon after, and Mr. Wagstaff assured me that he would not bother Susan or me again if we remained in New York."

"Did Mr. Reynolds leave because he was threatened?" Alexander paused. "Or because he was paid?"

Maria was stumped by the question; she had never considered the latter. "I-I don't know. I was just thankful he was gone," she said truthfully.

"Have you heard from him since arriving in Philadelphia?"

"No. Mr. Burr is the only one who knows I am here. Besides you, of course," she added quickly.

"Did Mr. Wagstaff give you an allowance in addition to providing you with household necessities?"

"No," she said. "I charged everything we needed, and Mr. Burr paid all the accounts monthly."

Why did it matter how I was paid?

"So, you had no money of your own, and you were entirely dependent on Mr. Wagstaff and Mr. Burr for everything." It wasn't a question.

"I suppose." She paused. "But we didn't need anything else. I was thankful for Mr. Wagstaff's generosity," she insisted.

He was silent for several seconds as he digested the information, and Maria held out hope that it meant he had finally run out of questions. But it was not to be.

"What happened after Mr. Wagstaff's death?"

"He'd made arrangements with Mr. Burr to pay our accounts through the spring, but after that, he made no further provisions. I had grown used to the security Mr. Wagstaff provided, and I did not want to return to my former life. Then Mr. Burr offered to pay for our passage to Philadelphia—so we left."

"Did Mr. Burr intend on replacing Mr. Wagstaff as your protector?" His voice had a steely edge to it.

"No," Maria insisted. "He has never behaved improperly toward me. I swear!"

"What was his reason for bringing you to Philadelphia, then?"

"I believed it was strictly benevolent. We had formed a friendship during the time he worked for Mr. Wagstaff, and he had expressed considerable concern for our future. Since he would be relocating to Philadelphia to take his seat in the Senate, he thought the change in scenery would be good for us."

"Then how did you come to end up on my doorstep?"

Maria swallowed hard. "I missed New York, and I wished to return. I had heard that you were very generous to those in need, so I endeavored to appeal to you for funds to return home." She looked down, unable to continue to look at him as the lies slipped off her tongue.

"Why did you not appeal to Mr. Burr for funds to return?"

"I did not want to appear ungrateful for his generosity." Her voice wavered, and her eyes welled up with tears. "I do not know anything more, sir. I have told you everything."

He waivered for only a few seconds before pulling her into his arms to comfort her. She closed her eyes, laid her head on his shoulder, and breathed in his scent.

"I do not want to think about it any longer," she said.

He pressed his lips to her forehead. "I know that was difficult, and I am sorry. But I needed to know the truth before I decided my next course," he said.

Maria lifted her head from his shoulder, suddenly fearful. "Are you going to set me aside?" Her voice wavered.

Alexander pulled her away to meet her eyes, his own legitimately confused. "Why would I have secured this house for you if I was going to set you aside?"

Maria's cheeks flushed, and she smiled at him in relief. "I was afraid you would leave me if I told you the truth of my past."

"The fault is more your husband's than your own. My own mother faced some of the same difficulties, so I understand more than you know." He paused before continuing. "I needed to know the truth of how you came here, and of your connection to Senator Burr in case he decides to use this against me. I don't think I could set you aside even if I wanted to." His words sounded more like a confession than an endearment.

With a groan, he pulled her back to him and bent his head to capture her lips with his, his tongue eagerly exploring her mouth. Maria moaned.

"If only you were not still suffering under your monthly courses," he whispered.

"I am certain I can think of some other way to ease your suffering," she whispered coyly, glad the previous conversation had ended.

Alexander moaned and swung her up into his arms. She wrapped hers around his neck as he started walking toward the bedroom.

"Wait. The candlestick. It's the only one here."

With a frustrated groan, he put her down. She quickly returned the kitchen table and grabbed the candlestick. He took her free hand in his, and they silently made their way up the stairs.

Twelve

S he woke to his kiss just as the sun was beginning to rise over the horizon.

"Good morning, my beauty," he said with a smile. He brushed a stray blonde curl out of her face with his fingers.

"Good morning." She smiled back at him and stretched languorously, thankful to be in her own bed, in her own house—and that she didn't have to get up immediately to return to the boarding house.

"Your trunks should be delivered this morning," he said as he stood. "And you will need to go out and purchase some things for the house." He grabbed the linen shirt he had tossed over the back of a chair the night before and pulled it on over his head. "I'm surprised you did not go shopping yesterday."

"I did not know what I was allowed to buy," she said as she pushed herself into a sitting position. The thin sheet fell from her shoulders, leaving her bare from the waist up.

He turned to her as he tucked his shirt into his breeches. "You are allowed to buy whatever you need, Maria. You don't need my permission. The girl I've hired to help you should arrive this morning as well."

"How long will she be staying, sir?"

He seemed momentarily confused. "I've hired her to be a maid to you. She will stay here. She can quarter in the third story room." He paused. "Have you not had a maid before?"

Maria shook her head. "No, sir. Mr. Wagstaff hired a housekeeper to come daily to prepare meals and clean, but she didn't live with us."

Alexander stopped in the middle of buttoning his waistcoat and sat down on the bed beside her. "Elijah Wagstaff was one of the richest men in the city. You could have lived in luxury if you had wanted."

"I was content with what I had," she said.

"Did you ever ask for anything more?"

"Yes," she admitted. "I asked for a tutor for Susan."

"And did he grant you that request?"

"Yes."

He reached out to put his hand on her face. "You never cease to amaze me, Maria. Just when I think I have you figured out, you surprise me." He leaned forward and kissed her softly on the lips. "I must go home and get ready for work, but I will return later tonight to check on you."

"I will look forward to it, sir," she said with a smile.

He grabbed his jacket and paused at the bedroom door to look back at Maria, half-naked and sitting in the middle of the rumpled bed. Which prompted him to return for one last kiss before departing and closing the door quietly behind him.

The next few weeks passed quickly as their lives fell into a comfortable pattern. Her new maid, Sarah, turned out to be a spunky, emancipated black girl of eighteen. She was taller than Maria by several inches (even without the white turban she wore around her head), slender, and straight as a rod. At first, Sarah was aloof and professional, but as the two women got to know each other, Sarah began to share her story.

She had been born into slavery in New York City, only two years old when the city fell to the British in the opening years of the War of Independence. Although her owners were Loyalists, Sarah's first memories were the cruelty and chaos of occupying British soldiers. She was ten years old when the British finally left the city at the end of the War; she and the other household slaves were sold to pay their owners' debts. That was the last time she had seen her mother. When Sarah turned sixteen, she petitioned the newly formed New York Manumission Society, of which Alexander was a founding member, for her freedom. She was purchased by the society and emancipated.

Because she could read and write, she had quickly found employment as a nursemaid to the young daughter of a wealthy New York family—the first time she had been paid for her labor. But the child had died from typhoid fever a month ago. The connections Sarah's former employers had to Colonel Hamilton got her the position with Maria here in Philadelphia. Susan adored her immediately.

From day one, Sarah quickly went about setting the small household in order with a no-nonsense demeanor and a competence that belied her years, for which Maria was incredibly grateful. While Maria was Sarah's senior by five years, the younger woman's domestic proficiency made Maria wish she had paid more attention to her mother's lessons and done less daydreaming about the handsome soldiers who'd frequented their tavern.

Since moving into the house, Maria had become extremely reluctant to go out in public, fearful she would run into Burr, or anyone else she knew from the boardinghouse. She was happy to relegate shopping and errands to Sarah, including delivering messages to Alexander. Susan often went with her.

Maria knew it was good for Susan to get fresh air and exercise, but she also knew that Susan's presence provided Sarah some protection from the horrendous practice of kidnapping free blacks and selling them back into slavery in the South. With a white child by her side, Sarah would less likely be detained and questioned than if she traveled alone. She carried papers proclaiming herself a free woman whenever she left the house, just in case.

Instead of setting up accounts for her as Elijah had done, Alexander gave Maria an allowance every week, which she turned over to Sarah to purchase food and anything else they needed for the household. Maria carefully stashed any extra money in her dresser drawer. Even though it wasn't much, just knowing she wouldn't be left completely helpless (if something unforeseen happened) filled her with a sense of security she never had before.

With his family still in Albany, Alexander slipped into the house most evenings after Susan and Sarah retired. Maria's bedroom became their own private world, one in which—if only for a few hours—outside responsibilities and stresses were set aside and forgotten. The lovers continued to find comfort and pleasure in each other's arms.

He never talked to her about politics or current events, and she had no interest in pressing him. Maria came to accept that Alexander viewed her as a sort of sanctuary from which he could escape the everyday stresses of his position. Often, she read of his political struggles in the paper, but she never brought them up or asked him about any of it.

In the quiet moments she lay in his arms, he told her stories of his exploits during the War instead. As General Washington's chief aide, he had been by the general's side in most of the major battles and had attended every war council. But Alexander's favorite stories involved the more intimate moments, the camaraderie among the general's "family," as they referred to themselves. The dances, formal dinners, and flirting with countless women (respectable and otherwise) who flocked to the general's young officers were an integral part of relieving the tension of being at war. As were the good-natured teasing and practical jokes they often played on one another.

Less often, he shared memories of his childhood in the West Indies, his words painting a vivid picture of incredibly blue waters, palm trees, and vast fields of sugar cane. Intermixed with his descriptions of a tropical paradise, however, were the dark and ugly realities of life on the islands like the stench of slave ships as they unloaded their human cargo at the docks, and the brutal horrors of the auctions he had witnessed as a boy.

He was proud of his status as a founding member of the New York Manumission Society, and passionately pointed out the incongruency between the words of the Declaration of Independence and Mr. Jefferson's status as a slave owner. Conspicuously absent were any stories about Alexander's father, or the death of his mother—and Maria did not ask.

For the first couple of weeks after they moved into the house, he came to her almost every night, leaving at sunrise just before the rest of the household awakened. Midway through the month of September he was plagued by a recurrent kidney ailment he had had since the War, and Maria applied warm compresses to his lower back to help soothe the ache, curling up next to him until he fell asleep.

Mrs. Hamilton and the children returned from Albany at the end of September, and the obligations and responsibilities brought by that meant she and Alexander no longer shared the luxury of spending entire nights together. With his family home and his health restored, Maria feared that his need and desire for her would subside.

But these added challenges only seemed to increase his hunger. With his wife once more in residence and the social season in Philadelphia in full swing, making predictable rendezvous became increasingly difficult. More often than not, he showed up unannounced at her door late at night, still dressed in formal attire and tasting of wine.

When those late-night opportunities were no longer enough to satisfy their desires, they began planning rendezvous during the day while Sarah and Susan were out running errands. The added intrigue and danger of discovery only added to their passion, at times making it difficult to focus on anything else but their next assignation.

As September slipped into October and the summer heat gave way to the cool crispness of autumn, Maria found herself lethargic and out of sorts. For two days in a row she took to her bed with a severe headache, muscle aches, and a slight fever. When the fever worsened, Sarah made her tea of white willow bark, lemon balm, and elderberry. The tea provided temporary relief, but the fever kept returning.

Thinking changes in the weather were the cause, Maria wasn't concerned. She rarely got sick. Even when she came down with a seasonal cough or sore throat, she usually recovered within a day or two. But this time seemed different. By the second day she had no interest in eating, and soon developed a cough severe enough to make her ribs sore.

When her fever worsened, Maria quarantined herself in her room. She also wrote out a short message to Alexander and sent it by Sarah, warning him to stay away in case she was contagious.

As the day progressed, she continued to decline. By that evening the fatigue and weakness were so severe, she could barely find the strength to get out of bed to relieve herself. Her body had begun to shake violently. She huddled under the coverlet, trying to still the chills.

As her fever rose higher and higher, Maria began to drift in and out of delirium. She briefly remembered Sarah, despite her weak protests, coming into her room and helping her change out of her soaked shift into a clean, dry one. She also remembered how alarmed the girl seemed to be at her condition. Maria told her to go, and Sarah left the room.

She had no idea how long Sarah had been gone by the time male voices and sudden activity all around her pierced through her consciousness. She felt the mattress shift as someone sat down beside her, and Maria struggled to pull out of her mental fog. She opened her eyes to see Alexander sitting on the side of the bed. He put his hand on her forehead.

Or at least, at first glance, it looked like him. But something didn't seem quite right to her fever-addled brain. Some things were familiar, others weren't. This man's nose wasn't quite as sharp as Alexander's, his eyes not as blue. Confused, she could only blink her eyes while her brain struggled to make sense of what she saw.

The man removed his hand from her forehead and picked up her limp arm, pressing his fingers against the inside of her wrist with practiced proficiency. She felt the mattress dip again as someone crawled into the bed on the other side of her.

"Maria."

She immediately recognized Alexander's voice. With tremendous effort, she turned her head toward the sound and tried to focus on his face. His features were etched with concern, and she saw fear in his eyes. As Maria started to drift, he put his hands on her shoulders and shook her gently. She wanted to reassure him she was awake enough, but she couldn't seem to move or find her voice.

"This is Dr. Stevens," he said, indicating the man sitting on the other side of her. "You're burning up. We must get your fever down. Do you understand me?" he asked. He held her face in his hands, eyes staring into hers—as if he could force a response through sheer will alone.

Does that mean the doctor is going to bleed me?

Panic began to bubble up around the edges of her fog. Bleeding was the accepted practice in cases of illness or fever, but she didn't like it. She knew then she had to trust Alexander explicitly, with her life if need be. He would not let anything happen to her.

Maria struggled to keep her eyes open and nodded slowly. She heard the two men, one her lover and one a total stranger, say something between them she couldn't make out. Then, Alexander's hands were gone from her face, and the mattress shifted again as both men stood.

"Maria," Alexander was standing by the side of the bed now, bending over her. "Stay with me, sweetheart. Look at me."

She forced herself to focus on his face and struggled to keep her eyes open. He slid his arms underneath her and lifted her out of the bed in one quick motion. Her shift was soaked through again, the wet fabric instantly cool on her skin.

He pulled her tightly against his chest and carried her across the bedroom. She caught a quick glimpse of the metal tub she used for bathing in the corner without any recollection of when or how it had gotten there. He stopped beside the tub and gently lowered her into the water below.

Maria gasped as the shock of the cold water took her breath away, and for a brief minute she struggled with every last vestige of energy she had left. Alexander was kneeling beside the tub, talking to her again. Comforting words, yet she had no idea what he was saying. She gave up the battle to keep her eyes open and slowly sank into the water.

She heard words pass between the two men but no longer had the energy to try to make sense of them. The shock had worn off now, and she allowed the feel of the cool water to carry her away as her head fell back against the edge of the tub. Alexander's hands were her only lifeline, keeping her from sliding underwater completely.

Maria had no idea how long he held her there. She could feel the cold water displacing the heat on her skin bit by bit before she started shuddering violently. Alexander quickly picked her up out of the water and held her against him, an embrace that soaked him through and left a puddle soaking through the floorboards. Racked by chills, her body convulsed hard enough to make her teeth rattle. Both men worked together to remove her shift and wrap her in a quilt.

With her bundled securely in a cotton cocoon, Alexander clutched her tightly while Sarah came in, quickly stripped the sweat-soaked linens from the bed and replaced them with fresh ones. A little more alert, Maria could only shiver and watch. Sarah left, and Dr. Stevens pulled back the clean sheets. Alexander laid her on the bed—still wrapped in the quilt—and pulled the coverlet tightly around her. Maria closed her eyes in relief as the extra warmth surrounded her, and her chills began to subside.

She only opened them again when Dr. Stevens sat down on the bed beside her and put his hand to her forehead. He held it there several seconds before he nodded in satisfaction.

"Her fever has broken," he said to Alexander, who stood behind him. Alexander hadn't changed, Maria noticed, the front of his shirt and breeches still soaked through.

"But it is probable it will return in a few hours, and we will have to repeat the process," he added.

"What do you think is the cause?"

"My best guess is some sort of bilious typhoid. All we can do is try and keep her fever down. I'll give your girl a list of some dried herbs to use to make up some tea that should help with the fever. See if you can get some down her."

Alexander nodded. "Sarah is quite knowledgeable about such things and keeps a well-stocked pantry. I'm sure she will have what is needed."

Dr. Stevens nodded, stood, and looked at Alexander pointedly. "And you best see about getting out of those wet clothes Alex, before you get sick as well."

Alexander put his hand on Dr. Steven's shoulder and gave him a relieved smile. "You're always worrying about me, Neddy. You would think you were the older, not I."

Dr. Stevens laughed softly. "You always have liked to hold that over me, haven't you? But no matter, you would do your best to mind what I say in this. I should not like to have to explain to Mrs. Hamilton the circumstances under which you became sick," he added more seriously.

Alexander put his hands in the air in mock surrender. "All right, all right. Point taken."

Maria lay perfectly still and silently watched the two men's easy banter in confused fascination. They were similar not only in appearance, but mannerisms as well. Dr. Steven's words were tinged with an accent she couldn't quite place—the same accent she sometimes heard in Alexander's voice when he was distressed, or during unguarded moments of passion.

Dr. Stevens picked up his leather bag and Alexander followed him to the door.

"Thank you for coming, Ned. I greatly appreciate your discretion."

"Of course." Dr. Stevens stood silently for several seconds, as if debating with himself. "You are playing a dangerous game, Alex.

You have enemies all around you just looking for information to use against you." He lowered his voice. "I hope you know what you're doing."

"I appreciate your concern, but I can take care of myself, as you well know. And I don't need a reminder of my moral failings from my oldest and dearest friend," he snapped, his words suddenly sharp and defensive.

An uncomfortable silence settled between them before Alexander spoke again. "I apologize. I didn't mean to be short with you," he said, his words more contrite now.

"No offense taken. It's been a long day, and I'm afraid we have an even longer night ahead of us. She is not out of danger yet."

"I cannot lose her, Neddy." Alexander's voice sounded choked with emotion.

"I will do everything I can, and God willing, you will not. I'll be back in a couple of hours to check on her. You need to try and get some sleep while you can. I will think of a proper excuse to tell Mrs. Hamilton to explain your absence."

Maria heard the bedroom door close. She watched as Alexander walked to the dressing table and began unbuttoning his wet breeches and shirt, his back to her. He laid them carefully on the back of the chair and pulled it in front of the fireplace. Not wanting him to think she was eavesdropping, Maria quickly closed her eyes and pretended to be asleep when he turned around and walked to the other side of the bed. She felt the mattress dip as he crawled in beside her and rolled toward her, his arms automatically reaching for her.

There were so many questions swirling around in her head, but she didn't have the energy or ability to ask. The chills eased as the warmth of the blankets and his body enveloped her, and soon she no longer had to pretend she was asleep.

The hours that followed were an endless cycle of fever, chills, sleep, and confused wakefulness. Apparently, they were taking turns because sometimes when she opened her eyes, Alexander was beside her applying wet, cooling cloths to her forehead, and other times, Sarah—both periodically pressing a cup of warm liquid to her lips and urging her to drink. Much to her mortification, she vomited anything they were able to get down her.

Dr. Stevens occasionally appeared in her delirium as well. She no longer had any concept of day or night, but when the worst of it came upon her, the room was lit by candlelight, a small fire in the fireplace.

Caught in the throes of a fever dream, she began to moan and thrash until she had completely dislodged the blankets carefully tucked in around her. She could feel the mattress shift and someone in the bed beside her as she frantically tore at the thin shift covering her nakedness.

Her eyes were wide open, but everything was blurry. Even the soft candlelight seemed unbelievably bright. Somewhere in the recesses of her mind, she realized she was no longer sweating. Her skin was hot and dry, and her throat felt like it was on fire.

Alexander was standing above her, his hand pressed against her forehead. She could see his lips moving and hear him calling her name. He was right there, but his voice sounded so far away. She couldn't make sense of any of it. Without an explanation or preliminaries, he bent down, gathered her up in his arms, and carried her across the room again. He stopped next to the tub and without a word and plunged her into the frigid water.

Maria gasped in shock as soon as the water hit her body. As she sank down and the water enveloped her, the room began going in and out of focus, everything becoming dimmer and dimmer, as if the room were receding entirely. In its place came darkness around the edges of her consciousness, encroaching closer and closer. Peaceful, though—and she felt no fear or panic as she began to surrender to it completely.

Then, Alexander was directly in front of her again, shaking her by the shoulders. Even in her confusion, she realized he had crawled into the tub with her. She could see his lips moving, but the words were too far away for her to grasp. Her mouth fell open, and her eyelids started to flutter as the yawning darkness threatened to overtake her again. Without warning, he pushed her head underwater, completely submerging her.

Maria came back up sputtering and gasping, her arms flailing frantically before finding purchase against the lean firmness of his body. Her fingers curled into tight fists in the wet fabric of his linen shirt.

"Don't leave me." She could hear Alexander's voice clearly now, his words desperate and choked with emotion. "Fight for me, Maria." He shook her once more as her head started to fall back again. "Fight for Susan."

His words penetrated through the fog and, using every ounce of strength she had left, she pulled her head up. With cold water still dripping down her face, his slowly came into focus in front of her, and she met his eyes.

"Yes, sweetheart, that's it." His fingers dug into the tender flesh of her upper arms, but she knew if he let go, she would fall into the darkness and never find her way back out. She tightened her grip on his shirt, drew in a deep breath, and released it as a ragged sob.

He pulled her onto his lap, his hand on the back of her head, and tucked her face against his neck. Their clothing floated in the water around them while little by little, the fever began to retreat.

Awareness of her surroundings began returning in increments. The steady rise and fall of his chest under her cheek, the feel of his wet linen shirt under her fingers, the crackling of the fire in the fireplace, the soft cast of candlelight reflecting on the top of the water. She also realized he was shaking. Maria opened her eyes. His face was white, and his lips had taken on a blueish hue. His eyes were closed but his face was far from peaceful. She could tell by the way his jaw was set, his teeth clenched together tightly.

How long has he been sitting here holding me like this?

With great effort, she lifted her head. He opened his eyes and looked down into hers, his relief evident and palpable. She opened her mouth to speak, but nothing came out.

He bent and pressed his lips to her forehead. As he closed his eyes again, a great cry tore from his chest. He pulled her against him even more tightly and buried his face against her neck, his body racked with tremors having nothing to do with the cold. Unable to hold back, she began to sob as well, setting off an avalanche of emotion they could do nothing to contain.

They sat clinging to one another in the frigid water until Alexander shifted her sideways on his lap. With some effort, he managed to stand with her clutched tightly in his arms. Water sloshed out of the tub as he stepped over the side.

Maria heard footsteps on the stairs and a soft knock on the door.

"Come in."

Over Alexander's shoulder, Maria could see Sarah open the door, her dark eyes widening as she took in the scene.

"Is everything all right, sir?" she asked, concern evident in her voice. "I heard you up."

"Please come in and help me with her."

Sarah nodded, closed the door behind her, and rushed into the room.

"We need to get her out of these wet clothes," he said, his teeth clenched tightly.

Even though the fever was gone, Maria's senses felt dulled. Everyone spoke slowly. Moved around her slowly. All she could do was watch passively.

At this point, Maria was beyond any semblance of modesty. She didn't protest as Sarah began pulling the soaked shift up over her bare hips while Alexander held her. Her body twisted like a rag doll as the girl pulled the wet fabric up over her head and arms. The shift landed on the floor in a wet pile, and Sarah opened the dresser drawer to grab a clean one. Alexander stopped her.

"Don't bother dressing her. She'll most likely sweat through it again. I'll just wrap her in the quilt."

Sarah nodded and grabbed a quilt that had been tossed across the footboard. She spread it out on the bed as Alexander deposited Maria in the middle of it. They wrapped the edges around her naked body and tucked them underneath her. Maria closed her eyes in relief as the warmth began sinking into her skin.

"She's stable now, but can you get a message to Dr. Stevens telling him to come at first light?" he asked. "And please, ask him to bring me a set of clean, dry clothes as well," he added.

"Of course, sir."

"Thank you. I'll stay with her for the remainder of the night. Please show Dr. Stevens straight in when he arrives."

She heard Sarah leave the room and close the door quietly behind her.

Alone with Alexander once again, Maria opened her eyes and looked up at him. She wanted to tell him to change out of his wet breeches and shirt before he got sick as well, but she had no voice. She could only stare up at him until she was no longer able to keep her eyes open.

Maria heard him tugging out of his wet clothes and felt the mattress sag as he crawled in beside her and pulled the coverlet over them both. He lay on his back beside her and shivered for several minutes;

she could feel his tremors through the quilt.

She wanted nothing more than to feel his body directly against hers, but she didn't have the strength to move. As if he could read her thoughts, he opened the quilt and pulled her body on top of his in one smooth motion.

After shifting around a bit, he wrapped her tightly in his arms and found a comfortable position for them both. She gave a contented sigh as he settled her head in the curve of his shoulder.

His body felt like a block of ice, before skin-to-skin contact began working its warming magic. His tremors lessened and diminished entirely as she drifted off to sleep—a natural sleep this time, not the yawning darkness that threatened to overtake her only a short time ago.

"Je l'ai sauvee, Maman. Je n'ai pas pu te sauver, mais je l'ai sauvee," he whispered the words against her still-damp hair, his voice barely audible.

She had no idea what he had said, and she didn't care. She was alive in Alexander's arms, and that was enough.

Thirteen

Although the fever returned off and on over the next several hours, it never came back with the same vengeance. Alexander remained at her side for the next two days, sleeping beside her while she slept. He barely left the room. Maria had no idea what sort of excuse he and Dr. Stevens had concocted to explain his absence to his family, but she was thankful for his presence and attentiveness.

When her fever was absent for a full day and night, Dr. Stevens declared her out of danger. Susan could finally come visit her. The events of the past few days had obviously taken a toll on the normally easy-going, talkative child. After running to the bed and climbing up by her mother, she sat silently, grey eyes wide as she clung to Maria and cautiously watched Alexander.

Despite the frequency of his visits, the two had never met during waking hours, and Susan was not sure what to make of her mother's companion. He was obviously comfortable around children and didn't seem put off by her initial wariness. Alexander teased her lightheartedly until she finally rewarded him with a shy smile, then launched into a cleaned-up version of a soldier's drinking song.

Maria knew he had truly won her daughter over when Susan

started giggling, and soon they were all laughing at his improvised lyrics. Her heart swelled as she watched the two people she loved most in the world laughing together beside her.

By the time Sarah came to get Susan, Alexander had taught the child how to count to ten in French. Maria learned for the first time that Susan was exactly one year younger than his daughter, Angelica, and one year older than his second son, Alex Jr. She was the same age as his foster daughter, Fanny, an orphan the Hamiltons had taken in when she was two. They had two other sons—an older and a younger as well. Maria had no idea how Mrs. Hamilton could manage that many children so close in age.

Even though the fever hadn't returned, Maria still struggled to take nourishment, and her stomach rejected everything except the bland panada made of milk softened bread that Sarah prepared for her several times a day. She picked at it while Alexander fussed over her like a nervous hen, sitting on the side of the bed—imploring, cajoling, then finally hand-feeding her.

When Maria was finally able to hold down something more substantial and get up on her own to relieve herself, he relented somewhat and returned to his daily schedule—but only after making Sarah promise she would attend to making sure Maria ate and drank as much as he had. Even then, he stopped by to check on her every morning on his way to work and every afternoon on his way home.

She got stronger each day, and her forced convalescence quickly became unbearable. She wanted nothing more than to be away from the four walls of her bedroom, to join Susan and Sarah in the rest of the house. Although Susan visited her several times a day, Maria desperately missed being part of normal, everyday activities.

She expressed her frustrations to Alexander when he visited that morning, and he said if Dr. Stevens declared her well enough to leave her bed, she would be allowed to move about. Maria desperately hoped that would be the case, determined to do her best to convince the doctor of her improvement.

Finally able to sit up in bed for extended periods of time, she was reading the newest issue of the *Gazette of the United States* Alexander brought her this morning when Dr. Stevens arrived.

"You are looking much better," he declared as he stepped into the room.

"I am feeling much better." She put the newspaper down on her lap and gave him her most convincing smile.

"Colonel Hamilton tells me you are beginning to grow restless."

"Yes. I am not used to lying about in bed, and it's becoming intolerable. I am perfectly able to be allowed out of my bedroom."

"Well, that's for me to decide, young lady." He sat down on the bed next to her and picked up her hand, pressing his fingers against the inside of her wrist.

Next, he reached up to feel the glands in her neck. For several minutes she sat perfectly still as he poked and prodded, looked down her throat, and pressed his ear to her chest and back while she coughed.

"Well," he finally pronounced, "I see no reason that you should be further confined to your bed."

Maria smiled in relief. "Thank you."

"You have lost quite a bit of weight, though. And you did not have much to spare to begin with. I'll share some dishes with your girl on my way out, ones to prepare for you that will be easy to digest. Alex assures me that she keeps a well-stocked apothecary cabinet, so some teas with dandelion root, stinging nettle, and red clover will help improve your strength. As long as you go slow and get plenty of nourishment, you should be restored to full health in no time."

He paused before continuing. "You are very fortunate, Mrs. Reynolds. I do not think you realize how close you came to death. If it had not been for Colonel Hamilton's quick thinking, you would have surely perished."

Maria quietly absorbed the truth of his statement as he stood to take his leave.

"I know you don't approve of me," she blurted out.

"I assure you, it's nothing personal," Dr. Stevens said, not even trying to deny her assessment. "You are quite fetching, and in fact, under different circumstances, I would be in danger of falling for your considerable charms myself. But considering I am fond of Mrs. Hamilton and being somewhat protective of my oldest friend—not to mention the moral implications of adultery—I think you are both making a big mistake," he said matter-of-factly. "It is painfully obvious that you are both deeply in love, though I do not see what good could possibly come of it."

She looked up at Dr. Stevens in surprise.

"Surely, you have realized that he is mad for you? Why do you think he would not leave your side to return to his family for almost three days?"

Maria was unsure of how to respond to such bluntness—she could only lower her eyes and stare at her hands folded neatly on her lap.

"I apologize for my candor, Mrs. Reynolds. I have said much of the same thing to Colonel Hamilton, and he did not deny it or attempt to assuage my concerns, either. My dear friend has the uncanny knack for making powerful enemies, and I am only worried about what would happen should your dalliance be discovered by one of them."

She was silent for several seconds as she absorbed what he was saying. *How much stronger would his concerns be if he knew the truth behind the circumstances that had led to my arrival on Alexander's doorstep, and that at least one of his enemies already does know?*

"I am aware my concerns fall on deaf ears," he continued. "You will both do as you like, and nothing I can say or do will stop that. Even as a young lad, once Alex set a course, he was not easily dissuaded from it."

Maria shifted uncomfortably, but his reference to Alexander as a boy piqued her interest.

"How long have you known Colonel Hamilton?" she asked.

"Since we were both lads in St. Croix. My family took him in after his mother died."

Maria raised her eyebrows at the revelation about her lover's childhood, a couple of new pieces sliding neatly into the puzzle. She wanted to know more, but she was unsure how far to push it. Curiosity finally won out.

"How did his mother die?"

Dr. Stevens hesitated briefly before answering. "Both she and Alex were sick with some sort of tropical fever. The doctor bled and purged them both until she finally succumbed. He was twelve when she died, covered in her own blood and vomit, in bed beside him." He paused at the sight of Maria's horrified expression. "I apologize for the graphic nature of my description, Mrs. Reynolds," he said, visibly embarrassed by his choice of words. "I tend to get carried away sometimes. I only know the details because I overheard my parents whispering about it shortly before he came to live with us. Alex has never spoken to me about what happened," he added quickly. "It is a subject we carefully avoid."

Maria nodded and closed her eyes as her mind instantly conjured up the horror of the scene painted by his words. She was sorry she had asked because she could now imagine her lover as a child, one who suffered from the same horrific ministrations as his mother—while knowing he could do nothing to help her as she slowly died in front of him.

Maria shivered and felt slightly queasy at the thought. "Do you not believe in the practice of bleeding?" she asked. "I know it is the accepted treatment for illness and fever."

"No. I think it's barbaric, and in my experience, it does far more harm than good," he said with surprising vehemence. "It hardly makes sense in an enlightened world to still be using medical practices of Medieval times."

Maria was silent as his words sank in, thankful that Dr. Stevens had tended to her, which very possibly spared her the same fate as Alexander's mother. Witnessing his passionate response, Maria was once again surprised at his resemblance to her lover.

"The most important thing for you right now is to continue to get plenty of rest, to begin building back your strength. Your girl is capable of looking after you, and, of course, I have no doubt that Alex will continue to monitor your recovery with his usual unflagging dedication and proficiency." He couldn't hide the disapproval in his voice, but Maria noticed even this was coupled with grudging admiration.

"I'll be back in a few days to check on you. If anything changes, please don't hesitate to send for me. "Maria nodded. "Thank you again for everything you have done."

"Of course." He turned to leave the room.

"Dr. Stevens?"

He turned back around. "Yes?"

"Are you and Colonel Hamilton brothers?" The question—the one that had been on her mind since the first time she saw the two of them together—tumbled out of her mouth before she could stop it. Maria fought to hold his gaze, instantly ashamed of her forwardness.

Dr. Stevens did not appear to be shocked or even surprised by her question. He paused on his way out and smiled enigmatically. "That, my dear girl, is the question, isn't it?" He turned and left the room without answering.

Maria didn't have time to dwell on his evasiveness, though. She waited until she heard the front door close behind him, threw back the covers, and climbed out of bed, determined to put on some proper clothes and leave this bedroom. She walked to the dresser and searched through the drawers for a pair of clean stockings and stays.

By the time she had pulled the wool stockings up to her calves and tied them with a under her knees with a ribbon garter, she was out of breath. She sat down on the side of the bed to rest a minute before attempting the next step.

This recovery might be more difficult than I thought, she admitted grudgingly.

After resting for a moment, she stood, pulled the stays on over her linen shift, and laced them up in front. Even with the lacings as tight as they would go, the bodice hung loose on her formerly curvy frame, and she understood for the first time why everyone was so insistent on her eating.

Determined to finish what she had started, Maria took a deep breath and proceeded to pull on and tie her petticoat. She lifted a navy wool skirt to her waist and pinned a short jacket over her stays. Although this was her normal, everyday clothing, everything felt so big and heavy, like a child wearing adult clothes for the first time.

She slid her stockinged feet into her heeled shoes but left them unbuckled. Each simple activity seemed to require a great deal of energy, and since she didn't plan on walking beyond the house or yard, she decided to leave off the buckles. Sarah had brushed her hair this morning, and a quick look in the dresser mirror told her the blonde curls still looked somewhat presentable. She quickly tied a linen cap on her head and made her way to the bedroom door.

Sarah and Susan looked up in surprise as Maria walked into the kitchen. Sarah was up to her elbows in flour from kneading bread dough on a flour dusted board as Susan looked on.

"Mama!" Susan immediately abandoned her watch, ran to her mother, and hugged her around the waist.

"It's good to see you out and around, missus," Sarah said with a smile. She had a smudge of flour across her nose.

"It's good to be out and around." Maria gave Susan a tight squeeze back.

"Be careful, little miss," Sarah said. "You're getting flour all over your mum."

Maria looked down to see white handprints across her dark skirt. "It's all right." She laughed and brushed the white powder off as best she could. "A little flour won't hurt me."

Sarah smiled. "Are you hungry?"

"No. But I've been told I need to eat."

"Yes. I have some griddle cakes and fried pork left over from breakfast. Or I can make you some panada."

Maria wrinkled her nose and put her hand on her stomach. "I do not think I could bear another bowl of panada. But I will have a griddle cake."

"Let me get that for you."

Maria put her hand up to stop her. "Finish kneading your bread. I am certainly not so weak that I can't get my own food."

"Yes, ma'am." Sarah smiled and turned back to her work, plunging her hands into the ball of dough. Maria picked up a pewter plate with two thin griddle cakes and sat down at the table with Susan.

"I can heat those up for you and pour some syrup on them," Sarah offered.

Maria shook her head. "No need. It won't help them go down any easier." She dutifully rolled up one of the round flat cakes with her fingers, took a bite, and tried not to wince as she swallowed it.

Susan sat by her side as Maria somehow managed to finish both griddle cakes by picking at them slowly and deliberately. Feeling somewhat proud of herself for accomplishing even that small task, Maria stood and took the empty plate back to the worktable. She watched as Sarah placed a ball of dough in a wooden bowl, covered it with a small cloth, and put it on the warm hearth to rise.

"I think I would like to walk outside for a while. The fresh air will do me good," Maria said. She was exhausted, yet reluctant to go back to her bedroom. "I promise I won't leave the backyard," she added in an attempt to allay her maid's obvious concerns.

"Don't overdo it, missus," Sarah said skeptically. "Colonel Hamilton will have my hide if I let you get sick again."

"I won't, I promise," Maria said as she stared out the window into the backyard. The warm beams of sunlight cutting across the kitchen floor were too inviting to ignore. "Would you like to walk with me?" she asked Susan.

Susan nodded her head enthusiastically and the two stepped outside, down the steps, and into the overgrown garden. For fall, the day was uncharacteristically warm. Maria lifted her face toward the sun, closed her eyes, and smiled as the sounds and smells of the city hit her all at once—sounds of horses and carriages on the main road in front. Signs that life had gone on uninterrupted while she was ill.

Holding Susan's hand, they walked slowly through the unkept beds. The tall, gangly weeds would soon die off with the first frost, but for now even the tallest ones were unaware of the fate that awaited them. They grew with abandon, spilling over their boundaries and threatening to overtake the dirt path winding its way through the small yard.

Perhaps if she and Susan were still here in the spring, they could plant their own garden. Maria had no experience tending a garden, but she was certain Sarah did, and at the moment, anything seemed possible.

Sounds of heavy footfalls on gravel startled her, and Maria looked up through the metal gate separating the backyard from the alley, surprised to see a well-dressed young man in the middle of the road staring at her.

"Good day, ma'am." He lifted his top hat off his head a few inches and nodded in greeting. "Beautiful morning, is it not?" He was trying a bit too hard to sound casual, she noticed.

Maria studied him for a moment between the bars before answering. He seemed familiar, like she had seen him somewhere before, but she couldn't put her finger on it. He was young, probably close to her own age, and wore a well-cut brown jacket and breeches fitted to his slender figure. He had intense, dark eyes and equally dark curls visible beneath his expensive beaver hat.

"It is," she answered noncommittally, measuring the distance back to the house as she pulled Susan along.

The young man didn't appear to be getting the hint, though. He cleared his throat nervously and shifted his feet.

"M-my deepest apologies," he stammered as he stepped up to the gate. "I seem to have forgotten my manners. Jacob Clingman, at your service." He bowed slightly.

Mr. Clingman was handsome, for sure, and extremely well-spoken. While he presented like a gentleman, something about him didn't seem authentic. His eyes bore a cleverness beyond his years that contradicted the youthful, awkward persona he was attempting to portray.

"And who might I have the pleasure of meeting?" he asked.

Maria paused as she considered his question, knowing the dictates of polite society required her to answer. She gripped Susan's hand a little more firmly, thankful the child had elected to stay silent.

"Mrs. Reynolds," she said.

"Pleasure to meet you, Mrs. Reynolds," he said with a smile, his dark eyes locked with her green ones.

Maria, growing increasingly uncomfortable with interaction, quickly looked away. This time, however, he seemed to take the hint.

"I regret that I must be on my way. I had been enjoying my walk in the sunshine, but now I can truly say that the beauty of the day has been eclipsed by the beauty of your countenance."

Maria wasn't sure how to respond to his exaggerated compliment. She certainly didn't feel beautiful today; she felt frail and vulnerable. What had seemed at first like a day of renewal and promise suddenly felt dark and foreboding.

"Good day, sir," she said before turning around to head back inside the house. She could hear his footsteps retreating behind them as he continued his walk. As if in response to her sudden shift in mood, a cloud floated across the sun, briefly plunging the backyard into shade as she opened the kitchen door.

Fourteen

Maria relayed the odd meeting to Alexander when he stopped by after work a few hours later. The more she thought about it, the stranger it seemed.

Why was a gentleman like Mr. Clingman walking down an alley behind my house in the middle of the day? Where was he going? What was he looking for?

"I am not familiar with any families here in Philadelphia by the name of Clingman," Alexander said as they sat alone together in the parlor. "But I have heard that name before. Congressman Muhlenberg has a young clerk with the surname Clingman, but I don't recall his first name. I will make some inquires."

"Thank you, sir."

"I am certain it is nothing to be bothered by, though," he said with a smile. "One can hardly blame a young man for stopping to talk to a beautiful woman. Do not concern yourself with it."

His words eased her mind somewhat, yet something didn't feel right about the encounter, especially after the revelation that the young man might be connected to a prominent politician.

Was Congressman Muhlenberg a Federalist like Alexander or a

Democratic Republican like Burr, she wondered? She lowered her eyes as the guilt once again washed over her. Yet another reminder of the possible political ramifications to the encounter and the part she played.

"I must say I am extremely relieved that Dr. Stevens has declared you well enough to be out of your bed," Alexander's words broke her train of thoughts. "Your girl said you ate well. Just be mindful that you do not try to do too much too fast. You could relapse."

"It does feel good to finally be out of bed," she acknowledged with a sigh. "But I will be glad when our conversations are no longer about what I ate, or if I did too much."

Alexander patted her hand. "Do not worry," he said. "There will come a time when you will be fully recovered, and our conversations can turn elsewhere again."

"I certainly hope so."

She suddenly longed to feel his lips on hers. Not the way he kissed her now, with affection and loving concern—but without the fire of passion that previously consumed them. Maria remembered he once told her that he stayed away from his wife's bed for several months after she became ill.

Is that going to be my fate as well? She did not think she could bear it.

Her eyes unexpectedly welled up with tears at the thought. She and Alexander did not share a name, a home, or a family. All they had were those moments of passion he managed to sneak in between his myriad duties. And if she could no longer offer him even that, what could possibly make him want to stay? She looked down to hide her tears.

Alexander stood up to leave. "I must be getting home for supper. But I am extremely heartened by Dr. Steven's report and your improvement." He leaned forward and kissed her on the forehead. "I will stop by again in the morning to check on you."

Maria took a deep breath and forced the tears back down. "I am thankful for everything everyone has done," she said, "but I feel like a child. I look forward to a time where I am once again treated as a woman." She looked up at him through her lashes, her expression leaving no doubt about what aspect of adult behavior she was referring to.

To her surprise, Alexander actually reddened.

"The full restoration of your health is my primary concern," he said somewhat defensively. "I would not be so selfish as to allow my own desires to jeopardize your recovery."

"I assure you, sir, that I am quite stronger than I appear to be." As if to prove her point, she stood up in one smooth movement and stepped toward him, her face suddenly just inches from his. She put her hands on his chest, curled her fingers around the lapels of his jacket, and lifted her face for a kiss.

Alexander was unable to resist the invitation. His lips played around hers—gently at first, then with increasing urgency.

"I need you," she whispered against his mouth. "You can come back later tonight."

Her words seemed to break him out of his momentary trance, and he took a step back.

"As tempting as that may be, Maria, I cannot risk it. I would never forgive myself if the satisfaction of my passions were to further jeopardize your health."

Tears once again sprang unbidden into her eyes. This time, however, she was unable to hide them from him.

He reached out and lifted her chin with his finger. "Do not fret, my beauty." He wiped the tears from her cheek with his thumb. "When the time is right, I will return to your bed with renewed vigor."

She looked up at him, all the earlier bravado gone now. "I am afraid I will become too much of a burden, and you will no longer want me."

"I could never stop wanting you, Maria," he said, his hands on either side of her face, his eyes boring down into hers with an intensity that made her tremble. "You have a hold on me that I am helpless to resist."

Maria sniffed and gave him a weak smile. "And I, you, sir."

He leaned forward to give her a proper kiss, and she melted into him, lifting her arms to encircle his neck while his tongue teased her lips open—and gently, but very thoroughly, explored her mouth. He pulled her tightly against him, leaving no doubt about the effect she had on him. When he finally lifted his mouth from hers several minutes later, she was breathless and slightly dizzy.

"Soon, Maria. Very soon. That I can promise," he whispered with a smile. He took a step backward and quickly changed the subject.

"Sarah tells me she is preparing a beef pie for supper. It would please me to hear you ate heartily of it when I stop by to check on you in the morning."

"I will do my best, sir," she said, her stomach automatically turning in protest at just the thought of a heavy meal. To regain her strength, she would do it, though.

"Good girl," he said with a smile. "Sleep well, my beauty." With a final kiss goodbye, he discreetly adjusted the crotch of his breeches, walked out of the parlor, and closed the door behind him.

Maria suddenly felt drained. Tonight would require an early bedtime of her for sure. Still, she counted today as a success and a good start to a complete recovery.

Only after managing to eat and keep down a piece of the meat pie did Maria remember her strange encounter with Mr. Clingman this morning. Hopefully, Alexander would find out more information about him, and that meeting would turn out to be happenstance.

For the time being, she forced herself to put aside Clingman as she crawled into bed just after dark—where she fell into an exhausted sleep, dreaming of a time when she could welcome Alexander into her bed once again.

at sunrise feeling stronger than the day before. She slipped into her stays and petticoats, followed by a simple gown—one that once fit snugly. She was encouraged when she was able to accomplish these simple tasks without getting out of breath and slipped out of her bedroom to meet Sarah going down the stairs.

"Good morning, missus," Sarah said with a smile. "It's good to see you out of bed this morning."

"It's good to be out."

They both walked down the last flight of stairs and into the chilly kitchen, and Sarah headed straight to the fireplace. After shoveling the cold ashes from yesterday's fire into a metal bucket, she gathered several pieces of wood from the rack beside the hearth, carefully stacking the small logs inside the fireplace before lighting them with tinder. Within minutes, a heathy fire blazed, and Sarah gathered what foodstuffs she needed to prepare breakfast from the pantry. Maria took a seat in one of the wooden chairs close to the fire, enjoying the heat.

They heard footsteps on the stairs, Susan stumbling into the kitchen still rubbing the sleep from her eyes. Knowing the child had been anxious and worried during her mother's illness, Sarah had taken Susan to her third story bedroom to sleep with her for the past week. Last night was her first night back in her own room. Her eyes widened in excitement when she saw her mother sitting in the kitchen already.

"Good morning, sweetheart," Maria said with a smile, inviting Susan to come and sit on her lap.

"Are you all better now, Mama?" Susan climbed onto her mother's knees.

"Yes, I think so."

Susan seemed to consider her answer for a moment before she smiled, seeming satisfied. Without another word, she hopped down off Maria's lap, pulled a small wooden stepstool up to the counter beside Sarah, and stood on top of it. Sarah was cracking brown eggs into a stoneware bowl while Susan looked on intently. Maria quickly got the impression that this had become their regular custom during her illness.

"I'll need to go to the market later this morning, missus." Sarah cut off a chunk of fresh butter, poured a jill of cream into the eggs, and began whisking them all together. "We're out of meat," she added somewhat apologetically, and poured the egg mixture into a cast-iron skillet on a grate over the fire.

"Do not worry. I am content without meat for one meal. Do you need some money?" Maria realized with a start that she had no idea how the household finances had been managed while she was sick.

"Oh no, ma'am," Sarah said quickly. "Colonel Hamilton has been providing for whatever was needed while you were ill." Her maid's expression was just short of worshipful.

"I like him. He's funny," Susan interjected, her face breaking out a toothy smile.

Clearly, Alexander had managed to endear himself to the rest of the household while she was sick. They had been secretive and cautious for so many months, it seemed odd for the other members of her household to talk about him so openly.

Of course, Sarah had delivered her messages to Alexander without any spoken acknowledgment of their relationship, any discussion of it at all. The fact that Sarah had taken it upon herself to contact Alexander when Maria first became ill had probably saved her life, though, so for that she was grateful. Still, she was a little put off by the ease with which he had charmed her entire household.

"I would not have normally let the food stores run so low," Sarah continued, "but I was told by Colonel Hamilton not to leave you alone."

"I am perfectly capable of being left alone for an hour or so," Maria assured her, her voice a little shorter than she had intended. "I'll be fine."

Sarah seemed to consider the situation as she sliced off several thick pieces of bread from a loaf she baked yesterday. "I'll just check with Colonel Hamilton when he stops by this morning."

Maria felt a flash of irritation at her maid's automatic deference to her lover, although she could hardly blame her. After all, Alexander was the one paying her wages, a fact obviously not lost on Sarah. Yet another reminder that she was being treated like a child. Alexander had shown no interest in managing the day-to-day activities of the household before she got sick, and she wasn't sure she liked it. She needed to talk to him about it the next time they had a private moment.

Maria watched the fire in silence as Sarah finished putting together the simple breakfast. A few minutes later, she and Susan were at the table enjoying buttered eggs and toast. For the first time in what seemed like forever, Maria dove into her food with real enthusiasm—the first time in days she had eaten breakfast outside of her bedroom. As was her custom, Sarah ate while she cleaned away the breakfast pots in between bites.

Maria was sitting in her chair next to the fireplace enjoying a cup of hot tea when Alexander stopped by for his morning visit. He came through the back door without knocking, and Maria watched in disbelief as Susan, squealing, ran to hug him around the top of his leg. He smiled down at her and tousled her hair affectionately. Things had certainly changed over the past week.

"Can Miss Sarah and I go to the market this morning?" Susan asked.

Maria's immediate response was to curtail her daughter's presumptiveness, but Alexander didn't seem surprised by Susan's familiarity. He picked her up and balanced her on his hip as if it were the most natural thing in the world.

"Do you promise to be good and stick close to Miss Sarah?" he asked. Susan giggled and nodded.

"Yes, sir."

"Then you can go."

"I wasn't sure if it was all right to leave Mrs. Reynolds alone or not," Sarah added quickly.

Maria sat momentarily speechless, watching the scene unfold in front of her as if she were not present.

"I don't have any meetings or pressing business this morning. I can stay with her while you are both gone."

Maria opened her mouth to protest, but a quick look from Alexander caused her to forgo even that.

"Now, go finish getting ready," he told Susan and set her back down on the floor. She scampered quickly back upstairs to her room.

Sarah finished clearing away the breakfast dishes and dried her hands on her apron. She picked up her market basket and opened a small box on the mantle containing several coins. Sarah slid them into her pocket.

"Do you need any additional funds?" Alexander asked.

"No, sir. I have plenty for what we need."

"Good." He nodded about the time Susan bounded back downstairs, fully dressed like clockwork for the short excursion. "No need to hurry back," he told Sarah as she took Susan's hand and headed toward the door. "We'll be fine here while you're gone."

"Well, what do you propose we should do to pass the time while they're away?" he asked with a smile as soon as the door closed behind them.

"Do not tease me, sir," she said with a sigh. Only a short time ago, she would have jumped at the opportunity that just presented itself, but this morning's events had left her emotionally shaken. She was suddenly feeling far too frail and vulnerable to partake in their usual teasing banter.

The laughter in his eyes was quickly replaced by concern. "Are you feeling unwell? I did not mean to imply that I expected anything. I only thought that after our conversation yesterday you were—much recovered."

"I am feeling much recovered," she said. "But things seem very different today." She struggled to find the words to articulate how watching his familiar interaction with Susan had made her feel.

"How so?" he asked. He took a seat in the chair beside her.

"For one, it is quite shocking to see that my maid and my daughter now defer to you for decisions on household matters in which I think I should at least be consulted."

Alexander seemed taken aback by her comments. "If they do, I can assure you it was quite unintentional," he said. "I am sorry if it seems that way, but you were incapacitated for a period, and I supposed they looked to me to make decisions. Now that you are back on your feet, I will gladly relinquish any authority I have on the matter of the running of your household," he said with a flourish.

Maria immediately felt bad for bringing it up. "I am sorry, sir. I do not wish to seem ungrateful for everything you have done. Clearly, my daughter adores you, but now I fear my choices will cause her to be hurt."

"Why would she be hurt?"

Maria hesitated slightly before continuing. "What would have become of Susan if I had died?" she asked, tears welling up in her eyes.

"I don't know," he conceded. "I had not considered it. I suppose her father would have been sent for, and she would have been sent to him."

Maria took a deep breath and struggled to keep her emotions at bay. "When Susan was returned to me, I made the decision to do whatever I had to do to protect her. It is painful beyond measure to think that all my sacrifices would have been for naught."

"Do you think he would harm her?" Alexander's voice rose.

"I don't know," Maria answered truthfully. "I would hope he would not be so vile of a character that he would do harm to his own child, but he took her from me once, so I do not doubt what he is capable of."

"You are a wonderful mother," Alexander said, his words slow and careful. "And Susan is a good girl. Very smart. You should be proud of her. If something were to happen to you, I would do what I could to see that she was protected. But I could never be a father to her."

Maria knew what he meant, even if he hadn't said it outright. He had already demonstrated his willingness to take in a child who wasn't his. But he could never bring his mistress's child into his house to be raised alongside his own children.

"I am not asking you to be," she said, her voice sharper than intended. "I well understand our place in your life."

Alexander drew back as if he had been slapped. "I am sorry, Maria, but it is all I can offer. My feelings for you don't change the facts of my situation. I have never hidden my intentions from you or led you to believe it would ever be any different, have I?" he asked defensively, his voice rising in frustration. "What is it you want me to do? I cannot change the way things are."

She was immediately sorry she had brought it up. Maria looked up at him, her eyes wide and glistening with unshed tears. "I do not expect anything more from you, sir," she said softly. "I am happy here," she continued, the words tumbling out before he could interrupt. "As you have stated correctly, you have not lied or hidden anything from me. I entered into our agreement with my eyes wide open." In fact, I'm the one who initiated it, she added silently. "You have already given me more than I could have ever imagined."

"I wish it could be more."

"I am well provided for, sir. And it is not the pecuniary compensation that I am referring to. I have never been with the man who makes me feel the way you do. There are times when I can think of nothing but your kisses and the way your arms feel around me."

Her words instantly dissolved his frustration, and he reached out to gently stroke her cheek with his thumb. He brushed an errant blonde curl out of her face. "My need for you is so strong, it often frightens me to think what I might do to satisfy it," he whispered. "But you deserve so much more, and at times I do not think it is a fair exchange at all."

He dropped his hand from her face and leaned back in his chair. They sat in silence for several seconds, his words heavy in the air.

"I am content with our situation, sir," she said finally, "and do not wish to change it or jeopardize it. I am just feeling a bit melancholy this morning. That is all." She sniffed, wiped her eyes with the back of her hand, and straightened in her chair. "Please forgive me."

"There is nothing to forgive, Maria. I did not mean to distress you."

"Nor I, you."

"Good," he said with a smile. "We are in agreement, then. We will speak no more about such things on this fine morning."

Maria smiled at him. "Thank you, sir."

"What shall we discuss, then?" he asked, his eyes teasing now. "I suppose I could read to you from a report I am compiling on useful manufacturers."

"That certainly sounds stimulating." She smiled. "But I have a better idea." She stood, her expression leaving little doubt as to what she was suggesting.

"Are you sure?" Alexander asked. "I was only teasing before. I am perfectly content with just the pleasure of your company."

"I am sure," she said simply, reaching her hand out to him. He took it, stood, and followed her upstairs to her bedroom.

They had just finished dressing and had barely made their way back into the kitchen when Sarah and Susan returned. Sarah's basket was overflowing with fresh vegetables and paper bundles of meat held together with twine.

"I am sorry we were gone so long. The market was more crowded than normal this morning." Sarah set the basket on the table and began unloading it.

"It is perfectly fine. Mrs. Reynolds and I found plenty to occupy our time while you were away."

Maria feigned interest in the dry goods to hide her embarrassment.

"Do you remember the man you were talking to in the garden yesterday, Mama?" Susan broke in.

"Yes, sweetheart. What about him?" Maria asked warily.

"He was at the market this morning."

Maria glanced quickly at Alexander, her eyes tinged with alarm.

"Did he say anything to you?" Alexander asked Susan, his voice edgy.

"No. He looked like he was shopping, but he didn't have a basket in his hands."

"I'm sure it's nothing to be concerned about," Alexander said, placing his hand on Maria's shoulder. Susan had already turned around to help Sarah put away their purchases.

"I will make some inquiries when I get to work today," he added under his breath.

"Thank you, sir," she whispered back.

"Now that everyone is home, I'm afraid I must be getting to the office," he announced.

Susan immediately dropped the bundle of carrots she was holding and ran to him for a goodbye hug.

"Be a good girl, and listen to your mama and Miss Sarah," he said. He squatted to return Susan's hug. "Promise?"

Susan smiled and nodded before running back to help Sarah.

He turned once again to Maria. "I will be back later this afternoon and will let you know if I find out anything," he whispered.

"Thank you."

As soon as he was gone, Maria sank down into a chair, feeling suddenly overwhelmed by the events of the morning. The euphoric flush from their lovemaking had quickly been replaced by the sudden fear she felt from Susan's observation. Mr. Clingman's appearance at the market was not a coincidence. Of that she was certain.

But what did it mean? Who was he exactly, and why was he following them? Hopefully, Alexander would have an answer when he returned later this afternoon.

Fifteen

Maria tried to push the incident from her mind and threw herself into the business of the day as best she could. Despite Sarah's protests, she helped take the laundry off the line and clumsily wrangled the load of petticoats and wool stockings into some semblance of neatness. Sarah prepared a light lunch and made a pippin pie with fresh apples she bought at the market.

By the time Maria was finished with the relatively simple task, she was exhausted. She ate a small pastry that Sarah had baked with the leftover pie crust and sat down to rest in front of the kitchen fireplace. The combination of a comfortable chair and a full belly soon had her nodding off.

Her head fell forward, and Maria jerked awake. She sat up and looked at the clock on the mantle, surprised to see that it was not yet two o'clock.

She glanced over at Sarah, who watched her with concern.

"You should rest, missus. You look tired," she said.

Maria didn't argue. "I am," she admitted. "I think I'm going to take a short nap. If I am not up already, please wake me before Colonel Hamilton arrives."

"Yes, ma'am."

Maria walked upstairs to her bedroom, closed the door, and stripped down to her shift before crawling under the rumpled covers where she and Alexander had made love only a few hours before. His comforting scent wafted her nose as she pulled the covers up to her neck, closed her eyes, and fell asleep instantly.

The feel of Alexander's lips on forehead woke her a few hours later. Still half asleep and disoriented, she moaned and opened her eyes. As he sat down on the bed beside her, she struggled to sit up in bed as quickly and gracefully as possible.

He looked concerned. "Sarah said you were sleeping, and I became worried."

"What time is it?" she asked, still confused. It felt like she had only been asleep for a few minutes, but the angle of the soft light coming in through the windows indicated it was late.

"It's four thirty."

"I'm sorry," she said with a yawn. "Sarah was supposed to wake me before you arrived. She must have forgotten."

"Judging from the smells coming out of the kitchen, I'd say she's been busy making use of this morning's purchases."

"I should get up and help her." Maria pushed the covers off her legs and started getting up.

He put his hand on her arm to stop her. "I'd say she has everything well in hand." He paused for a few seconds before continuing. "She told me you insisted on taking the laundry off the line after I left this morning."

Maria looked down, suddenly feeling like a ten-year-old version of herself being scolded by her mother after her older sister, Susannah, tattled on her for daydreaming instead of doing her chores. Only this time, she was in charge of her own household being scolded for doing chores.

"I am not a helpless child," she said defensively. "I am quite recovered enough to be able to do simple tasks."

"I would have thought the strenuousness of this morning's activities would have rendered you unable to do anything more for the rest of the day." His voice was light and teasing now, and any frustration she felt evaporated.

"That's exactly why I was sleeping so hard when you woke me," she quipped. "I just didn't plan on sleeping this long."

He smiled, leaned forward, and kissed her softly on the lips. "I can hardly be blamed for worrying about you, though. You gave us all quite a scare. Perhaps I should better control my passions if you won't learn to display prudence in limiting your *other* activities," he bantered.

"If it means your continued presence in my bed, I will lay about all day like a contented cat with a belly full of cream."

"Then I shall supply all the cream my kitty desires," he said, grinning from ear to ear.

Maria pretended to be shocked. "I don't know what you mean, sir." She looked up at him through her lashes.

"Perhaps I should demonstrate my ability to keep my little kitty well fed, then," he said, leaning toward her so that his lips were only inches from hers.

"Perhaps you should," Maria challenged back, her voice low and husky. She held her ground by staring into the endless oceans contained in his eyes.

Alexander was the first to break. With a groan of frustration, he took a deep breath and sat up.

"If only I could create more hours in the day," he said with sigh. "Mrs. Hamilton and I have an engagement tonight, so I cannot stay long."

Maria nodded, and they sat in silence for several seconds, the mood broken. "Were you able to find out anything more about Mr. Clingman?" she asked.

"Oh yes, I almost forgot," Alexander said. "The mysterious Mr. Clingman did indeed work as a clerk for Speaker of the House Muhlenberg but has since left his employ. It appears he has found another patron, but I was unable to ascertain who. Another gentleman mentioned that he had seen Mr. Clingman leaving Senator Burr's office, but I was not able to confirm a connection between them."

Maria's stomach churned at the mention of Burr's name. *Would he really have hired someone to track me down and follow me?* She would not put it past him.

"Is Mr. Muhlenberg a Federalist?" Maria asked, mentally trying to place the various men on both sides of the political chess board.

"He is what we call a 'low' Federalist, supportive of the administration, but not completely supportive of all the president's policies. He is no friend of Mr. Jefferson's, though, if that's what you're asking."

That was indeed what she was asking, and Maria relaxed somewhat.

"I would not be overly concerned, though," Alexander continued. "Mr. Muhlenberg attests to Mr. Clingman's good character. Perhaps his appearance at the market was simply a coincidence."

"Do you believe that?"

"No," he conceded. "But based on what I've learned about Mr. Clingman, I do not think he represents a threat to you or Susan. Perhaps he was just intrigued by your beauty and wanted to learn more about you." Alexander smiled. His words were light and playful again, although their levity didn't seem to match the concern in his eyes.

Maria sighed. "I know you are jesting, sir, but I hope you are right about him not being a threat," she said, not at all convinced.

The possible connection to Burr was too convenient. For a few seconds, she considered telling Alexander the whole story of her alliance with Burr—before dismissing the idea as quickly as it had occurred. She had seen the full display of Alexander's temper where Burr was concerned and did not want to be responsible for what he might do should he discover the extent of Burr's machinations against him.

"Do not concern yourself about it," he assured her. I will make some inquiries at the president's reception tonight and let you know if I find out anything more." His tone made it clear that the matter was settled.

"I'm afraid I must be on my way." He stood and bent down to give her a quick kiss goodbye. "I don't know if I will be able to come by to see you for the next couple of days. We are expecting diplomatic guests from abroad, and I will be required to play the part of the amicable host during their visit. They are staying through Sunday, so it will probably be Monday morning before I can stop by to check on you again."

Maria nodded, ever reminded that they inhabited very different spheres of society. "I understand. I'll be fine," she said, trying hard to hide her disappointment. It was only Friday afternoon, and Monday suddenly seemed so far away. She had grown far too dependent on Alexander. She did not want to appear clingy or needy, even if such was true.

"You do not have to worry about me," she reassured him.

"I know I don't have to, but I do," he said. "If you need me, you can send a message by Sarah. Will you do that, if something happens?"

"Of course, sir." Maria tried to smile.

As if assessing the truthfulness of her statement, Alexander hesitated for a moment. He bent down and gave her a longer kiss this time.

"Promise me that you will eat well and rest during my absence, and I will give you something clever upon my return," he said with a smile.

Maria couldn't help but smile back at him. "How could I resist such an offer?"

"Do you promise, then?"

"Yes."

Satisfied, Alexander stood and righted his cravat and jacket. "Good night, my beauty. Eat a good supper, sleep well, and dream of me."

"I will," she whispered as he closed bedroom door. Susan's high-pitched voice floated up from the kitchen as he said his good-byes to the rest of the household.

Maria remained sitting on the side of the bed for several seconds after she heard the back door close, trying to resist the urge to crawl back under the covers.

How did my world suddenly become so small? Even before she got sick, she hadn't left the house in weeks. Her entire existence was contained within these walls. Maria no longer thought about leaving or her previous plans of operating a boardinghouse.

Yet, she was happy, Maria told herself. The two people she loved the most in this world were here, even if one of them resided else-where. She was secure and comfortable; she had everything she need-ed. But it wasn't good for her to be this isolated. And certainly not for Susan. Thankfully, Sarah offered the child some outside company, and her daughter left the house upon occasion. After this morning's incident, however, the urge to keep Susan inside was stronger.

In New York, Maria had loved the energy of the city, the hustle and bustle of people around her. Philadelphia, though, had become a frightening place, a city full of political intrigue and shadowy men who were following them. Now it would be at least two days before she saw Alexander again. Perhaps Dr. Stevens had been right when he told Alexander they were playing a dangerous game.

Maria pushed those unpleasant thoughts from her mind and stood. She grabbed her simple wool gown from the back of the chair and slipped it on over her shift before walking into the kitchen to join the rest of the household.

Much later, when Sarah was about to head to her room for the evening after taking up the supper dishes, she approached Maria hesitantly.

"Excuse me, missus, may I ask you something?" Sarah poked her head into the parlor where Maria was reading.

"Certainly. What is it?"

"Now that you are better, I was wondering if you'll be needing me Sunday? I would like to attend church. There will be lunch on the grounds afterward. I have not been in the past two weeks."

"Yes, of course, Sarah," Maria said, immediately feeling guilty for Sarah's lapse in worship. She knew Sarah attended the African Episcopal Church of St. Thomas faithfully every Sunday, and Maria also suspected there might be a motivation of the male persuasion there too.

"Despite what you and Colonel Hamilton may believe, I am quite capable of taking care of myself and Susan for a few hours. If he says something about it, I will tell him I insisted on allowing you to go," Maria assured her.

"Oh, I've already discussed it with Colonel Hamilton, ma'am. He said it was up to you."

Once again, Maria felt a brief stab of irritation that Sarah had spoken to him first. At least Alexander had done as he had promised and deferred the final decision to her.

"Then, it is settled." Maria forced a smile. "Go to church and spend time with your friends."

"Thank you, ma'am." Sarah gave a little curtsy.

"I will leave shortly after breakfast and will return by late afternoon."

"Take all the time you need. We will be fine," Maria repeated. "In fact, since Colonel Hamilton won't be back until Monday, I am looking forward to a day alone to catch up on my reading," she added with a smile. *That wasn't really the truth, either.*

"Thank you again, ma'am. Good night. I will see you in the morning."

Sarah ducked out of the parlor and closed the door. Maria could hear her footsteps on the stairs. She glanced down at the book she had been reading, a novel from Alexander's own private library, one she no longer had any interest in.

Stop being silly, she told herself. *I am a grown woman, not a girl. Susan and I are perfectly capable of entertaining ourselves for a few hours.*

Why, then, did she have this sense of foreboding that she couldn't seem to shake?

Sixteen

Two days later, the temperature dipped below freezing, and Maria bundled up with Susan on the couch in front of the parlor fireplace. Last night's dip had turned the morning dew into a light frost that glistened on the grass outside the window, the first real freeze of the season. This October day was overcast and not about to warm up much, even by noon.

Sarah had stoked and added more wood to all the fireplaces before she left, so the room was truly toasty and comfortable. But Maria couldn't seem to shake a chill that crept into her bones.

Susan had her favorite rag doll in her arms, her face also pensive, her forehead wrinkled in thought.

Maria curled up her legs beside her, her quilt spread over her lap and tucked underneath. She leaned against the armrest and tried to focus on the book in front of her.

"Why hasn't Colonel Hamilton come to visit today?" Susan asked.

"He was just here two days ago," Maria reminded her.

"I know, but he usually comes every day." Susan paused. "Is he sick now too?" Her voice quivered slightly.

"No, sweetheart," Maria hastened to assure her. "He's just been busy at work, that's all. He'll be back to see us in the morning."

While Susan seemed to accept her answer, Maria could tell that she was still stewing over it in her mind. Things were infinitely more complicated now that her illness had forced Alexander to reveal himself to the entire household.

Maria was not worried about Sarah. The very livelihood of anyone who worked as household staff was largely dependent on the ability to be discreet. But her precocious daughter was another matter entirely. Marie didn't want to lie to Susan, but she also didn't want to take the chance that her daughter would blurt out damning information to just anyone who asked. It was best to keep things simple, she decided, to answer questions as they came up.

"What does Colonel Hamilton do at work?" Susan asked.

Maria froze. Of all the questions for the child to ask, this one was probably the most dangerous. After all, she could hardly tell her daughter that the man who had stayed constantly by her mother's side while she was sick was one of the most powerful men in America. Susan knew he worked at the Treasury because she tagged along with Sarah to deliver messages to him there.

"He helps take care of our country's money and keeps the accounts," she said carefully. Although it was an oversimplification, at least it wasn't a lie.

"Is that why he gives you and Miss Sarah money?"

"No, sweetheart. He does that because he wants to make sure we have the things that we need." It was the best explanation Maria could come up with on such short notice, but it seemed to satisfy the child's curiosity for the time being.

Susan returned her attention to the doll on her lap and sat in silence for several minutes. Maria finally relaxed, and looked back down at the book she was reading.

"Why didn't you use money to buy things when we went to the stores in New York?" Susan asked a few minutes later.

Maria lifted her head in surprise. She had no idea her daughter paid that much attention to her shopping habits. "Because we had accounts at the stores in New York. When we bought things, they wrote it down in a big book called a ledger, and it was paid at the end of the month," she answered as patiently as she could.

"Why don't we have accounts at the shops here?"

"Because we don't know anyone here."

"We know Colonel Hamilton."

"But we can't tell anyone that."

"Why not?"

Maria sighed in exasperation. "Because we can't," she said, a little shorter than she had intended. "Why don't you read to me from your book?"

Susan picked up her own book and opened it to her favorite story. Slowly and carefully, she began to read, using her finger to mark her place on the page. Two paragraphs in, the child's attention started to waver.

"When is Miss Sarah coming home?" Susan asked.

"She'll be back later this afternoon."

"Why couldn't I go with her?"

"Because she was going to visit her friends, and they live on the other side of the city," Marie said simply.

Susan gave a resigned sigh, put her book down beside her, and sat back onto the couch cradling her doll. Maria knew her daughter was bored, and while she sympathized, there was nothing she could do about it. Maria also feared their increasingly isolated existence would only make things more difficult for her outgoing and inquisitive daughter as she grew older.

She was glad that Susan enjoyed helping Sarah with the household chores and thankful for Sarah's patience with her, but this was going to be a problem if Sarah's absence for only a few hours was this difficult. Even though their only clock was in the other room, Maria knew it was not yet one o'clock. The specter of a long afternoon of being peppered by insistent and potentially dangerous questioning loomed in front of her.

As a little girl growing up along the Hudson River, Maria had spent most of her days playing outside with the other children in a close-knit Dutch community, and not necessarily because she liked being outdoors. If she stayed inside, her mother yelled at her for being underfoot. Maria didn't want it to be like that for Susan. She wanted her daughter to enjoy her company—anywhere. But Maria could only do so much to entertain her, especially since she was still recovering. And Maria knew only so much she could teach her. As the youngest child, Maria had run buck wild most of the time. She was too clumsy for household chores and had never learned any of the domestic arts like cooking, knitting, or needlework.

Things got better after she turned twelve, old enough to help serve in the family tavern. She found she was good at it—mostly because their largely male clientele adored her—and she enjoyed the attention. Work was especially exciting during the War when the surrounding conflict brought a steady stream of soldiers stopping by for a hearty meal. Here and there they discreetly slipped her small trinkets, which she collected in a box hidden under her bed. By the time she met James Reynolds at the age of fifteen, her box was overflowing with ribbons, notes, and dried flowers.

A knock on the front door startled Maria, and she looked up from the book on her lap, her heart beating loudly in her chest. Susan glanced up as well. Alexander or Sarah would have come to the back door. The only other people who knew she lived here were her landlord and the mysterious Mr. Clingman.

Maria threw off the quilt, swung her legs off the couch, and quickly slipped her stockinged feet into the satin shoes on the floor beside her. She walked to the window, pulled aside the lace curtain, and wiped away the condensation from the glass with the fabric of her sleeve. From this angle, she couldn't see who was at the door. No horse or carriage in front that she could see, either. Whoever it was had arrived on foot.

Susan had followed her to the window, her eyes wide with excitement at the prospect of a visitor.

"Stay here," Maria said sternly, her hand up as a warning. "I'll be right back." She didn't wait to ensure her daughter's compliance before opening the parlor door and stepping out into the entryway, though. Outside the parlor, the rest of the house was cold. Maria shivered, wrapped her arms across her chest, and headed quickly down the hallway.

She slid the bolt across the heavy wooden door and opened it only wide enough to peek outside. The man standing on the doorstep was alone. Tall and thin, he wore a navy-blue wool greatcoat over his fashionably cut jacket and trousers and an elaborately tied cravat around his neck framed by a high, stiff collar. His short, light brown hair was topped with an expensive beaver hat. With the afternoon light behind him, he stood in silhouette. For a few seconds Maria could only blink in confusion while her eyes adjusted. His features slowly came into focus, and recognition dawned on her face.

"Hello, Mary." He smiled as he removed his hat and tucked it under his arm. "It's been a long time."

Seventeen

"What are you doing here?" Maria whispered, the only response she could find at the moment. She didn't like it that her voice shook, either. She gripped the edge of the door with one hand and twisted the other hand into the folds of her skirt to keep it from trembling. He smiled again. Hard to believe she had once found that same smile so endearing.

"That is no way for a wife to greet her husband."

Maria's head spun with unanswered questions.

"What do you want?" she asked, louder this time.

"I want to talk to you, of course," He held his hands up in a nonthreatening way. "I wish you no ill will," he assured her. "I only want to see my daughter."

"Why would I allow you to see her? You tried to take Susan away from me." She started to shut the door, but he quickly stepped closer and put his foot into the gap.

"I was desperate, Mary. I knew I had already lost your love, and I was afraid I would lose Susan as well." He hesitated, and Maria could see emotion in his grey eyes. He *almost* looked sincere. "Please. Can I at least come inside?"

"No. This is not a good time," she said. She certainly didn't want him in the house with them while they were alone.

He took a step away from the door, and Maria relaxed slightly. At least he wasn't going to try and force himself in.

"When can I return, then? You are still my wife, and I have every right to be here—to see my daughter. I can hire an attorney if necessary."

Her eyes widened. "Is that a threat?" If he wanted to go down that path, she could play that game too. After all, her lover was one of the most prominent lawyers in the country. But, despite her bluster, she knew he was right. Even Alexander couldn't help her with this.

"I am not threatening you. Please, Mary," he continued, his voice plaintive now. "I just want to speak to you. That is all."

Her heartbeat pounded in her ears as she struggled to maintain control and figure out what to do. There was no way she was going to be able to avoid a meeting, but she wanted that meeting to be a time and situation of her choosing, not a surprise visit while they were alone. She needed to wait until Sarah returned, when she was able to get a message to Alexander.

"You can come back later tonight. After supper."

James nodded and put his hat back on his head. "Thank you, Mary," he said. He paused briefly before turning around to leave. "Whatever you may believe, I have missed you both. I will be back." His last words were spoken both as a promise and a threat.

Maria didn't respond as she watched him turn around, walk down the stairs, and out onto the street. Only after her husband disappeared over the horizon did she finally close the door and slide the bolt shut.

All the rage coursing through her body seemed to leave at once. She collapsed against the door and covered her mouth with a shaking hand. She forced herself to close her eyes and take deep breaths.

Maria immediately opened them when she heard the parlor door open. Susan stuck out her head, her eyes widening as she caught sight of her mother.

"What's wrong, Mama?" Her voice trembled. "I heard a man's voice at the door." Susan ran to her.

Maria hugged Susan tightly and took a deep breath. "Let's go sit down, and I'll tell you."

Susan nodded, and they walked back into the parlor together. Maria felt numb, her mind a jumble of thoughts she needed to unscramble. She'd sit down and figure this out.

Maria sat back down, pulled the discarded quilt back over her lap, and clutched it to her chest. She was suddenly so cold. Susan sat down beside her on the couch, as close as possible without being on her lap. Maria extended the quilt over Susan's lap and they sat in silence for several minutes.

"Is that man coming back to hurt us, Mama?" she asked, her lip quivering in fear.

Maria pulled her daughter close and gave her a reassuring smile. "No, sweetheart. He's not going to hurt us," she said as confidently as she could. "It was your papa, who came back to see you."

Susan's eyes widened, and Maria watched the emotions—shock, fear, confusion, and finally, excitement—float across her daughter's face.

"Did he come to Philadelphia on a big ship?" she asked. Maria couldn't help but give a weak smile. *Always about the ships.*

"I don't know," she answered honestly. "Perhaps you can ask him when he comes back later."

Susan nodded as she continued to process the news.

After several seconds, "Why were you sad?"

"I suppose—just the shock of seeing him again," Maria answered slowly. She knew it wasn't much of an answer, but it seemed to satisfy

Susan for the time being.

"Is he going to come back here to live with us?" she asked.

"No," Maria said quickly.

"Why not?"

Maria considered the question in silence. She had never considered her husband's return as a real likelihood, so she had never entertained the idea of living as his wife again. But from her daughter's point of view, she knew the possibility was not an unrealistic expectation.

In fact, how many times had Susan heard her say that her husband was away on business and would return in the future? She had told their landlord, Mr. Otis, that very thing just two months ago. And now, this convenient falsehood had come back to haunt her. Maria could hardly tell Susan that she had been lying the entire time.

"Because he probably has another place to stay here in the city," Maria said frankly, hoping and praying that was true. Suddenly everything was so complicated, and there were too many questions.

Her mind immediately went to Alexander. What would his opinion be on the matter? Would he set her aside now that her husband had returned? Her eyes filled with tears. James's return was a circumstance neither of them had discussed. She needed to get a message to Alexander as soon as possible.

"Come upstairs with me." She took Susan's hand firmly, not wanting her daughter out of her sight for even a few minutes. As soon as they got to her bedroom, Maria leaned over the basin and splashed cold water on her face, the shock of it enough to instantly stop any threatening tears. She patted her face dry with a towel while Susan stood quietly beside her.

"Sit with me while I write a message to Colonel Hamilton," she said, patting the end of the bed. Maria retrieved her supplies from her stationery box and Susan crawled onto the bed behind her.

Maria dipped her quill into the ink, took a deep breath, and started writing.

> *Sir,*
>
> *I Can not begin to tell you the seriousness of our current Situation. Mr. Reynolds has returned Unannounced and wishes to once again meet with myself and Susan. I have put off this Proposed reunion until this evening after I was able to Consult you regarding it. Please, Sir, do not be distressed with me. I had no knowledge of his return to the City and do not know how he Obtained the place of our current Residence. Please send word back by Sarah what your Advice would be regarding his Proposed reunion. I will abide by whatever Your wishes are in the matter.*
>
> *Maria*

She blew on the letter to dry the ink, carefully folded it, and sealed it. There was nothing left to do now except wait for Sarah to return so she could deliver it. Maria briefly considered delivering it herself before dismissing the idea. Aside from the fact that she was probably still too weak from her recent illness to comfortably walk to his home, it was far too dangerous to show up on his doorstep with his family and guests present.

"Are we going to take the message to Colonel Hamilton?" Susan asked hopefully.

"No. Sarah will be back in just a little while, and she will do it." Maria braced herself for more questions, but Susan was uncharacteristically silent on the matter. Nothing more to do but wait.

Sarah returned an hour before sunset, her cheeks windburned from the long walk home in the cold. Before she even removed her red wool coat, Maria quicky pulled her into the parlor to talk privately.

"Something has happened," Maria said, her words coming out in a torrent. "Mr. Reynolds has returned unexpectedly and will be back tonight after supper. I need you to take a message to Colonel Hamilton as quickly as possible."

Sarah stood wide-eyed, trying to process it all. Maria took the letter she had written earlier out of her pocket and pressed it into Sarah's hands. "Wait there until you receive an answer.'"

"Yes, missus," Sarah said, still trying to digest all the information. "What about supper?"

"Don't worry about cooking. This is more important. I can find something for us to eat tonight."

Sarah looked skeptical, but Maria ignored her. She wasn't *that* helpless. They had bread, cheese, and milk in the pantry—as well as the remains of the pippin pie Sarah made a couple of days ago. More than sufficient to fill their bellies for one night.

"I'm sorry. I know that you must be tired from your walk home." Maria immediately felt guilty for sending her back out into the cold before she had a chance to warm up. "I wouldn't ask you to do this if it wasn't urgent."

"I understand, ma'am." Sarah nodded, not a hint of irritation in her expression. "I'll return as quickly as possible."

"Thank you. You have no idea how much I appreciate you." Maria squeezed Sarah's hand to emphasis her point.

Sarah seemed taken aback by the unexpected praise. "I'll be back as soon as I can," she said quickly. She tucked the letter into her pocket, fastened her coat once more, and left.

With Sarah gone, they were alone again, and it would be dark soon. Maria folded her arms across her chest and shivered. The wood in the fireplace had burned down to a bed of coals, and it was getting colder outside. Maria needed to do something to keep her mind occupied while she waited.

Maria walked back into the kitchen. "Let's go get some wood and bring it inside before the fires go out," she told Susan. The woodpile was just outside, against the back wall of the house.

"Hold your skirt up, so I can put some sticks in it," she said. Susan complied and stood silently as Maria filled the makeshift basket with several smaller and lighter branches. She filled her own skirt with kindling, and together they carried their loads back into the house.

"Is Sarah going to be back to cook supper?" Susan asked.

Maria unloaded the sticks from sticks from her skirt and laid the branches down carefully beside the kitchen fireplace. "No. We'll have to fix something for ourselves."

Susan nodded without any further comment. She had been uncharacteristically quiet all afternoon, no doubt still processing her father's unexpected appearance.

After stacking the sticks from her own skirt onto the hearth and brushing the dirt, bark, and dried leaves out as best she could, Maria squat down in front of her daughter and put her hands comfortingly on her small shoulders. While Susan's initial reaction to the news that her father had returned was excitement, she now seemed much more uncertain, probably due to Maria's own reaction than anything else.

"There is no reason to be worried, sweetheart," she assured her. "Your papa only wants to see you. Perhaps you can ask him about the ships he sailed on while he was away," she added with a smile, knowing Susan wouldn't be able to resist.

Susan pursed her lips, and Maria pulled her into her arms for a hug. "It's going to be all right, I promise," she whispered, and pressed her lips against her daughter's soft, pale curls. *If only I could convince myself it was true.*

Maria turned her attention back to the dying fire, throwing on some smaller sticks, then a couple of logs onto the pile of coals. Using the metal poker propped up against the brick hearth, she poked the logs into position and watched for several seconds, gratified to see flames licking around the fresh wood.

Maria took a couple more logs into the parlor and added them to the fireplace there as well. A quick glance out the window told her it was already dark. Sarah should be returning soon with a response from Alexander. And the darkness would soon bring her husband as well. She pressed her hands to her belly and took a deep breath to soothe her nerves, but it didn't help.

If Maria were completely honest with herself, she would prefer her husband and her lover handle this between themselves and leave her out entirely, like Burr and Elijah had done years earlier. But she knew that wasn't a fair or reasonable expectation, and in retrospect, Elijah's arrangement hadn't really worked out that well for her, anyway.

No. James was her mistake and ultimately hers to deal with. What she needed most from Alexander right now was his support and reassurance that even this would not cause him to set her aside. But she'd be lying to herself if she didn't admit a part of her wanted him to swoop in as her dashing protector and make it all go away.

Maria and Susan had just sat down at the table to share a small plate of cold cheese and bread when Sarah returned from her errand. Susan ran to give Sarah a hug. Without stopping to take off her coat, she walked straight to the fireplace and held out her gloved hands to warm them.

Maria stood, exchanging a knowing glance with Sarah. Her maid's expression assured her the mission had been successful. Maria quickly joined them in front of the fireplace where the three stood side-by-side for a time, staring silently into the flames.

Susan, still hungry, decided to make her way back to the table.

Maria turned to Sarah. "Were you able to speak to him?" she asked quietly.

"Yes, ma'am. They were having a grand dinner party, and there was a line of fine carriages in front of the house that went to the end of the block." She paused to catch her breath. "I had to wait a goodly while for Colonel Hamilton to be summoned, but I was able to get your message to him. He sent this in return." Sarah pulled a sealed letter from her pocket.

Maria ignored the brief sting she felt, the last to know about the dinner party. Just another reminder of her place in his life. A world he didn't talk to her about, and she would never be a part of. She took the message from Sarah's fingers as her maid stretched her hands once more toward the warmth of the fire.

"He asked me how you were."

"What did you tell him?"

"That you were anxious but handling it well."

Maria certainly didn't feel like she was handling it well. She felt weak, vulnerable, and on the edge of falling apart completely.

"Thank you, Sarah. For everything."

"Of course, missus." She lowered her eyes and walked across the kitchen to hang her coat up on the hook by the back door.

"I'm going to heat something up for the young miss," Sarah said, no doubt horrified by the idea of letting Susan go to bed with only a cold supper. Maria didn't know how much Alexander was paying her, but it wasn't nearly enough.

She popped open the seal on the message in her hand and tilted it toward the fire so she could read the words inside.

Maria,

I regret that my Responsibilities make it impossible for me to get away tonight or in the morning to discuss recent developments with you in person, as I have guests until Tuesday. Although the situation is Unfortunate, considering that Mr. Reynolds is still your legal Husband and Susan's Father, neither you nor I can prevent his contact with her.

Do not think for a moment that I place any blame on you for your current Misfortune or that it is my wish to discontinue our Friendship, although I understand that this new development will bring new Challenges and Complications.

I will be Indisposed for the remainder of the evening, but please send word by Sarah to my office in the Morning to assure me you are well and what has transpired at the proposed meeting. I will remain,

Yours very Truly,
A. H.

Maria carefully refolded the note as she contemplated the words written across the page. While it was unreasonable to expect him to drop everything and come to her, she hadn't expected him to brush her off so easily. Not a word of advice about what she should do when her husband arrived later this evening, either.

"Would you like me to heat up something for you too, missus?" Sarah's question and the ping of a cast-iron skillet interrupted her thoughts.

Maria slid the letter into her pocket and turned away from the fire.

"No, thank you. I'm afraid I don't have much of an appetite." She half expected her maid, skillet in hand, to give her another lecture about eating—but Sarah merely nodded instead.

"Yes, ma'am. You should sit down and rest while I fix up something for Susan."

Maria agreed and took a chair near fireplace, for she knew she had to come up something to say when James arrived.

She didn't have much time to think about it. Sarah had just heated up leftover meat and vegetable pie and served Susan when a loud rap on the front door startled them all.

Maria stood quickly and glanced over at her daughter. "Finish your supper and stay here with Miss Sarah until I come and get you. Do you promise?"

Susan nodded, her eyes registering a combination of excitement and trepidation.

Satisfied with her daughter's compliance, Maria walked down the hall to the front door. She stood in front of the door for several seconds before nervously tucking an errant strand of hair behind her ear and smoothing the front of her calico gown down over her stomach. Her hand shook as she reached out and opened the door.

Her husband stood on the doorstep, dressed in the same clothes he had worn earlier in the day and holding his top hat in his hands.

"Hello, Mary. Is this a good time?" he asked.

Maria shrugged, trying her best to remain as cool as possible. "As good a time as any, I guess." She opened the door wider and stepped aside.

He nodded respectfully as he stepped into the entry way. "Thank you," he said as she closed the door behind him. He shrugged out of his coat and handed it to her along with his hat. She hung it on the large hook beside the door.

"Let's talk privately in the parlor," she said, opening the door to the more formal and private room.

James nodded and followed her inside. She sat in her usual spot on the sofa while he lowered his lanky frame down onto the upholstered chair beside her. He stretched out his long legs in front of him, and they sat in uncomfortable silence for several minutes, the crackling fire the only sound in the room.

"You look skinny, Mary," he said, his voice laced with concern.

"So I've been told."

"Are you well?

"I was recently ill, but I have recovered."

"I am glad you are better," James said with seeming sincerity, and they lapsed once more into an uncomfortable silence.

He glanced around the room. "You seemed to have done well for yourself in my absence."

"I could say the same for you," she countered. Everything he wore looked new, from his freshly polished shoes to the elaborately tied cravat and cut of his jacket. She noticed when she took his coat that it was unstained despite the rain and mud that had dogged the city the past few days, and his hat looked like it had barely been worn. Whatever money he had come into, it was obviously a recent development.

He nodded. "Yes. I have been very fortunate of late and have made a tidy amount speculating in Virginia. I have more than enough to provide for you and Susan in comfort."

Maria ignored the last part of his statement, keeping her face carefully deadpan and divulging no emotion while her mind spun wildly behind her mask of indifference.

"How did you know where to find us?" she asked, the one question she had been pondering all afternoon. Only a handful of people knew she was here, so there weren't that many options.

James shifted uncomfortably in the small chair. "I made some inquiries concerning the whereabouts of my wife upon my arrival in Philadelphia. Men tend to notice when a woman such as you arrives in a new town."

Maria knew immediately he was lying. She had not left this house in weeks, nor had any interactions with any men besides Alexander.

Except Mr. Clingman, the voice in the back of her head reminded her. She remained perfectly still, her pulse beating loudly in her ears and her stomach twisting into a tight knot.

"What is it you want from us?" She tried to keep her voice steady to avoid betraying her real feelings.

"I want to once again be a husband to you and a father to Susan," he said, his grey eyes earnest.

"You left me and tried to take her away from me. Why should I trust you now?" she asked, her voice rising. She hated how her hands shook as those long-buried emotions started to bubble up to the surface.

"You will not win if you wish to fight me on this, Mary" he said. "You have no right to keep her from me." His grey eyes flashed with the same quick anger she remembered from years ago before slipping under his new, more genteel persona. "Not even whoever is paying for all this"—a wave of his hand indicating the room—"can deny me my rights as your husband and Susan's father."

Maria instantly stiffened. *How much does he know about who is paying for all this?* "What makes you think I have any sort of benefactor paying my bills?" she challenged.

"Don't play coy with me, Mary. You wasted no time welcoming

Mr. Wagstaff into our bed within days of my departure, so I can only assume you've found someone new to pay your bills now that he's dead."

"Oh, don't you play the aggrieved husband. We both know the truth. *You* were the one who set up the arrangement with Mr. Wagstaff in the beginning," she snapped back. "If you had not tried to take Susan from me, I would have had no need for Mr. Wagstaff's protection and generosity."

The vehemence of her words seemed to take James by surprise. "You were no longer acting as a wife to me." His words sounded petulant, like a child whose favorite toy had been taken away.

"Perhaps if you had not insisted on whoring me out to pay your debts, I would have been more conciliatory toward you," she spat, surprising even herself. "You didn't treat me as a wife, so why should I have acted as one?"

"I didn't ask you to do anything you weren't already doing," James snapped back.

"What choice did you leave me? You deserted us repeatedly to pursue your own desires, never once thinking about how I was supposed to make a way for us. Then, as the final straw, you tried to take the one thing I love most in this life to punish me for my perceived failures as a wife. I will never forgive you for that." Maria's eyes were filled with tears, but her voice was strong and unwavering.

James had no response to her accusations. He looked down at his lap. "I am sorry I was not a better husband to you, Mary." His words, however, were clipped and short—not at all an apology. "You have no idea of the machinations against me. You think your precious Mr. Wagstaff and Mr. Burr saved you from me, but you have no idea what the truth is."

"Enlighten me, then," she challenged.

James gave her a cold, sadistic smile that sent shivers down her spine. "They set me up, Mary."

"Why should I believe you?"

James shrugged. "I suppose you have no reason to believe me, but I think that deep down, you recognize there is some truth to what I'm telling you."

Maria held her ground, not wanting to give James the satisfaction of seeing her doubts. "You are the one who tried to take Susan from me. Your own actions caused me to seek out Mr. Wagstaff's assistance in getting her back."

"Susan is my daughter, and I had every right to take her with me wherever I pleased."

Maria knew that he was right. The law didn't make any provision to force him to return Susan to her.

Did they threaten him, or pay him? She could hear Alexander's words in the back of her consciousness.

"How did they force you, then?" she challenged.

"We were already on board a schooner bound for Boston when the Magistrate and one of his thugs dragged me off the ship like I was the lowest sort of criminal," he said, drawing himself up. "When he searched me, he pretended to find three hundred dollars tucked into my jacket pocket. Money I had no knowledge of." His voice rose in indignation. "They took me to Mr. Burr's office where Mr. Wagstaff was waiting. He told me if I kept the three hundred dollars I had in my pocket as payment for leaving you and Susan in their care, they wouldn't file charges against me. Charges I had no way to defend myself against. After all, who would believe someone like me, a working man with a criminal record, over a powerful businessman like Elijah Wagstaff and his henchman, Aaron Burr?"

Burr told me that he was a man without morals or character, who would do anything for money, including selling his own wife. Alexander's words echoed in Maria's head once again.

"Why should I believe you?" She tried to hide the tremor in her voice.

"Because you know in your heart that it's true, Mary. Your great hero and savior, Elijah Wagstaff, purchased you from me to use as his own personal whore."

Eighteen

Maria sat in shocked stillness as she desperately tried to maintain her composure. She knew James had intended to shock and wound her, but she was not going to give him the satisfaction of allowing him to see how much his words had hurt.

James sat back in his chair with a frustrated sigh. "I didn't come here to fight with you, Mary. I am not your enemy. Mr. Wagstaff and Mr. Burr are the ones to blame, not me."

Maria was silent as she sorted through a myriad of conflicting emotions. "What would you have done with Susan had they not stopped you from boarding that ship?" she asked, her voice hardly above a whisper.

"I would have kept her safe with me, Mary. I would not have allowed any harm to come to her."

Despite her best efforts, her eyes began to fill with tears. "But she would have been without her mother. And I would have been without my daughter."

"I knew I couldn't stop them from taking you from me, and I thought I could at least keep Susan from witnessing her mother's shame. But I was wrong, Mary. I should have confided in you, and we could have left New York together and made a life for ourselves in the South, far away from Mr. Wagstaff and Mr. Burr's scheming." As he leaned toward her, his words seemed so earnest—and his grey eyes so much like her daughter's, beseeching her to believe him.

All the *could haves* suddenly flashed before Maria as she considered what her life would have been like in that scenario. Had her husband not left her, she would have been able to live a respectable life instead of living secretly and lying to everyone about an invisible husband who would someday return. Instead, she'd had to exist on the outskirts of polite society and live every day with the fear of discovery and ruin.

She would have been able to make friends and go out in public without the fear of being seen, or having someone ask questions she had no way to answer. She would not have had to lie to Susan about her own father. She would have been a wife, sharing a name and a home with her husband, with every expectation of respectability. Not a mistress who slept alone most nights, the days spent pining for a lover who was not hers and never would be. Not someone subsiding solely on the crumbs of time and attention Alexander was able to afford her.

Of course, she had no reason to believe that James would have suddenly changed his ways upon leaving New York, or that their marriage would have been any different than it was the first several years. In truth, he was a liar and thief. Her life as his wife would have no doubt continued to be difficult. But she would never really know what the future could have held for her in that scenario because she wasn't given a choice.

"Why did you not confide in me?" she said, her voice rising once again. "You should have talked to me instead of stealing Susan away in the middle of the night," her voice broke, the confusion and uncertainty finally too much to bear. "You shouldn't have just left me there alone, with nowhere to go, and no other option but to turn to Elijah and Burr for help." She took a deep breath.

"I would have returned for you, Mary, but I was told by Mr. Burr that I would be arrested and prosecuted if I ever set foot in New York again. I made a nice life for myself in North Carolina. I could have sent enough money for you and Susan to come to me. I would have provided for you both in comfort. I wrote you letters. But you never wrote back, and I knew they had turned you against me."

He's trying to make it sound like he's the victim in this whole sordid scenario.

"After I received word that Mr. Wagstaff died, I returned to New York to try and find you and Susan, but you had left. Only by pure chance did I come upon someone who remembered you and was able to tell me where you had gone."

Another lie. Maria had told no one where she was going when she left New York, and only Burr knew of her change in residence. Obviously, James's arrival was another set up. *But who were they setting up—me, James, or Alexander?*

"I would like the opportunity to win back your love, if you will allow me."

Maria shook her head without even taking time to consider his proposal. Allowing him back into her life as her husband would mean giving up Alexander. And that was the one thing she could not do.

"The time has already passed for a reconciliation. I don't trust you. I cannot deny you access to your daughter, but I will never agree to act as a wife to you again."

"I hope I can convince you of my sincerity," he said. "Until then, I will be content just being a father to Susan."

They sat in uncomfortable silence once again as Mary sniffed. She felt broken and exhausted from the emotion exchange. So much information to sort through, so many conflicting thoughts to figure out.

"How long do you plan on staying in the city?" she asked.

"Only a week. My business partner and I need to return to Virginia to finish some business we have there. But I will return to Philadelphia before the end of the year."

Maria lifted her head at the mention of a business partner. *What sort of hapless soul has he managed to trick into participating in his schemes?* In the past, he had always worked alone. Regardless, Maria was relieved James would be leaving again in a few days, however brief the reprieve. She needed to see Alexander, to feel his arms around her once more. Only he could quiet her fears and make her feel like the world was right again.

"I will go get Susan and bring her in."

"Thank you."

Maria stood slowly and brushed the wrinkles from the front of her gown. She hesitated at the door. "You should be proud of your daughter. She is a good girl and very smart. She already knows her letters and numbers and can write her name. She is my world."

"You have been a good mother to her, Mary. I give you my solemn word that I will do my best by her."

Maria didn't respond as she opened the door and walked into the kitchen. A few minutes later, she returned with Susan in tow. The child pressed herself into Maria's side as if she were trying to disappear within the folds of her mother's skirts. Maria clutched her hand tightly as they stopped a few feet from James. He stood, then took a knee in front of his daughter.

"Hello, Susan," he said, smiling at her. She squirmed closer to Maria, eyeing him warily.

"You have certainly grown since I saw you last," he went on. "I've missed you so much. I think about you every day."

Not sure how to respond, Susan pressed her hand to her mouth and slowly pulled away from Maria's side.

"Your mother tells me you are very smart and can already write your name."

Susan continued eyeing James nervously. "I can read, too. And count to ten in French," she added proudly, finding her voice.

James's eyes widened in surprise. "Who taught you that?"

"Col—"

Maria put her hand on her daughter's shoulder, and Susan immediately closed her mouth.

"We had a neighbor who spoke French and taught her," Maria interjected quickly. *God, I hate lying in front of her like that.* She glanced quickly at James's face—any indication he noticed anything amiss—but he was smiling at Susan instead.

"You are a very smart girl, then," he said. "I am very proud of you."

Susan returned his smile and took a tentative step toward him.

"Did you come to Philadelphia on a ship?" she asked, no longer able to curtail her curiosity.

"Yes, I did. I sailed from Virginia on a merchant ship called *The Jamaica.* Would you like me to take you down to the river sometime and show you the ships docked there? Your mother can come with us, of course," he added quickly.

Susan nodded enthusiastically at the idea, her face brightening instantly.

"Then we will make plans," he said, and stood.

"Are you going to come here to live with us now?" Susan asked.

Maria's sharp intake of breath brought his eyes to hers, her own warning to him to tread carefully.

"I'm only going to be in Philadelphia for a few days. I have some business to take care of in Virginia."

Susan's face fell in disappointment.

"But I will return in a month, and your mama and I will talk about it," he added quickly. Maria knew then he wasn't above using their daughter to try and get her back.

"I'm afraid I must be going now before it gets too much past your bedtime. Can you come give your papa a hug?" he asked. He held out his arms toward her.

Susan hesitated and looked up at her mother.

"It's all right, sweetheart," Maria said, nudging her lightly.

Susan stepped into her father's arms, and he pulled her to him and hugged her tightly. When he finally released her, Maria swore she could see the sheen of unshed tears in his eyes.

"I would like to come and see you again tomorrow," he said. "If that is acceptable to your mother, of course."

Susan looked back at Maria expectantly. Maria nodded, and Susan smiled at her for the first time since the meeting began.

James smiled back at them. "I will come tomorrow at the same time then, and we will get to know each other even better." He turned to Maria with a polite nod. "Thank you, Mary. I can see myself out."

Maria could hear him gathering his coat and hat before leaving by the front door. So much more to contemplate now, so much new information to dissect. Since she had made it past this first meeting without completely falling apart, she would count it as a major victory.

She tapped Susan on the shoulder. "Let's go get ready for bed. It's been a long day."

Susan looked up at her. "Why does Papa call you Mary?" she asked.

Maria hesitated; she hadn't even realized he had used her given name. "Because that's the name I was given when I was born, what I was called when your papa and I married."

"Why does Colonel Hamilton call you Maria?"

"Because that's the name I use now," she said unreservedly. "Come on. It's time to head upstairs." She walked out of the parlor.

Susan dutifully followed her back into the kitchen, where Sarah, needle in hand, looked up from her seat in front of the fire. She was letting out the hem in one of Susan's gowns.

"Has she outgrown another one?" Maria asked. Soon there would be no more hem, and Maria would have to use some of the money she had set aside to purchase fabric to have more dresses made for her daughter. Maria had a wardrobe full of fine gowns Elijah had purchased for her in New York, gowns she no longer wore because she no longer left the house. Perhaps Sarah was skilled enough with a needle to use the fabric from those gowns to fashion them into something that would fit Susan.

Sarah nodded and smiled affectionately. "Growing like a weed, that one is."

"My papa said he would take me down to the river and show me the ships," Susan told her enthusiastically. "Mama is going to go with us," she added.

"That sounds like great fun, miss." Sarah smiled at her warmly.

"Go upstairs now, and get into bed," Maria reminded her gently. "I'll be there in a few minutes to tuck you in."

Susan nodded and scampered up the stairs.

"Will Mr. Reynolds be moving into the household now that he has returned, missus?" Sarah asked.

"No," she said quickly. "Mr. Reynolds will be leaving again for Virginia in a few days and will not return until the end of the year. He will occasionally come to visit Susan. Nothing in the household will change otherwise. Your position here is secure," Maria assured her.

"Yes, ma'am." Sarah nodded and turned her attention back to

the dress on her lap. Maria noticed she did not appear to be totally comforted by that, either.

Maria could hardly blame her maid for being concerned, though. Considering Alexander paid her wages, Sarah had ample reason to be fearful of her continued employment now that James had returned so unexpectedly.

A silence fell over the room, and the sound of the fire crackling in the fireplace seemed unnaturally loud. Maria could tell that Sarah wanted to ask more about how her husband's return would affect her relationship with Alexander—but she would never bring it up on her own. While their household was a very informal one, that was a line not to be crossed. Probably for the best, Maria thought. She really didn't have an answer for her, anyway.

"I'm finished for the night, missus," Sarah said. She tied a knot in the thread, broke it off with her teeth, and put the folded dress back into a mending basket on the floor beside her feet. "If you'll not be needing anything more, do you mind if I retire to my quarters now?"

"Of course," Maria said, weighing Sarah's sudden aloofness. After Maria tucked Susan in bed, the two usually stayed downstairs by the fire for a little while, chatting amicably while Sarah worked on the seemingly never-ending pile of mending. Maria could hardly blame her, however, for wanting to escape to her room early tonight. This had been a long day for everyone, and Sarah was no doubt exhausted from being out in the cold and wind. Maria was spent as well.

"Thank you again, Sarah, for everything," Maria added, and began gathering up the mending.

"Of course," she said with a nod. "Good night, missus."

"Good night. I will see you in the morning."

Sarah nodded and then she was gone, leaving Maria alone in the kitchen to sort through the emotions running through her head. She needed to write an answer to Alexander's last message, but she was far too exhausted to be able to put her thoughts into any sort of order tonight. She would do it first thing in the morning.

After tucking Susan into bed, Maria locked the front door and retired to her room. There was nothing more she could do now but prepare for bed and try to get some sleep.

But that proved elusive. Maria tossed and turned all night, finally giving up when she heard Sarah going down the stairs to start her morning chores. She dressed quickly and walked into the kitchen just as Sarah got the fire going. Susan was not yet awake, and Maria stood in front of the flames trying to warm herself while Sarah silently went about her morning chores. A knock at the back door surprised them both.

Who can possibly be at our door at this hour of the morning? Maria wasn't expecting Alexander—he still had guests until tomorrow. This was much too early. Maria's next thought was that James had returned to wheedle her to a nub. But James would come to the front door. She exchanged glances with Sarah.

"I'll get it," Maria said, and went to the backdoor, her heart beating loudly in her chest. She slid the bolt and opened the door, sighing in relief when she saw Alexander standing in front of her. What she really wanted to do was throw herself into his arms, but propriety won out. She smiled up at him, her relief evident.

"Good morning."

"Is this a good time?"

"Of course, sir." She opened the door completely. "Please come in. I didn't expect to see you," she continued. "I was going to write you a letter later this morning."

"I didn't mean to startle you. I apologize for my unannounced appearance at your door so early, but I was concerned and wanted to see for myself that you were safe and well." He looked over to Sarah. "I hope there are no adverse effects from your adventures in the cold last night."

"I am well, sir," she said, and turned her attention back to her morning chores.

He leaned closer to Maria. "Can we speak privately?"

"Of course."

Maria led the way down the narrow hall to the parlor. The fire had gone out in the night, so the room was still chilly. As soon as she closed the door behind them, Alexander took a step toward her. Maria wanted nothing more than for him to take her into his arms and kiss her into oblivion, but instead, his arms remained respectfully by his sides. She pulled her wool shawl tighter around her shoulders.

He looked as if he hadn't slept well, either. His eyes were bloodshot, and his face looked puffy. Of course, she reminded herself, he had hosted a dinner party last night, and a late night with too much wine could very well have produced the same results.

"I couldn't sleep for worrying about you," he said, as if he'd read her mind. "I didn't receive a message last night, and I was worried. I needed to see you and ensure that you were safe." He paused. "Did you arrive at a decision?"

"I told Mr. Reynolds that I will never again be a wife to him, but that I would not stand in his way of renewing a relationship with his daughter," she answered. "He accepted my decision, and the meeting ended amicably." Maria could see the muscles in Alexander's jaw instantly relax. He reached out and pulled her into his arms.

"I was so afraid that I would no longer be able to see you," he whispered, his eyes desperate and beseeching. He put his hands on either side of her face and looked into hers, sealing the truth of what he'd just admitted.

Maria was suddenly overcome by his pain. Based on the dispassionate tone of his last letter, she did not expect him to be so affected.

Then again, his letters rarely displayed the emotions he expressed to her in person. She needed to tell him about James's tale of coercion, about Burr and Elijah—but that could come later. For now, all she wanted was to be in Alexander's arms.

His fingers tightened in her hair as he took her lips with his in a kiss more possessive than tender, and for the first time since her illness, she could feel the original fire and intensity that had marked the beginning of their affair. But she could taste something else too. Something new, something almost primal. A potent combination of fear, passion, anguish, and jealousy.

What would Alexander have done if he had arrived to find James still here with me?

She didn't want to even consider the repercussions. Showing up on her doorstep at this hour of the morning had been stupid and reckless on Alexander's part. But she didn't care. The fact that he wanted and needed her so badly made her heart sing.

Maria lifted her arms to encircle his neck, the woolen shawl falling onto the floor as she gave herself over to the madness. His kisses grew more and more fervent as he backed her up against the parlor wall, his mouth and body demanding no less than her complete and total surrender. He unbuttoned the front of his breeches with one hand, the other was twisted in her hair, pinning her to the wall even more securely. She raised the white flag willingly as he lifted her skirts, caught up in a tidal wave of emotion she was helpless to resist.

It was over quickly, and they collapsed against each other, his forehead pressed to hers, their breaths commingled, their faces covered with a fine sheen of perspiration.

For several minutes, the only sound was their labored breathing. Slowly, the room began to come back into focus. Alexander took a small step back and Maria stood once more on her own two feet, her skirts falling back into place. The night's sleeplessness followed by their own ardor had her legs quivering, however—enough to threaten total collapse. She took a deep breath.

Alexander's face reddened with embarrassment. The knowledge that Sarah was just on the other side of the unlocked door was not far from either of their minds. He reached down, quickly tucked the tail of his linen shirt into the waistband of his wool breeches and buttoned up the front.

"I am sorry," he whispered. "That was not well done of me. I'm afraid I allowed myself to get carried away. I was just so afraid . . ."

Still slightly out of breath and unsure of her ability to form a cohesive sentence, Maria pressed herself against him, instinctively finding the spot on the inside of his shoulder where her head fit perfectly. She buried her face against the side of his neck. Alexander pulled her tightly against him once again and pressed his lips into her soft, tousled curls.

In that instant, the events of the past twelve hours struck her full force. The flimsy dam she had built to hold back all the emotions she had quelled since her husband's unexpected arrival suddenly burst, a flood of tears poured forth with no warning and intensity she was powerless to stop.

No longer trying to be strong, she poured every fear and sorrow she had felt in the past eighteen hours into the fine wool cloth of Alexander's buff colored jacket, leaving an ever-widening wet spot beneath her face. He put his hand on the back of her head and pressed her more tightly against him to absorb the sound of her cries as she broke.

"What is wrong? Did I hurt you?" His voice rose with concern.

Unable to speak, Maria shook her head vehemently.

"What is it then? Did Mr. Reynolds do something to you?"

Maria shook her head once again, unable to find the words to express the emotions crashing in on her.

"Please don't leave me," she finally managed to whisper between sobs. She curled her fingers around the lapels of his jacket and held on as if her very life depended on it. "I could not bear it."

"I won't, Maria. I promise," he rasped, his lips pressed tightly against her hair.

A small, rational part of her mind knew that his situation precluded any ability to make such a promise, but she didn't care. Those were the words she needed to hear. She struggled to stop her tears, but her attempt was in vain.

At the root of her emotional display was no longer just her fear of losing Alexander, but the entirety of the revelations of the past twelve hours. She still didn't know whether she could believe any of the story James had told her. Even so, her naive, idealized view of Elijah as her protector and rescuer was gone. What were once fond memories were now tainted and ugly.

She cried for Susan and for the isolated, secretive life she had foisted upon her daughter by her own decisions. With a single word, Maria could once more be a wife to her husband, and Susan would have a father once again. But if it meant losing Alexander, Maria couldn't do it.

What kind of a mother chooses a love affair over the wellbeing of her own daughter? She cried harder at the realization of her failures.

When several minutes passed with no sign of her tears abating, Maria began gasping for air, and Alexander looked down into her eyes, his own narrowing with concern.

"Maria, sweetheart, you're going to make yourself sick." He took out his handkerchief and gently wiped the tears from her cheeks. "You must tell me what is wrong. Come, let us sit down. Whatever it is, I can make it right. But you must talk to me."

He gently maneuvered her toward the couch, sat, and pulled her down beside him. She exhaled with a sob that, much to her mortification, came out as a very messy, unladylike snort. Her hand flew to her mouth, and she hiccupped.

Her eyes immediately locked on Alexander's face. Rather than the disgust she expected, his eyes held a look of tender affection. He reached over and wiped her nose with his handkerchief while she sat very still under his ministrations, hiccupping again halfway through. At least she wasn't crying anymore.

"There," Alexander pronounced when he had finished wiping her face. "Now tell me why you are so distressed. I have told you sincerely that your husband's return will not cause me to put you aside. Did Mr. Reynolds say something more to you?"

Maria nodded and took a deep breath. "Mr. Reynolds claims Mr. Wagstaff and Mr. Burr tricked him, that he was forced to leave me under threat of prosecution." She paused a moment before continuing. "They searched him and found three hundred dollars. He claims they told him he would be arrested for stealing it if he didn't leave. If he left, they said he could keep the money as consolation."

Alexander didn't seem surprised. "I didn't know the details, but I suspected as much when I confronted Mr. Burr about his connection to you several months ago, and he warned me about Mr. Reynolds. I am quite certain I mentioned the conversation to you at the time."

Maria nodded, sniffed, and ran her hand across her nose as she struggled to maintain control. "You did. But I dismissed it," she admitted. "Do you believe Mr. Burr?"

He shook his head. "No. But regardless of who initiated the exchange, I believe that both sides took advantage of you for their own purposes. Mr. Reynolds for the money, and Mr. Wagstaff for his own private satisfaction," he said matter-of-factly.

Maria lowered her head as tears threatened once more, suddenly feeling very foolish. *How could I have been so naïve and so stupid? How did I not see the true nature of the exchange?*

Alexander lifted her chin with her fingers. "Do not blame yourself, Maria. You had no way to know. You are innocent in the designs of such men."

If he only knew how much. She didn't even want to think about the repercussions of what would happen should he find out.

"Did Mr. Reynolds tell you how he came to learn of your address?" Alexander asked.

Maria's eyes widened. "He claimed he made some inquiries of men in New York and here in Philadelphia, that they told him where I was. But that is a lie, sir," she said, her voice rising. "I have not left this house in weeks. None beside you, Mr. Otis, and Mr. Clingman know I am here—and I am confident neither you nor Mr. Otis would have cause to reveal that information to a stranger."

Alexander sat up straighter, instantly alert. "There is no chance that Mr. Clingman's sudden appearance in the alley and market was a coincidence," he stately flatly.

Maria nodded her head in agreement.

"Did Mr. Reynolds say anything more about his business partner or what sort of speculation they were engaging in?"

"No, sir. Only that they had made a tidy sum."

"Did he share his immediate plans with you?"

She nodded. "He said he would be leaving Philadelphia to return to Virginia at the end of the week to finish business there, but that he would be back in December for good."

Alexander furrowed his eyebrows in thought, then said something Maria would never have anticipated.

"I would like to arrange a private meeting with Mr. Reynolds before he leaves the capital."

Nineteen

Maria could only stare at Alexander in disbelief for several seconds. *Why would my lover wish to speak to my estranged husband alone, in private?* She could not imagine a more nightmarish scenario.

"Why?" The only thing she could think of to ask.

"I want to ascertain for myself what sort of speculation he is engaged in and what part Mr. Clingman has played."

Maria wasn't sure that was the entire truth, either—but she didn't want to push it.

"Do you think they are engaging in something illegal?"

"I don't know," Alexander said, "but considering Mr. Clingman's connection to several prominent politicians, I feel it necessary to at least inquire. Do you know where Mr. Reynolds is lodging?"

Maria shook her head. "No."

"Can you find out for me?"

She nodded hesitantly, still not completely convinced this was a good idea. "How are you going to explain how you came to know of Mr. Reynolds and his activities?"

Alexander was silent for several seconds. "I don't know," he admitted, "But I am sure I will be able to come up with a suitable excuse that doesn't reveal our—particular friendship." He added special emphasis to the last words and grinned at her.

Marie blushed. .

"Has he planned another visit with Susan?"

"Yes. Tonight, after supper."

Alexander nodded. "How is she? I would imagine her to be quite shaken by the sudden reappearance of her father."

His concern for her daughter's emotional state made Maria's heart skip a beat. "She was. But she is also very curious and will probably warm up to him quickly."

"Do you think he will try to take her from you again?"

"Yes," she nodded. "It is my biggest fear." Tears welled up in her eyes at the thought. *That, and being set aside by you.*

"Then I will do my best to see that it does not happen," he said. He leaned forward and kissed her softly on the lips. "I'm afraid I must take my leave." He stood and adjusted his jacket and cravat. "I am expected at breakfast shortly."

Maria nodded and stood to see him out. "Of course."

"But I will plan a longer visit soon where we can indulge our passions in a proper bed, not up against your parlor wall." He took her face in his hands, a little more serious now. "I promise I will do my best to see that no harm comes to you or Susan." His eyes bore down into hers, and she found herself lost to their depths.

He kissed her one last time, and they walked out of the parlor as if nothing had happened. *Save my red, puffy eyes and the large wet spot still visible on the shoulder of Alexander's jacket.*

Susan had emerged from her bedroom in her nightdress, now standing next to Sarah at the kitchen worktable watching her mix flour, butter, and milk together for bread dough. They both turned to look as Maria and Alexander emerged from the parlor. Susan gave a delighted squeal and ran to hug Alexander.

"My papa has come back to see me," she told him proudly as he swung her up into his arms. "He's going to take me to the river and show me the ships docked there."

"That sounds terribly exciting," he said, and glanced over at Maria.

"I will be accompanying them as well," Maria added.

"Have you ever been on a ship?" Susan asked Alexander.

"Yes," he said, smiling at her. "When I was a young lad of fifteen, I left my home in the West Indies and traveled on a big sailing ship all the way to Boston. It took three weeks." He shifted her weight more comfortably onto his hip. "But before we could get there, a fire started in the hold and soon traveled up the masts and burned all of the sails and ropes." He waved his free hand as Susan, clearly caught up in this story, widened her eyes in alarm.

"What did you do?" she asked breathlessly.

"The crew tied ropes to wooden buckets and threw them over the side of the ship to collect water. Everyone on board helped pull them up and throw the water on the fire to put it out," he said with a flourish, clearly enjoying Susan's reactions to his dramatic tale.

"Were you frightened?"

"Yes. Everyone was. Fire is a very dangerous thing when you are at sea. We all would have drowned if we had not gotten the fire out."

"Did you make it to Boston?" Susan asked in breathless anticipation.

"Yes, but barely."

"What did you do then?"

"I got on another ship and sailed to New York. And do you know what?"

"What?" Susan leaned forward, her eyes wide with anticipation.

"I haven't sailed on the ocean since." He laughed and sat her down on the floor beside him. Susan attempted a smile, but the furrow between her eyebrows indicated she was clearly concerned.

"I want to go on a ship someday, but I do not think I would like it if it were to catch fire," she said.

"A ship wouldn't dare catch fire with such precious cargo as you aboard." He smiled down at her.

Susan giggled, her fears instantly evaporating.

"It's time for Colonel Hamilton to be on his way now," Maria broke in. She had no idea whether the story he had just told was truth or a tall tale, but watching Alexander interact with Susan was twisting her heart to pieces. Maria silently cursed the fates that had made Susan her husband's daughter and not Alexander's.

"I will see you out," she said quietly, lightly touching his sleeve.

He got the hint and said his goodbyes before heading toward the back door, Maria directly behind him. Since Sarah and Susan had turned their full attention back to the bread dough, he leaned forward and gave Maria a peck on the cheek.

"I will return in the morning at a more decent hour," he whispered, "although it was quite worth rising early to be able to indulge in your particular charms." He gave her his most lecherous grin.

Maria's cheeks flushed, and she remained in the doorway, watching him mount his dappled grey mare. He kicked the horse into an easy canter and headed down the alley—away from the main road and prying eyes—for Maria very well knew he shouldn't be seen leaving her house at this hour of the day.

Then he was gone. Back to his home. Back to his wife. Back to his children.

Maria wanted nothing more than to retreat to her bed, pull the covers over her head, and stay there the rest of the day. But in the end, she didn't. She did her best to pretend that nothing was wrong as she went through the rituals of the day instead. The telltale sign, however, was her loss of appetite—a fact that didn't escape Sarah's keen observation. Maria caught Sarah watching her more than once as she pushed her food around on her plate without eating it.

She will no doubt report this to Alexander the next time he comes over, Maria thought wryly. But she couldn't really work up the energy to be to cross with Sarah, for she never doubted that Sarah's concern was sincere.

James returned shortly after supper as promised. By that time, Susan was in such a state of excitement, he had barely taken a seat in the parlor before she began peppering him with questions.

Knowing her daughter as she did, Maria should have guessed that one of the first questions Susan would ask about would be one concerning fires on ships.

"Have you ever been on a ship that caught fire, Papa?"

The minute the question left her daughter's lips, Maria knew they were in dangerous territory, but it was too late to stop it.

"No," James said. "Where did you hear a story about that?"

"Colonel Hamilton told me."

Maria's sharp intake of breath caused Susan to spin around and confirm her error in her mother's eyes, her own widening as she realized what she had done. Maria gave her a little smile to indicate she was not angry with her. What was done was done, and it would be cruel to traumatize her daughter over an innocent mistake.

Besides, six-year-old children shouldn't be required to keep secrets about their mother's lovers from their father in the first place, Maria reminded herself.

"Colonel Hamilton, as in Secretary of the Treasury Hamilton?" James quickly looked over at Maria.

"Yes," Maria said softly, her mind working feverishly to come up with an acceptable explanation. "Colonel Hamilton was very kind, and he helped us find a place to stay when we first moved to Philadelphia. He befriended Susan, as he has several children of his own, and indulged her with many fanciful stories." The best she could come up with off the top of her head.

"I am surprised you did not look to Mr. Burr for assistance, now that he's been elected to the Senate." James's words were angry and clipped.

"I am no longer on speaking terms with Mr. Burr." *At least* that *is the truth.*

James raised his eyebrows in what might be genuine surprise, and once again Maria wondered how much he knew, or what Jacob Clingman had told him.

"If you are still in touch with Secretary Hamilton, do you think you can pass along a message from me requesting a meeting?" James asked. "I have some knowledge regarding a member of his department who is offering lists of money owed to the Virginia Line to speculators for a handsome price. Perhaps he would offer me a reward for the information, or even a position in the department." He smiled at Maria.

Could it really be that easy?

"Give me the address where you are staying before you leave, and I will send a message to Colonel Hamilton with your request for a meeting," she said, finding it hard to believe he had bought her story so easily.

"Thank you, Mary," he said, his eyes shining with excitement. "A position in the Treasury would be quite a prize and would allow me to move to Philadelphia permanently."

Maria couldn't think of a worse place for him to be. *Would Alexander really hire him?* Surely he would have the good sense to deny James a job in the Treasury—although being the employer of your mistress's husband would be a good way to keep track of him.

No, it was a terrible idea. Besides, James's lack of pecuniary integrity would hardly make him a trustworthy candidate for any government position.

"When are you going to take me to the river, Papa?" Susan's voice broke in.

"Why don't we plan an outing for tomorrow afternoon?" he asked. "If that time is acceptable to your mother, that is," he added quickly.

Both turned to look at her with identical grey eyes, and it was all Maria could do to nod her assent. With everything arranged, James and Susan chatted for a while longer. By the time he was ready to leave, Susan had crawled up on his lap on her own to give him a goodbye hug.

"I will be here tomorrow at one o'clock, and we can walk to the river together," he said.

The first time I have left the property in almost a month, Maria realized. "I will need the address where you are lodging, so I can send a message to Colonel Hamilton about arranging a meeting with you."

"Oh, yes." He pulled out a small, printed card from his waistcoat pocket with the name and address of a tavern where he was staying and handed it to her. "Be sure and let him know I will be leaving for Virginia in a few days, and I would like to get the information to him before I go."

Maria glanced down at the card before slipping it into her skirt pocket. The address was unfamiliar to her—somewhere along the river in the northern part of the city—a section she knew had a reputation for its abundant brothels and rougher inhabitants.

He may dress like a respectable gentleman now, she thought to herself, *but it seems his choice in company hasn't changed one bit.* She walked with James to the front door and watched him walk down the road, locking up only after he disappeared from view.

Twenty

The next morning dawned cool and clear, and much to Maria's disappointment, Alexander didn't stop by as expected. A short message arrived midmorning.

Maria,

I regret that I will not be able to see you today, as my guests from abroad will not depart until this evening, and there will be yet another formal send-off. Please send word back if you were able to obtain the place of Mr. Reynolds' lodging so that I can arrange a meeting before he departs.

Yours truly,
A. H.

She tried to hide her frustration as she carefully refolded the letter. She had wanted to tell Alexander about last night's conversation in person, so he would know what to say when he contacted James. The idea of having to write it out in a letter seemed overwhelming right now. But there was no other option. She slipped into her bedroom and wrote out a message in return.

Dear Sir,

Enclosed please find the address of Mr. Reynolds lodgings. He will remain in the City until the end of the week. Susan accidentally brought up your name during his visit last night. When asked how I had come to make your Acquaintance, and what your connection to the Household was, I told him you had been sympathetic to our plight when we arrived in the City alone, and that you had been a very kind and generous friend, which is the truth. He did not ask any further questions but unprovoked, he then mentioned that a member of your Department had offered him a list of Monies owed to the Virginia Line for a hefty sum, and he asked if I would convey his wish to meet with you. He made it clear that he desired some type of Reward for providing this information. Mr. Reynolds is coming at one o'clock to take Susan on an excursion to the River. I will be accompanying them. We expect to be home by supper.

Maria

She set the quill down on the desk with a sigh and looked at the letter. Hopefully, it made sense and she had explained it adequately. Maria folded the letter and carefully tucked the card James had given her into the folds before sealing it securely. She had so much more she wanted to say in person. This would have to do for right now.

Maria stepped back into the kitchen and slipped the sealed letter to Sarah. "I'll need this delivered as soon as possible," she whispered.

Sarah nodded. "Yes, ma'am," she said as she tucked the note into her pocket.

"Thank you."

"I'll return as quickly as I can." Sarah headed out the back door.

She returned quickly as promised, and Maria spent the remainder of the morning trying to decide what would be appropriate to wear on an outing to the river with her husband and daughter. She hadn't been out of the house in public for so long, just thinking about it made her brain foggy. Funny, she didn't remember having this much difficulty before her illness.

Maria didn't want to wear any of the plain dresses or worn wool skirts and short jackets that had become her daily uniform. Without any good reason to dress up, she had slipped into dressing for convenience. She had a wardrobe full of fashionable gowns she had not worn since moving into the house, and she had no reason to dress like a serving girl, anyway.

Maria finally decided on a long-sleeved cotton gown printed with tiny sprigs that had been a favorite when they lived in New York. When she pulled it on over her shift, stays, and petticoats, it hung loosely from her shoulders like the rest of her clothing. It did have a fashionable, lower neckline that dipped below the top of her stays and exposed the tops of her breasts. Despite the weight she had lost during her illness, her breasts remained as full as ever— even more so, actually. Strange, but true. She checked her reflection in a small wall mirror. While her lover may have appreciated the remaining softness of her decolletage, it was much more skin than she was comfortable showing in public.

She opened the bottom door of her dresser and pulled out a delicately made lace scarf, draped it around her shoulders, and tied it across her chest in the front. Another quick glance in the mirror told her she looked perfectly respectable. Maria tucked her curls under her best linen cap and pinched her pale, gaunt cheeks in an effort to bring some color back to them. In truth, her appetite hadn't significantly improved since her illness; she even picked at her breakfast this morning.

She *did* want to eat and gain back the weight she'd lost. She really did. Shortly following her illness, her appetite seemed completely restored. Lately, however, eating seemed much more difficult—requiring a level of energy she no longer seemed to have. Most mornings just the thought of food made her nauseous.

The clock on her mantel struck one o'clock, breaking Maria out of her thoughts. James would be here any minute. The sun had come out, the temperature quite pleasant for midmorning in November. A perfect day for a family stroll.

Maria stepped out of her bedroom to find Susan in her best dress, looking out the parlor window and anxiously awaiting her father's arrival. Shortly, James arrived to collect them, and with Susan leading the way in hops and bounds, they began walking toward the river.

They had only made it a few blocks before Maria realized she was far weaker than she cared to admit. James noticed her difficulty and slowed down to allow her to catch up. He silently offered his elbow, which Maria took with a begrudging smile.

Leaning more heavily on her husband than she liked, Maria feared she would pass out by the time they made it to the river. He led her to a bench along the riverfront path where she sat, grateful to be off her feet.

"Thank you," she whispered, her face flushed with exertion.

"Of course," he replied, his expression earnest. "You are still my wife, and despite what you may believe, I do not wish to see you in discomfort."

With Susan's hand clutched in his, they walked to the water's edge while Maria sat and watched them from behind. She noticed then that Susan's dress was several inches shorter than it should be, even after the hem had been let out. There was no way around it; she would have to use some of the money she had saved to buy her daughter some new clothes.

Maria looked on as James squatted down to Susan's level, put his arms around her shoulders, and pointed out certain boats and ships near the dock. She heard him explaining the various sails and rigging to Susan, who listened without a word. Maria could tell from her posture, though, that her daughter was blissfully happy.

Maria's heart squeezed painfully in her chest. *This is how it is supposed to be. Susan deserves to have a father all the time.* She closed her eyes and took a couple of deep breaths, letting the warmth of the sun on her face dispel the chilling sadness. When she opened them, James was standing directly in front of her.

"Are you feeling strong enough to walk with us a little farther down, or would you like to stay here and rest?" he asked.

Maria hesitated. She still didn't trust him, but so far, James had not done anything to indicate he would leave with Susan again. Even if he did, she was too weak to try and stop him. At this point, Maria was seriously worried about her ability to get home.

"I will sit here and wait for you."

"We won't be long," he assured her. Maria sat and watched them walk away and out of sight. Her only recourse now was to trust that everything would turn out all right.

After that first outing to the river, their lives fell into a comfortable routine. James ate supper with Susan and Maria every evening and stayed until it was time for Susan to go to bed. Sarah—while taking the changes in stride—seemed nevertheless uncertain about the situation, enough to quietly retreat to her room each night as soon as James left.

Maria measured each visit closely, looking for any signs of the husband who had abandoned her to another man only a year ago. She found none. James was respectful and polite, and he clearly adored his daughter. Despite his questionable lodgings, she had not detected the smell of alcohol on him. Nor had he given any indication he was indulging in any of the vices so prevalent in his current neighborhood. Perhaps he had truly changed, she conceded. Still, one week was hardly enough time to judge sufficiently. Susan, on the other hand, was the happiest Maria had ever seen her.

The day after their first visit to the docks, James presented Susan with a large white box tied with a ribbon. Susan squealed in delight when she opened it to find three new dresses inside. Maria had not said a word to him about Susan's need for new clothes, but obviously, he had noticed. Alexander, on the other hand, had seen Susan almost every day for the past month. If he had noticed, he'd never mentioned it.

But that's not fair, Maria scolded herself. Alexander wasn't Susan's father. James was.

James had taken a seat in the chair beside Maria, and they sat in uncomfortable silence as they waited for Susan to return. Only a few minutes later, Susan came down the stairs, a huge smile on her face as she twirled around to show off one of her new dresses.

"You look beautiful," James said. He stood up and swung Susan up into his arms.

She threw her arms around his neck. "Thank you, Papa. I love them!"

"I'm so glad," he replied, and held her close, closing his eyes as he pressed his face into her hair. Too much for Maria to handle at this point. She looked away.

Maria remained silent all through supper, watching her daughter and husband talk and jest. She picked at her food except to make a show of taking a few bites of the roast capon on her plate and force them down each time she caught Sarah watching her.

As soon as James said his goodbyes and left to go back to his lodgings, Maria tucked Susan into bed for the night, and Sarah retreated to her upstairs room. Normally Maria sat in the parlor after supper and read for a while, but tonight, she headed straight up to bed. Even exhaustion, though, couldn't settle the ache of crawling under the covers alone. She pulled the quilt up to her chin, willing her mind to be quiet. Eventually, her mind obeyed, and she fell into a fitful sleep.

She had barely made it out of her room for a late breakfast the next morning when a message arrived.

Maria,

I have sent a message this Morning to the place Mr. Reynolds is lodging requesting a meeting before he leaves the City. I will inform you as soon as I hear back when the meeting is scheduled to transpire.

I remain yours truly,
A. H.

As it turned out, she heard the news of the planned meeting from James first. As soon as he'd arrived the previous afternoon to see Susan, he told her they would be meeting at the Treasury the day before James was to leave for Virginia.

The idea of her husband and lover alone in the same room was terrifying, and Maria was driven to distraction the entire day. She made a mess of the laundry by trying to help, eventually just giving up and retreating to the parlor to read. There was nothing she could do, anyway. This was completely out of her control.

A messenger arrived with a note shortly after the meeting took place, and she opened it with shaking fingers.

Maria,

The scheduled meeting with Mr. Reynolds has occurred, and in the course of our interview, he confessed that he had obtained a list of claims from a person in my department which he had made use of in his speculations. I invited him, by expectation of my Friendship, to disclose the person, which he did. As the person named resigned from the office some time ago, it was not very important, but I appeared to set value upon it in order to continue the expectation of Friendship. Mr. Reynolds told me he was going to Virginia and upon his return would point out something that I could do to serve him. I remained noncommittal, but I expect he was referring to a job in the Treasury. He did not inquire about the history or nature of our acquaintance, which I took to assume he had accepted whatever explanation you had provided. The meeting ended amicably. Please send word as soon as Mr. Reynolds leaves the city.

I remain yours truly,
A. H.

Maria carefully refolded the letter and added it to her collection of correspondence now filling the top drawer of her dresser. She was relieved that the meeting had gone well and that nothing disastrous had occurred but was surprised Alexander would even consider the possibility of employing her husband.

When James arrived for supper a short time later, he told much the same story, only in her husband's version of their meeting, he was fully convinced he would soon be offered a job at the Treasury.

Maria and Susan saw James off at the dock the following morning, where he and Jacob Clingman boarded a ship to Virginia. Mr. Clingman acknowledged Maria with an exaggerated bow and the same open admiration he had shown the first time they met. He never acknowledged their first meeting, so Maria remained silent about it as well. *Something not quite right about his behavior, though.* His smile was a little too calculating, and he watched her too closely for her comfort. Clingman didn't linger, however, for their goodbyes. He quickly walked up the gangplank instead and disappeared below deck.

Maria didn't protest when James pulled her to him for a farewell embrace, but she didn't reciprocate, and turned her head just in time to avoid his kiss. His lips glanced off her cheek instead.

"Please take care of yourself while I'm away, Mary," he urged, his eyes sincere and clouded with concern. He gently held her by her shoulders as he looked down at her. "If not for yourself, do it for our daughter," he added more seriously.

Maria staved off a flash of anger at his unspoken suggestion she wasn't being a good mother.

"Do you promise?" he asked.

Maria nodded, still fighting the sudden irritation she felt. *How dare he lecture me about being a mother when he was the one who deserted us.* But that wasn't exactly right, either. He had only deserted *her*, not Susan. He had tried to take Susan from *her*, she reminded herself.

He took her hand in his and pressed something cold and hard into her palm. Surprised, Maria glanced down at several coins.

"Use this for anything you and Susan may need until I return," he went on. "As your husband, you are my responsibility, and I do not wish to leave my family dependent on the charity of others when I now have the means to provide for you."

Maria could only look up at him in confusion.

James turned next to Susan, dressed in her favorite of the new gowns—a blue calico print— her fine, yellow curls held back in a matching bow. He swung her up into his arms, holding her in front of him as they said their goodbyes. Maria could tell that Susan was trying to be brave, but her lower lip quivered as she clung to her father. The ship's bell rang out a final boarding call.

"Be a good girl and mind your mum," James said to Susan as she struggled to hold back tears. "I will return in four weeks, and we will all be together for Christmas." When Susan brightened somewhat, he touched her chin. "See, that's better. Now give your old papa a hug and a kiss before I leave."

A tear ran down her delicate face, and Susan gave him a peck on the cheek. She hugged him tightly around the neck until he set her back down on the dock.

Maria immediately took Susan's hand, and they watched him walk up the gangplank. *Four more weeks until he returns, this time for good*. It felt both like a reprieve and a sentence to Maria. *Four weeks of normalcy*. Even then, Maria knew in her heart that things would never be normal again.

Twenty-One

"In the course of a short time, she
mentioned to me that her husband had
solicited a reconciliation, and affected to
consult me about it. I advised to it, and
was soon after informed by her that it
had taken place."

Alexander Hamilton, the *Reynolds Pamphlet*, 1797

As the days grew colder and shorter and November quietly turned into December, life returned to a more familiar schedule, the only difference being that Alexander no longer visited Maria in the daytime hours. Daily visits and interactions with Susan were much too dangerous, he explained, lest she let something else slip to her father. And it was unrealistic to expect a six-year-old to keep such a secret.

Maria understood Alexander's logic—even agreed with it—but it didn't make answering Susan's questions any less difficult. In one way or another, they had been openly and foolishly playing house since the summer. Maria had grown used to it, but it was only reasonable to expect it would come to an end at some point.

As soon as James left town, their amorous activities resumed. Alexander slipped into her bedroom under the cover of darkness several times a week, where they continued to indulge their passions. Her estranged husband's unexpected appearance seemed to only have increased her lover's hunger for her, and Alexander was as insatiable as he had been those first weeks they were together.

Maria reveled in the intensity of his passion and matched it with her own, even if it left her weak and slightly fuzzy-headed the next day. She had no idea how he was able to work all day and somehow tend to his multitude of additional responsibilities on so little sleep. If he was anywhere close to being as exhausted as she was when he left her bed, he certainly didn't show it.

Things seemed different between them too—an intensity in their kisses that hadn't been there before. Maria flushed just thinking about the variety of shapes she had assumed over the past few weeks. With each night they spent wrapped in each other's arms, the specter of time lurked in the background, counting down the hours and days until they would no longer be able to indulge their passions so freely.

At times when Alexander got dressed to leave, she clung to him so tightly, he had to gently pry away her fingers and reassure her repeatedly he would return. If her heightened emotional state bothered him, he didn't show it. In fact, he seemed to revel that she needed and wanted him so badly. They never spoke of her husband or about what would happen once James returned to the city.

As the four-week mark came and went with no word from James, Maria allowed herself to imagine the possibility that perhaps he wouldn't return after all, and her world would go back to how it was. She would immediately feel guilty then for what that would do to Susan. For every day, Susan asked when her father would return, and

Maria was running out of things to tell her.

A letter arrived by post halfway through the fifth week of James's absence. As had become her habit of late (mostly due to her frequent late-night activities and the recent, ever-present nausea), Maria had slept in until midmorning. She had just dressed and joined Susan downstairs when Sarah put the letter into her hand. Maria stared at the name written on the outside in messy, ink-smeared script. *Mrs. James Reynolds.* She had not been addressed by that title in years.

The morning was a particularly frosty one, and the fire in her bedroom had died several hours ago—what had finally driven her from her bed to seek out the warmth of the kitchen. Maria clutched the heavy woolen shawl more tightly around her shoulders and sat down in one of the wooden chairs in front of the fireplace. She stared warily at the missive for several moments like it was a snake coiled to bite.

Gathering her courage, Maria finally popped open the seal, unfolded the letter, and struggled to read the cramped, hastily written words inside.

Mary,

Our business in Virginia took longer than we anticipated, but I will be returning to Philadelphia within the week. It is my desire upon my return to live once more with you and Susan as a Husband and Father, and I prevail upon you as an Honorable Wife and a Loving Mother to allow us to once again be a happy Family. My present situation allows for me to provide for you both in some comfort, especially once I have secured a position in the Treasury as promised to me by Mr. Hamilton. I understand you would need time and I will share a room with Susan until you make your determination. What can I do to convince you that I have become an Honorable man? I beg of you, please allow me to prove my sincerity. I will Call upon you as soon as I arrive.

I remain, your Husband,
James

Maria's first instinct was to rip up the letter and toss it into the fire. She was being manipulated, and she hated it. From the very beginning, James always had the ability to twist things up in her mind and make her feel simultaneously confused and guilty.

Even though he had presented the prospect as a choice, the cold reality was she had no say in the matter. The law allowed him to live with her as her husband, no matter what she wanted. Should he decide to push it, she could do nothing to stop him. *Except divorce him, that is.* But she had neither the money nor the energy to pursue legal action. Besides, being someone's wife gave her a veil of respectability and protection within society that a divorce would strip away. Things had been so much easier when James had simply been a vague, shadowy figure she could use to explain her situation, an absentee husband she hoped would never return.

Then too, was the thorny subject of money. Currently, Alexander was paying for everything, including Sarah. It wasn't fair or right to expect Alexander to continue supporting her with her husband in residence. That also meant she would be entirely dependent upon James again. *That didn't work out so well the last time, did it?*

And what about Sarah? Would there be enough money to keep

her on? And if there wasn't, how could Maria possibly be expected to manage the household without her?

And what will happen when James isn't offered the job in the Treasury Department that he expects? As evidenced by his letter, James obviously expected a job upon his return, even though Alexander hadn't promised him one outright. He would be angry that that job didn't pan out, of course. Beyond that, Maria had no idea how he would react.

More importantly—how will I be able to continue seeing Alexander with James living in the same house? How long can I continue to deny James his conjugal rights? To expect her proposed arrangement of separate bedrooms to continue indefinitely was pure wishful thinking on her part.

So many questions. Just thinking about them made her head hurt.

She would send Alexander a message immediately. Every day since James left, he'd asked her if she had heard anything from Virginia. Up until now, the answer had always been *no.* Perhaps Alexander was half hoping, as she was, that James wouldn't return at all.

Without a word Maria stood up, walked back upstairs to her cold bedroom, and sat down at the desk to write out a quick missive.

Sir,

I have received a letter by Post this morning from Mr. Reynolds with the news that he will return to the City within the Week. He has asked for a Reconciliation and that we live once more as a Family. I do not know how to respond to his request. Please advise and I will do as you suggest.

Maria

Maria stared at the finished letter. She had no idea what Alexander's response would be. She guessed she'd find out soon enough.

Twenty-Two

M aria quickly sealed the letter, wrote Colonel Hamilton's name on the front, walked back down to the kitchen where Sarah was busy making her a late breakfast.

"Can you arrange to have this delivered this morning?" she whispered as she slipped the missive into Sarah's hand.

"Of course. I'm going to the market shortly, and I can do it then."

"Thank you."

Maria sat down at the table and woodenly ate the piece of plain toast and boiled egg Sarah had prepared. Simple, bland food was the only thing Maria could stomach anymore, and she ate it without even tasting it while Susan began cheerfully telling her about a dead pigeon they found on the back steps earlier this morning when they brought in logs from the woodpile. It took everything Maria had not to lose what little breakfast she had eaten as Susan told the story with great relish and detail.

Maria somehow managed to finish her food and didn't interrupt her, though. She felt guilty enough as is without snapping at Susan to be quiet. As near as she could tell, her daughter's main concern was *how* the pigeon's death had occurred—whether at the hands of the rowdy little boys who lived next door, or by one of the feral cats who lived in the alley.

Susan was leaning toward the boys as the culprits, but they were also frequent scapegoats in her daughter's daily drama, so Maria didn't put much stock in it. While she didn't have an opinion one way or the other about what had caused the pigeon's demise, she didn't think a dead bird on their doorstep was a particularly good omen.

Sarah broke into the conversation when Maria brought her empty plate to the worktable. "Would you like to go to the market with me and the little miss this morning, missus?"

Maria looked at her curiously.

"It would do you good to get out," Sarah offered.

Maria's first instinct was to politely decline and retreat to the parlor with her book. But she knew Sarah was right; she needed to get out and get some fresh air. Despite the chill this morning, the sun was out, and it looked like it was going to be a beautiful day.

Maria looked down at her dress, the third or fourth day in the row she had worn this same plain navy-blue gown. It looked quite wrinkled; she would have to change.

"Let me put on something more appropriate, and I will accompany you," Maria said quickly.

Sarah smiled.

Wearing a clean and much more stylish gown thirty minutes later, Maria set off with Sarah and Susan to the market two blocks away. Her mere presence seemed to have marked this regular outing as a special event, and Susan bounced along happily beside her. Maria had briefly considered telling her daughter her father would be returning within the week, but decided to wait until she heard back from Alexander. She was sure Susan would have many questions, and Maria didn't have answers to any of them.

Susan talked non-stop the entire way, with Maria only half listening, distracted by the unaccustomed sights around her.

"You're going to talk your mum's ear off, missy," Sarah broke in. "She won't ever come with us again if you don't let her be." Although her words were firm, Sarah was smiling down at Susan, Maria noticed. And Susan piped down immediately. They continued the short walk together in silence.

As they got closer to the market, Sarah turned to Maria. "Is there anything in particular you would like me to get for supper, missus?"

"I have no preferences," Maria answered truthfully. One meal seemed about the same as another these days.

The crowds began to thicken, and Maria could see the first of a series of long market sheds extending down the center of High Street (referred to as Market Street for obvious reasons) for several blocks ahead. The impressive sheds were made of red brick, with high ceilings and wooden roofs supported by arches running their lengths. They were open at each end.

Maria's breathing quickened as the crowds closed in around them and the sounds and smells assaulted her all at once. She took Susan's hand in hers as they entered the first shed and pressed her free hand to her mouth.

When Sarah stopped at one of the booths with a large display of cabbages, Maria sighed in relief, thankful for a moment to rest. Sarah quickly picked out a couple of heads and slipped the vendor a coin before placing the cabbages in the basket on her arm.

Maria took the opportunity to look around and take in her surroundings. Even though she had noticed the sheds several times since moving to Philadelphia seven months ago, this was the first time she had been inside one. Maria didn't particularly like crowds or shopping, and there had been no need to come here when she was living in the boarding house. Sarah had taken over all the household tasks and shopping once she and Susan moved into their current home.

Most of the shoppers were women and ran the gamut of social status from the very poor to well-dressed ladies accompanied by their servants. A few men too. Several women shopped alone or in pairs, dressed in simple uniforms or modest gowns that identified them as members of a household staff.

Children were *everywhere*. Some, well-behaved and standing quietly with their parents, while others chased each other up and down the arcades and dogged shoppers without any adult supervision. Apparently used to the chaos, Susan watched nonchalantly and remained by Maria's side.

The sounds were the most overwhelming—echoing off the walls and captured under the roof—the bark of vendors hailing shoppers to buy their wares, the high-pitched greetings, the women negotiating their purchases, the screams of children at play, the occasional crying baby thrown in for good measure.

"Mrs. Hamilton!"

Maria heard the woman's voice behind her. Before she could stop herself, she glanced over her shoulder to see a plump, middle-aged woman dressed in a burgundy gown covered with ruffles and lace. *Far* more embellishment than was flattering for someone her age, with her girth. She was frantically waving down another woman in the market.

Maria turned back to see who she was calling, and her eyes widened in surprise. Whatever she had imagined her lover's wife to look like, it didn't match the reality before her. Dressed in a simple, but fashionable rust-colored gown made of lightweight wool, Mrs. Hamilton was quite tall for a woman, the same height or taller than Alexander. She wore a black shawl tied around her shoulders.

Elizabeth Hamilton was thin and fit, no doubt the result of

chasing after young children all day. So different from Maria's petite stature and soft, rounded curves. Her features were attractive enough to be considered pretty, but she would probably never be considered a great beauty. Her dark brown hair was styled simply under her linen cap, and her eyes—almost black, betraying a steeliness of purpose and determination that Maria knew she would never want to test.

The first two words she could think of to describe Mrs. Hamilton were sensible and capable. She seemed like someone who was not likely to indulge in unwarranted emotional displays or hysterics, and who would always know exactly what to do in every situation. A woman sure of her place who could manage a large household with seeming ease.

Maria's cheeks reddened at the comparison. So unlike her own recent tendencies to break down emotionally at the drop of a hat and her utter dependence on Sarah to manage just for her and Susan. A younger woman—probably a maid—accompanied Mrs. Hamilton and her four children in various sizes from ages three to eight.

Maria's breath caught in her throat as her eyes rested on each child, one by one. Even if she hadn't heard the name, she would have recognized their paternity immediately. Although they were dark-haired like their mother, each one was strongly stamped with their father's features. All except for the youngest girl, that is. She looked distinctly out of place with her light hair and round face.

The two girls walked quietly beside their mother, the youngest one holding a small boy by the hand. The older boy seemed on the verge of bolting any minute and would have no doubt done so if not for his older sister's firm grip on the back of his jacket. Maria knew of another older boy as well, but he was probably away at school.

"Mrs. Hamilton!"

As Elizabeth turned to greet the matron, those dark, resolute eyes

Maria knew she never wanted to test gave her maid an ever-so-slight eye roll, so quick that Maria almost missed it. Not wanting to gawk, she turned away and pretended to study the rows of smoked sausage hanging from racks above the booth in front of her. Maria couldn't help but smile at Mrs. Hamitlon's brief lapse of decorum despite the knots in her stomach. She got the impression that Mrs. Hamilton did not particularly enjoy her social responsibilities and did not suffer fools lightly.

"I've finished here, missus," Sarah said, breaking Maria's concentration as she strained to hear the conversation going on behind her.

"We need to head to the next shed now."

Maria nodded and reluctantly followed Sarah down the wide aisle. Probably for the best, anyway, Maria thought. While the older woman's voice was shrill and obnoxious, Mrs. Hamilton's words were so soft, so Maria couldn't hear any of her replies. Maria stole a quick glance behind her as they left the first shed. It appeared Mrs. Hamilton had managed to disengage herself in record time, and their group was once again making its way down the center of the aisle.

Maria continued following Sarah as she efficiently worked her way from stall to stall and filled her basket. They had barely made it halfway through the second shed when the combination of sights, smells, and unaccustomed activity finally became too much. Maria's stomach lurched into her throat, and she stopped in the middle of the aisle, hand covering her mouth. Her face felt clammy, and she almost swayed into an oncoming shopper.

"Mama, are you unwell?" Susan asked, wide-eyed with concern. Sarah quickly stepped up to Maria's side and gripped her upper arm tightly to steady her.

"What is wrong, missus?"

Maria closed her eyes and took several deep breaths, willing her stomach back down. She would die of embarrassment if she lost her breakfast right here in the middle of the market. Several seconds passed before she could trust she wasn't going to retch when she tried to speak.

"I think I'm fine now," she said slowly as she opened her eyes.

Sarah and Susan clung to her, their brows furrowed with concern.

"Obviously, breakfast did not agree with me," she said lightly, forcing a simper. "But it seems to have passed. Just give me a few more minutes, and I will be able to continue."

Sarah didn't look at all convinced. "You need to sit down." With a bossiness that belied her age and circumstance, she pulled Maria toward one of the stalls.

"My mistress is not feeling well," she told the vendor. "Do you mind if she sits here while I go fetch someone to help?"

Maria put her hand up to stop her. "No. Really. I'm fine now." Maria turned to the confused vendor. "I am sorry to have bothered you." She could see other shoppers glancing her way, no doubt wondering what was going on. Her cheeks grew hot.

She stood a little straighter and met Sarah's eyes. "I can make it home," she said firmly, "but I'm afraid you will have to come back later to finish your shopping."

"I don't care about that, missus." Sarah gave her a doubtful look. "I was almost finished, anyway."

The basket on her arm *was* almost full, Maria noticed. "Once we get home, I promise I will lay down and rest for the rest of the afternoon."

Sarah considered her words for a moment before acquiescing to Maria's wishes with a quick nod. Maria could tell Sarah wasn't totally convinced, however, by the way she clutched her arm to steady her and continued walking right by her side. They slowly made their way back outside, going out the same way they had entered.

As soon as they were outside in the open air, Maria stopped and took a deep breath, instantly revived by the crisp, cool breeze. She had no idea what had come over her, but she was thankful it seemed to have passed. She felt the blood rush back into her face.

"I'm much better now," she said more confidently. "I can make it the rest of the way home."

Sarah relented and dropped her hand from Maria's arm. "We'll walk slowly, though," she countered.

True to Sarah's word, the journey returning from the market was much slower than going, but the trio made it without further incident. As soon as they walked in through the back door, Maria quickly made her way upstairs to her room—and the closest chamber pot—to empty her bladder.

When she returned to the kitchen a few minutes later, Sarah had already finished putting her purchases up in the pantry. She looked up as Maria entered the room.

"You are looking better now, missus," she announced.

"I feel better," Maria answered truthfully. "But I believe I will keep my promise to rest for the remainder of the day."

Sarah nodded. "I am sorry, but we left the market before I was able to have your message delivered," she said, pulling the letter to Alexander out of her pocket. "But I can go now and deliver it myself. If you think you will be all right here alone until I get back."

Maria nodded. "Yes. Of course I will. Susan can stay here and keep watch over me." She smiled at Susan, more grateful for her company now than anyone realized. She really didn't want to be completely alone, even if only for a short time.

"I won't be long," Sarah said. She gathered her shawl again for the excursion.

"Thank you."

When Sarah was gone, Maria turned back to the small fire still burning in the fireplace. While she had every intention of making good on her promise to rest, she needed a cup of nice, hot tea to settle her stomach.

She filled the tea kettle with water, set it on the grate over the fire, and beckoned Susan to sit beside her while she waited for the water to boil. The child had been uncharacteristically quiet during the walk home.

"I received a letter from your papa this morning," Maria said. Susan would want to know the news, she'd decided. This morning had been stressful, and Susan needed something to distract her.

Susan's eyes widened in excitement. "Is he coming back to see me?"

"Yes. He will be here by the end of the week." Maria smiled down at her daughter, one that didn't have the energy to reach her eyes.

Just as Maria had hoped, the news of her father's return superseded Susan's memory of the events of the morning, and Susan chattered away as Maria prepared her cup of tea. She'd just added a pinch of mint to soothe her stomach when Sarah, out of breath, bustled in through the back door.

"My papa is coming back to see me," Susan announced.

"Is that right, missy?" Sarah tousled her curls affectionately. She went about her business hanging up her shawl on the hook beside the door, seemingly unfazed by the greeting.

"Yes," Susan said, her expression earnest. "Mama said he'll be here by the end of the week."

Sarah smiled down at her but didn't offer any comment.

Maria stood. "Now that you have returned, I think I'm going to go lay down."

Sarah looked away and nodded.

Maria turned to Susan. "Come with me so we can let Miss Sarah finish her chores in peace." She glanced over to Sarah. "Please wake me if a message arrives."

"Yes ma'am," Sarah said, but she avoided Maria's eyes. Susan, while not terribly keen on the idea of taking a nap, obediently followed her mother up the staircase.

As soon as she had closed the door behind them, Maria and Susan stripped down to their shifts and crawled up onto the soft, thick mattress. Maria's nausea seemed to be under control for the time being, but she was exhausted. She stifled her racing thoughts and forced her eyes closed as she settled in beside Susan.

She woke much later to the soft touch of a hand on her cheek. Maria opened her eyes with a jolt, surprised to see Alexander standing next to the bed. She stole a quick glance beside her. Susan was already awake and gone. *How long have I been asleep?* She struggled to sit.

"I did not expect to see you here at this time of day, sir." She yawned.

"Sarah delivered your message and told me about what happened at the market this morning. I was worried."

"Nothing to concern yourself with," she said quickly. *So, Sarah had taken it upon herself to tell him what had happened. No wonder she wouldn't look her in the eyes earlier.*

"That is for me to determine."

Maria was briefly taken aback by his tone, but her irritation toward Sarah dissolved when he took her hand in his. His eyes were clouded with worry and—something else she couldn't quite put her finger on.

"Sarah tells me you became ill and almost fainted." He sat down beside her on the bed.

Maria gave him a weak smile. "It wasn't as bad as all that," she said, trying to sound light and casual. "I ate something this morning that did not agree with me and, with the walk there—and the crowds—I was overcome. I made it home under my own strength, and all is well," she quickly added.

His fingers tightened around her hand. He hesitated. "Sarah also tells me you have not bled for the past two months."

Maria's eyes widened and her face reddened, embarrassed that Sarah would disclose something so personal and intimate, even if it happened to be true.

"O-only because of the fever and my recent illness," she stammered, not quite certain how to respond. "I am certain it is nothing more than that."

"Even if it is a natural result of your sickness, it is concerning that you have not made a more thorough recovery from it. I have arranged for Dr. Stevens to stop by later this afternoon to assess your condition for himself."

Maria opened her mouth to protest, but quickly gave in when she saw the determined set of his jaw. "I am certain he will report to you that all is well," she said with a confidence she didn't feel.

"We can only hope," Alexander said as he stood up from the side of the bed. "I must be getting home, but I will return later tonight, and we will discuss Dr. Steven's findings as well as Mr. Reynolds's imminent arrival."

He bent down and gave her a soft kiss on the lips. "Do not fret, my beauty, everything will be made right, regardless."

Maria could only nod as she watched him walk out of her bedroom.

An hour later, Dr. Stevens arrived and confirmed what was at the same time her most fervent desire and her worst nightmare.

Twenty-Three

B y the time Sarah retired to her quarters for the night, and she tucked Susan into bed, Maria had worked herself into a nervous frenzy.

How is Alexander going to react? Will he be angry with me, or worse yet, will he think I lied to him or tried to trick him?

Maria paced back and forth across the parlor floor in her nightgown, waiting for Alexander and repeatedly kneading one hand into her still flat stomach.

She could still hardly believe it was true. Dr. Stevens estimated the baby would arrive in July. One year from when the affair had begun.

Years ago, Maria had resigned herself to the belief that she could never have another child, so *this* wasn't something she had even considered might happen. Even when her menses failed to arrive after her illness, it never even crossed her mind that pregnancy might be a reason for it.

She knew, of course, about certain herbs she could procure for a tea that would bring on delayed menses, and her problem would cease to exist. *Will Alexander ask that of me? And if he does, will I be able to do it?* She took a deep breath to still her nerves. No sense in bringing up questions she had no way to answer. She would know soon enough what he wished her to do.

Four years had passed since her last pregnancy had ended in tragedy. Just the thought caused her to cross her arms protectively over her stomach. The one thing she knew above everything else was, she wanted this baby—Alexander's baby—more than anything she had ever wanted in her life.

But worries consumed her. The fact was, she was not in good health. She hadn't truly recovered from the fever and had not eaten enough over the past few weeks to sustain herself, much less a baby. *And what possible effects could that sort of illness have on my unborn child?* She had either conceived shortly before or after the fever. Either way, the timing was not an indicator of a positive outcome.

A soft tap on the door heralded Alexander's arrival, and Maria rushed to unbolt the front door. As soon as the door closed behind him, he pulled her into his arms, and all the emotion she had been holding back for the past several hours burst forth.

"Please, sir!" she cried, her fingers curled tightly around the lapels of his jacket. "Don't be angry with me." Her voice rose. "I truly believed I could not conceive. I did not do this on purpose or to try to trick you." The words tumbled out of her mouth before she could stop them.

Alexander put his hand on the back of her head and pulled her to him tightly, her face pressed into the cloth of his jacket. She felt him take a deep breath, trying to control his own emotions.

"Shhh . . . " he whispered comfortingly, his lips against her hair. "I am not angry with you, Maria. I could never be angry with you." He gently pulled her away from his shoulder and looked into her eyes. "A child is always a blessing," he assured her, "no matter the circumstances."

She relaxed and gave him a soft smile. At least he didn't want her to do something rash. Still, she noticed his words didn't exactly match the worry in his eyes.

"I am deeply concerned about your health, though, and your ability to carry this child."

"I promise I will not be so stubborn, and I will eat and rest and do whatever I need to do," she hastened to assure him.

"I know you will, beauty, but some things are in God's hands, not ours."

Maria nodded and looked away.

"Come. Sit down. There is more we need to discuss." He sat on the couch and patted the upholstered cushion beside him. Maria quickly complied and took a seat next to him.

His voice grew serious. "We need to decide what to do about your husband's imminent return and how you will explain your condition."

Maria nodded, feeling anxious about what he would say again. She saw a look of hardness and resolve on his face she had never seen before, and she mentally braced herself for what might come. Alexander took a deep breath and looked down at his hands.

"My mother married very young," he began. "Her husband was a cruel man, and she tried to run away from him. He had her thrown into prison. When she was finally able to secure a divorce, it stipulated she could never marry again, thus dooming any further children to illegitimacy." He looked up and met her eyes. "I was born a bastard, Maria, and I would not wish that hell upon any child, much less my own."

Maria's eyes widened, and her stomach twisted. *Why is he telling me this? I don't care about the circumstances of his birth.*

"What is it you want me to do, then? There is nothing to be done to prevent that now." She held her breath, her heart beating in her ears.

"I want you to take your husband into your bed."

"No!" She let her breath out with a gasp, shocked and horrified by the very idea of it. Whatever it was she had expected him to say, that wasn't it. She could only stare at him and shake her head vehemently.

She started to stand, but Alexander put his hands on her upper arms, forcing her to remain seated. "I would not ask you to do this if there were any other way, Maria." His deep blue eyes implored her. "This is as difficult for me as it is for you, but it's the only way this child will not be born into shame and ruin." His voice shook with distress.

"But I cannot . . . " Maria struggled to process what he was asking her to do.

"I will not force or coerce you," he said. "It will be your decision. But please, consider the consequences."

Maria bit her lip and started to cry.

"When my mother died," he softly continued, "my legitimate half-brother, born of her marriage, stepped forward and claimed her entire estate. I was twelve, and my brother James and I were left with nothing but the clothes on our backs. At the probate hearing we were called whore's children because of the unfortunate circumstances of our birth. *Whore's children*, Maria." His fingers tightened painfully on her arms.

Maria could only stare at him, her mouth agape, as tears streamed down her face.

"If you do this," he continued, "our child will be legitimate, and will have opportunities that would not otherwise be afforded to it."

What about you? she wanted to scream at him. If he had overcome the unfortunate circumstances of his birth, their child could too.

"We will know the truth, Maria, even if the world does not," he said, his voice rising with passion. "And I will ensure that you and our child will always be provided for. I will help you secure a divorce from Mr. Reynolds after the baby is born, if that's what you want. And I will provide you the funds to set up the boardinghouse you told me about. You'll have your own income and your own home. "

Is he really trying to use my dream to bribe me?

"But if James thinks the child is his, he can take it from me," she argued.

"I won't let him, Maria."

"I-I don't know . . . " she stammered. She was so confused by everything swirling around in her mind.

"You don't have to decide right now," he said, his voice calmer. "We still have a few days until Mr. Reynolds arrives from Virginia. You need to rest now. Come, let's go upstairs and let me tuck you into bed."

Maria wiped her eyes, sniffed, and nodded. She suddenly wanted nothing more than to close her eyes and forget. They stood up from the couch and silently walked up the stairs to her bedroom. Alexander turned back the covers, and without a word, Maria obediently crawled up on the mattress and rolled onto her side.

Alexander shrugged out of his jacket, crawled in behind her, and curled his body around hers. His arms pulled her even closer, one hand resting protectively on her stomach.

"It will be all right, Maria," he whispered, his mouth against her ear. "I promise."

A stifled sob was her only response. But soon, as the warmth of his body enveloped her and exhaustion overtook her, she drifted off to sleep in his arms.

Twenty-Four

Maria marked the days until her husband's expected arrival like counting down her final days of freedom to a prison sentence. Once she invited him back into their bed, her life would never be the same again. If her fate, however, meant a better life for her unborn child—Alexander's child—she accepted it.

Her focus now was keeping the baby safe. True to her promise, she forced herself to eat regular meals—even when the nausea was bad enough to lose everything she managed to get down. Slowly, day by day, she got stronger. Eat and rest. That was her job for the rest of her pregnancy.

Alexander checked on her every day. If he couldn't stop by in person, he sent a message, and most days she sent Sarah out two or three times to deliver messages of her own. She wrote so much that Alexander began playfully calling her his "great scribbler." Writing was the only activity that kept her from going completely mad, though, so he indulged her and brought her more paper and ink when she ran out.

Alexander still visited Maria on the nights he was able to get away. They sought comfort in each other's arms, their activities curtailed to a much more tender and gentle nature. Mostly, they used whatever time they had left to plan.

They decided that once her husband was in residence, Alexander would cease paying her allowance directly, and James would take over the household expenses as expected. Alexander in turn would deposit Maria's allowance into an account he set up in her name that her husband couldn't access.

She also gave Alexander the cash she had hidden in her dresser drawer for deposit—over seventy dollars—fearing that her husband would stumble upon it and help himself to it. Maria was surprised by the amount of the cash she had secreted away, a combination of monies received from three different men: her husband, her lover, and Burr. If Alexander wondered where it all had come from, he didn't ask.

She had no time to reflect on the realities of her life and pushed away any guilty feelings she had. The nest egg provided a sense of security she never had before, and Maria allowed herself to believe for the first time that their plan might work after all. She only had to keep the child within her safe and get through these next few months.

Alexander insisted on keeping Sarah in the household at his own expense as the final part of their plan. Maria didn't know how she was going to explain that to her husband, either. She had to think of something since lover wouldn't budge on it.

Maria had gradually forgiven Sarah for telling Alexander about the incident at the market, for she couldn't blame the girl's concern, and her condition would have revealed itself in due time anyway. At least this way, they had time to prepare and make plans before James's arrival. She still despised the plan nonetheless.

Her relationship with Sarah had been affected by the breach of trust, also. They no longer shared the casual banter they had enjoyed in the beginning. Polite but aloof, Maria no longer pursued any conversation after supper, and Sarah retreated to her quarters where she remained until morning. Maria missed her company, but she also knew it was probably for the best. Sarah already knew far too much.

When she told Sarah that James would be moving into the house when he returned, she didn't seem surprised by the news. She said nothing, which confirmed Maria's suspicion that Alexander had probably already spoken to her privately when she delivered one of Maria's many letters to his office. No doubt they had concocted a plan for Sarah to keep an eye on James, which Maria couldn't really fault them for.

Maria was much more frightened by the possibility of James running off with Susan again. James, while pushy and manipulative, had never struck Maria. He had sold her to another man and had tried to take her only child from her, methods of punishing her for perceived shortcomings crueler than any blow he could inflict on her body.

Maria had resigned herself to the idea of being a wife to her husband again, although she wasn't sure she could hide her disdain. The thought of being intimate with him again made her nauseous.

Her biggest concern about her husband's imminent arrival was *how* she would be able to see Alexander. He had sworn he would not set her aside, and she believed him. With her husband living in the household, however, their ability to see each other would surely be limited. Just the idea left her melancholy. She hoped they would somehow find a way to have some time alone together, unrealistic as it seemed.

In the early part of their marriage, James had not been domestically inclined, electing to spend most evenings drinking with his friends in the tavern below their room. That vice seemed absent during his recent visit, but Maria found herself hoping he would revert to his old habits once he moved in permanently. She and Alexander could still exchange messages during the day too.

The last task Alexander asked her to complete before her husband's arrival was to destroy all his letters. She knew he was right; keeping them in the house where they might be discovered was reckless. A little piece of her heart shattered as she sat in front of the parlor fireplace late one night and fed his letters to the flames one by one.

When a week had passed since James's last letter, and he had not arrived as expected, Maria began to hope that perhaps he had changed his mind. Sometimes she secretly fantasized that his ship would be lost at sea, and she would be a respectable widow, the child within her legitimate. No one would ever know except Sarah. Of course, Susan would be devastated by the loss, but even she would recover in due time. And she would have a new sibling.

Maria's dark imaginations did not come to fruition, though. On a wet and blustery afternoon ten days later, James showed up on her doorstep with his luggage in tow and very much alive.

Maria had barely ushered him inside when Susan came running down the narrow entryway to greet him.

"Papa, you're here!"

"Of course. I promised I would return." He picked her up in his arms and swung her around. Susan howled with delight.

"It's good to see you too, Mary," he said. He set Susan down and looked at Maria approvingly. "You look healthier."

Her first instinct was to tell him her improved health was certainly none of his bidding, but she managed to hold her tongue.

She looked down at the floor. "I am trying," she said instead.

When James stepped forward to embrace her, she didn't pull away, standing quiet and still as he pulled her into his arms. His tall, lanky body felt strange against her, his hands hard and cold.

After a quick hug, he picked up his battered leather portmanteau. "Where can I put my bag?" he asked, the implications of the question clear.

She took a deep breath. "Let me show you," she said, turning toward the stairs to her bedroom. His eyes darted back to her face, but he didn't respond otherwise. He silently followed her up the stairs instead and set his bag just inside the door. Maria pointed to the top drawer of her dresser, *the very one* that held Alexander's letters only a few days before.

"You can put your clothes in there," she said. "If you need more room, I will try to empty another drawer for you tomorrow."

"This should be good for now," James said, his voice low and contrite.

"I will leave you to get settled, then," she said. "Sarah will have supper ready in about an hour."

"Thank you, Mary," he said sincerely, and tried to meet her eyes with his. Maria looked down, nodded, and walked out of the room. Susan could keep her father company while he emptied his bag into the drawer.

As she made her way downstairs, Maria could hear Susan peppering her father with questions. Without a word to Sarah, she filled the teakettle with water, hung it on the hook over the fire, and sat down in the chair in front of the fireplace. She needed to send a quick message to Alexander with the news James had arrived, but she couldn't seem to find the energy for it.

A few minutes later the kettle was whistling, and Maria poured the boiling water over the tea leaves in her porcelain cup. She set the saucer on top to steep just as James and Susan walked into the kitchen. Her daughter had a huge smile on her face as she held her father's hand. Maria tried to return the smile, but she couldn't work up the enthusiasm to make it look convincing.

"I finished putting my clothing away," James announced. "To-morrow, I will make arrangements for the rest of my things to be delivered."

Maria nodded as she stirred a little bit of sugar into her teacup, pulling her shawl tighter around her shoulders. Although the temperature in the kitchen seemed to be comfortable for everyone else, she couldn't seem to get warm.

"Are you going to live here with us now, Papa?" Susan asked.

James glanced at Maria. "As long as it's all right with your mama," he said.

Susan looked at her mother.

"Yes, he will be living here with us," Maria answered, forcing a smile.

Susan squealed with delight and hugged Maria roughly, causing her tea to slosh over the sides of her cup.

Maria held her tongue; she could hardly be angry at her daughter's excitement. Susan had been unusually subdued over the past few weeks, no doubt worried about her father's absence and what she perceived to be her mother's illness. Susan undoubtedly remembered the fever that had almost killed her only a few months before too.

Despite the circumstances, Susan's happiness proved infectious, and by the time they sat down for supper, Maria's mood had lightened somewhat. If she hoped to secure legitimacy for the baby within her womb, she was going to have to make their reconciliation look convincing. She even managed to eat a decent sized helping of the mutton stew Sarah had prepared, something James noticed as well. He smiled at her from across the table.

Sarah, on the other hand, was unusually quiet as she served supper.

And Maria grew more and more nervous as darkness fell, and the bedtime hour approached. Sooner than she would have liked, Susan was in bed, Sarah had retired to her room, and she found herself alone in the parlor with her husband.

"Thank you again, Mary, for allowing me to once again be a husband and father," he said. "I will endeavor to prove to you my sincerity. You will not regret your decision."

She forced herself to give him a convincing smile. For this to work, she would have to accept to his advances. "I have determined to once again be a wife to you. In all ways," she said softly. "I hope I don't regret my decision," she added as an afterthought.

James stood, walked over, and sat next to her on the couch. When he took her hand in his, his fingers were rough and callused, his touch cold. Nothing at all like Alexander's soft, warm caresses that caused her skin to tingle with sensation. James tightened his grip on her hand as he leaned forward to kiss her, lips hard and demanding at first. His kiss softened somewhat after Maria forced herself to relax against him. If she was going to do this, she might as well make it as pleasant as possible.

After several seconds, he lifted his mouth from hers and smiled. "Shall we retire to the bedroom?" he asked.

Maria nodded her assent, unable to trust her voice.

No sooner had she stripped down to her shift, pulled back the covers, and crawled into bed, than he was on top of her, pressing her into the mattress with all his weight and no preliminaries. Memories of their previous intimacies came back to haunt her in an instant. She spread her thighs as he tugged the hem of her shift up over her hips, knowing it would be over quickly.

True to her recollections, he soon finished with a groan and collapsed on top of her. She lay perfectly still beneath him for several minutes until it became difficult to breathe. Afraid he might fall asleep on top of her, she pushed him off and rolled onto her side. Maria instinctively pulled up her legs and she wrapped her hands protectively over her stomach. It was done. No one would ever question it.

She forced herself to lay very still beside him as her heartbeat slowly returned to normal. Within minutes, he was snoring loudly. As Maria lay in the darkness, she made a quick mental assessment, surprised to find no tears threatening. Mostly, she just felt numb. She took a deep breath, closed her eyes, and willed herself to go to sleep.

James slept through the night and didn't try to touch her again, which suited Maria just fine. So different from her lover. Alexander craved physical affection, and if she were within arm's reach, he was touching her somehow, even as they slept. She always slept best wrapped tightly in his arms.

In bed with her husband for the first time in years, Maria slept fitfully. When the first rays of light streamed in through the windows, she could no longer stand to lay beside him. She got up quietly and didn't bother with dressing. Thankfully, James didn't stir as she wrapped a blanket around her nightdress to ward off the chill and softly closed the bedroom door behind her.

"Good morning, missus." Sarah looked at her with surprise when she walked into the kitchen. "I didn't expect to see you up so early." She hesitated. "Is everything all right?"

Maria took a seat next to the fire and pulled the blanket more tightly around her, not quite certain how to answer her simple question.

"Yes, everything is fine," she said after a few seconds, realizing that much was true.

Sarah turned back to her task of adding wood to the fireplace.

"Mr. Reynolds is still sleeping," Maria added after a minute or so of uncomfortable silence. "He is very tired from his journey, so I don't want to disturb him." She paused. "I will need you to deliver a message later this morning."

"Of course," Sarah said. "Are you hungry? I could make you some toast to break your fast."

Maria thought about her maid's offer for a brief second, amazed that her stomach didn't roil in protest at the thought. Her usual morning nausea was absent this morning. In fact, a piece of dry toast sounded quite good.

"Yes, I would like that," she said.

Sarah's eyebrows shot up, but she offered no further comment. She sliced off a piece of bread and slid it into the metal toasting rack in front of the fire while Maria grabbed a cup from the cupboard and filled it from the coffee pot sitting on the hearth.

That wasn't lost on Sarah, either. She brushed her skirt, pretending not to notice. "I need to get more wood," she said, and walked out the back door.

For the past several weeks tea had been the only thing her stomach could handle this early in the morning, but today a cup of the stout coffee, Sarah's favorite, seemed to be just what Maria needed. She quickly added some cream and a little bit of sugar to the inky black liquid before turning back to the toasting rack to flip the bread over to the other side while Sarah was gone.

Sarah returned momentarily and began transferring the wood from her apron to the hearth. "You must be feeling a mighty bit better today," she finally said.

"Yes," Maria answered, a piece of toast in one hand and a cup of coffee in the other. Despite the circumstances, she did feel better this morning. *Strange.* She didn't feel happy, or sad, or even resigned. The word that best described her mood was *relieved.*

No longer was her mind thinking up new ways to torture her when she thought about what she had to do. No longer did she have to wonder whether she could go through with it. No longer did she have to worry about what Alexander would say if she couldn't. No longer did her stomach reel from just the thought of it. The deed was now done, with a profound sense of relief and an odd sense of triumph in tow.

While she hadn't enjoyed it, the experience hadn't been as bad as her imagination had foreseen. Clumsy and quick, James hadn't hurt her. She hadn't lost the contents of her stomach, and he'd never noticed the ever-so-slight curve of her belly.

Maria heard footsteps on the stairs and turned to see James—wearing only the same linen shirt and trousers he arrived in yesterday—walk into the kitchen. He casually held his boots in one hand and his jacket and cravat in the other. He leaned over the back of her chair and gave Maria a kiss on the top of head.

"Good morning, Mary," he said.

She gave him a soft smile, earning a look from Sarah. For now, Maria chose to ignore it.

"I'm surprised to see you up so early," Maria said. "I thought you would still be tired from your journey."

"I have too much to do today to sleep in." He sat down in the chair next to her and tugged on his boots over his thick socks. "I need to make arrangements for the rest of my belongings to be delivered. Then I need to stop by Mr. Hamilton's office to see if he will make good on his promise of employment."

Out of the corner of her eye, Maria caught Sarah's startled expression. *Of course she didn't know, did she?*

"Are you going to want some breakfast before you leave, sir?"

Sarah asked, trying very hard to act like nothing was askew.

James considered the offer briefly before shaking his head. "No. But I will return for supper."

"Yes, sir." Sarah turned back to her morning meal preparations.

James unbuttoned the front of his trousers and tucked in the folds of his shirt before buttoning them back up and haphazardly tying his cravat around his neck. He slid his long arms into the sleeves of his jacket and pulled it on.

Embarrassed, Maria turned back to stare at the fire. Alexander would have never finished dressing in the kitchen in front of the maid, no matter how informal they might be. Then again, Maria had never described her husband as a gentleman, either.

James bent down and gave her a quick kiss on the cheek before heading out the back door. Maria sighed and sat back in her chair as soon as the door closed behind him, relieved that he would be gone for the next several hours. She needed some time to sort things out in her head.

The first thing she needed to do was to get a message to Alexander to warn him before James showed up in his office unannounced. Just the thought of those two men alone together in the same room made her stomach twist into a knot.

"I'm going to go write a quick message," Maria said to Sarah. "I'll need you to deliver it just after breakfast, as soon as Colonel Hamilton gets to his office."

Sarah nodded. "Yes, ma'am."

Maria stood up, adjusted the blanket around her, and made her way back to her bedroom. She was surprised that the nausea remained gone. Perhaps she had just reached the point in her pregnancy where it went away. She hoped that was the case. Anything, to make the entire situation more bearable. She sat down at the small desk and started to write.

Sir,

Mr. Reynolds arrived in town Yesterday Evening. What you have asked of me has been done. He has just left to fetch the rest of his belongings from his previous lodgings and says he will be visiting your Office later this morning to speak to you about employment in your Department. I am Certain you will know best how to respond to his Request. I am well but long for the time when I can see you once again.

Maria

She supposed this was her life now, caught at every turn between her husband, her lover, and clandestine messages going back and forth. She wondered how long she and Alexander would be able to hide both their relationship and her condition. She carefully folded the letter and sealed it.

As it turned out, the discovery was made much faster than either of them could have ever anticipated. And how fitting, that her constant scribbling would eventually lead to their downfall.

Twenty-Five

Alexander declined to offer Mr. Reynolds employment in the Treasury, claiming (if somewhat truthfully) there were no open positions in his immediate office. The appointment of clerks in the other branches, he said, were left to the chiefs of those respective branches. James was angry but brushed off his disappointment within a few hours and seemed to forget about it.

The genteel veneer James had adopted since his reappearance, however, began to slip. Within days, Maria began to see more and more frequent glimpses of the husband she remembered. Now that he had what he wanted, he spent less time with Susan. He was distant and on edge. At night he took Maria without any preliminaries. She accepted his advances without argument because she believed the more husbandly rights she allowed him, the more convincing his "fatherhood" would be.

When Maria asked for money for Sarah to buy provisions at the market, James sullenly handed over a few coins, and only enough for a few days of food. Maria was quickly reminded of the early years when he had doled out money strictly on an as-needed basis. He had *never* given her any extra.

Such a simple, yet welcome relief when Mr. Wagstaff arranged for me to purchase anything I needed by simply signing a ledger. Even if society branded her a harlot and an adulteress for how she earned those luxuries, the security it provided had been a worthwhile trade-off. Pretending to rely on her shifty husband was a ruse she'd sworn to employ once more, even if only temporarily. Thankfully, the private account Alexander had opened for her gave her financial security she hadn't had those years ago as James's teenage bride.

As she feared it would happen, James began questioning the need to keep Sarah on and asked Maria where the maid's wages came from. Some quick thinking enabled Maria to fabricate a story on the spot about an alleged agreement with Sarah's impoverished family to hire her in exchange for room and board. He seemed to accept her explanation and dropped the matter after a sneering remark about his wife's inability to cook.

With every passing day, Mary doubted more and more the course she and Alexander had chosen, and her despair grew. On more than one occasion James caught her crying when he came home in the evening. She blamed it on various things like the book she was reading, and she really didn't care if he believed her anymore. Perhaps her unhappiness was the result of her condition, or the fact that she hadn't seen Alexander since James's arrival. She felt herself slowly slipping away.

At that point, she estimated she only had a couple of weeks before the baby quickened, and her condition would become apparent. Each day was one step closer to the time when she would no longer have to pretend to be a dutiful wife and she would be free of him. Still, it was difficult. She wasn't sure how long she would be able to hide her pregnancy from her husband, although James never saw her completely naked. He only seemed to be interested in one thing and, much to her relief, did not seem inclined to explore beyond that. So different from Alexander, who had mapped out her body with his caresses from the very beginning, noticing every change in the hills and curves.

Just the thought made Maria sigh in frustration. She craved the sound of her lover's voice, the feel of his lips on hers, and the sensation of his fingers on her bare skin. Without his touch she was withering inside, like a flower too long deprived of water. She closed her eyes and took a deep breath. *Only for a season*, she continually reminded herself.

She had tried to abide by their truce, but yesterday, she caved to the desperation and wrote Alexander a frantic letter.

Sir,

Please do not be offended with me, but I do not think I can continue long without seeing you. Please, I beg of you, help me find a time in which we can once again be Alone together. Mr. Reynolds will leave in the Morning on unknown business in Town, and if I know you can Come to me, I can think of some errand on which to send Sarah and Susan. Please, do not be distressed with me for trying so hard to see You. Just Come to me and help Ease this Sorrow which I find myself plagued with daily. It is my fervent wish that Mr. Reynolds will once again leave this City and things will be once again as they were . . .

Fearful that Alexander would be angry with her desperate pleas, she'd hidden the unfinished letter in her desk drawer. By yesterday evening, when she could no longer contain her desperation, she finished the letter and sent Sarah out into the night to deliver it to his home. James left shortly afterward to meet with a friend from New York and returned home late, smelling of rum and tobacco smoke. Maria had pretended to be asleep, and thankfully he did not bother her when he crawled into bed beside her.

When Maria woke up this morning, she immediately regretted sending the emotional missive to Alexander. She knew it would worry him, and she dreaded his response. It wasn't his fault he hadn't been able to see her since James arrived, either. He'd continued sending her a note every day telling her how much he missed her, that they would be together again very soon. That was all she could expect of him.

As it had become his pattern, James left early in the morning without telling her where he was going. He always promised to return in time for supper. Over the past few days as Maria reviewed her proposal to Alexander, she began to realize the foolishness of it. A daytime interlude at present was a highly risky proposition. If James found out about Alexander, all would be lost. Everything she had done to secure legitimacy for their child would be for naught.

Maria had no idea what James did while he was out, but she suspected that whatever money he had come into in Virginia was rapidly disappearing. He was probably working on another scheme to revive his pocketbook. The night before last, she had found him poring over some sort of ledger in the parlor. He had immediately covered the numbers with his arm when she walked in to fetch the teacup she had left on a side table next to the couch. Although she couldn't see exactly what it was, she suspected it was not entirely aboveboard. Perhaps if she were lucky, he would leave to resume dealing his business in Virginia.

A messenger arrived midmorning with a letter from Alexander plus a small square package wrapped in brown paper and tied with twine. By the shape, Maria immediately recognized it as a book, and her sadness lifted immediately when she took both from Sarah's hands. If he had sent her a book in return, he couldn't be too cross with her.

She untied the twine and carefully tore off the brown paper. Inside was a beautifully bound novel, and Maria eagerly flipped through the pages. While Alexander was very generous in loaning her books from his own library, they had very different reading tastes. Maria had grown bored with the dry treatises, highbrow fiction, and poetry he passed along to her. This was a gothic novel, her favorite. He had obviously bought it especially for her.

Sounds of a soft rain had played on the roof since early this morning—cold and dreary weather. What had at first seemed designed to match her miserable mood now became the perfect weather for curling up on the couch to read in front of the fire. She would write and thank him later, but for now, she clutched both items to her chest and headed to the parlor. She laid the book carefully on the side table, stood in front of the fireplace, and opened the letter.

My Dear Maria,

For Heaven's sake, do not yield too much to the little adverse circumstances that must attend us. Be mindful that your recent melancholy may well have adverse effects upon your health. I can only hope that this small token of my affection will help revive your spirits. It is newly published, having just arrived from England. The bookseller assures me it is quite popular. Remember, this is only for a season, and soon we will once again be able to reacquaint ourselves with one another. Think of me, my Beauty, and be assured of my affection during this time of trials.

A. H.

Maria sighed. Her lover always wrote the most beautiful letters—and unfortunately, this one was resigned to the same ill fate as all his others. She leaned forward and dipped the corner of the letter into the fire, watching the flames lick their way toward her fingers. She waited until the last second to release the missive into the fire.

Sounds of loud voices from the kitchen startled her, and Maria recognized the heavy thud from James's boots coming down the narrow hallway. She glanced down quickly into the fire, gratified to see that all traces of the letter were gone already. The footfalls stopped in outside of the parlor. Maria watched in horror as the door flung open with enough force to bounce off the wall behind it.

James loomed in the doorway, his eyes hard, an expression on his face she had not witnessed since the early years of their marriage. She instinctively took a step back and cast a quick glance at the book lying on the table. He followed her gaze, his eyes narrowed. Maria's heart skipped a beat as James walked to the table and picked up the book. She cringed as he roughly thumbed through the pages before slamming it shut.

"Is this the book that makes you cry every night when I come home?" he demanded.

"No," she said defensively, her mind scrambling for an explanation. "I haven't read that one yet," she admitted, regretting those words as soon as they left her mouth.

"Where did it come from, then?"

"A-a friend sent it to me," she stammered.

"Would that friend be Mr. Hamilton?"

Maria glanced in desperation toward the open parlor door, hoping for Susan or Sarah to interrupt. Susan usually never left her father's side from the moment he came home, and Sarah watched everything like a hawk. But the house was oddly silent beyond the doorway.

James followed her glance. "If you're looking for your protector, she's not here," James said. "I wanted to speak to you privately, so I sent her and Susan on an errand."

Maria's breath quickened. Her heart was beating so loudly, she was sure he could hear it.

"What did you want to speak to me about?"

"This." He pulled a piece of paper from his inside pocket and unfolded it. Maria's blood turned to ice as he began to read out loud.

"Please, do not be distressed with me for trying so hard to see you. Just come to me and help ease this sorrow which I find myself plagued with daily. It is my fervent wish that Mr. Reynolds will once again leave this city . . . "—he looked up at her—"Do I need to go on?"

Maria stood frozen in place, her eyes wide with terror. "How did you get that?"

"I was looking for some paper last night and found it in your desk drawer. I copied it," he said smugly.

Anger and indignation began to replace her fear. "You had no right to go through my things!"

"As your husband, I have every right to know who my wife is spreading her pretty little legs for." He took a step toward her, hedging her backward. Maria nearly tripped over the small table behind her.

She knew James had intended his words to sting, and she fought back tears as her mind frantically calculated some sort of response. At least she had not mentioned Alexander's name in the portion of the letter he had copied. Perhaps he didn't know anything more.

"And don't think you can lie to me anymore, Mary," he continued. "I followed Sarah last night when she delivered the finished letter. Followed her all the way to Mr. Hamilton's house," James muttered through clenched teeth.

Maria sobbed and closed her eyes, not knowing what to say. Denying it would be fruitless, for James had the proof in his hands.

"How long have you been Mr. Hamilton's little whore, Mary?"

Twenty-Six

"... I am determined to have satisfaction.
It shant be onely one [f]amily thats
miserable ... I am determined to leve
her and take my daughter with me that
She shant see her poor mothers Lot."

Letter from James Reynolds
to Alexander Hamilton, December 15, 1791

Maria lifted her head and angrily wiped the tears from her eyes. No more reason to placate her husband, now that he knew.

"What do you care?" She stepped toward him. "You sold me to another man and left me. What was I supposed to do? I was alone in a new city and applied to Colonel Hamilton for help. It was I who suggested physical consolation in exchange, not him," she added defensively.

James seemed caught off guard by her angry parry. "I already told you," he said, "I was forced to leave you."

"I don't believe you," she said flatly.

"I don't care if you believe me," he sputtered. "It is the truth."

Maria suddenly wanted to wound him with her words, to somehow hurt him as much as he had hurt her. "There is no other man I care about in his world anymore except Colonel Hamilton. He is twice the man you will ever be."

Her words hit their desired target, and she watched James's eyes narrow in anger. He took another step toward her, but she stood her ground. She'd half expected the stinging retribution of his hand across her face, but he didn't come any closer this time. His thin lips turned up at the corners into a grin instead.

"If Mr. Hamilton is so great, then why did you feel the need to take me into your bed as well? Are you so greedy that you require two men just to satisfy your appetite?"

The verbal assault hit her straight in the heart, for Maria had no answer. She couldn't possibly tell James the truth. She subconsciously wrapped her arms across her stomach and looked down at the floor.

"You are my husband," she said modestly. "I have no legal right to deny you."

"Don't try to play the victim with me, Mary," he snapped. "I never forced you. You spread your legs for me quite willingly."

Her face flushed with embarrassment. "What is going to happen now?" She needed to get word to Alexander somehow, to warn him about what was coming.

He obviously hadn't thought about that, Maria observed. James went silent for several seconds. "I suppose my actions will depend on Mr. Hamilton. But I will have satisfaction for what he has done." His voice rose in anger and indignation.

Is he really considering challenging Alexander to a duel? The idea seemed preposterous.

"I wrote Mr. Hamilton telling him of my discovery and asked

him to name a time and place to meet so we can discuss this like gentlemen. If he doesn't agree to see me today, I suppose that I will write to Mrs. Hamilton."

So, blackmail is his intention. In that instant, Maria knew all James wanted was money, that he had no intention of provoking a physical confrontation.

"No one knows anything yet, though," he went on. "So I suppose it all rests on his shoulders. He can make it difficult, or he can make it easy."

Maria actually felt a brief glimmer of hope at the realization. James had sold her to another man and left once before. What price would be a sufficient salve for James's wounded honor now, and would Alexander be willing to appease it?

"Are you the reason he went back on his word to offer me a position in the Treasury? Did you tell him not to hire me?"

Maria was momentarily taken aback. *What an odd question, after everything they just revealed in the past few minutes.*

"No," she said honestly. "That was Colonel Hamilton's decision."

"Did he think I would leave to find work elsewhere, and he could take you from me for nothing? I came to him as a sincere friend," he continued, his voice rising. "And he has treated me as his worst enemy, as if I were some annoying fly he could get rid of with a flick of his fingers. I will have satisfaction for what he has taken from me, Mary. Ours won't be the only miserable family."

The sound of the back door slamming echoed down the narrow hallway.

"Mama! Papa!"

Maria sidestepped James when she heard Susan running toward the parlor. The child ran to the room with a half-eaten peppermint stick clutched tightly in her fist and stopped just inside the doorway. Maria took a deep breath and tucked a stray curl behind the little girl's ear as Susan looked from her mother to her father to her mother again.

"Is anything wrong?" Susan asked.

"Of course not," Maria assured her, willing her own voice to sound normal. "Where did you and Miss Sarah go?"

"Papa sent us to deliver a letter to Colonel Hamilton," she announced. "Miss Sarah bought me a stick of candy on the way home." She held out the sticky treat to show her mother.

Maria protectively pulled Susan closer to her. She glanced up at her husband's face to see that he was grinning.

"Well, it seems that the game is afoot," James announced. "I am afraid I must be on my way. I am meeting with a gentleman to discuss some new business investments while I await Mr. Hamilton's reply. I will return for supper." He looked down at Susan. "Come give your papa a hug goodbye." It was not a request.

Maria's hand tightened on her daughter's shoulder, and Susan looked up at her doubtfully. She turned to her father, who reached out and pulled her against his leg.

"Maybe we can take a little trip sometime," he told her. "Just you and me. Would you like that?" Although he was talking to Susan, Maria knew his threat was clearly meant for her.

Unsure what to make of the tense situation, Susan looked to her mother for the answer, and Maria could see the fear in her daughter's eyes. Maria reached out her hand to reassure her, but James pulled the child just out of her reach. Maria bit her bottom lip to keep herself calm when she saw tears welling up in Susan's eyes.

James is just trying to scare me, Maria told herself. And she would not give him the satisfaction of seeing her in tears again.

"No," Maria said firmly. "Susan is too young to go on a long trip with you all alone." She held out her hand to Susan. "Come. Your papa has business to attend to. Let's go see if Sarah needs help in the kitchen." Susan gave her mother a relieved smile and took her hand. Maria led Susan, still clutching the peppermint stick firmly, out of the room. Maria heard the front door close as soon as they reached the kitchen. She closed her eyes and sighed.

"Is everything all right, missus?" Sarah asked, her forehead wrinkled with worry.

"No," Maria answered honestly. "But I hope it will be soon. I need to write a message to Colonel Hamilton, and I will need you to deliver it to him as quickly as possible." Hopefully, fast enough before James *or Alexander* did something rash.

"Of course," Sarah said. She paused. "If it is helpful, missus, when I delivered Mr. Reynolds's message earlier, Colonel Hamilton was in a cabinet meeting at the president's house and not expected back for at least another hour."

Maria wanted to hug her with relief. *The fates have given me a brief reprieve*—to dash this next letter out as quickly as possible. She picked up her skirts and made her way up the stairs.

Dear Sir,

I have not time to tell you the cause of my present troubles, only that Mr. has written to you this morning. I know not whether you have gotten the letter, but he has sworn that if you do not answer it or if he does not hear from you today, that he will write Mrs. Hamilton. He has just gone out. I think you had better come here that you may know the cause, then you will know better how to act. Do not write to him, no not a line, but come here soon. Do not leave anything in his power.

Maria

She put her quill back in the stand and blew on the ink to dry it before folding and sealing the letter. Tears stung the back of her eyelids, but she was determined not to give in to them. Alexander would come to her as soon as he got her letter, and they would figure it out together. She ran her hand over the slight curve of her belly and took a deep breath before heading back downstairs to the kitchen.

She pressed the letter into Sarah's hands. "I cannot stress how important it is that Colonel Hamilton reads this before he responds to Mr. Reynolds's note," she said.

Sarah nodded. "Yes, ma'am. I will make certain."

Maria squeezed her hand. "Thank you." She watched Sarah put on her cloak and gloves and head out the back door. A gust of cold, wet air blew in through the open doorway before Sarah closed the door behind her. Maria pressed a hand to her stomach. Although her nausea had eased over the past couple of weeks, she suddenly felt like she was going to retch. She went to the window and watched Sarah hurrying toward the alley in the drizzling rain. There was nothing left to do but wait.

Susan sat on the kitchen floor in front of the fire, absently sorting a handful of glass marbles by size and color. Maria put on the kettle to heat and decided to leave the child be. She was no doubt still frightened and confused by the scene in the parlor earlier. Maria simply didn't know what to say anymore.

Maria had barely finished her cup of hot tea when Sarah returned. Neither mother nor daughter had spoken since Sarah left.

"Were you able to get the message to him?" Maria asked.

"Yes, ma'am." Sarah removed her red wool cloak and hung it by the door. "He had just returned."

Maria gave a sigh of relief, thankful her message had gotten to Alexander before he had a chance to react to James's explosive missive. Now they would decide together how best to handle her husband. As it turned out, she didn't have to wait long.

A knock on the back door came in merely minutes. Maria was ready. "I'll get it."

She opened the door to find Alexander standing on the top step. Outwardly he appeared calm, but his hair looked tousled on one side, and his normally clear blue eyes, cloudy with emotion. No longer worried about being discreet, she threw herself into his arms.

"Thank God you've come, sir," she sobbed into his jacket. "I didn't know if you would."

He tightened his arms around her and pressed his face into her hair. "Of course, I've come. I do not blame you," he assured her. "We can make it right, but first we need to go inside before someone in the alley sees us."

"Of course," she whispered back. She took a step back into the kitchen as he followed her and closed the door behind them.

Upon seeing Alexander, Susan gave a delighted cry, jumped up from her spot on the floor, and ran to hug him.

"Why haven't you come to see me?" she asked, her bottom lip properly pouted.

Maria reddened, but Alexander didn't seem fazed by the awkwardness of Susan's question. He squat down and returned her hug.

"I've been busy with work," he said. "Besides, your papa is here now."

Susan scrunched up her face. "Papa told me he was going to take me away on a trip, but I do not think I would like to go without Mama."

Alexander looked up at Maria. She nodded. He turned back to

Susan. "If he tries to make you go with him, go tell your mama or Miss Sarah as fast as you can. Do you promise?"

Susan nodded.

Alexander stood and turned toward Maria. "Can we speak privately?" he whispered.

"Of course, sir." Maria wiped her eyes and led the way down the hall. As soon as Alexander closed the door behind them, she threw herself into his arms once again. "How can you ever forgive me?" She sobbed. "I feel more for you than for myself, and wish I had never been born to give you so much unhappiness."

Alexander pulled her away so he could look down into her face. "Don't talk like that. I don't blame you. But I need you to tell me everything that has transpired today," he said. "Start from the beginning, and don't leave anything out. Can you do that for me?" His voice was comforting but stern.

Maria nodded, wiped the tears from her eyes, and sat down on the couch. Her thoughts spun as she tried to find a starting point. *This is all so complicated.* She took a deep breath. Alexander stared at the floor while he began pacing back and forth in front of the couch, waiting for her reply.

"Mr. Reynolds came home about ten o'clock this morning and confronted me with a copy of the letter I had written you yesterday. He said he had found it in my desk drawer while he was looking for paper, and he copied it down. Then he returned the original to the drawer." The words tumbled out of her mouth in a torrent. "When I finished the original letter and sent Sarah to deliver it to you last night, he followed her to your home." She took a deep breath before continuing. "He told me this morning that he had sent you a message informing you of his discovery, and that he was trying to see you. He said he will have satisfaction for what you have done."

Alexander stopped pacing and looked at her. "Does he mean to provoke an interview with me, then?"

Maria shook her head. "I do not think so, sir. I believe it is money he wants, not a duel."

"Then, as much as it is within my power, I will gratify him if possible."

"He threatened to take Susan away from me," she said with another sob.

Alexander nodded. "Yes, he expressed as much in his letter to me."

"Please don't let him take her!"

Alexander sat down on the couch beside her and took her hands in his. "I will do what I can within the bounds of the law, but if Mr. Reynolds wishes to take Susan from you by reason of adultery, the law would support him, and there is nothing you nor I can do to stop him." He paused while Maria cried harder. "I am sorry, but it is the truth."

"I could not bear to lose her, sir!" She broke down as she said the words.

"I know, but in a few months, God willing, you will have another."

She stared at him in disbelief, tears running down her face. "Do you really believe you can simply replace one child with another?"

Alexander had the decency to see his misstep. "Of course not," he said quickly. "That's not what I meant. I know that no child could ever replace Susan, but the reality is that no court in America would deny a husband the right to take his child away from an adulterous wife." He tightened his hands around hers to emphasize the point. "That is why we must seek to resolve this in private. If our *amour* were to be revealed to the public, the resulting scandal would not only ruin Susan's hopes for the future, but the futures of my children and future children as well." He gave a meaningful glance at her belly.

Maria sobbed harder. *It isn't fair. None of this is fair.* "So, you are saying I should just let him take her from me?" she asked, horrified by the very idea of it.

"You may not have a choice in the matter."

She knew what he was saying was true, but her mind refused to accept it. There had to be some way around it. She would do whatever she had to do to keep from losing her daughter, even if it meant taking her and running away.

Alexander pulled Maria against him to try to comfort her. "Do not work yourself into a state of distraction," he said soothingly. "It is not good for you or the baby. Perhaps Mr. Reynolds and I will come to a solution that is agreeable for everyone, and the things you are worried about will never come to fruition after all."

His words gave her hope for the first time since this whole nightmare started. She sniffed and let out a little moan. He held her against his chest and patted her back until the tears stopped. They remained in that position for several minutes until her breathing returned to normal.

"Does Mr. Reynolds know of your condition?"

Maria shook her head against his chest. "No."

Alexander nodded in satisfaction. "Good. I pray that it remains so." He paused. "Does anyone else know?"

She lifted her head from his shoulder and looked up at him. "Only yourself, Sarah, and Dr. Stevens," she said.

He nodded again, and they sat in silence for several seconds as she wiped her cheeks and tried to compose herself.

"How do you propose to answer Mr. Reynolds's letter?" she finally asked.

"I will send him a message as soon as I return to the office and propose a meeting this afternoon. If money is what he is after, perhaps we can come to an agreement that will be mutually beneficial and does not involve him taking Susan from you."

Maria pulled herself up into a sitting position. "Thank you, sir."

"I am concerned about leaving you here alone with him, though."

"I will be all right. Sarah is here, and I will not let Susan out of my sight," she agreed.

Alexander nodded, but his expression belayed his continued concern. "Promise me you will send a message if anything happens."

"I promise."

He seemed satisfied. "Do not fret and make yourself sick, my beauty. Hopefully, Mr. Reynolds and I can come to an agreement, and the matter will be settled swiftly."

Maria didn't think it would be that simple, but she gave him a weak smile anyway. He leaned forward to kiss her.

"I must return to my office now, but I will endeavor to keep you abreast of any developments." He stood.

Then, he was gone. Maria sat back against the couch, crossed her arms protectively, and stared into the fire. Here she was again, hoping against hope it would really be as easy as Alexander suggested.

Twenty-Seven

"I have this preposial to make to you . . ."

Letter from James Reynolds
to Alexander Hamilton, December 19, 1791

James made the next three days as hellish as possible. Maria's nightmare walked into her waking hours while her lover and her husband politely negotiated her future behind closed doors.

She could clearly see from Alexander's messages that he was rapidly growing frustrated with James's seeming unwillingness to finally name a price for his wounded honor. According to James, Alexander had used a divisive and angry tone with him when they met the previous evening at the George Tavern. He had expressed visible anger and frustration, James said.

Maria didn't understand why James was dragging this out. Surely he'd had a sum in mind when he sent the first letter informing Alexander of his discovery. *Does he intend to prolong it out of cruelty, or as a way to further punish me?*

Maria avoided James as much as possible when he was home.

Unwilling to let her daughter out of her sight (especially at bedtime), Maria moved Susan into her bed while James slept in Susan's room or didn't come home at all. Susan didn't argue or question the new arrangement, but Maria saw fear and anxiety in her child's eyes when she watched her mother jam the back of a chair under the bedroom doorknob every night before they went to sleep.

Four days after the initial discovery, James came home midmorning and asked to speak to Maria alone in the parlor. She met Sarah's eyes across the kitchen and glanced over at Susan. Sarah understood her unspoken request and nodded, dark eyes wide with concern. Maria twisted her hands into the folds of her skirt to stop them from shaking as she followed her husband down the narrow hallway toward the parlor.

James closed the parlor door behind them. "I have presented Mr. Hamilton with a final proposal this morning," he said without any introduction. "I guess we will see what he thinks my silence is worth, won't we?"

Maria lifted her chin and met his eyes, determined not to give him the satisfaction of seeing her fear. She knew that while Alexander had power and position, he was not a wealthy man. He also had a large family and household to care for. *What if James was too greedy, and Alexander is unable to meet his demands?* Her stomach twisted as guilt washed over her.

"What was your proposal?" she asked cautiously.

James smiled and pulled a piece of paper from his inside jacket pocket. "Why don't you see for yourself? This is a copy of the letter Mr. Hamilton is just now receiving at his office."

He held the wrinkled, ink-splotched page out to her. She took it from him with trembling fingers, her stomach in knots. As she read, James sat down in a chair across the room from her. He stretched out his long legs, tented his fingers together in front of his face, and positioned himself so he could watch her reaction. Maria took a deep breath as she read the words her husband had written.

Sir,

When we were last together, you said you wished to know my Determination and you expressed a wish to do anything that was in your power to Serve me. It is true it is in your power to do a great deal for me, but it is out of your power to do anything that will Restore me to my Happiness, for if you should give me all you possess, it would not do it. You have been the cause of Winning her love, and I don't think I can be Reconciled to live with her when I know she loves another. Now Sir, I have considered on the matter seriously. I have this proposal to make to you. Give me the sum of a Thousand Dollars and I will leave town and take my daughter with me and go where my friends can't find me and leave her to Yourself to do for as you think proper. I hope you won't think my request is in view of making Satisfaction for the injury done to me, for there is nothing you can do that will compensate for it. I will expect your answer This evening or in the morning early, as I am determined to wait no longer till I know my lot.

Yours,
James Reynolds

Maria stared at the letter she clutched tightly in her fingers. Her eyes filled with tears, and the handwriting swam in front of her. She couldn't fathom that amount of money. *Does James really expect Alexander to pay such an extravagant sum?*

The words following the amount were what cut her to the core. This was not about blackmail, James's wounded honor, or the pain of losing her lover as the letter suggested.

This was a sale, pure and simple.

For the price of one thousand dollars, James would give her to Alexander, "to do for as he saw proper." Maria felt faint.

She would not give James the satisfaction, though. She closed her eyes and took a deep breath, willing herself to keep her head and not fall apart. Honestly, she would be ecstatic if James left her with Alexander, but her daughter was more than she was willing to pay for that happiness.

Alexander would figure out a way to help her, she silently assured herself. He would also come up with a way to keep James from taking Susan. But doubts crept in. *Would he really?* He had been ready to concede Susan's loss only a few days ago.

"Colonel Hamilton will not pay you if you take Susan from me," she declared, the words leaving her mouth before she had time to think. In truth, she had no idea whether Alexander would pay anything. She just wanted to knock that smirk off her husband's face.

Maria saw the brief flicker of doubt in his eyes. "I won't let him," she continued. "I will tell him that I will no longer continue seeing him if Susan is gone." She paused. "If you take Susan, I will run away, and neither of you will have me." Her voice was convincing enough, even if she doubted she could ever really leave Alexander.

"He will pay for my silence," James said.

"Silence about what? An affair? Rumors of Colonel Hamilton's supposed lecherous activities appear in the *Aurora* every week. Why would this be any different?" She could see that her words were beginning to have an effect.

"I will write to Mrs. Hamilton."

"With what proof? A copy of a letter supposedly written by her husband's lover? And Colonel Hamilton would no doubt deny it. Why would she believe a lowly criminal like you over her own husband?" Maria knew *that* hit him hard when he sat up suddenly. "I don't think you have thought this little scheme of yours through to its ultimate conclusion," she continued. "Your silence is worthless, and without my cooperation, you have nothing. Besides, even if you do agree to let me keep Susan, what makes you believe he would pay such an exorbitant price for me in the first place?"

"I think you underestimate yourself, Mary. I've seen the look in his eyes when he talks about you." He gave her a lecherous grin. "Or perhaps it's not really you, but that pretty little triangle between your legs that he's so enamored with. "

Maria knew James meant his words to hurt her, but she wasn't about to give him the satisfaction. "It's something you will never see again, I can assure you of that," she spat back.

"Oh, I could take you anytime I want. It's my right. And I have no doubt you would spread your legs willingly for me." He paused. "Does your lover know you've been spreading your legs for me too?" James asked. "What would he think of you if he knew that?"

Maria stifled a smile. Better for James to think she was frightened of disclosure than to know their marital bedtime hour was Alexander's idea in the first place.

"If you hope to get top dollar for me, it would be in your best interest to at least maintain the illusion of my fidelity, " she retorted.

Maria watched James's face as the truth of her words slowly sunk in. He could threaten her all he wanted. She now knew James wouldn't try to force himself on her because the money far outweighed any spontaneous lust or a desire to hurt her.

"Do you promise to leave Susan with me if I allow myself to be sold to enrich your pocket?" The very sound of words coming out of her mouth sickened her, but Maria pressed on. "My agreement to participate is the only way your plan will succeed."

"I will not promise anything," he stubbornly said.

"Then don't be surprised if you find us gone one morning without warning, and you will be left with nothing to bargain with. If you agree to leave Susan with me, I will do everything in my power to see that Colonel Hamilton pays the money you are asking for."

Maria didn't wait for James to respond. She slowly turned around and walked back to the kitchen where Sarah and Susan waited for her. A few minutes later, she heard the front door close. Maria collapsed in the chair next to the fireplace, put her face in her hands, and wept, feeling like she had just made a deal with the devil himself.

Twenty-Eight

"Received December 22 of Alexander
Hamilton six hundred dollars on account
of a sum of one thousand dollars due to me."

James Reynolds to Alexander Hamilton, December 22, 1791

Three days later, Alexander made his first payment of six hundred dollars. The transaction seemed treacherously surreal as Maria watched James carefully write out a receipt of payment and hand it to Alexander. Maria knew that Alexander had struggled to pull the money together, and her stomach twisted with guilt as she watched him hand the check over to her husband. Alexander was quiet, his jaw tight with barely constrained anger. The remaining four hundred dollars would come after the first of the year—he insisted it couldn't be paid any sooner.

In a few days it would be Christmas, but none of them were feeling very festive. Perhaps James was with his newfound windfall. The entire household was on edge. Even Susan quietly kept to herself. Maria had barely slept at all for the past two nights. When she washed her face and cleaned up at the washstand this morning, she could see dark circles under her eyes.

On his way out, Alexander tilted up her face with his finger and admonished her to get some sleep before kissing her goodbye. Other than that, no conversation between them had transpired. And so terribly strange for Alexander to kiss her in front of her husband, although there was no longer any need for secrecy.

Maria also suspected Alexander had done it to make a point. After all, he was paying a lot of money for the privilege. Their one remaining secret Maria dared hope James never discovered, though. He would no doubt charge extra if he knew the deal also included Alexander's unborn child.

Their original plans had shifted wildly since James's discovery of the affair, but they had not talked about it. Maria supposed that once James disappeared as promised after collecting the remainder of the money, she could continue as if nothing had happened. She could say her husband had left her, which was the truth, and no one would question the legitimacy of the child.

If Alexander had doubts or questions about James's sudden change of heart regarding custody of Susan, he didn't express them. Maria had not yet told Alexander of the deal she had struck. She had pleaded with James not to take Susan, and he had relented, she said. Keeping to her end of the bargain, she encouraged Alexander to pay the money, although she now had little doubt he would have paid regardless.

Although Alexander was certainly angry about it, there also seemed to be some level of penance involved, as if the money would make up for his own moral failings and sense of honor. James had certainly gone out of his way to exaggerate the harm done, so a good amount of guilt was involved in Alexander's immediate acquiescence to James's financial demands.

For the next few days, Maria was in a daze, living in some sort of volatile, transitory world. Until the balance of the money was paid, their lives were in a holding pattern. Maria had no guarantees that what she hoped for would transpire.

With the fear of discovery removed, Maria and Alexander could send messages freely. But Alexander grew distant and distracted, and his notes seemed obligatory rather than loving. Maria started to worry that he would soon decide the constant drama surrounding them was too much, that she was more trouble than she was worth. Each day Maria became more and more convinced that Alexander would leave her once the money was paid.

Part of the reason she was so surprised to receive a message the day after Christmas. Just two sentences, with no pretty words or endearments.

I wish to see you tonight. Send Susan to sleep with Sarah.

He hadn't asked where James was, either. Perhaps he no longer cared.

Weeks had passed since he'd visited her bed. Instead of anticipating the thrill of her lover's touch, however, Maria's first thought was that something was wrong. Perhaps this wasn't a night of passion he had planned. Perhaps he was coming to tell her goodbye. Perhaps he had grown to hate her for all the problems she had caused. Her anxiety grew with each passing hour while she waited for darkness to fall.

By the time he arrived at her door, it was almost midnight. A light dusting of snow had covered the sidewalks earlier that evening and sparkled under the streetlamps. Alexander was wearing a heavy greatcoat, his tricorn hat slightly askew on his head. He looked disheveled and did not meet her eyes when she opened the door.

He had arrived in a hired coach, not like him at all. With a wave of his hand, he dismissed it, and the driver drove the black coach away, down the cobblestone street. Alexander swayed slightly, and the smell of brandy wafted to her nose.

No wonder he had hired a coach; he could barely stand. Maria had never seen him like this, and her heart pounded fearfully in her chest.

She opened the door wider, and he stepped inside. "Is everything all right, sir?" she asked.

"Not really." He closed the door behind him and began struggling with the buttons on his coat.

"Here, let me do it." She stepped forward and deftly slid the buttons free from their buttonholes. He stood quietly while she pulled the heavy wool coat off his shoulders and arms. Underneath, he was wearing a formal jacket and waistcoat. So, he had just come from a party.

Maria hung his coat on a hook in the entryway and placed his hat on top. "Let's get you into bed before you pass out." She took his hand.

Alexander hung his head like a dejected child and silently followed her up the stairs. As soon as he stepped into her bedroom and closed the door behind him, he kicked off his buckled shoes and began pulling at his elaborately tied cravat. Without a word she took over, pulling his cravat loose and helping him out of his heavily trimmed satin jacket, waistcoat, and breeches. She left off with his linen shirt and stockings, led him to the bed, and pushed him to sit on the side of the mattress.

"I'm sorry, Maria," he mumbled. "I should have never come." He hung his head in shame.

Maria didn't respond as she bent down, grabbed his ankles, and swung his legs up onto the bed. He groaned as his head fell back onto the pillow. Whatever activities she had hoped for this evening, they certainly hadn't included helping her intoxicated lover into bed.

Maria sighed, tucked the bedsheets around him, and blew out the bedside candle. When she crawled into bed beside him, he rolled toward her and clumsily pulled her into his arms.

"I wish I were strong enough to leave you," he whispered into the hollow between her breasts.

Maria closed her eyes and took a deep breath as the pain of his words washed over her. She knew it was the brandy talking, that he didn't fully realize what he had said. *That's what makes this so painful.* He had not said it to hurt her, but because it was true.

She put her arms around him and pressed his face more tightly against her. "Shhh . . ." she whispered, her lips against the top of his head. She shushed him to both comfort and silence him because she was truly afraid of what he might say next.

He pressed on. "I have become everything that I despise. I can't even look at myself in the mirror anymore." He caught his breath with a strangled sob, and she could feel the wetness of his tears against her skin.

Please stop talking, she pleaded silently. But he didn't.

"Mrs. Hamilton is once again with child," he continued.

Maria closed her eyes as hot tears slid down her cheeks.

"How could I have betrayed her like this?"

"It's going to be all right," she whispered, even though she knew it was a lie.

"Please don't leave me," he begged.

Her heart twisted in confusion. *Why would I be the one to leave?*

"I have despised my father for leaving us since I was ten," he went on. "Now, I want nothing more than to do the same thing. But I couldn't live with myself if I did."

Maria had no idea whether he was talking about leaving her or his family. She didn't want to know.

Finally, his impulsive confession seemed to have played out, and he lay still and silent against her. Maria held him until his breath became slow and even. Sleep would surely elude her again tonight, she knew, as she settled in next to him. Her treacherous mind would see to it as she repeated his words over and over in her head.

Maria woke with a start just as the first rays of light began to march slowly across the wooden planks of the floor, surprised to find herself still in Alexander's arms. She slowly disentangled herself and struggled to sit. Alexander rolled over with a groan. Considering his condition when he had arrived, she was not surprised he had slept through the night in her bed. But what excuse was he going to give his wife to explain his absence? Her stomach clenched as she remembered what he told her.

As if he could sense her watching, he opened his eyes. She halfway expected him to panic once he realized where he was, but he simply smiled at her instead. *Does he even remember what had happened last night?*

"Good morning, beauty," he said in a husky voice.

She couldn't help but smile. "Good morning. I am sorry I did not wake you earlier, but I just woke up as well. I did not realize you had stayed all night."

He winced as he struggled to sit up and brought his hand to his forehead. No doubt he felt miserable.

"Will you need to go home soon?" she asked.

He shook his head and rubbed his eyes. "No. Mrs. Hamilton and the children have left to visit her father in Albany for the holidays. I will be joining them for Twelfth Night."

The first she had heard of his holiday plans, but she nodded as if this was old news. In the tight-knit Dutch community where Maria was raised, Christmas was celebrated not just as one day, but a season. The annual Twelfth Night marked its official end. She wondered if Alexander even remembered what he had told her last night.

They sat in uncomfortable silence for a moment before she pulled back the covers, swung her legs off the side of the bed, and crossed her arms over her chest against the chill. Maria walked to the fireplace and shuffled the coals around with an iron poker before tossing a log from the rack onto the exposed embers. A tendril of flame slowly licked its way up the outside of the log.

"Maria, honey, what happened?"

Maria turned and looked at him in confusion. "What do you mean?"

"There is blood on your shift."

Maria looked down to see two circles of dried blood staining the white cotton over her hips. She pulled it away from her body to study the discovery more closely, her stomach lurching. Alexander was beside her in an instant.

"What happened last night, Maria? Did I do anything to hurt you?" His eyes clouded with fear as his fingers tightened around her arm.

"No, no." She shook her head. "You did not do anything." At least not *physically*, she added silently. "We spoke briefly, and then you fell asleep."

She watched the emotions play out across his face. First relief, then remembrance, then shame and regret. His cheeks reddened, and he took her hands in his.

"I should not have come last night." He looked down at the floor. "I am sorry if my words caused you pain. That was not my intention,

I assure you." He paused. "But it cannot be taken back, and your health is always my main concern. Have you been sick? Any cramping or discomfort?"

She shook her head and tried to think. Her stomach had been twisted into knots for weeks now. Yet, in her condition, how could she possibly distinguish normal responses from signs of potential problems?

"It may not be anything to be concerned about, but I will send a message to Dr. Stevens asking him to come by as soon as possible. Until then, you need to clean up, change out of your shift, and rest for the remainder of the day. Will you do that for me?"

Maria nodded.

"I will need to return home to change into some more suitable clothes, but I will be back."

He turned away and began picking up his clothes off the floor.

Maria walked to the washstand, pulled the stained shift over her head, and tossed it onto the floor. She shivered as the cold air hit her bare skin. While Alexander dressed behind her, she filled the ceramic basin with clean water from the pitcher and dipped a white linen towel into the cold water. Maria made a quick pass between her legs and stared at the streaks of blood— enough to make her close her eyes and bite her lip with a sob. This was how it had started the last time.

Alexander was suddenly behind her, wrapping his arms around her naked body and pulling her against him. "Do not make yourself sick with worry, my beauty." His hand rested on the curve of her belly. "Let's get you dressed and back into bed, so you don't catch cold." He gently pried the cloth out of her fingers and tossed it into the basin. The water instantly turned pale pink.

Maria stood motionless. Numb.

Alexander grabbed a clean shift from her dresser drawer, pulled it on over her head, and led her across the room. He gently tucked the covers in around her as she stared silently at the ceiling. Last night, she had taken care of him. Apparently, their roles had reversed today.

He leaned forward and pressed his lips to her forehead. "I'm not going to bother with a message. I will stop by Dr. Stevens's house on my way home and ask him to come. I will return as soon as I can. I will let Sarah and Susan know you are not feeling well, and you are resting. Do you know where Mr. Reynolds is?"

Maria shook her head. She no longer felt the need to keep track of her husband. Sometimes he came home at night, sometimes he didn't. She had no idea which one it was today.

"No matter. I won't be gone long enough for him to bother you." He bent down and kissed her softly on the lips this time. "Try and rest. I'm sure Dr. Stevens will find all is well and there is nothing to worry about." His eyes belied his confidence, she noticed. She closed hers as he left the room.

Maria listened to Alexander's footsteps as he descended the stairs and walked into the kitchen. Susan's excited voice drifted upward as she greeted him. She heard more muffled voices too—male and female—but Maria couldn't make out what was being said. With a moan, she rolled over onto her side, pulled her legs up into a fetal position, and pressed her face into the softness of the pillow.

She was going to lose him. She knew that with certainty now. No way they could sustain this. The stakes were too high and the emotions, too painful. This baby was the only part of him that might be hers to keep. She did not want to live if she lost it too.

Dr. Stevens arrived just as Maria had drifted off to sleep. He sat down beside her without any preliminaries. "Colonel Hamilton tells me you had some bloody discharge in the night," he said.

Maria nodded, still trying to find her voice.

"How much blood was there? Was it as heavy as your regular

menses?"

She shook her head. "No. I only saw blood on my shift. Nowhere else."

"Have you experienced any cramping or pain recently?" he asked. She shook her head.

"Has there been any unusual physical exertion?"

At the implication of his question, Maria looked away and shook her head again. Of course, she hadn't counted helping to maneuver her drunk lover into bed last night. That couldn't have helped.

"I would not be too concerned about it, then," Dr. Stevens said. "Sometimes it happens. I would like to examine you to be sure, though."

Maria nodded her consent. His casual demeaner had always given her some degree of comfort. She closed her eyes as he pushed and prodded her abdomen before lifting her shift. Maria felt his fingers between her legs and closed her eyes as she felt them inside her. Thankfully, the examination only lasted a few seconds.

"Well, the good news is, you are almost five months along," he said as he pulled her shift down to cover her. "Past the time to be concerned about a miscarriage. As I said earlier, I do not think it is anything to worry about."

Maria looked up at him, a relief that was met with a familiar-looking expression betraying none of the antagonism he had shown her the last time she saw him. *Does he know of Mrs. Hamilton's pregnancy?* She lowered her eyes in shame.

The door opened, and Maria glanced away to see Alexander walking toward her. The two men made eye contact and nodded cool greetings without any signs of their previous closeness. Clearly there had been a recent rift in their longtime friendship.

"Thank you for coming, Ned," Alexander said.

"I was just telling Mrs. Reynolds that based on my examination,

I would say she's already five months along, past the time to be concerned about a miscarriage. But if the bleeding becomes heavier or is accompanied by pain and cramping, contact me immediately." He glanced back at Maria. "I would recommend bed rest today and limited activity for the remainder of the week."

"Thank you," she said. He nodded once again and collected his bag.

"I will see you out," Alexander said.

Dr. Stevens didn't respond as he opened the door and stepped out into the hallway.

Alexander gave Maria a quick kiss. "I will be right back," he whispered, and followed Dr. Stevens out of the room.

Maria slid back down under the covers as soon as they left. Two men—possibly brothers and certainly longtime friends—were now at odds because of her. One more item to add to the considerable list of things to feel guilty about. She closed her eyes and tried to hold back tears, but she wasn't successful.

Maria didn't move or open her eyes when Alexander walked back into the bedroom several minutes later. She heard him stripping out of his clothes and felt a gust of cold air as he pulled back the covers and slid underneath. She rolled over onto her side and looked at him. "Are you all right, sir?"

He gave a short, rueful laugh. "No. But it is my own damned fault. My head is pounding, and I feel like I've been dragged behind a horse for a half mile."

She didn't doubt it. He lay very still on his back for a moment, one arm tucked under his neck. Maria snuggled up against his side and laid her head on this chest. He wrapped his free arm around her shoulders and pulled her closer. Maria knew that at some point they would have to sort through everything. Until then, she could think of nothing more she wanted or needed from Alexander than to be in his arms.

Twenty-Nine

"Received Philadelphia January 3, 1792
of Alexander Hamilton four hundred
dollars in full of all demands."

James Reynolds to Alexander Hamilton

On January 3, Alexander paid James the remaining balance of four hundred dollars before leaving to join his family in Albany for the remainder of the holiday. For the following week, Maria had no way to contact Alexander if something happened. And she was completely on her own with her husband.

For the most part, the days passed uneventfully. She tried to stay out of her husband's way and ignore him as best she could. Maria had hoped James would leave immediately after collecting his payoff, but he didn't. When she tried bringing it up to him, he candidly told her he was leaving soon and refused to elaborate any further.

Maria also knew that Alexander expected James to be gone by the time he returned, part of their agreement. At least James had not been adversarial toward her. With his windfall money in hand, he was quite jovial and accommodating.

Three days into Alexander's absence, Maria received a letter delivered by post. She anxiously popped the seal and opened it. A bank note rested inside the folds, which she quickly slid into her pocket.

Maria,

I am currently on a sloop traveling up the Hudson to Albany but will no doubt have reached my destination by the time this letter arrives. It occurred to me after I had already left that I had not ensured you had funds on hand to pay for any expenses during my absence, and I wished to remedy my oversight. Please rest and take care of yourself while I am gone. I am well and maintain every happy expectation that Mr. Reynolds will be gone by the time I return, and we can put this dark season behind us for good.

A. H.

Maria released her breath with a sigh and carefully refolded Alexander's letter before consigning it to the flames in the kitchen fireplace. She was grateful for the money, and that he was thinking about her. But what would happen if he returned and James was still here? Would he be angry and somehow blame her? Maria's stomach twisted at the thought. What could she do about it? She couldn't force James to leave.

Sarah looked up from what she was doing. "Is everything all right, missus?"

Maria nodded. "Yes." She pulled the bill from her pocket and held it out to her. "Colonel Hamilton sent this. Please use it for anything we need. I don't want to ask Mr. Reynolds for anything."

Sarah wiped her hands on her apron and took the bill from Maria's fingers. "Yes, ma'am," she said, and slid the money into her own pocket.

Maria could see the relief in her dark eyes. Sarah wasn't any more comfortable depending on James than Maria was. A huge respite for everyone when he finally left.

Thankfully, the remaining days passed quickly, and soon Alexander was back in the city, none too pleased to find James still in residence when he called on Maria the evening of his return. The two men were cordial to one another, but the next morning, Alexander sent a message summoning James to his office for a meeting in the afternoon.

Maria could do nothing but pace back and forth across the parlor as the meeting was taking place. Either her husband or her lover would return and inform her what had transpired. By the time James returned from the meeting, Maria had exhausted herself and was sitting on the couch. She had her legs pulled up next to her and a copy of yesterday's gazette on her lap, fare she hadn't been able to concentrate on enough to read. James was in a surprisingly cheerful mood, which she suspected did not bode well for her. When he walked into the parlor and closed the door behind him, her heartbeat began pounding loudly in her ears.

"I have been thinking on the matter for the past few days," he began without preamble. "And I informed Mr. Hamilton this afternoon that it has become disagreeable to me for him to continue to call on you."

Maria could only blink her eyes and stare at him as the words slowly began to sink in. "What did he say?" she asked, barely able to get the words out of her mouth.

"Only that I knew best how to handle my domestic situation, and that he would abide by my decision."

James was lying. He had to be. Alexander would not have given in so easily. He would fight for her and their child, she told herself. Perhaps he was working on another plan.

"You can't do this," she declared with far more confidence than she felt. "I won't allow it."

"You have no choice in the matter," he stately bluntly. "You are my wife. I can do whatever I want."

"I ceased being your wife when you sold me to Colonel Hamilton." She watched as her verbal arrow found its mark and the smile on his face evaporated.

"The money he paid was only to assuage my wounded honor and make up for the loss of your love," he sputtered defensively.

"The loss of my love was of your own doing. Colonel Hamilton had no hand in that." She paused. "You promised to leave if Colonel Hamilton paid what you asked. He has held up his end of the bargain. Are you of so vile a character that you would fail to hold up yours?"

James took a step toward her as those words hit home. "Do not ever question my character again," he threatened.

Maria anchored herself as tightly to the back of the couch as she could and refused to give him the satisfaction of seeing her fear.

"I said I would take Susan and leave if Mr. Hamilton paid what I asked," he continued. "Without Susan, there is no agreement. If she is here with you, I will be too." He smiled as Maria's eyes widened in shock and horror. "Did you really think you would be able to keep them both?"

Maria could only stare at him as her mind struggled to process the words he was saying. He was going to make her choose between her daughter and her lover—her worst fear come to life.

She closed her eyes and took a deep breath, trying to control the hysteria bubbling just underneath her seemingly calm surface. That's when she felt it. A tiny flutter in her belly. She froze and resisted the urge to put her hands on her stomach. Then, she felt it again. Proof of life coming at the very same time her own was collapsing around her.

James broke the silence. "I will not say anymore on the subject. If you want your lover back in your bed, all you must do is say the word, and Susan and I will be gone. Otherwise, I will remain here, and we will live together as a family."

Maria refused to look at James or respond in any way. She sat silently instead, staring down at her lap until he finally gave up and left the room.

For the next two weeks, Maria did the only thing she could think of—make her husband's time at home as miserable as possible. She refused to speak to him or acknowledge his presence in any way. Although Susan had no knowledge of the circumstances surrounding her parents' hostility, she followed suit and refused to speak to her father in an unspoken act of solidarity with her mother.

What James didn't know was, Sarah worked for Alexander, and every time she left the house to run errands, she usually had a letter hidden on her person. Despite James's declaration that Alexander could no longer call, the messages continued unabated—short, un-signed, and in disguised handwriting. Alexander was indeed working on a plan.

Sarah discreetly slipped his latest message into Maria's hands as soon as she got home from the market. James was out, but Maria didn't take any chances now. She locked herself into the parlor and opened the carefully folded paper.

> *Please do not despair. All is not lost. I have written to my branch offices in both North Carolina and Virginia asking them to investigate Mr. Reynolds' business affairs while in those states. I am confident that evidence of some crime with which he can be arrested will come across my desk shortly. Be strong in your faith that I will use every tool at my disposal to remove him from our lives for good.*

So, that was Alexander's plan. She had to admit, it was a pretty good one. Maria had no doubt her husband's business dealings in the South had been of an illegal nature. If Alexander's agents could find that proof, James would be sent back to face the consequences. He would no longer be a problem.

This plan would take time, though, and time they didn't have. Every day her belly grew a little rounder. Soon, Maria would no longer be able to hide it under her skirts. She carefully tossed the note into the flames and headed back down the hall toward the kitchen.

A knock at the front door had the two women and Susan raising their heads at the same time. No one came to visit anymore.

"I'll get it," Sarah said quickly. She set aside the knife she was using to pare potatoes for tonight's dinner and headed down the hallway.

Maria heard the door open and a male voice outside. The door closed again, and Sarah walked back into the kitchen.

"Mr. Clingman is here to see Mr. Reynolds, missus," she said. "He said they were supposed to meet at two o'clock."

Maria glanced up at the clock on the mantel. It didn't make sense to send him away since it was already one forty-five. "See him into the parlor until Mr. Reynolds returns."

"Yes, ma'am." Sarah headed back down the hall.

Maria's eyes narrowed in suspicion as she stared into the flames. She hadn't seen Mr. Clingman since seeing James off to Virginia two months ago. James hadn't mentioned him anymore, and she assumed he had stayed behind. *What, if anything, does his sudden reappearance in Philadelphia mean?*

By the time Sarah returned to the kitchen after showing Mr. Clingman into the parlor, Maria had decided proper manners dictated that she ought to at least speak to her guest. She also didn't particularly like the possibility of him alone snooping around in the parlor.

Maria looked at Susan. "Stay here with Miss Sarah," she said. Maria walked into the parlor just as he was taking off his coat. He laid it over the back of the chair and looked up in surprise.

"Mrs. Reynolds," he said, nervously wiping his hands on his trousers. "Thank you for letting me wait inside."

Maria nodded curtly and sat down on the couch. "Please, have a seat while you wait, Mr. Clingman." She pointed to an empty chair across from her.

He quickly took a seat. "Please, call me Jacob."

Maria nodded noncommittedly. "When did you return to the city?" she asked, feigning small talk.

Jacob cleared his throat. "Only yesterday," he said. When he didn't elaborate further, Maria didn't question him. She picked up her book instead and started reading while he sat uncomfortably and waited. Maria knew she was being rude, but she didn't particularly care. When James arrived a few minutes later and greeted him warmly, Maria closed her book, stood, and left the room without a word to either of them.

Her cold reception proved to be the only influence Maria had. After that, Jacob became a frequent guest in their house, even supping with them on occasion. Coinciding with Jacob's arrival, James abruptly changed his mind about allowing Alexander to visit.

Maria could only stare at it in disbelief when James showed her a copy of the letter he delivered to Alexander.

> *Sir,*
>
> *When I conversed with you last, I told you it would be disagreeable to me for you to Call, but since I am pretty well convinced she would only wish to see you as a friend, and since I am reconciled to live with her, I would wish to do everything for her happiness and my own. So, don't fail in Calling as soon as you Can make it convenient.*
>
> *Yours to serve,*
> *James Reynolds*

For his part, Alexander wasted no time in taking advantage of James's offer. He showed up at the house that very afternoon, and after fielding Susan's enthusiastic greeting and insistent questions, Alexander finally retired to the parlor with Maria where they could talk in private.

The second the door closed behind them, Maria threw herself into his arms. While they had been able to exchange short messages during his banishment, those had not been enough, and she had missed him terribly.

"Thank God you are here, sir," she said with a sob, hanging onto his neck as if her very life depended on it. She lifted her face for a kiss despite James's strange pronouncement that she would *only want to see him as a friend*. They didn't even try to control their passion. When Alexander finally lifted his lips from hers, Maria sighed and laid her head contentedly on his shoulder.

"Come, let's sit down and talk," he said. They sat side-by-side on the couch, and he held her out at arm's length. "Let me look at you." Maria sat perfectly still as his hand traced a line down her body, reacquainting himself with her curves from the top of her head to her burgeoning stomach.

"I am pleased to see that you are well, and that you have been taking care of yourself," he said. "I think you are even more beautiful now than the day I met you."

Maria put her hands over his, closed her eyes, and wished this moment would never end. "The baby has already quickened," she said, "and I'm afraid I will not be able to hide it much longer."

"Do not fret about it. I have found that men are often ignorant of the timing of women's bodies," he said with a wry smile. "He will mostly likely not be able to ascertain with any certainty the paternity of the child or do anything rash."

"I hope you're right," she said, still not quite convinced.

He changed the subject. "What do you think caused Mr. Reynolds's change of heart regarding my visits?"

Maria shrugged her shoulders. "I do not know, sir. I have tried to make his time at home as unpleasant as possible, but I'm not convinced that I dissuaded him in full. I fear he may have more sinister plans in place." Her forehead furrowed with worry.

"No matter," Alexander said. "Any nefarious intentions will reveal themselves in time, there is no sense in worrying about it now." He leaned forward and kissed her lightly on the lips. "Let us take advantage of the time and opportunity that has been afforded us. Now go lock the door so that we can renew our particular friendship without interruption," he added.

Maria couldn't get the door locked fast enough.

Thirty

T hus began for the next month a strange truce between her husband and her lover, with Alexander coming and going seemingly at will to and from the house. After Alexander was allowed to visit her again, Maria backed off her silent treatment. Even if they didn't speak warmly, when her husband was home, they were at least civil to one another.

Maria didn't have to wonder long about James's motivation in allowing Alexander to see her again. When he sent a note to Alexander's office the next day asking for a "loan" of thirty dollars (including a receipt with the letter), his motives became crystal clear. Alexander promptly paid it.

The pattern continued over several weeks, a request for another loan every time James knew Alexander had been to see her. Maria was not fooled by James's insistence on calling these "loans," and she held no illusion that James would ever pay back the money. This way, she supposed, James could continue to deny to others that he was whoring his wife out to another man.

They continued the farce—now even more absurd because she could no longer hide her burgeoning belly. Maria had determined that if her husband were to ask her about the pregnancy, she would not lie. He never broached the subject, however; he simply seemed to ignore her condition. No doubt he was probably including the baby in his financial calculations. Every player on this pitiful stage seemed caught up in their bizarre roles, politely pretending not to know what they knew.

Neither she nor Alexander brought up his drunken confessions the night she bled, but his words haunted her, and Maria sensed Alexander was rapidly growing frustrated with the situation. While he continued to be loving and attentive, a look of anxiety replaced the original twinkle in his eyes, and as the intervals between his visits increased, Maria's desperation grew. If it weren't for the baby in her womb, James's continued demands would probably cause Alexander to leave her altogether. This Maria knew too well.

During this time, James didn't seem interested in staying at home or resuming their marriage relationship, which suited Maria just fine. He came and went without explanation, which made it much easier to maintain the illusion. Jacob Clingman, on the other hand, came to the house with increasing frequency for meetings with James and went out of his way to talk to Maria when he was there. Although their conversations were polite and superficial, she had caught him (more than once) staring at her in a way that made her uncomfortable.

On one such evening, she and Jacob were alone in the parlor making small talk while waiting for James to arrive when they heard a knock at the door. Maria started to stand, but Jacob put his hand out to stop her.

"It's more than likely just Mr. Reynolds. I'll get it."

Only later did it occur to her, why would James knock in the first place?

Maria realized something was wrong when she heard Alexander's voice. She jumped up from the couch and made it to the door just in time to see the two men staring at each other in surprise. She stepped forward to try and salvage the situation.

"Good evening, Colonel Hamilton," she said as casually as possible. "Mr. Reynolds is currently out but is expected shortly." She fought down the shakes. "Mr. Clingman happens to be waiting for him as well."

Alexander slipped a piece of paper into Maria's hand. "I've been told to deliver this to Mr. Reynolds," he muttered. Then he was gone, leaving Maria standing at the doorway, her heart pounding.

"Who could order the Secretary of the Treasury to deliver a message to Mr. Reynolds?" Jacob asked, clearly puzzled as she was.

Maria shrugged her shoulders. "I suppose he doesn't want it to be known," she replied. "Colonel Hamilton assisted Mr. Reynolds a few weeks ago, I think," she added in afterthought.

Jacob didn't ask any more questions, and they sat in uncomfortable silence for several minutes while Maria tried to process what had just happened. She glanced down at the note Alexander had pressed hastily into her hands, *a receipt for a ream of paper and some ink?* Alexander had obviously given her the first thing he found in his pocket to explain his presence at her house. Perhaps she would have found it comical if hadn't been so startling.

Maria picked up her open book and stared blankly at the page. So many unanswered questions. *How much do I really know about my husband's business partner, other than he always seemed to be in the right place at the right time?*

"Are you originally from Philadelphia, Jacob?" she asked.

He seemed surprised by her question. "Yes, I was born here," he said. She waited for him to expound on the subject, but he remained silent.

"How did you end up in North Carolina?"

Jacob cleared his throat and hesitated slightly before answering. "I was hired as an agent to do some business there," he said, not elaborating any further.

Maria waited. Undaunted, she continued. "I assume that's how you met Mr. Reynolds?"

"Yes, ma'am."

She could tell he was growing more and more uneasy with her line of questioning, so she pushed onward. "Mr. Reynolds mentioned that you worked previously as a clerk for Speaker of the House Muhlenberg?"

That got his attention. "I don't member mentioning that to Mr. Reynolds."

Maria casually shrugged her shoulders. "Perhaps I was mistaken. I was almost positive Mr. Reynolds told me. I don't know where else I would have heard it," she said innocently.

Jacob shifted and cleared his throat. "Yes. I did work as a clerk for Speaker Muhlenberg."

Maria smiled in an attempt to ease his sudden defensiveness. "A congressional clerkship sounds very exciting," she said in her most coquettish voice.

He relaxed instantly. "Not really," he said with a slight laugh. "It was all pretty tedious and boring."

"Is that how you came to know Senator Burr?"

When she saw the look of panic flash quickly across his dark eyes, she knew she had her answer. He recovered quickly, though.

"I met a great number of congressmen during my employment," he said smoothly. "Why do you ask?"

Maria smiled again. "Just curious. Senator Burr was the person who encouraged and facilitated my relocation from New York to Philadelphia. Perhaps he was the one who told me about your previous employer," she lied.

Confusion clouded Jacob's dark eyes.

"But I am probably mistaken," she added, smiling sweetly.

In that instant, everything suddenly became clear. Jacob Clingman's strange appearance in the alley. His presence at the market, where he followed Sarah and Susan while they did their shopping. His improbable arrival in North Carolina, where James just so happened to be. Coincidences so carefully orchestrated.

The front door opened, and Maria heard James's footsteps coming down the hall to the parlor. She stood and picked up her book. "It sounds like Mr. Reynolds has arrived. I will take my leave now," she said politely. "Thank you for a most enlightening conversation, Mr. Clingman."

Without waiting for his reply, she left the room and closed the door behind her. Her thoughts whirled. *Now that I have all the answers I want, what am I going to do with the information?*

Maria woke early the next morning and dressed completely before coming downstairs for breakfast. She wore the same pale green gown she had worn the day she arrived in the city almost nine months ago because it seemed appropriate for this morning's errand. The fashionable, high waistline allowed it to fit easily over the soft swell of her belly. A quick check in the mirror assured her that she looked perfectly respectable. She hadn't left the house in months, and even the short walk ahead of her seemed daunting. But this was something she needed to do.

Sarah looked up at her with a surprised smile. "It's good to see you dressed up for a change, missus," she said. "Where are you off to?"

"I have a meeting first thing this morning," she lied. *Although not a lie, really.* She intended on meeting someone indeed. He just had no clue she was coming.

After a quick cup of coffee and a slice of buttered toast, Maria said goodbye to Susan and stepped out into the early morning fog. Winter was finally loosening its grip on the city, some patches of snow still visible up against the sides of the row houses and along the edges of the cobblestone roads. Maria pulled her shawl more tightly around her shoulders and began her daunting walk toward the courthouse on the corner of Sixth and Chestnut Streets where she knew congress met.

With a smile and a discreet inquiry of the first man she approached, she learned the location of Burr's office. She knew she was being impulsive, but she had to know. She certainly wouldn't be able to repeat this process in a few weeks and might possibly lose her nerve in the interim too.

As it turned out, her early venture was more than worth it, just to see the look on Burr's face when she stepped into his office unannounced. She closed the door behind her. He was practiced in regaining his composure quickly, though, and a smile slowly crept across his face. He put his quill into a stand on his desk and stood to greet her.

"Mrs. Reynolds," he said. "What a delightful surprise!" He studied her for several seconds, his dark eyes darting to her belly. "I must say, you have positively blossomed since the last time I saw you. It looks like congratulations are in order for you and Mr. Reynolds."

Now that the initial shock of her appearance had worn off, he was just playing with her, trying to get a reaction. He knew good and well whose baby she was carrying. Her eyes narrowed. Stay focused and remember why you came, she reminded herself.

"Forgive me, I seem to have forgotten my manners. Please, come in and have a seat." He gestured toward the chair in front of his desk.

Maria hesitated for a second before accepting his offer. She smoothed her satin skirt down over her stomach and sat about the time the baby executed a perfect backflip. Maria caught her breath and self-consciously sat up straighter.

"And to what do I owe the pleasure of your visit, Mrs. Reynolds?"

Maria had already decided a direct approach was the best. "Did you hire Jacob Clingman to spy on me?"

Burr seemed genuinely surprised by her question. "Your condition becomes you. I don't remember you being this direct before."

Maria saw something that almost looked like—*admiration*—in his dark eyes.

"I will try to be just as forthcoming, then. The short answer is yes, I hired Mr. Clingman to find you when you left the boarding house."

"Why?" she asked.

"I was concerned for your safety," he said. "You left the boarding house in such a hurry, and I was worried something might have happened to you."

She didn't believe his explanation for one second. She also wasn't completely ready to navigate around his lies. "Did you also send Mr. Clingman to North Carolina to find Mr. Reynolds and tell him where we were?"

Burr didn't smile this time. "I—only thought your husband had the right to be informed of the whereabouts of his daughter."

Maria sat up even straighter, instantly indignant. "You didn't seem concerned about his paternal rights when we were in New York and Mr. Wagstaff was paying you to keep him away."

For the first time in their lengthy acquaintance, Burr looked ruffled. "That was different," he said, his words tinged with a defensiveness she had never heard from him before.

"How so?"

Burr cleared his throat. "I don't have to explain myself."

"Is that because you don't want to admit that you were the one who helped broker my sale to Mr. Wagstaff?"

Burr at least had the decency to look down at the top of his desk as the truth of her words struck home.

"And now, Mr. Reynolds has returned and repeated the process. You may be surprised to learn that my price has more than tripled," she practically spit the words at Burr. She stood, hands clutched into fists, growing angrier by the second. "Why couldn't you leave things as they were?" she continued, her voice rising. She could feel her face growing red and hot. Something within her had snapped, and she couldn't stop. "Do you hate losing so badly that you are willing to destroy other people's lives in retribution?" She took a deep breath to maintain some semblance of control. "You hired me to find proof of Colonel Hamilton's corruption," she continued in a lower voice, "which does not exist, I can assure you. And now, because of your meddling, Mr. Reynolds is set on a course for Colonel Hamilton's financial ruin while he threatens to take away my own daughter to keep me in line."

"I warned Colonel Hamilton about Mr. Reynolds," Burr replied, his words flat and without emotion. "I will not take responsibility for something that you yourself agreed to willingly."

Maria gave a cynical laugh and ran her hand over her belly to try to still the soft kicks from within. "You are right," she admitted. "I did agree to participate in your scheme against Colonel Hamilton, and I will regret that decision for the rest of my life." She was suddenly so tired. "While I am racked with guilt, I am certain that in your own mind, you will be able to absolve yourself of any responsibility in this."

"I sleep quite well at night, Mrs. Reynolds."

"I am sure you do, Mr. Burr." She sighed. "I only have one more question. Is Mr. Clingman still in your employ?"

"No." He admitted it so quickly and with such conviction, she knew it was the truth.

Why then is Jacob still hanging around if he isn't working for Burr?

"I don't mean to be rude, Mrs. Reynolds, but I am expected in chambers shortly." He met her eyes. "I am truly sorry for the circumstances in which you now find yourself. I acknowledge my own part in it, but in the end, we are all responsible for our own decisions and the unfortunate consequences that may arise from them."

Maria was taken aback by the sincerity in his eyes. While it was not a true apology, this was more than she'd thought she would ever get from him.

"I wish you the best, Mrs. Reynolds. Truly, I do. But I will not be painted as the villain in your story." With that, he broke eye contact and reached down to pick up a stack of papers on his desk.

Maria turned to leave without another word.

Thirty-One

Maria rolled onto her side and pressed her hand into the small of her back to try to ease the dull, nearly constant ache she'd had for the last several hours. Just uncomfortable enough to make sleeping impossible.

With a frustrated sigh, she struggled to sit and propped up her pillow against her back, hoping a change in position would bring some relief. The repositioning helped, but a full bladder made her need to move more urgent.

Light from a full moon was just enough to make out the outline of the furniture in her bedroom. With a groan, Maria swung her legs over the side of the bed and stood, bracing the small of her back with one hand. Something didn't seem right; she didn't remember having this kind of back pain in her pregnancy with Susan. Maria pulled the chamber pot out from under the bed and emptied her bladder, which relieved her somewhat—but not enough.

She stood beside the bed for several seconds considering what to do. *Should I wake Sarah and have her get a message to Dr. Stevens? What if it is nothing?* She didn't want to summon him in the middle of the night unless it was necessary. *That will make me look even more foolish.* Maybe it was just something she had eaten, something she had done. Today had been particularly stressful, and even the short walk to the courthouse and back was more exercise than Maria was used to.

She would wait and see if it got any worse before waking anyone, she decided, and crawled back into bed. Perhaps the throbbing would go away on its own once she got some rest. Satisfied with her decision, she rolled onto her side and tried to get comfortable. But her mind wouldn't let her.

After leaving Burr's office, the day had been otherwise uneventful. James came home, changed clothes, and left again after supper with barely a word. Jacob had not been by, and she hadn't heard from Alexander since yesterday. Exhausted by her emotional exchange with Burr, she had retired early to bed, although the onset of back pain made it impossible to sleep.

She still didn't know what she was going to do with the information she had gotten from Burr concerning Jacob. Her first thought was to tell Alexander, but she couldn't think of a way to tell him without admitting her own culpability in setting him up in the first place. She didn't think Jacob was a threat to her or Susan. What she still couldn't figure out was why he was still here after he'd finished the job Burr hired him to do.

Every one of them was keeping a secret about something. She didn't think James knew Jacob had been working for Burr, or that he had been paid to find her. She didn't think James knew that their meeting in North Carolina was orchestrated, either. As for his part, James seemed to have conveniently neglected to inform his business partner of his recent windfall money and his foray into extortion and blackmail. Only she and Alexander knew that agents were scouring North Carolina looking for proof of illegal activity to have James and Jacob arrested. The most damning secret of all, though, was the one she kept from Alexander: Burr's plot against him, and her own culpability.

Maria was stuck in the center of a web of secrets, lies, and half-truths. One wrong move, and it would collapse around her. No wonder she was having trouble sleeping.

The ache in her lower back finally eased enough to allow her a couple hours' sleep until a full bladder compelled her out of bed again. This time, the sun was already creeping over the horizon. Perhaps Alexander would come by to see her today, incentive enough to keep her from crawling back onto the inviting softness of her mattress. She was still tired, but at least her backache seemed to have resolved.

She heard Sarah going down the stairs to the kitchen, and Maria grabbed the wool shawl she from the back of her desk chair to wrap around her shoulders. She had made it halfway down the stairs when a strong pain in her abdomen seized her. She gasped and grabbed her stomach.

Maria gripped the railing until the pain finally released. After several short breaths, she looked up and caught Sarah staring at her. She rushed forward and grabbed Maria's arm to steady her.

"I think you should go fetch Dr. Stevens," Maria said, trying to keep her voice calm.

"Let's get you back upstairs, missus," Sarah said, guiding Maria slowly back the way she came. They had made it only a couple of feet into her bedroom when Maria suddenly stopped. Sarah's hands tightened on her arm as Maria's knees threatened to collapse beneath her. A gush of fluid came out from between her legs and splashed across the wooden planks. When Maria noticed the blood-tinged puddle between her feet, the implication slowly hit her.

No! This can't be happening! It's too soon.

Maria looked up at Sarah. "I can get into bed on my own. Go get

Dr. Stevens and get a message to Colonel Hamilton!"

Sarah hesitated, reluctant to leave her side.

"Hurry!" Maria said more strongly this time, enough to spur the maid into action.

"I'll be back as quickly as I can." Sarah ran out of the room. Maria had never seen Sarah this ruffled before, which only fed her fear.

Slowly and carefully, she took a few steps toward her bed, put her hands on top of the mattress, and leaned over the side as her stomach tightened with another contraction. Instinctively, she closed her eyes and began to pant through the pain until it passed.

A sound behind her caught her attention, and she turned to see Susan standing in the doorway in her nightshirt, her eyes wide with fear, fixated on the spots of blood on her mother's shift.

"Is everything all right, Mama?" Her voice shook.

Maria tried to reassure her with a smile. "Of course, sweetheart," she said.

Susan didn't look convinced.

"Come here and give me a hug," Maria said softly.

Susan walked carefully around the puddle on the floor, and Maria weakly pulled her against her side. She knew she shouldn't tell her daughter too much about what was going on.

"Are you sick?" Susan asked.

"No, I'm not sick," Maria tried to reassure her. The warmth of Susan's body gave her the comfort and strength she needed to continue. "Remember when I told you that you would have a new little brother or sister soon?"

"Well, it looks like the baby is anxious to meet you." She tried to smile.

Susan's eyes widened in surprise. "You mean today?"

Maria closed her eyes and nodded. "Yes. Today." She didn't dare tell Susan that the chances of a baby being born this early and surviving were extremely low. Based upon Dr. Steven's last examination, she was barely into her seventh month. Maria bit her lip fought her own emotions as she pulled Susan closer. Her legs were growing weak; she was running out of time. *Maybe they are wrong. Maybe I am farther along than they all think.* She clung desperately to that one small hope.

"I need to lay down now," she said after several seconds. "Miss Sarah has gone to get Dr. Stevens and Colonel Hamilton. Would you like to sit with me until they get here?"

Susan nodded and anxiously watched Maria crawl up onto the bed on her hands and knees. "Where's Papa?" she asked.

Maria rolled onto her side with a sigh. She had totally forgotten about her husband; she had no idea where he was. She hadn't heard him come home in the night, either.

"I don't know," she answered honestly. Thankfully, Susan didn't persist like she often did. She dutifully walked around the other side of the bed and crawled up beside Maria instead.

Another contraction came again without warning. Not wanting to frighten Susan, Maria closed her eyes and bit her lip to keep from crying out. The contractions were coming closer and closer together.

Maria heard the front door open, followed by heavy footsteps on the stairs. She sighed in relief when Dr. Stevens entered her room, Sarah right behind him.

Dr. Stevens quickly took in the scene, walked over, and sat on the side of the bed. He glanced over at Susan, his eyebrows furrowing in disapproval. "She shouldn't be here." He glanced back at Sarah. "Come and get the child, take her downstairs, and then come back up and clean up the floor before someone falls."

Sarah nodded and walked around to the other side of the bed to collect Susan.

Maria looked into her daughter's terrified face and squeezed her hand. "It will be all right," she assured her before Sarah led her away.

As soon as she heard the door close, Maria looked back at Dr. Stevens. "It's too early for the baby to come, isn't it?"

He patted her hand sympathetically. "Yes, but there is nothing we can do to stop that now."

Maria closed her eyes and started to cry. *Where is Alexander? I cannot do this without him.*

"Colonel Hamilton is on his way," Dr. Stevens said. "When did the contractions start?"

Maria forced herself to think, to remember. "Early this morning. About an hour ago, I believe." She really had no idea how much time had passed, but she needed to tell him something. "I was up all night with a backache," she added.

"When was the last time you felt the baby quicken?"

"I don't know," she answered honestly. Although the baby had been unusually active yesterday afternoon, she hadn't felt any movement at all this morning. She took a deep breath and bit her lip as another contraction hit her.

That contraction had just eased when Sarah returned with an armful of cotton toweling to soak up the puddle. She tossed the fabric on the floor, and it quickly soaked through.

As Sarah gathered the toweling up, Dr. Stevens turned to her. "Thank you. You can go down and stay with the child now. Please send up Colonel Hamilton as soon as he arrives."

Maria could see in Sarah's eyes that she really wanted to stay.

"It's all right, Sarah," Maria said. "Susan needs you more than I do right now."

"Yes, ma'am," Sarah said. She was in no way totally convinced, but she left.

Dr. Stevens's expression betrayed nothing as he turned back to Maria, gently prodded her belly, and lifted her blood-splattered shift.

Another contraction took her breath away, and Maria cried out in pain. She instinctively drew up her knees, and as soon as the contraction released, she felt his hands between her legs.

She could see the shock in his eyes when he looked back up at her. "It is already time to push," he said.

No! I have to wait for Alexander!

Before she had time to collect her thoughts, her stomach tightened once again, accompanied by the overwhelming urge to bear down. She cried out in pain, grit her teeth, and held her breath—using every ounce of strength she had to resist what her body was telling her to do.

"You must push, Mrs. Reynolds," Dr. Stevens admonished her.

"No!" she screamed, collapsing back onto the pillow as soon as the contraction ended. Her breath came in hard gasps, her body racked with sobs. "The baby will die if I do."

"If you do not push, you will die as well," Dr. Stevens stated, his voice raised and hard.

"I don't care," she cried through the pain. She tightened every muscle in her lower body to resist the instinct to push as another contraction took hold. *Where is Alexander?*

"Damn it!" Dr. Stevens finally lost his patience. "If you do not assist, I will be forced to remove the babe myself."

Maria opened her eyes as he reached into his black leather bag and pulled out a metal contraption that looked like a device from the Middle Ages. She screamed. It was all happening so fast, and she was going to lose the battle.

The door opened, and Alexander burst into the room.

"What is happening?" he asked loudly.

"The baby is coming, and she refuses to push. I will have to remove it manually if she does not cooperate."

Alexander reached down to gently stroke the side of her face.

"Maria, honey, you have to help."

"The baby is too early," she sobbed, her voice desperate. She had to try and make him understand that their child would die if she did not resist.

"There is nothing you can do to stop what is happening," Alexander said, his voice soft but firm. "If you continue on this course, you will die too." She saw Alexander and Dr. Stevens exchange looks. *They think I'm crazy.*

Perhaps she was out of her head with pain and exhaustion, Maria thought. Before she was able to respond, her stomach tightened again, and she cried out.

"Push, Maria. You must push." Alexander's hand tightened around hers, and she lost the will to fight any longer. She bore down as hard as she could and felt the baby slip from her body.

Maria fell back against the pillow with a cry of defeat and closed her eyes tightly, terrified of what she would see if she looked down between her knees. She held her breath and listened intently, straining her ears for any sounds of life. *A cry, a gasp, anything.* But the silence was deafening. Maria looked up at Alexander, and his eyes told her everything she needed to know.

"I am sorry," Dr. Stevens said. "She was not ready to be born yet." *She. It's a girl.*

In that moment, Maria's world came crashing down around her and she screamed as if her heart were being torn out of her chest. Delirious with grief, she began struggling as she felt another contraction. Alexander held her down while Dr. Stevens delivered the afterbirth.

Maria knew then that she had passed the point where any rational thought could reach her—and she didn't care. Something in her mind had snapped, and she knew that nothing would ever be the same again.

In the end, Alexander forced open her mouth for Dr. Stevens to give her some laudanum to calm her. As the opium began taking effect, she heard Sarah's voice. Bloody bedsheets moving underneath her. Alexander lifting her up. Someone cleaning the blood off her legs and thighs. Alexander crawling into bed beside her and holding her as she slipped away.

Thirty-Two

"I can neither Eate or sleep and
have Been on the point of doing
the moast horrid acts . . ."

Letter from Maria Reynolds to Alexander Hamilton, 1792

". . . if I could take all of her Greif
upon myself I would do it with pleasure,
the excess of which alarms me untill
now I have had no idea of . . ."

Letter from James Reynolds to Alexander Hamilton,
March 24, 1792

The days that followed were a blur while Maria waited for the fever to come like it had the last time she lost a baby. But it did not. In fact, her body began to recover at a most frustrating and remarkable pace as she sank deeper and deeper into grief. She knew that her behavior was concerning—and she was embarrassed by it—but she lacked the will or ability to do anything else.

The memories of that morning played like a loop in her mind and taunted her unmercifully. She wished she'd had the courage to look at her baby, to hold her, to say a proper goodbye before they had taken her away. Maybe then she would have had some sort of closure. On some days she could almost convince herself it had never happened.

At night, though, she was haunted by what happened. Alone in her bed each night, the nightmares came in the same way, over and over again. Her infant daughter was crying, and she couldn't find her. In the first few days when her body was still trying to feed a baby that didn't exist, she would wake to find milk dripping from her swollen nipples.

The days were only slightly better. Alexander came by to check on her every morning and evening, but Maria spent most of her days alone in her bedroom crying. Not even Susan's visits provided any comfort.

At first, James was sympathetic. He even sat at her bedside to try and comfort her as she drifted in and out of sleep. But his efforts were half-hearted at best, and he quickly gave up.

After a few days, the danger of infection passed, and Dr. Stevens declared her able to return to a light schedule. But Maria had no desire to rejoin the household. Even Alexander had returned to his normal schedule as if nothing had ever happened.

But that wasn't really fair, she chastised herself. She had no doubt he was grieving too. She could see the sadness etched onto his features and hear it in his voice. But he had another baby to look forward to in only a few months, one that would no doubt be robust and healthy like all the others his wife had already borne him.

When two weeks had passed and Maria still refused to get dressed or leave her bed, Alexander became frustrated with her. It wasn't healthy for her to stay abed all day, he gently told her. He told her again more forcefully when that didn't seem to work. No doubt his strong and sensible wife would have never found herself completely prostrate with grief—lying in bed, crying all day, and hoping to die.

Maria calculated that if she refused to eat or drink for an entire week, she might just slip away. Even that failed only a few days into her self-induced hunger strike when Alexander threatened to hold her down and force-feed her himself. Unwilling to test his resolve, she relented—and grew more resentful every day.

Alexander too, grew more and more distant. Within six weeks of their daughter's stillbirth, he was limiting his visits to a few times a week. When she eventually found the energy to get out of bed and get dressed, Maria spent her days on the couch in the parlor, reading or staring at the wall. Alexander's visits seemed more obligatory somehow, and she had no desire to renew their previous passionate pursuits. He did not press her.

James still came and went at will but remained surprisingly gentle with her. He even reached out to Alexander, not to ask for money—but out of concern for the seeming depth of Maria's grief.

She didn't know why Alexander bothered to come around at all anymore. The only things that had connected them were their previous passion and their unborn child. Both of those were gone. But Alexander wouldn't leave her, even as the time neared for his new child to be born. He continued to try to pull her out of her depression, even offering to make good on his previous promise to help fund her boardinghouse. A dream she no longer had any desire to pursue.

Surprisingly, though, Jacob brought her the most comfort. Unlike Alexander or even James, he didn't pressure her to eat or move. As the frequency of Alexander's visits decreased, Jacob's increased. At first, he used the excuse of meeting with James, but eventually he dropped the pretense altogether. When James was gone, Jacob was there. He'd just sit beside her on the couch and chat casually about nothing whether she responded or not.

Alexander remained frustratingly loyal at times, continuing an unspoken commitment or responsibility that no longer existed. When she expressed as much to him, he responded the next day by presenting her with her a delicate, heart-shaped locket in silver filigree with a lock of his hair inside.

She almost wavered when he pinned the locket onto the bodice of her gown right over her heart. But Maria knew she was dead weight now, sinking slowly. She didn't want to be the shackle around his ankles that pulled him down with her. If he would not save himself, she would cut him loose, even if she must sacrifice herself in the process.

Day by day, she slowly built up the strength to act upon her resolve. When that day finally came, Alexander had arrived to find her once again in bed. She had just drifted off to sleep when she heard the sound of footsteps as he walked into the room. Maria squeezed her eyes shut and lay perfectly still as she heard him kick off his shoes and take off his jacket. She felt the mattress dip as he pulled back the covers, crawled in behind her, and wrapped his arms around her waist.

"Please come back to me, Maria," he whispered, his lips against her ear. When he pulled her to him and began kissing the side of her neck, she almost gave in. So easy to yield to the passion of his kisses, to roll toward him and once again surrender to the pleasure she knew could still be found in his arms. She opened her eyes and lay perfectly still, a single tear sliding down her cheek.

"I went to Senator Burr's office the morning before I went into labor," she whispered, staring blankly at the wall in front of her.

He immediately stopped kissing her neck and propped himself up on his elbow to look down at her. "Why? What business did you have with him?"

She could hear his surprise, and squeezed her eyes shut. "I asked him if he had hired Mr. Clingman to find me and to tell James where we could be found."

She felt Alexander's hand tighten around her waist. "What makes you think Senator Burr had any connection with Mr. Clingman?"

"Because he was angry and wanted to get back at me."

"For what, Maria?" Alexander's voice was tinged with confusion, no doubt trying to make sense of this. "Why would Burr be angry with you?"

"Because I refused to continue the job he had hired me to do." Her voice sounded empty. Tears streamed down her face.

Alexander moved his hand from her waist to her upper arm. "Turn around and look at me, Maria," he said, his voice hard. "What did he hire you to do?" He said the words very slowly.

She rolled over to face him, determined to finish the course she had chosen. "Seduce you," she said.

In the end, it wasn't anger, but the look of pain and betrayal in his eyes that almost undid her. She covered her face with her hands and began to sob, no longer able to look at him.

"Was everything you told me a lie, then?" He flung the covers back, swung his legs off the side of the bed, and stood.

Maria sobbed harder as the full ramifications of her confession slowly dawned on him.

"Look at me. Answer me, dammit!"

With every ounce of resolve she had left, Maria lowered her hands from her face and met his eyes. "Yes," she said, although *that* wasn't accurate, either. She pushed herself into a sitting position and watched him pace back and forth beside the bed, one fist clutched tightly in his hair, the other against his thigh. He didn't seem to know how to respond to her simple confession.

"Are you not going to defend yourself?" he finally asked. "Are you not going to at least give me an explanation?"

Truth and lies—she no longer had strength or desire to separate them. Maria remained silent in the face of his mounting anger.

"Did you even love me at all, or was it just a job from the very beginning?"

She caught her breath. "I love you more than I have ever loved another man in my entire life," she added tearfully.

He searched her face as if to ascertain the truth. "Then why did you not confide in me earlier?" His voice was softer now, pleading. "We could have figured this out, if I had known Burr was behind it all."

"I was afraid."

"Afraid of what, Maria?"

"Afraid I would lose you."

"Then why are you telling me now?"

"Because I know nothing will stop that."

The silence hung heavy in the room as he took his jacket off the back of the chair and pulled it on. He slid his stockinged feet into his shoes, and she started crying again.

"What are you going to do?" she asked.

He stopped and looked at her. "I don't know," he said. "But I won't stay here."

In that moment, Maria wanted to throw herself at his feet and beg for forgiveness. But what would that get her? Another month? Perhaps two? Her confession had ensured he would never trust her again. Without trust, all the love in the world couldn't hold them together anymore.

"Are you going to confront Burr?"

"I haven't decided yet. But I do know that from this moment forward, I will make it my religious duty to oppose his career. I will do everything I can to ensure that he *never* obtains the reins of power." He spit out those last words through clenched teeth, and she had no doubt he meant them.

My God, what have I wrought?

She watched in silence as he walked out and slammed the door it behind him.

Thirty-Three

If Maria believed that confessing the truth to Alexander would put an end to her guilt or emotional volatility, she was sorely mistaken. In the months after he left, she felt like she was set adrift in a boat with no oars. She allowed the current to carry her along, no longer caring where she went or what happened.

Without the money Alexander paid to see her, she outlived her usefulness to James, and he moved to new lodgings along the river. Sarah stayed with Maria and Susan for a while, but eventually she left too, and married a respectable young man she met at church.

Only Jacob stayed. Over the past six months, he had gone from platonic friend to tender confessor to devoted lover. He moved in with them shortly after James left. Despite her misgivings regarding his part in the plot against Alexander, Maria entered the relationship willingly, desperate for the stability and physical comfort Jacob provided. At times she felt like she sincerely cared for him. At other times, it felt like she merely played the part. She had no desire to introspect or determine which was true.

When her husband left and another man moved in to take his place, her landlord evicted them from the house, declaring his property *a respectable residence in a respectable neighborhood,* that he didn't allow *degenerate and immoral behavior.* Nevermind what she and Alexander had done.

Jacob found a smaller house to rent in a neighborhood close to the river. Still better than a single room in a boarding house, and Maria took it as a bit of a blessing in disguise. Living with the memories contained in the walls of their previous house for much longer would have probably sent her down a path of madness.

She kept up with Alexander's political activities in the newspapers and knew that his wife had given birth to a healthy son three months ago. For his part, Jacob took on the role of Maria's savior and avenger and began meeting with politicians directly opposed to Alexander. He was often out late at meetings, although she never questioned him too closely about what he was doing.

In mid-November, when the first snowfall of the winter dusted the city streets and rooftops overnight, Maria woke early to find Jacob up already, pulling on his clothes. A quick glance at the window told her it wasn't yet light outside.

"It's still early," she said with a yawn. She stretched her arms overhead and sat up.

"I know. I have a meeting before work this morning. I will return for supper."

Something didn't seem quite right. He looked nervous and edgy, and he wouldn't look her in the eye. She brushed aside her concerns, though, and swung her legs over the side of the bed. He gave her a quick kiss goodbye and walked out.

It didn't make sense to go back to sleep, she thought. She might as well get an early start on the day. They didn't have the money to hire another girl to replace Sarah, so Maria had learned how to cook and manage a household out of necessity. She was not particularly good at it, but her skills were sufficient to keep them adequately fed and their clothes clean. Susan was getting big enough now to help too, and had picked up a surprising amount just by watching Sarah.

The day passed uneventfully enough. When Jacob didn't return for supper as promised, Maria tried not to worry. The hour grew late—past time for bed, and he still hadn't arrived. Maria fretted, imagining every sort of disaster from a carriage accident to being robbed, stabbed, and left dying in the street. She could only worry and wait.

Sleep proved elusive, and when morning broke with still no word, Maria was determined to go out and find him herself. She emptied the ashes from the kitchen fireplace and had a fire blazing in the hearth by the time Susan came downstairs. Maria was still trying to figure out the best course of action when they heard a knock at the door. Her heartbeat in her ears, Maria opened the door to find a young black boy standing on the doorstep with a letter in his hand.

"Message for Mrs. Reynolds," he said.

She looked at him in confusion for several seconds before the name sunk in. She had used the last name of Clingman since they moved here—not necessarily to be deceitful—but to avoid getting kicked out of another house for the sin of living with a man who was not her husband.

"I am Mrs. Reynolds," she said, and reached out with shaking fingers to take the message from his hand.

He nodded, released the letter, and headed back into the street.

Maria clutched the letter tightly as she closed the door. *No name or address on the front.* She didn't recognize the seal, either. Bracing herself for bad news, she unfolded the paper and began reading the words inside. Because it was written in a disguised hand, she was halfway down the page before she realized who the sender was.

> *Maria,*
>
> *I hasten to inform you that Mr. Reynolds, along with Mr. Clingman, were picked up yesterday morning on a warrant issued by the Comptroller of the Treasury, Mr. Wolcott, and are currently being held in jail on charges of forgery and intimidating a witness stemming from business conducted last year in North Carolina.*
>
> *Mr. Burr and Mr. Muhlenberg have already petitioned me on Mr. Clingman's behalf, and Mr. Clingman has indicated his willingness to pay restitution and return the lists that were illegally obtained. If he abides by these conditions, I have given Mr. Wolcott permission to release him shortly.*
>
> *I do not wish to see you or Susan suffer because of the actions of your husband and Mr. Clingman, in which you had no part. Please let me know what I can do to provide relief. Burn this letter upon reading.*

Maria dropped the letter into the fire as if the paper itself had burned her fingers and watched the flames quickly consign it to a pile of ash.

"What's wrong, Mama?" Susan asked. "Where is Mr. Clingman?"

Maria swallowed hard. "He and your papa have been arrested and put in jail." No reason to lie. The truth would come out eventually, anyway. It always did.

"For what?"

"Something that happened last year when they were in North Carolina. I'm sure it will soon be resolved, though," she added.

Susan frowned. She was old enough now to hang onto these things, Maria knew. A series of conflicting emotions ran through her own mind, and Maria didn't know whether to be shocked, angry, or relieved.

Her thoughts went first to Jacob, relieved that he was safe and not dead or injured, but angry that he hadn't notified her himself. She was not terribly surprised, however, that Jacob had gotten caught up in one of James's schemes last year.

Her thoughts turned to Alexander. He couldn't be angry with her if he had offered to help, she reasoned. And by his own words, Jacob would be released soon, so there didn't seem to be any retaliation involved. Perhaps Alexander's concern was sincere. She shook her head as if to dispel the thought. After everything she had done, the possibility that he still cared about her was more than she could fathom.

She needed to see Jacob and hear the story from him personally before she made any rash decisions or responded to Alexander. It didn't occur to her to be concerned about her husband's fate. James could rot in jail as far as she was concerned.

"I'm going to the jail to talk to Mr. Clingman," she said quickly. "You stay here. I won't be long." She hated leaving Susan, but the city jail was no environment for a child, and she would not be gone long.

Once Maria made her decision, she acted quickly and ran upstairs to wash. She wiped a smear of soot from her cheek, pulled a ruffled linen cap on over her messy curls, and tossed her stained apron onto the floor.

She hugged Susan goodbye, wrapped a wool scarf around her

shoulders, and headed toward Walnut Street where she knew the jail was located. The plain, red brick building was easy to find, and she paused for a second to fortify her resolve before stepping inside.

The smell of urine and unwashed bodies assaulted her all at once, and Maria was glad she had left Susan behind. A large, roughly dressed man stepped out of the shadows to meet her.

"What kin I do for ya?" he asked, punctuating his question with a wad of tobacco he spit onto the brick floor.

"I'm here to see Mr. Clingman."

The man was silent for several seconds as he looked her up and down. "Follow me," he said, and walked away without waiting for her to respond.

Maria walked quickly to catch up to him. The guard stopped in front of a heavy wooden door, pulled a brass key ring from the pocket of his trousers, and painstakingly sorted through the keys until he found the one he was looking for. When the key slid into the lock, the bolt opened with a loud clank.

Maria followed the guard into a long hallway bordered by jail cells where even stronger smells assaulted her. She wrinkled her nose in disgust while they paraded past. Prisoners stood when they saw her, thrusting their arms through the iron bars and calling out to her. Maria tried to focus on the guard's back and ignore their taunts. He stopped in front of one of the cells.

"Maria!" Jacob said, rushing toward her. "How did you know I was here?"

"I received a letter this morning telling me you had been arrested," she answered. "Why did you not send word to me yourself? I've been worried sick."

She could see by the light from the guard's lantern that Jacob's face was flushed with embarrassment. His face and clothes were streaked with dirt, and he reeked from the filth of his environment.

"I'm sorry." Jacob reached through the bars to take her hand. "I should have told you, but I thought I would be released quickly."

"This is all Mr. Hamilton's fault," a voice spoke up from the back of the cell. Maria's eyes narrowed as she watched her husband step out of the shadows and walk toward them. "We have done nothing wrong. He did this to get back at us." His voice dripped with anger.

"I would think that your own actions are to blame for your current circumstances, not Colonel Hamilton's," she shot back. She hadn't even considered that they might be confined in the same cell, and the idea of those two men alone together for the past twenty-four hours was not a comforting one. She knew from experience just how convincing James could be.

"This has all been a terrible misunderstanding, Maria," Jacob interrupted. "Mr. Burr and Mr. Muhlenberg have spoken to Secretary Hamilton, and he has promised to secure my release. I hope to be home before nightfall."

"The bastards wouldn't speak on my behalf, though," James added, his voice shaking with anger. "Even though I assured them I had information that would make some department heads tremble."

A chill went down her spine at his obvious threat. She had no doubt he would do or say whatever he needed to ensure his own freedom.

Jacob didn't react to James's words. "Go home and wait, Maria," he said, squeezing her hand. " Do not speak to anyone about this. I will return as soon as I am released. This is no place for a lady."

James snorted dismissively and turned back into the shadows. Maria chose to ignore the insinuation. Jacob could've defended her, but he was obviously choosing his battles carefully.

She turned to the guard. "I am ready to leave now."

Without a word, the guard turned and started back down the hallway. Maria struggled to keep up with his long strides, her mind reeling from the events of the past couple of hours.

Thirty-Four

"The charge against me is a connection
with one James Reynolds for purposes
of improper pecuniary speculation. My
real crime is an amorous connection to
his wife, for a considerable time with his
privity and connivance, if not originally
brought on by a combination between the
husband and wife with the design to
extort money from me."

Alexander Hamilton, the *Reynolds Pamphlet*, 1797

Susan ran to greet Maria as soon as she walked back into the
house. "Is Mr. Clingman coming home?" she asked. "Did you
see my papa?"

"Yes," she replied. "It was all a misunderstanding. Mr. Clingman
will be home soon, and your papa was with him. He sends his love,"
she lied. Susan smiled in relief. Maria knew that her daughter still
missed her father, or at least the father he had pretended to be when

he first arrived in Philadelphia.

The smells from the prison still clung to her, and Maria knew she would not be able to concentrate on anything else until she cleaned up. She hung a pot of water on a hook over the fire and carried it up to her bedroom as soon as the water was warm enough. She wasted no time stripping naked and scrubbing her skin with the last little bit of the rose scented soap she had saved. When she was finished, she changed into a clean gown and went back downstairs to finish her daily chores. The entire morning was now gone, and she had so much to do.

Maria hoped Jacob would be home by midday, but the hours came and went with no word. She and Susan ate the simple supper she had prepared in silence. She couldn't put Alexander's words out of her head, and briefly considered responding to his letter before dismissing the idea. *Jacob asked me not to speak to anyone. Plus, Alexander has already promised to release Jacob. What good could possibly come from renewing our correspondence or accepting his offer of relief?*

When darkness fell and she still hadn't heard anything, she began to get anxious. Her mind was full of questions. Alexander had said Jacob would have to pay restitution. *How much money was involved in their illegal scheme? And where was he going to get the money to pay it back?* As it was, Jacob barely gave her enough money each week to maintain their modest household.

By midnight, she finally gave up waiting. This would be the second night in a row she would have to sleep alone. The one thing she liked the most about her arrangement with Jacob was that someone was with her every night, that she didn't have to be alone anymore.

A knock on the door startled her, a cadence of the raps emblazoned into her memory. After all, she had heard it scores of times. Maria briefly considered snuffing out the candle and not answering.

But he would have seen the light in the window and known that she was still awake. Maria stood frozen in place, her heart pounding loudly in her ears. *What if Jacob was home and I wasn't alone?* Then she remembered that Alexander had complete control of Jacob's release.

The knocks came again, more insistent this time. She would not be able to avoid this meeting. She walked to the door and opened it a crack.

"Can I speak to you, Maria?" Alexander asked. His voice was slightly hoarse, his eyes boring into hers. "Please," he added when she didn't move, as if he could persuade her by the sheer force of his will. "Can I come inside?"

Maria merely nodded and opened the door wider. He stepped inside, closed the door behind him, and brushed a light dusting of snow from the shoulders of his heavy coat.

"What is it you want?" she asked, finally finding her voice.

"I want to warn you."

"About what?" she asked.

"Let's sit down." He didn't wait for her response before finding his way toward the kitchen. Still somewhat stunned by his appearance on her doorstep, Maria followed him and took a seat. He took a chair beside her and reached out to take her hand.

She pulled hers away, for she knew she would not be able to think clearly with his hand on hers.

The candlelight cast a soft glow across his features, and he looked down. "I'm sorry. That was out of line." He didn't try to make an excuse for it.

"What is it you wanted to warn me about?"

Alexander looked up and met her eyes. "Mr. Reynolds is so desperate to be released from jail, he has been telling anyone who will listen that he has information to take me down."

Maria nodded. "Yes. He said the same thing to me when I visited

Mr. Clingman earlier. But it's just talk. He has no evidence against you." She paused. "Except that concerning our *amour*," she added.

"We know that, but two congressmen from Virgina, both friends of Mr. Jefferson's, are entertaining Mr. Reynolds's accusations after interviewing him in jail. They may try to speak to you as well."

"What is it exactly that Mr. Reynolds is claiming?"

"That the money I gave him was for improper speculation."

"But that's a lie!"

"You and I know that, Maria, but others may believe him. Especially since he did receive money from me. Quite a bit of money," he added.

Maria's blood boiled, and she hated James more than ever. She looked down at her lap. "Is Senator Burr involved?" she asked.

"No," Alexander said sharply. "He knows what the money was for." A pause. "He petitioned me to obtain Mr. Clingman's release. That is all."

Maria nodded, feeling momentarily overwhelmed by guilt over her part in the whole thing. "What do you want me to say if they ask me about your financial dealings with Mr. Reynolds?"

"If they ask you directly, tell them the truth, and I will do the same."

Maria's shifted in her chair. Alexander's knee brushed against the side of her skirt, and suddenly, the proximity of his body to hers was all she could think about.

"About—everything?" she asked.

"Yes. They cannot use Mr. Reynolds's claims against me if I tell them the truth about our arrangement."

Maria paused as she considered the implications of such a confession. "But what about Mrs. Hamilton?" Maria couldn't imagine that he would willingly confess to adultery—even to avoid accusations of financial impropriety.

A blush crept across his fair features. "I have already told her, and she has forgiven me." He looked down.

"Does she know you are here now?"

"No."

"Then you should probably leave."

Alexander's blush deepened as he looked up at her. When his eyes met hers, she felt like she was drowning.

"I know I shouldn't have come, but I needed to know that you were safe."

Maria wasn't sure how to respond, so she changed the subject. "When will Mr. Clingman be released?"

"I signed the order for him to be released first thing in the morning."

"Thank you." She stood up. "I will see you out."

He stood as well, and they were once again face-to-face. The energy between them was overwhelming.

"Does he treat you well?" Alexander asked.

"Yes. I am content with him." She'd started to use the word *happy*—but that would be a lie. Content was good enough to describe her current circumstances.

"Is he providing for you and Susan?" He looked around the room, taking in the dirty teacup and plate sitting on the table, the ashes in front of the fireplace she hadn't bothered to sweep up.

"Yes," she answered, her voice a little more defensive than she intended. She could tell by his expression that he was not convinced.

"Please know that I am here if you have any concerns."

"I'm still afraid that Mr. Reynolds will try and take his anger out on Susan and me," she blurted out. Although she didn't want to acknowledge it, worry had been building inside her since seeing James in jail this morning. She knew James was desperate, and desperate men do dangerous and unpredictable things. She was not confident that Jacob would protect her, either.

Alexander nodded. Obviously, he had some of the same concerns. "I cannot hold him indefinitely, so he will be released at some point. But I will do everything in my power to see that he never threatens you or Susan again."

Maria swallowed hard, comforted by the conviction of his words. "Thank you," she whispered as her eyes met his. "And do not worry about the men investigating Mr. Reynolds's claims," she added. "I will not provide any information they can use to harm you."

The words hung between them as they stared at each other in silence for several seconds, the tension palpable.

Alexander was the first to break. "I should be going home now," he said softly.

"Yes. That is probably for the best."

Without another word, he walked into the hallway, retrieved his coat from the hook by the door, and slid into it. Maria watched silently as he prepared to leave. With one last glance behind him, he opened the door and disappeared into the wintery darkness.

Thirty-Five

Jacob was released the following morning as promised. He had just gone out again when two men showed up on Maria's doorstep and asked to speak to her privately. They introduced themselves as Congressman Venerable and Senator Monroe from Virginia. They were polite enough, although Mr. Monroe seemed colder and more aloof.

Trying to act as if this were merely a casual, social visit, Maria ushered the men inside and offered to take their coats before leading them into the kitchen. She invited them to take a seat, her mind spinning.

The men remained standing until she had taken a seat, and she took the opportunity to study them. They both were about the same age as Alexander. They dressed and spoke like gentlemen. The shorter of the two, Congressman Venerable, seemed decidedly nervous, while Senator Monroe watched her with an icy stare. Monroe was tall and handsome in a stoic, reserved sort of way that might have been intimidating if not for the soft dimple on his chin.

Maria steeled herself for the questions ahead. If they were determined to get information from her that they could use against

Alexander, she was equally determined to thwart their effects using every tool at her disposal. They were flesh and blood, after all.

In the end, it really wasn't that difficult. She had no intention of giving Alexander's political enemies information they might use to accuse him of something he didn't do. When they asked her what she knew about her estranged husband's financial dealings with Colonel Hamilton, she forced out a single tear.

Congressman Venerable quickly pulled out his handkerchief and handed it to her. She dabbed her eyes and sniffed, making a show of trying to compose herself. When their questions became more pointed, she met their inquiries with even more tears until she had worked herself up into an emotional lather, sobbing into her hands and taking deep, shaking breaths. She didn't think either man realized she had not actually answered a single question.

Congressman Venerable lost his nerve first. Even Senator Monroe gave up shortly afterward. When they stood to take their leave, they apologized profusely for causing her any distress and practically ran out the door.

While Maria could count her emotional display as a victory, she knew in her heart that this would not be the end of it.

James was released from jail a week later. According to an unsigned note from Alexander, her estranged husband had agreed to meet with the same congressmen who had questioned her. James was intent on providing proof that Alexander was engaging in speculation with him.

But the meeting never happened. Alexander met with James at daybreak that morning instead. He never told Maria what transpired, but he assured her James would never disturb her or Susan again.

After James left the city, she went to visit Burr again, this time to file for divorce. Maria had no money to hire an attorney on her own, and she figured Burr owed her for his part in instigating the whole scandal. Whether from guilt, obligation, or just a natural outcome of their long, sordid, history—Burr agreed to represent her pro bono. By the end of the year, her legal connection to James was permanently severed. She and Jacob married on the day her divorce was final, and they immediately left for Virginia.

Jacob had been offered a lucrative new position there, and despite her initial reservations, Maria liked Virginia. Life was somehow slower there, more genteel. Jacob's new job provided them with enough for a modest, but comfortable home and the money to lease an enslaved woman to help Maria run the household.

She was uncomfortable with the conspicuous presence of enslaved people in all areas of life here and had at first resisted the idea. But Jacob reminded her that the practice of owners leasing their slaves was common in the South, so she acquiesced and found a way to justify it.

In Virginia, she was Mary Clingman, a woman who bore no resemblance to the scandalous Maria Reynolds. She had female friends who visited for tea and gossip. They were invited to dances and barbeques at the plantation homes surrounding Richmond, and for the first time in her adult life, Maria was in truth the respectable wife and mother.

They returned to Philadelphia in time for the presidential election in 1796, but the worst was about to come. Alexander had resigned his position as Secretary of the Treasury a year earlier and returned to his law practice in New York. Soon after Mr. Adams was elected, charges of improper speculation between Alexander and her ex-husband were dredged up and published in an explosive new pamphlet entitled *The History of the United States for the Year 1796*. Maria had not spoken to Alexander in years, but she was not surprised when he soon answered with a bombshell pamphlet of his own.

The fallout from his pamphlet with the unfortunate title, *Observations on Certain Documents Contained in No. V & VI of The History of the United States for the Year 1796 in which the Charges of Speculation Against Alexander Hamilton, Late Secretary of the Treasury, is fully refuted. Written by Himself,* more commonly known as the *Reynolds Pamphlet*, was swift and vicious. To refute the charges, Alexander felt compelled somehow to publicly confess their entire affair in excruciating and humiliating detail. He insisted he was extorted by James, and the money he paid was in restitution for adultery, not illegal speculation.

The moment Jacob laid the pamphlet into Maria's hands was seared into her memory. First, disbelief—then pain, anger, and finally, the crushing weight of humiliation and betrayal. The words Alexander had written about her were memories still emblazoned in her mind.

> *"All the appearance of violent attachment, and of agonizing distress at the idea of a relinquishment, were played off with a most imposing art."*

Then, later:

> *"The variety of shapes which this woman could assume was endless."*

He held nothing back regarding the extent of their amour. *". . . I had frequent meetings with her, most of them in my own house, Mrs. Hamilton and her children being absent on a visit to her father."*

Maria recalled the strong urge to burn it. *Was nothing sacred? What was the point of including details that would only hurt me, the woman he claimed to love? And what of the children who would now have to bear the burden of their parents' disgrace?*

Worst of all, though, were the letters Alexander published in the back of the pamphlet. Private letters Maria had written to him when she was at her lowest. The words scrawled across the page were desperate and hysterical. Countless declarations of love, begging, pleading, and threats to harm herself if he left her. Words she had meant for his eyes only now printed for anyone to read. She barely recognized those messages as her own. But there they were.

For months, the shame and pain of Alexander's betrayal was almost too much to bear. Maria vacillated continually between righteous anger and deep depression. Thankfully, his public confessions contained no information or details about the loss of their daughter. Perhaps even Alexander considered that subject too sacred and painful to revisit.

The anti-Federalist newspapers attacked both Maria and Mrs. Hamilton with a vengeance she had never seen. Eventually, it all became too much. The depression won out, and Jacob soon determined that the only way to save her was to leave the country entirely. Maria didn't object when they packed up their entire lives and boarded a ship under the cover of darkness to start a new life in England, where Alexander's words could no longer reach them.

Thirty-Six

JULY 1801
SCHUYLKILL RIVER, PENNSYLVANIA

Maria sat on the expansive porch and stared out across the river with its sounds of the roaring falls just out of her sight. The summer air was hot, but a steady breeze coming in off the water made it quite pleasant. She had arrived here only yesterday, but she could already feel the anxiety of the past few months slipping away in the fresh air and quiet stillness of the Pennsylvanian countryside.

Alexander's cursed pamphlet had been reprinted by his political enemies only a month ago, and Burr had advised her to stay low and keep out of sight. Maria had boarded in the city until she learned of a retired couple on the banks of the Schuylkill River with rooms to rent. She could spend her summer there in relative seclusion and anonymity, so she left Philadelphia and settled into the expansive country farmhouse using the name Maria Clement.

Six months ago, she and Susan—now fourteen, headstrong, and difficult—booked passage on a ship back to America from England.

Maria had hated England from the beginning. The cold and the rain. The way the British looked down their noses at her the second they heard her American accent.

But Jacob was content in their adoptive home. He had accepted a lucrative position as a partner in an accounting firm and used his new connections to pursue and catch a seventeen-year-old English beauty—also named Maria—behind her back. So, she quietly filed for divorce and left him there with his new love. No fight, no argument.

Maria wasn't surprised at all that it hadn't worked out. She and Jacob hadn't started out on solid ground, and when the scandal revealed *his* name and details of *his* involvement in the unfortunate situation, she knew it was the beginning of the end of their time together.

In England, she and Jacob began drifting apart. Maria was moody and suffered with frequent bouts of melancholy. She supposed she had once loved him in her own broken and dysfunctional way, but whether that love had arisen out of gratitude or desperation, she had no idea.

There was another pregnancy two years into their marriage, but it had ended in miscarriage only a couple of weeks after she realized she was expecting. If God was really determined to take her babies from her as some sort of cosmic retribution for her sins, at least this one was mercifully taken before it quickened. After that, her body gave up trying to carry a baby to term and, at the age of thirty-two, she was effectively barren.

Susan was gone too. For the first time in her life, Maria was truly alone. As soon as they arrived from abroad, she had once again sought Mr. Burr's help. This time to secure a place for Susan at a respectable boarding school. The recently elected vice president agreed, and after Maria made him swear an oath that he would protect her, Burr became Susan's legal ward. He sent her to reside in the Boston household of William Eustis—a wealthy politician and longtime friend of Burr's—who used his influence to get Susan into a school where she would soon begin her studies. Something Maria had always hoped for her daughter. The chance for an education and a better life than hers.

But Alexander's pamphlet nearly destroyed that dream. As it was, Susan had to be enrolled in school using Maria's maiden name of Lewis to avoid any connections to her now infamous parents. Mr. Burr said he wasn't sure when Maria would be able to see her daughter again, for any hint of connection to her mother's scandal would ruin Susan's hope for a respectable marriage. Yet another of the unexpected consequences of being the notorious adulteress in America.

Maria suspected that the help Burr had afforded her over the years was his own form of restitution for the part he had played in her downfall, although he never directly admitted any feelings of guilt to her. She often wondered what their lives would have been had she refused to participate in his plan.

The affair would certainly not have happened had she not initiated it. But she also knew that sort of rehashing was worthless. She had nothing to gain from going down that path. Maria tried instead to focus on the future. She knew the public was notoriously fickle and would soon grow bored and move on to the next new scandalous thing. Her story would be relocated to the bin of history. At least she hoped so.

Here in the countryside, her identity would remain secret, and she would be able to spend the next few months in relative seclusion while she figured out what she was going to do with the rest of her life. One thing she knew for certain: she was no longer interested in finding another husband or lover. Her choices in that arena hadn't exactly worked out so well, had they? She had funds to live in relative comfort through the summer before she had to seek out respectable employment of some sort.

Only two other boarders lived in the house, both young men of wealthy backgrounds just out of college and enjoying a summer holiday before embarking on their professional careers. Mostly Maria stayed to herself, only engaging with them at the dinner table where manners dictated she at least attempt polite conversation. On the weekends they were joined by another young man named Peter, and it soon became clear that the three of them had determined to learn the history of their secretive housemate. Peter's attempts were not as clumsy as the others, and in his eyes, she could see compassion over curiosity.

Over the course of the summer, Maria shared her story bit by bit, and Peter listened without judgment or condemnation. She suspected he might be somewhat infatuated with her despite their age difference. If he was, he never acted on those feelings. Peter remained her respectful, platonic friend.

At the end of the summer, they parted ways with a promise to continue their new friendship through letters. Peter used some of his connections, and Maria was offered employment managing the household of a bachelor doctor named Dr. Mathew in Philadelphia. So, Maria once again pushed away her fears and doubts when the time came to leave her summer sanctuary to embark upon a new life and a new adventure in the city she knew so well.

Epilogue

February 1802
Philadelphia

My Dear Friend Peter,

I am well and settled comfortably in my situation managing the household of Dr. Mathew here in Philadelphia. My employer has been made aware of the details of my unfortunate history and is not concerned by it. I am thankful for his kindness and for the employment.

Susan remains under the wardship of Vice President Burr and continues to be enrolled in school in Boston. It has been months since I've seen her, and I miss her terribly. I have petitioned Mr. Burr to ask that some arrangements might be made that would allow me to visit her, but he says her identity must remain hidden lest Her prospects for a respectable future be at risk.

Could I prevail upon you, my Dear Friend, to contact Mr. Burr and ask that some sort of an arrangement allowing Susan and I to meet that would not reveal our connection could be made? I would be ever in your debt.

Your Friend, Maria

July 13, 1804
Philadelphia

My Dear Friend Peter,

I am sure by now the news has reached you of Vice President Burr and General Hamilton's ill-fated interview. I do not have to tell you how affected I have been over the past several days or of the melancholy that has cast its dark shadow over me.

I continue to be content in my situation with Dr. Math-

ew and am forever grateful for the protection and comfort my position has afforded me. I am certain this dark cloud will disappear in time. I can write no more.

Maria

February 24, 1805
New York

Dearest Peter,

I recently traveled to New York with Dr. Mathew where I took the opportunity to call upon Mrs. Hamilton alone. Although she was still in mourning, she agreed to see me. She did not recognize me at first, as she had previously known of me only through my former name. When I informed her of my true identity, she received me not quite warmly, but without bitterness or animosity.

She appeared with her youngest son on her hip, a mere babe still in dresses. I cannot begin to tell you how affected I was at the sight of the fatherless child or of the guilt that struck me in that moment. She and I spoke privately for over an hour under the watchful gaze of General Hamilton's portrait.

I will not reveal the intimate details of our conversation, not even to you my Dear Friend, but suffice to say that while I did not receive total absolution for my actions, the heavy burden of my conscience was much lessened upon my leaving that day.

I remain your Sincere Friend,
Maria

May 18, 1806
Philadelphia

It gives me Great pleasure, my Friend, to share with you the happy news of my marriage to Dr. Mathew. You, more than anyone, know of my sincere fondness and gratitude to the Doctor, and I am content to live out my days with him. I know you share in my happiness. Dr. Mathew joins me in sending his best regards. Do not neglect to call on us the next time you are in town.

Your friend,
Maria Mathew

March 17, 1819

Dearest Peter,

I am afraid I must once again appeal to you for assistance regarding the unfortunate situation in which Susan now finds herself. She has become Intemperate and Unmanageable to the point her new Husband says he can no longer live with her. She is determined to leave for New York and nothing I can say will dissuade her. She has at least agreed to leave my granddaughter, Josepha, with Dr. Mathew and me, but I fear she is in mortal danger in her current state.

I do not know where else to turn. I know Susan looks upon you as a Brother and she will perhaps listen to you when no other can reach her. Please come soon, or I fear she will be lost.

> *I am forever in your debt,*
> *Maria*

> *October 22, 1823*

Thank you, my Dear Peter, for the words of sympathy in the wake of Susan's unfortunate passing. I know you loved her as a Sister and tried everything you could to dissuade her from the destructive path she chose. I am convinced in my grief that nothing either you or I could have said to her at the end would have prevented her tragic outcome.

I have tried not to dwell upon the many ways that I failed her in her youth, for I know that thinking upon such things for too long would only serve to cast me back into the dark pit of despair from which I swore I would never again surrender.

I am thankful that my Beloved Granddaughter is here

*with me now, and I am determined to provide for her
all the advantages I was never able to give her mother.*

*Your Sincere Friend,
Maria*

*November 7, 1825
Philadelphia*

My Dear friend Peter,

*Thank you for your kind expression of sympathy in the
passing of my husband. I am heavily grieved, but not
sunken under the weight of it because I know that we will
meet again in a better place. Most of all, I am full of
gratitude for the life of true affection and respectability
he provided me these past nineteen years. I found in him
an affectionate companion who knew all of my faults
and dared to love me anyway.*

I am content in my widowhood, and it is my desire to stay in the city and spend the remainder of my life in the charitable pursuits my position now affords me. Josepha is away at boarding school in New York, where she has recently endeared herself to my previously estranged Sister and her family, who have in turn showered her with affection. She excels in her studies, and I am certain she will remain free of the impulsive and reckless nature so prevalent in her mother. Give my best regards to your family, and do not fail to honor us with a visit the next time you are in town.

Your friend,
Maria

March 23, 1828
Philadelphia

This may be the last time, My Dear Peter, that I am able to write, as my current illness is quickly overtaking me. Josepha is here by my side and has been a great comfort to me at the end. She has become a fine and respectable married woman, and now carries within her all the hopes of our family. She is my proudest accomplishment.

Do not despair of me. I am content and have every expectation of soon joining my Dear Husband in a better world. It is my most fervent desire that Susan made her peace with God at the end, that we will be reunited in Eternity, and that I will likewise be reunited with the Daughter who never took a breath outside of my body.

Your friendship has been such a blessing to me over the years. You came beside me and listened to my sad history without judgment or condemnation, and for that, words seem inadequate to express the depth of my gratitude. Please know that as I look back upon the events of my life, I do so with the knowledge that my sins have been forgiven and that I will meet my Maker with a clear conscience. In these last years of my life, I have found the contentment and peace that eluded me in my youth.

I know that when the history of this Country is told, Posterity will not look kindly upon me, and I have reconciled myself to that probability. After all, I can hardly change the words that have been committed to print, nor can I control those who would read my history and ascribe dark motives to me that did not exist. I just hope there are those who hear my story and have compassion, if not quite understanding, regarding the events that transpired, and my unfortunate role in them. Remember me well when you speak of me.

I will remain in Death as in Life, your most Sincere and
Dearest Friend,
Mary

Author's Notes

I first heard the name Maria Reynolds in 2020 while watching Lin-Manuel Miranda's award-winning, blockbuster musical, *Hamilton*. In direct contrast to the other female characters in neutrals or pastels, the actress portraying Maria wore a scarlet gown. That simple design choice told me everything I was supposed to think about Maria and what her role in the story was.

After that, I fell down a research rabbit hole that consumed me for almost two years. I read everything I could get my hands on about Alexander Hamilton and the founding generation, with a particular interest in the Early National Period of the 1790s. I was shocked to discover just how much a part the Hamilton/Reynolds scandal played in the political machinations of that time. But one questioned continued to loom large for me. Was Maria Reynolds really the manipulative, mentally unstable adulteress and harlot that history (and the musical) made her out to be?

Well technically, yes. She certainly committed adultery (which at that time was legally defined by a woman's marital status, not a man's), and there is evidence she had dabbled in prostitution before the affair. While it's hard to determine with any accuracy the mental state of someone who has been dead almost two hundred years, the letters she wrote to Hamilton during the affair (which he published five years later) hardly suggest a mentally stable woman in charge of her emotions.

The question of manipulation is a much harder charge to answer, and trying to ascribe motives to a long-dead historical figure is a dubious exercise at best. While it may seem simplistic, I believe that like a lot of women of the time, she did what she needed to do to survive, and if that included pushing the bounds of what was considered socially acceptable then, so be it.

It would have been easy to simply roll my eyes and dismiss her as a crazy, manipulative harlot with no redeeming qualities. But the more I read, the more I began to question the two versions of her that historians had put forth: a vile seductress who conspired with her husband to manipulate and blackmail men (and ultimately bring down a powerful politician), or an abused wife who had been forced to prostitute herself to line her husband's pockets.

There is some evidence for both of those theories. What caused me to reject either of these versions, though, was what is known about Maria's life *after* the scandal. By all accounts, Maria spent the last half of her life as the wife of a respected physician, as a grandmother, and as a devout member of the Methodist Church. Hardly the lifestyle one would expect of a manipulative, blackmailing adulteress. Despite the drama and turmoil of her earlier life, she had not only survived, but also seemed to have found happiness and respectability. That inspired me to look deeper.

I ultimately came to believe Maria was neither an innocent victim nor a brazen harlot, but both, which made her infinitely more interesting. The more she came alive for me, the more I began to empathize with her. During a time when women had no agency and lived at the whim of their husbands or male relatives, I think that

Maria was doing the best she could for herself and her daughter with whatever tools she had at her disposal.

I struggled most with the letters that Alexander Hamilton published in the appendix of his infamous confession known as the *Reynolds Pamphlet, Maria's* letters. Private letters readily accessible to anyone with an internet connection even two-hundred-fifty years later. The letters are full of overwrought hysterics, desperate pleas, and threats of self-harm. They are so full of misspellings and so badly punctuated, it makes them difficult and painful to read.

Historians have used the many errors in Maria's letters to cast aspersions on her class or intellect, but it is important to remember that in an era where a woman's education was often limited to basic reading, writing, and household arts—if she were educated at all, it hardly seems fair to shame Maria for her lack of proper education.

Despite how overblown and ridiculous the letters appeared, the more I learned, the more I became convinced that the letters were the sincere pleas of an emotionally unstable, twenty-three-year-old woman whose world was collapsing around her. But, of course, truth is a slippery thing.

By the time I sat down to write *American Harlot,* though, I was fully on "Team Maria," and I'll be the first to admit that my personal feelings may have at times colored my representation of her. Since this is fiction, however, I am free to indulge those perceptions. For those interested, it is in these pages that I will endeavor to separate fact from fiction, and you can decide for yourself what you believe.

Maria Reynolds was born Mary Lewis in Duchess County, New York in 1768 to parents Susanna Van Der Burgh and

Richard Lewis. Her older sister, Susannah, was married to a member of the prominent Livingston family (and distant cousin to Alexander Hamilton's wife, Elizabeth). Her half-brothers from her mother's first marriage, Colonel Lewis DuBois, and Captain Henry DuBois, were officers in the Revolutionary War.

Maria married James Reynolds in 1783 at the age of fifteen. Their daughter, Susan, was born two years later. Maria's parents both died when she was twenty, and it doesn't seem like she was close to any of her siblings. Beyond those facts, the historic record is silent regarding Maria's childhood and early adulthood.

There are no portraits or drawings of Maria Reynolds available, none done during her lifetime, but I think it is safe to assume she was very attractive. In Hamilton's description of their first meeting, he refers to her as *"a beauty in distress."* Her ancestry on her mother's side was Dutch, so I gave her blonde hair and fair skin, but we really have no idea. For the other real-life characters, I stayed true to contemporary accounts and portraits.

We don't know what Maria's parents did for a living, so I made up a fictional tavern for Mary to grow up in. Elijah Wagstaff is a completely fictional character as well. There is also no direct evidence that Aaron Burr and Maria knew each other in New York, or that he paid her way to Philadelphia—although there is some circumstantial evidence that indicates a prior acquaintance. He pops up at several times at key points of her story often enough to raise questions.

Mary, who was by this time going by the name Maria, first appears in Philadelphia with her six-year-old daughter, Susan, sometime in 1791 and is listed in the city directory simply as Mrs. Reynolds. Her husband did not appear to be with her. Most historians believe, as do I, that Maria's appearance on Hamilton's doorstep was a setup. What is not certain is whether Maria was working alone or with a coconspirator. If she was working with someone else, who was it?

For the purposes of my story, I settled on Aaron Burr as the instigator of the plot. Hamilton and Burr had known each other for most of their military and political careers. They seemed to have been amicable with one another until Burr beat Hamilton's father-in-law, Phillip Schuyler, for a seat in the Senate in 1791, just prior to the beginning of Hamilton's affair. At the same time, Burr aligned himself politically with Thomas Jefferson's Democratic Republicans in direct opposition to Hamilton's Federalists.

What better way for Burr to gain the trust of his new allies than to uncover proof of official corruption by Hamilton, their sworn enemy? From Burr's perspective, the reward in loyalty and patronage would have been immense if he could deliver the evidence to take Hamilton down.

Hamilton also had a reputation for being extremely solicitous to beautiful women in distress. If Burr wanted to get information about Hamilton—a man he knew was susceptible to female histrionics—why not install a pretty, young spy in his bed? Of course that's all conjecture, but I am not the first to express the opinion that Burr and Maria knew each other prior to the affair.

It's important to remember that during this time, extramarital affairs were not uncommon. Unlike today, the revelation of a sexual liaison on its own would not have been enough to end Hamilton's political career. These types of relationships were considered by the elite class to be "private matters," and we can safely say that Hamilton was not the only Founding Father who indulged in such extracurricular activities. Burr himself was known for his many affairs. Therefore, it is reasonable to believe the goal of the plot was not to reveal the affair to the public, but something else—probably money or information. In today's parlance, it was a "honey trap."

The consensus among historians seems to be that the affair was a scheme created by Maria and her husband, James Reynolds, to extort money from Hamilton. And Hamilton expresses that belief in his pamphlet years later, although he can't quite bring himself to say with complete certainty that she was in on it. Those who are more sympathetic to Maria point out that she was probably a victim of domestic abuse and may have been forced against her will to participate in the plot. Maria references being treated "cruelly" by her husband on several occasions, and their letters reveal a tumultuous marriage full of gaslighting and threats. Maria was no doubt a troubled young woman.

The idea of James Reynolds being the instigator and driving force of the plot never rang true to me, either. Frankly, after reading his letters and researching his history, I don't think he was that smart. He was a low-level con artist and not a very successful one, having been caught and jailed multiple times for various failed financial schemes over his lifetime. There is also evidence that while he was with Maria in Philadelphia, they were not living together as man and wife (i.e., separate bedrooms), so I don't think she particularly liked her husband. This was a sophisticated plot targeting the second most powerful man in the country. While there is some evidence James had previously conspired to sell his wife's sexual favors, the targeting of Hamilton seems to be an awfully big leap for a small-time crook. So I focused on Burr instead.

In writing Maria and Hamilton's first meeting and the beginning of their affair, I used Hamilton's own description of the events of that night as a framework and filled in the details from my own imagination and knowledge of the personalities involved. The musical, *Hamilton*, suggests that the affair began after his wife and family left to visit her father in Albany, but according to Hamilton's own written account, the family was still in residence the evening Maria showed up on his doorstep.

After that first encounter, Hamilton was quite enamored with

Maria, and they continued to see each other more and more frequently. By his own admission, he had frequent sex with her in his own house after his family left. Although we don't have Elizabeth Hamilton's letters to her husband while she was away, we have his letters to her. It seems that while she wanted to come home, he was trying desperately to keep her away—claiming she needed to stay in the country for her "health."

I know that marital infidelity is difficult to excuse or dismiss by today's standards, but by all accounts, Alexander and Elizabeth Hamilton had a happy marriage. Theirs was a love match, and I have no doubt they loved each other very much. She remained loyal to him until her death at the age of ninety-seven. That she forgave him for the affair and scandal is equally clear. In fact, their last two children were conceived and born *after* the *Reynolds Pamphlet* was published. In total, she bore Alexander eight children (six sons and two daughters) over the course of their twenty-four-year marriage, all eight of whom lived to adulthood, which was very rare for that time.

Perhaps tellingly, though, the longest gap between pregnancies was between their fourth and fifth child, exactly when the affair with Maria started. At the time the affair began, their youngest was almost four years old. No gap in pregnancies of that length exists before or after.

Clearly, the Hamiltons were a very physical couple. Considering the absence of any children born between 1788 and 1791, we can probably assume that something had disrupted that. Those are also the years of President Washington's first term and Hamilton's first four years as Secretary of the Treasury, a very busy and tumultuous time. They had also moved from New York to the new capital in Philadelphia, farther away from her parents and siblings with whom she was very close.

We also know that Elizabeth and their youngest son, James, had been ill several months prior to the affair. The reason for their seeming lack of intimacy during that time could have been one of these things, a combination of these things, or none of these things. I chose to include it in the story—not to excuse Hamilton for his behavior—but because I believe it was true.

A quick note here regarding Hamilton's reputation with women: he was a notorious flirt, and no doubt very charming and charismatic. Rumors of his supposed lecherousness abounded, spread mostly by his political enemies. But that's where it seems to have ended. There is no direct evidence to suggest that Hamilton was in the habit of bedding women other than his wife. And with the notable exception of his complicated and close relationship with his sister-in-law, Angelica Church, no proof of any extramarital affair outside of Maria Reynolds exists.

In his definitive biography *Alexander Hamilton*, author and historian Ron Chernow describes Hamilton's affair with Maria Reynolds as a "sexual obsession." Considering Hamilton would eventually pay Maria's husband a third of his annual wages to continue sleeping with her, I would say that is a pretty accurate assessment. Since obsessions of this nature usually contain an emotional as well as a physical component—and given Hamilton's passionate personality in general (he never did anything halfway), I believe that his feelings for Maria went beyond the physical, although he downplays any possible emotional attachment years later.

I think that Maria was also in love with Hamilton. Given her history, it would not be a stretch to think that she would have viewed him as a sort of savior. More cynical authors and historians believe the histrionic declarations of love and desperate pleas contained in her letters were an elaborate act designed to keep Hamilton engaged in the affair so that her husband could continue to extort money from him. I believe she was truly a desperate woman in love. As with most things, the truth probably lies somewhere in between.

We know that the affair continued even after Hamilton's wife and children returned to Philadelphia in September of 1791, and it's possible that Hamilton was financially supporting Maria at that time. Sarah is fictional character, although not entirely. In her letters, Maria references sending messages back and forth by her maid. I invented a name, face, personality, and history.

Maria's near-death experience from a fever is also fictional. I used it to illustrate the parallels between her and Hamilton's mother, Rachel Faucette, who died of a fever when he was twelve while he also was sick in bed beside her. The striking similarities between the lives of Rachel and Maria have been pointed out by many historians, and it's often been suggested that Hamilton seemed to be working out some sort of issues from his own difficult childhood in his relationship with Maria. I thought that might be an interesting dynamic to explore, so I invented a situation that would bring those similarities to the forefront.

Dr. Edward Stevens is a real person, and Hamilton's childhood friend from the West Indies. The Stevens family took in Hamilton after his mother died, and the two men stayed close into adulthood. Dr. Stevens appeared in the Hamilton household from time to time when there was illness. He took care of both Alexander and Elizabeth when they contracted yellow fever in the epidemic of 1793, and attended Elizabeth when she suffered a miscarriage while her husband was away during the Whiskey Rebellion in 1795. Dr. Stevens was also known to be a staunch advocate of using cold water baths to bring down a fever, which was in direct opposition to the medical practice of bleeding and purging practiced during this time.

The two men apparently looked so much alike, it was speculated Hamilton was the illegitimate son of Dr. Steven's father. Neither man ever publicly acknowledged such a relationship, and no portrait or drawing of Dr. Stevens has been discovered—so we are left to our own imagination to determine the degree or significance of any supposed resemblance. Although it is possible, there is no evidence Dr. Stevens ever met Maria or knew about Hamilton's relationship with her.

Hamilton was quite knowledgeable about medical issues himself, and it is well-documented that he attended to his own family personally whenever they were sick, so the attention and dedication he shows to Maria during her fictional illness would not have been out of character.

We don't know exactly when James Reynolds appears in Philadelphia. According to Hamilton's account, "*. . . in the course of a short time, she mentioned to me that her husband had solicited a reconciliation, and affected to consult me about it. I advised to it, and was soon after informed by her that it had taken place.*"

In other words, her husband returned at some point, asked if they could get back together, and she asked Hamilton what he thought. Hamilton said to do it, she did, and their affair continued unabated. I changed the narrative slightly and added some context, but left that much intact—even if I don't understand it.

Jacob Clingman is also a real person. We know from his own signed statement published in the appendix of the *Reynolds Pamphlet* that he met James Reynolds in September of 1791, and a business partnership existed between them. But we don't know where they met or the circumstances of their meeting. Clingman had indeed worked previously as a clerk to the Speaker of the House (Pennsylvania Congressman Fredrick Muhlenberg), which I thought very interesting. It is also probable that he had some sort of connection to Burr, but the historical record is silent on when or how they met or what the nature of that connection was.

Maria's pregnancy is my own invention. According to historical record she had only one child, but miscarriages or stillbirths were often not recorded since they were unfortunately very common during that time. Her daughter, Susan, was born when Maria was seventeen, so it is probable there were other pregnancies—no way to know for sure. We do know that Elizabeth Hamilton became pregnant during her husband's affair with Maria and gave birth to their fifth child only two months after the affair ended.

In the telling of the discovery of the affair and James's subsequent demand for money, I used James and Maria's own letters to Hamilton, only correcting them for some of the spelling and punctuation errors to make them easier to read. James did indeed demand a thousand dollars, almost one-third of Hamilton's annual wages as Secretary of the Treasury.

Historians usually refer to Reynolds's demands as blackmail. James tells Hamilton if he pays the money, he will ". . . leave her to you to do for as you see proper." That sounds like an exchange of a different sort to me. Whatever the arrangement was, Hamilton paid the money in two separate payments and got receipts from James for both.

Also true is that James still threatened to take Susan after Hamilton paid the money he demanded. From what I could determine, Susan was with her mother in Philadelphia the entire time. After James returns and discovers the affair, he mentions two separate times in letters to Hamilton that he is going to take Susan and leave. But he never carries through on these threats, and we can only speculate as to why. No doubt Susan would have been privity to the drama taking place during the last few months of the affair, and it's not a stretch to think that the trauma at such an early age would have affected her deeply.

From January to May or June of 1792, it is not always clear (from the letters that Hamilton published) what was going on. At one point in January, James tells Hamilton he can't see Maria anymore. Then he reneges a couple of weeks later and invites Hamilton to renew his visits—which he does. For the next few months, the affair continues, Hamilton visiting frequently enough that (according to his signed statement and his own recollections) Jacob Clingman catches Hamilton at their house on at least two occasions. James then asks for small "loans" of money after each visit.

Strangely, James even writes Hamilton receipts for these loans with a signed promise to pay them back, although there is no evidence he ever did. Once again, writing IOUs to the person you are supposedly blackmailing doesn't seem consistent with the theory. That Hamilton paid the money for continued access to Maria, I have no doubt.

It seems that at some point during this time, Hamilton tries to distance himself from Maria. He is met with hysterics and pleading, for there is a period of profound grief and desperation in Maria's letters. It's so bad in fact that James writes Hamilton and expresses concern about the seeming depths of her despair. Of course, this could have all been an elaborate act designed to keep Hamilton engaged (and most historians believe this to be the case), but I chose to give Maria the benefit of the doubt and created a situation where she was truly grieving.

The affair probably ended in late May or June of 1792. Hamilton indicates it ended when James told him once again that he could no longer see Maria. *The interdiction was in every way welcome, and was, I believe, strictly observed,* " Hamilton wrote.

Strangely, though, James continues to write Hamilton asking for "loans" well into August. Elizabeth Hamilton gives birth to their fifth child on August 22. James writes and asks Hamilton for money on August 24 and then again on August 30. Interestingly, in one of those letters James asks for a loan of $200 to furnish a boardinghouse he and Maria are supposedly setting up. The loan requests seem to have been ignored, however, and there is no record of James asking again.

Reynolds and Clingman are indeed arrested by the Department of the Treasury for fraud only a few months later. Although James believed Hamilton was behind their arrests, there is no evidence that indicates Hamilton knew about those arrest warrants until afterward. Shortly following the arrests, both Muhlenberg and Burr appeal to Hamilton personally to solicit Clingman's release from prison, which he agrees to.

We know that Hamilton reached out to Maria either in person or by message after these arrests. In his statement, Clingman says that Maria had *". . . received money of Col. Hamilton since her husband's confinement, enclosed in a note, which note she burned."*

Although Clingman was released shortly after their arrest, no one came forward to speak on James Reynolds's behalf, and he remained jailed. It is true that while he continued to sit in jail, James began insinuating to anyone who would listen that he had dirt on the Secretary of the Treasury. Clingman brought James's claims to his former employer, Muhlenberg, thus setting in motion the ensuing investigation.

Senators James Monroe, Abraham Venerable, and former Speaker of the House Frederick Muhlenberg conducted the investigation. James claimed he and Hamilton were engaging in illegal speculation, and that Hamilton had given him money for that purpose. When the men confronted Hamilton with the accusations, he immediately confessed to the affair and extortion scheme, giving them letters written to him from James and Maria as proof.

The Congressmen professed to believe him and promised to remain silent about the affair. They also spoke to Maria—or at least tried to. According to a statement signed by Monroe and Venerable, they met alone with Maria, and "*. . . it was with difficulty that we obtained any information from her.*"

It is also true that Hamilton met privately with James on the morning he was released from jail, and that James disappeared shortly after their meeting, skipping out on a subsequent meeting with Monroe, Venerable, and Muhlenberg scheduled later that same morning.

Shortly after the investigation ended, Maria filed for divorce from her husband—Burr acting as her attorney at no cost—which seems to indicate at the very least a prior connection between the two. The divorce was granted by reason of adultery (James's, not hers), and Maria married Jacob Clingman on the same day it was final. They lived in Virginia after their marriage, which I thought was interesting—since neither of them had family there, or any previous connections to the state.

Was Jacob offered a position in Virginia by Hamilton's political enemies as a reward for his help in bringing the scandal to light? We will probably never know the answer, but it's an interesting theory.

Maria's relationship with Clingman was the one thing in my research that I could never quite wrap my mind around. Whether she married him out of desperation, convenience, or a real affection, there is no way to know. They were together until 1799 or 1800 (I could not find their divorce decree), when she left him in England and returned to Philadelphia with Susan.

Amazingly, and perhaps more telling of gentleman's views on adultery at that time than anything else, the details of the affair were kept quiet by Hamilton's political enemies for five years. By my own count, over a dozen of the most powerful men in America knew about it (including three future presidents) and remained silent. Thomas Jefferson made a note about the affair in his papers only two days after Hamilton's confession to Monroe, Venerable, and Muhlenberg.

Some historians theorize that the reason Hamilton never stood for president himself is because Thomas Jefferson warned him that if he did, they would release the details of the Reynolds affair to the public. But that remains only a theory. Whatever the reason for their previous silence, the story finally became public in the summer of 1797.

No one can say with any certainty who leaked the scandal to the press. The Hamiltons clearly believed James Monroe was responsible. The two men almost arranged a duel over it, which may very well have occurred if not for the efforts of Aaron Burr to squash it (oh, the irony!). For her part, Elizabeth Hamilton seemed to have held a grudge against James Monroe long after her husband's death, and there is a wonderful story passed down through her family about her confronting a contrite Monroe who came to make amends toward the end of his life.

Others point the finger at Thomas Jefferson as the real culprit, who passed along the sealed documents from the investigation to a muckraking journalist, James T. Callender (who was on Jefferson's payroll during the years he served as Secretary of State). Personally, I think it was a combination of Jefferson and Monroe, but we will probably never know for certain.

In his pamphlet, Callender claims the money Hamilton gave to James Reynolds five years prior was for illegal speculation, charges that Hamilton's enemies knew were not true. Nevertheless, culpability for speculation would have cast a shadow over his entire legacy of public service. In the process of defending himself from these accusations, Hamilton was forced to explain what the money he gave James had been for, and he did so in shocking detail in his infamous pamphlet entitled *Observations on Certain Documents Contained in*

No. V & VI of "The History of the United States for the Year 1796" in Which the Charge of Speculation Against Alexander Hamilton, Late Secretary of the Treasury, is Fully Refuted. Written by Himself, otherwise known as the "*Reynolds Pamphlet.*" The scandalous pamphlet became quite popular, and the Jeffersonian newspapers delighted in making the revelations as embarrassing and humiliating as possible for both Elizabeth Hamilton and Maria Reynolds.

After the publication of the *Reynolds Pamphlet* in late August of 1797, the attacks from the press became so bad that Maria and Clingman left the country for England. Elizabeth Hamilton (who had given birth to their sixth child only three weeks before the pamphlet was released to the public) remained by her husband's side.

We have no documents or letters written by either Hamilton or his wife that reference the affair and ensuing scandal directly, but vague references in letters written by close family seem to indicate that Elizabeth blamed the men who had leaked the documents rather than her husband. We don't know when she first found out about the affair. Five years had passed between the affair's end and the publication of the *Reynolds Pamphlet*, so there is a good chance Elizabeth had learned of the affair much earlier, having already worked out her own feelings on the matter years before Hamilton's public confession. We will never know for sure.

Maria returned from England in 1800 with Susan and without Clingman. By that time, Susan is fourteen, and whether by Maria's initiation or his, Burr becomes Susan's legal ward! He sends her to Boston to live in the bachelor household of a close friend, Massachusetts Congressman William Eustiss, who uses his connections to get Susan into a respectable boarding school.

In a letter to Eustiss dated December 1, 1800, Burr tells Eustiss regarding Susan *"I repeat and do assure you, she is to my belief, pure and innocent as an angel,"* and that *". . . she has not the most remote affinity to me."* In other words, she's a virgin and she's not my illegit-imate daughter. He also added that he was *". . . under a sacred oath to protect her."*

The fact that he refers to having taken a "sacred oath" is interesting and indicates a history and connection to both Maria and Susan that is not explained in historic record. This seems to indicate a length-ier and more complicated relationship. Whatever the case, Susan is enrolled in school using Maria's maiden name, Lewis, to avoid any connection to her infamous parents. We don't know who was paying for Susan's education, but it was almost certainly Eustiss, Burr, or a combination of the two men. To keep Susan's identity a secret, Maria is not allowed to visit her.

And thus begins the sad downward spiral of Susan's life. At the age of eighteen, she elopes with a man who deserts her three weeks later, and Eustiss finds her in a house *". . . frequented by young men. . . "* (i.e., a brothel). He brings her back into his care, although he tells Burr in a letter, *"I see nothing to be expected of our unfortunate charge but a gradual declension from reputable life down to what lengths or depths God knows."*

Susan marries again and has a daughter, Mary Josepha. There are conflicting reports about whether that husband leaves or dies, but she is left alone again. By this time, Maria is married to Dr. Mathew, and Susan and Josepha move in with them in 1808. There is a period of calm, and it seems that Susan is trying to get her life back together. She marries a third time, but that husband also leaves her. From that point on, Susan's life seems to be a downhill slide of alcoholism and mental illness until her death in New York at the age of thirty-one. In his memoir, Philadelphia merchant and longtime friend, Peter Grotjen, sums up the possible reasons for Susan's downfall:

"I have often pondered and reflected on the probable causes, which could have eventuated in so deplorable an issue; and am strongly of

the opinion that the desultory manner of her early education, the knowledge of the shame and exposure of her mother during the most interesting time of her youth, the secrecy and deceptions she was forced to practice in early life had greatly contributed to give a wrong direction to a mind naturally virtuous, innocent and amiable."

Probably the most well-known aspect of Hamilton's life is his death at the hands of Vice President Aaron Burr in a duel in 1804. Burr and Hamilton's bitter rivalry seems to have started in 1791. Most historians point to Burr's defeat of Hamilton's father-in-law, Philip Schuyler, for a seat in the US Senate as the origin of this conflict, which also corresponds with the beginning of Hamilton's affair with Maria. In September of 1792, three months after the affair ended, Hamiton writes these words about Burr: *"I feel it a religious duty to oppose his career."*

And Hamilton stuck to that promise for the next dozen years. When Jefferson and Burr tied in the Electoral College in the presidential election of 1800, Hamilton began a letter-writing campaign to try and convince his fellow Federalists in the House of Representatives to vote for Jefferson over Burr. It's impossible to know for sure how effective Hamilton was, but Jefferson was eventually elected president after thirty-six ballots.

Four years later, when it became clear that Burr would not be chosen by Jefferson as his running mate in the next election, Burr set his eyes on the New York governorship. Once again, Hamilton stepped up to oppose him, and spoke out against Burr at every opportunity. One of those opportunities happened to be a dinner party attended by a Dr. Cooper in which Hamilton expresses his opinion that he *". . . looked upon Mr. Burr to be a dangerous man, and one who ought not to be trusted with the reins of government."* What Burr seems to take most offense at, though, is Dr. Cooper's assertion, *"I could detail to you still a more despicable opinion which*

General Hamiton has expressed of Mr. Burr."

What exactly that "despicable opinion" was we have no way to know. Hamilton's refusal to disavow or apologize for those statements led them down the path to the duel. On July 11, 1804, both men along with their seconds and Hamilton's personal physician rowed across the Hudson to a spot on the cliffs overlooking Manhattan in Weehawken, New Jersey. What happens there is not entirely clear, but we do know that both men discharged their weapons.

Whether by accident or design (in a statement written the night before, Hamilton indicates he did not plan to shoot directly at Burr), Hamilton's shot misses and Burr's bullet goes straight into Hamilton's abdomen—shattering a rib, piercing his liver, and lodging in his spine. Mortally wounded, Hamilton is taken back to New York where he dies the next day surrounded by his wife and children.

Hamilton's death effectively ends Burr's political career. He is charged with murder in both New York and New Jersey, but the charges are allowed to lapse. After a short stay in the South, Burr returns to Washington to finish out his term as vice president, presiding over the impeachment trial of Supreme Court Justice Samuel Chase.

Three years later, Burr is arrested in Alabama and tried for treason for what is now known as the "Burr Conspiracy," and the real intentions of his dealings in the West remain a mystery to this day. Acquitted of the charges based on a very narrow interpretation of treason by Chief Justice John Marshall, Burr finished his life in relative obscurity, never having attained the political power he wanted so badly. There is no evidence that Maria and Burr had any further contact after his fateful duel with Hamilton.

All the remaining details we have about the later years of Maria's life come from a memoir Peter Grotjen wrote in 1846 when he was in his seventies, in which he chronicles his own introduction to

Maria at a boardinghouse on the Schuylkill River in 1800. There she shares her history with him. They stay in touch for the next twenty years, and in his memoir, Grotjen chronicles his negotiations with Aaron Burr on Maria's behalf to try and arrange a meeting between Maria and Susan while she was enrolled in school in Boston. He also chronicles Maria's happy marriage to her employer, Dr. Mathew, Susan's unfortunate demise, and Maria's subsequent raising of her granddaughter, Josepha.

Although the letters in the epilogue of *American Harlot* depict some true events, they are strictly a product of my imagination. There is no evidence that Maria visited Elizabeth Hamilton after his death. It is possible the two women met at some point, but we will probably never know. The idea of such a meeting was too incredible for me to ignore, so I included one.

It seems clear from Mr. Grotjen's memoirs that he was somewhat enamored with Maria, although there is no evidence to suggest that their relationship was more than platonic. His bias toward her is evident, though, so while most of the events he describes such as her marriage and Susan's death are verified by the historical record, he certainly sees her as an innocent victim in everything that transpired.

Mary "Maria" Lewis Reynolds Clingman Mathew died on March 25, 1828, just five days short of her sixtieth birthday. History does not record the circumstances or cause of death. Peter Grotjen ends his description of his lengthy friendship with Maria in this way:

Mrs. Mathew, soon after she was married to the Doctor, experienced a great change in her mind. She became serious, sedate, and religious without hypocrisy. She joined the Methodist Church, but retained all her former gentleness of manner. Her former life and adventures being only known to a few of her sincere friends, who had long ago buried the knowledge in oblivion; she enjoyed both for her own sake, and as the wife of a highly respected physician, a well-deserved rank in society, and the love and good will of all who were acquainted with her.

While we may never know the accuracy of Mr. Grotjen's recollections, I would like to believe they are true, and that in the last half of her life, the original "American Harlot" truly found peace, happiness, and redemption.

Acknowledgements

A project of this scope would not have been possible if not for the support of my family and friends. A special thank you to Terri Haney, Julie Rogers, and Rebecca Jones for the hundreds of hours they logged listening to me talk about Alexander Hamilton, Maria Reynolds, and the Founding Fathers, plus their help brainstorming countless plot points and ideas. It's not a stretch to say that this project would not have been possible without them.

A special thanks to Julie Rogers (author of *Falling Stars* and countless other published works) for her editing and formatting expertise. A special thanks too, to Rebecca Jones for her proofreading prowess and trusty red pen.

In researching *American Harlot*, it was important to me to use primary sources (letters or other documents written at the time by the historical figures themselves or their contemporaries) when possible, so for that I am eternally grateful to **founders.archives.gov**. Sponsored and maintained by the National Archives, the website contains the digitalized papers of the seven major Founding Fathers. This important resource is truly an American treasure.

For those things I couldn't find in the archives, I relied on countless other sources, most prominently, Ron Chernow's masterful biography, *Alexander Hamilton*. Other important resources included *Affairs of Honor* by Joanne B. Freeman, *Founding Brothers* by Joseph Ellis, *A War of Two* by John Sedgwick, *Fallen Founder: The Life of Aaron Burr* by Nancy Isenberg, *Duel with the Devil* by Paul Collins, *Revolutionary Characters* by Gordon S. Wood, *Jefferson and Hamilton* by John Ferling, *Thomas Jefferson: The Art of Power* by John Meacham, *Elizabeth Hamilton* by Tilar J. Mazzeo, *Alexander Hamilton, American* by Richard Brookhiser, and *The Essential Hamilton: Letters & Other Writings* edited by Joanne B. Freeman. I am grateful to them as well as to novelists William Safire, Stephanie Dray, Laura Kamoie, Elizabeth Cobbs, and Susan Holloway Scott for their fictional portrayals and insight into the characters inhabiting the pages of *American Harlot*.